HEART'S CONFESSION

Terrence gazed at Jezebel, his eyes softening. "You are the most beautiful woman here tonight."

"Thank you." Jezebel looked down at her ball dress, a figured red silk, cut low upon the shoulders and with a skirt fanning out to whisper with every movement. "I am still amazed the Duchess gave this to me."

"She is beginning to like you," Terrence said, stepping closer. "But then, who wouldn't grow to like you?"

Jezebel looked down, his closeness disturbing her. She had been in his arms for every waltz, touched hands with him in every country dance, and still it wasn't enough. She wanted to be in his arms once more. "I am certainly beholden to her," she said. "This is my very first ball, you know."

"You have handled it with aplomb, my dear," Terrence murmured. "Evidently, you were born for them."

"No," Jezebel said, shaking her head. "This is nothing like my life . . . my real life, that is."

"Perhaps this is your 'real' life instead." He raised a hand and lightly brushed her cheek. "Perhaps this is where you were meant to be."

"What do you mean?" Jezebel asked softly.

"You were meant to shine, Jezebel." Terrence slid his hand to the back of her neck. "To be the belle of the ball . . . to dance in my arms every night." His hand lightly commanded her to draw near, and he bent his head, his lips brushing hers. . . .

Books by Cindy Holbrook

A SUITABLE CONNECTION
LADY MEGAN'S MASQUERADE
A DARING DECEPTION
COVINGTON'S FOLLY
A RAKE'S REFORM
LORD SAYER'S GHOST
THE ACTRESS AND THE MARQUIS

Published by Zebra Books

THE ACTRESS AND THE MARQUIS

Cindy Holbrook

Zebra Books
Kensington Publishing Corp.

http://www.zebrabooks.com

ZEBRA BOOKS are published by

Kensington Publishing Corp.
850 Third Avenue
New York, NY 10022

First Printing: March, 1997
10 9 8 7 6 5 4 3 2 1

Printed in the United States of America

One

A hack, old and battered, pulled up to the back entrance of the theater. "Whoa, boys," the driver muttered as his team snorted. He waited a moment. Shaking his head, he leaned over and yelled, "We're here, miss!"

Another pause ensued and then the hack's door opened. A woman descended. Enshrouded in a dark cloak with a hood which hid her hair and face, she appeared mysterious. Theater people were always putting on odd airs, the driver thought as the woman stepped over to him and handed him the fare. He noticed her hands were encased in frayed black gloves with a hole in the thumb.

"Thank you, sir," she said softly.

Her voice was melodious, genteel sounding. "Yer welcome, miss." The driver hid his disappointment at the small tip she had added.

His fare nodded and turned from him. After two steps she halted. It seemed to the driver she stiffened. He frowned. "Ye best be going in, miss, ain't wise ter be loitering back here."

"Yes," the woman responded, her voice low. "I must go in there."

He saw her straighten and walk with a firm stride to the back door. Then he shook his head and whipped up his team.

* * *

The gleaming carriage came to a dashing halt in front of the theater. Its polished sides vaunted a coat of arms painted in gold.

"We're here, My Lord," the driver shouted.

The carriage door opened and a man alighted. His many tiered cape swirled with the lithe movement and fell open, displaying the most elegant of evening attire beneath. His cravat, tied in the intricate Waterfall, showed the hand of an expert. A large, square-cut emerald winked from within its folds. His mahogany hair favored the windswept style and lay in fashionable disarray. Severe lines, however, marred his autocratic, chiseled face. In his gloved hand he held a missive. He glanced at the heavily embossed letter, crumpled it, and tossed it to the ground. The evening breeze frisked it along the street.

"The show is most likely half over, My Lord," the driver said.

"That's all right, Bootle," the gentleman responded. The clouds in his dark, gray eyes evaporated. "I intend to stage my own production soon. One which, I make no doubt, shall send dear grandmama into the boughs." His laugh was deep and rich. "She cannot abide actresses, you know?"

He grinned and headed toward the theater's entrance with long strides.

"I beg of you to release him," Jezebel said, gripping her hands tightly together. It was far worse than she had ever imagined.

The actress Molly Flannigan, despite her years, was still a handsome woman. Her green eyes were perhaps made more brilliant by the heavy blackening around them, and the red glints of her hair undoubtedly had much to do with dye; yet the bountiful bosom spilling above her merry widow was unmistakably her own.

"But I be powerful fond of Josh, dearie," Molly said, leaning back in the old, scarred chair. "Powerful fond."

"He is but a boy," Jezebel protested, anger shooting through her.

"And what a boy," Molly said. Her deep sigh pushed her bosom dangerously past its bodice. Her green eyes glinted. "I'll bet you're trying to figure what Josh is doing with an old jade like me, ain't you?"

Jezebel flushed. "No, not really. Josh has always had a particularity for women with large . . ." She halted, biting her tongue. "Er, never mind. But what would *you* want with a boy like Josh?"

"What would I want with . . . ?" Molly choked up and then broke into hearty laughter. "Lud, ye speak as a sister would."

"I am his sister," Jezebel said, gritting her teeth.

Molly shook her head. "Well, dearie, just wait till you get to be my age. Then you'll be finding out why an old woman like me enjoys a young man." Her smile broadened. "His attentions, I meant ter say."

"His attentions to you are breaking him," Jezebel said. "He is not a rich man. If he continues to spend all his funds upon you, he'll not have enough to go up to Eton this year."

"And what do you want me ter do about it?" Molly said, straightening in her chair. "You asking me to be cheap?" She tossed her red curls back and threw up her chin. "Well, Molly Flannigan don't come cheap, I'll have you know. No, siree, she don't come cheap for anyone."

"What I'm asking is for you not to come at all," Jezebel snapped.

Molly stared at her. Then she hooted with laughter. "Gawd, I'd never thought to hear a fine miss putting it so bluntly."

Jezebel frowned, attempting to hide her puzzlement. "I am sorry if I appear bold. I did not mean to insult you, or insinuate you should hold yourself cheaply. I-I understand if a man squires you that you expect him to be able to pay. But that is the rub. Josh cannot afford to pay. Please, if you would only sever your ties with him, I am sure you can find another man who could afford you."

"Oh, no, ducky," Molly said, shaking her head. "Josh treats me right fine, and I don't intend to be shoving orf anytime soon."

"But don't you understand?" Jezebel exclaimed. "You are ruining his chances at schooling!"

"Oh, no," Molly said, grinning. "I'm schooling him right well, I am. In all the ways I like, in fact."

"Do you not care that you are ruining his life?" Jezebel asked, enraged.

"Ruining his life?" A sudden sly look crossed Molly's face. "Well, now, if you put it that way, 'course I don't want ter ruin sweet Josh's life." Her eyes narrowed. "But, as I said, I don't come cheap . . . or go cheap."

Jezebel frowned. "I beg your pardon?"

"Beg me pardon all you want," Molly laughed. "But if you want me ter leave brother Josh alone and find another ter 'squire' me, you'd best come over with the dibs."

Jezebel's mouth fell open. "You want me to pay you?"

Molly nodded. "Two hundred pounds ought to sever my affections fer him."

"Two hundred pounds!" Jezebel shouted. She stared at the woman. "You cannot be serious."

"Oh, but I am," Molly said, her chin jutting out. "I have ter make a living in this world, and I won't be tossing a fine catch like Josh away unless you make it worth my while."

Jezebel's eyes narrowed, and rage suffused her. "We are talking about my brother, Miss Flannigan, not a . . . a fish. How dare you ask for money simply to release him from a ruinous relationship when your own conscience should tell you to do so."

"Conscience?" Molly asked. "Hoity-toity, ain't you? My

conscience ain't the one with a bellyache. It's you taking snuff at this here situation, not me."

Jezebel hid her grimace. She had known her argument was weak, but she had thought it worth a try. "I don't have the money."

Molly shrugged. "Then I'll just have ter keep seeing Josh—he does."

"He does not, I tell you!" Jezebel said. "He is using funds that are not meant for . . . for, er, that purpose."

"I don't care. If you want me to help you, you'd best find me the ready."

"I have told you, I do not have it!" Jezebel gritted out. "If I had—"

"Excuse me," a male voice interrupted from behind. Jezebel, irritated, glanced over her shoulder. A tall gentleman stood within the door to the tiny, dressing room. "I am sorry to interrupt, but do you know where Lucy is?"

"No, I do not," Jezebel said quickly and turned back to Molly. "Now—"

"Lucy?" Molly asked, shifting to peer past Jezebel at the man. "She ain't here anymore, she broke her arm and won't be acting for a few weeks." She turned a narrowed gaze back to Jezebel. "Life in the theater is a hard one. A poor woman needs all the help she can get. And if someone won't pay when she ought to . . ."

Jezebel stiffened, quite embarrassed. "I told you, I do not have the money."

"Then I think you'd best just find it," Molly said. "You pay for your gent, or I won't be doing anything for you!"

" 'Tis too much," Jezebel said, flushing. She had actually stooped to heckling with this unprincipled actress. "It is far too much."

"That's the sum, dearie," Molly said. "Ye want to do business with me, then you pay up or I'll keep darling Josh."

"You are new here, are you not?" the male voice spoke again. Sighing in exasperation, Jezebel turned. The man had not left. In fact, he'd entered the room, all but filling up the tiny quarters. Jezebel frowned. "Sir, this is a personal conversation, if you please. Miss Flannigan and I are discussing business—private business."

The man's gray eyes twinkled, clearly in amusement. "Indeed, sweetings, I can tell that. But perhaps I might have some business here myself."

"I see," Jezebel said. Evidently Molly had a few irons in the fire other than poor Josh. She lifted her chin. "Then if you would be pleased to wait a moment, sir, I will try to finish my business with Miss Flannigan as swiftly as I can, so you will be free to discuss matters with her yourself." Misliking the man's twitching lips and bright eyes, Jezebel nodded briskly and turned quickly back to Molly. "Please, Miss Flannigan, would you not take less?"

Molly grinned. "Not one ha'penny."

Jezebel thought quickly. "Perhaps half?"

"Half?" Molly laughed. "Josh is a fine provider, and you want me to let you pay only half for him?"

The man's voice once again interrupted. "What is the sum?"

In exasperation Jezebel drew in a deep breath. Refusing to even look at the rude, intrusive man, she said over her shoulder, "Sir, I will be finished with Miss Flannigan shortly."

"It's two hundred pounds," Molly called, once again shifting to try to see the man. Jezebel stepped forward, determined to block her view.

A whistle filled the room. "Faith, that is steep!"

"See!" Jezebel said. "Even he agrees with me!"

"I don't sell anything cheap, my fine buck," Molly said, leaning back in her chair and crossing her arms.

"Indeed, she does not," Jezebel muttered. She jumped as the man suddenly appeared beside her. He stepped very close. "Sir!"

"May I?" he said with an odd smile. He reached out quickly and pushed the hood of her cloak back.

"I beg your pardon," Jezebel gasped, recoiling. She stared at the man as if he were deranged, which she highly suspected was indeed the case.

"Faith," he murmured. He gazed steadily at her. "What is your name?"

"That is none of your business, sir," Jezebel said, attempting to straighten her unruly mass of blond hair which was clearly the focus of the bedlamite's attention.

"Her name is Jezebel," Molly said.

"Jezebel!" the man exclaimed. He threw back his head and laughed. "Forsooth, 'tis even better."

"I find nothing amusing in my name," Jezebel gritted out. Even deranged men should not be so rude.

" 'Twould be perfect," the gentleman murmured, still gazing at her with sparkling gray eyes. "Would you please take off your cloak?"

"My cloak?" Jezebel asked, blinking. She stiffened. "No, sirrah, I would not. Now would you please leave us?" She turned back to Molly, feeling oddly breathless and disoriented. She frowned, trying to focus her scattered wits. "Miss Flannigan, please be reasonable. I do not have that much money. Will you not reconsider?"

Molly's eyes flickered between the man and Jezebel. The oddest expression crossed her face, and then her eyes lighted. "Just take orf your cloak for the gentleman, dearie."

"I most certainly will not!" Jezebel exclaimed. The man's insanity was apparently contagious. "Now if you would attend to the matter at hand—"

"Oh, I'm attending it, love," Molly chuckled. "I'm attending it."

"I'm only asking you to remove your cloak," the gentleman said in mild tones.

"That's all he's asking, Jezebel," Molly said. She smiled broadly. "And I won't be doing any business until you do."

"What?" Jezebel exclaimed. " 'Tis ridiculous!"

Molly shook her head. "You ain't being polite to the gentleman, Jezebel. Now you take orf your cloak and then we'll talk business."

"Oh, very well." Jezebel threw up her hands. "If that is what is necessary to conclude this matter." She undid the clasp of her cloak and flipped the garment from her shoulders. Then she glared at the two in her company. "There, are you satisfied?"

Molly nodded happily, while the man studied her. Jezebel flushed deeply. Never had a man perused her in such a manner, as if she were merchandise for his inspection. Trying to ignore the strange feeling growing in the pit of her stomach, Jezebel tore her gaze from the man. She looked desperately to Molly. "Ah . . . er, as I-I was saying, would you not accept less, M-Molly?" She peeked over to the man. Still he stared. She licked her lips nervously and added, "Ahm . . . perhaps one hundred and twenty-five. It—it would be hard for me to raise, but I shall."

"She's got some talent there, don't she?" Molly murmured, watching the man.

Jezebel blinked, bemused. "Talent?"

"She does indeed," the man said, suddenly grinning. "I don't believe this Josh deserves her."

Molly smiled back at him. "He be a mighty fine provider, I hope you know. I'm thinkin' it's three hundred now."

"Three hundred!" Jezebel squeaked. " 'Tis highway robbery."

"I want exclusive," the man said.

"That would be five hundred," Molly shot back.

Jezebel gripped her hands tightly, feeling totally out of her depth and out of control. The two were completely ignoring her, as if she were not in the room. "Molly, would you please attend to me first before dealing with this gentleman?"

The actress paid Jezebel no mind, her gaze trained upon

the gentleman, a look of expectation on her face. The man reached into his pocket and pulled out a roll of notes. Jezebel's eyes widened. Faith, if only she possessed that kind of money. 'Twas no wonder Molly gave the gentleman first consideration.

He handed the roll to Molly. "I only have four hundred and fifty. Take it or not."

"I'll take it." Molly's painted hands grasped it before Jezebel could even blink. The actress sprung from her chair, shoving the wadded notes into her cleavage. "Don't worry about your Josh anymore, love; I'll not be seeing or needing him." She sprinted toward the door and was out of the room in a flash.

"Heavens," Jezebel said, stunned. "Wherever did she go in such a hurry?"

The man looked at her in a disconcerting, proprietary fashion. "You are absolutely beautiful."

Jezebel flushed. "Er, thank you . . . I think." He gazed at her. She stared at him. The room suddenly became too small, the man too close. Jezebel swallowed hard and said, "Well, I guess my business here is done. Goodbye."

"Wait a minute," the man exclaimed. "Where are you going?"

Jezebel lifted a brow. "Why, home, of course."

"But you can't," the man said. "I wish to discuss my plans with you first."

"Your plans?" Jezebel frowned. "I am sorry, sir. Your plans are no concern of mine, so if you please, I am going home."

"No concern of yours?" His eyes darkened. "Since I just paid five hundred for you, they most certainly are."

"Four hundred and fifty," Jezebel said, frowning.

He waved an impatient hand. "Four hundred and fifty then."

Suddenly the full intent of his sentence hit Jezebel. "For

me!" Her mouth fell open. She shook her head. "You . . . you paid for me?"

"Of course for you," he said. "I bought you for—"

Jezebel stiffened. "You did not buy me."

"Yes, I did," he said. "I gave Molly the money, for God's sake. You just saw me do it."

Faintness overtook Jezebel. Her world whirled. "I saw you do that . . . but . . . but that had nothing to do with me." His gaze narrowed coldly upon her. "Did it?" His look remained steady, unflinching. "But . . . but that is impossible," she wheezed. She teetered past the man and fell onto the chair. "You—you could n-not have bought me. I-I am not for sale." She shook her head. "I-I am not a s-side of beef, or—or a furbelow some man can b-buy."

"But you are an actress," he said, his tone curt.

Jezebel lifted stunned eyes to him. "No, no, I am not."

His fine brows snapped down over the bridge of his nose. "Yes, you are. And you are doing a mighty fine performance right now, I would say." He stepped menacingly toward her. "Do you think you are going to gull me? Take me for a flat? Do you think you and Molly can diddle me?"

"I-I don't think I'm going to do any of that," Jezebel stammered, pressing back into the chair. "And as for Molly, I do not know. In truth, I—I am not an actress."

"Very well," he said, with a sigh. "It was my mistake. I merely assumed it, since you are here. No matter. If you are only a prostitute—"

"A prostitute!" Jezebel yelped. "I am no such thing."

He frowned. "What do you mean?"

"I am no"—Jezebel flushed—"lady of the evening."

He shook his head. "But you said you are not an actress."

"Indeed," Jezebel said, stiffening. "I am not an actress, and I most certainly am not a . . . a p-prostitute."

"Then just what in blazes are you?" He glared at her. "What did I just pay four hundred and fifty pounds for?"

Jezebel shook her head slightly. "I don't know wh-what

your business with Molly was, but it has nothing to do with me."

The muscle along his jaw jumped. "Oh, no, sweetings, it has everything to do with you. I don't know what game you're playing, but you can stop. Your playing the innocent isn't something I need. I am sure some men like it, but it's never appealed to me. Now, I gave Molly, your very excellent procuress, four hundred and fifty pounds for you, and that's that. Use whatever term you wish, but I did buy you."

Jezebel stood swiftly. "You did not!" She charged past him.

An iron hand clamped upon her arm and jerked her back. The man swung her around to him, his gray eyes volcanic.

"Let me go." Fear overrode decorum and she lifted her slippered foot and kicked him sharply in the shins.

"Blast it!" His grip only tightened, his other hand swiftly gripping her shoulder. He shook her slightly. "Stop that."

"Let me go," Jezebel gasped. She kicked him again, grimacing at the pain to her toe. "Let me go."

"I said stop that!" He jerked her to him, wrapping strong arms around her. Jezebel tried to move, but he effectively squeezed the air and fight right out of her. "Now, we are going to settle this," he rasped. "Were you or were you not going to pay Molly for this fellow Josh?"

"Yes," Jezebel said, regaining some of her breath and squirming. "If I could find the money."

"But you spent the money and didn't pay Molly when you should have, correct?"

"Spent the money?" Jezebel suddenly stilled. "What money?"

"The money Josh paid you," he said, his tone impatient.

"Josh never paid me," Jezebel said, shaking her head.

"You mean the blighter never paid you?" His hold gentled, even as his gray eyes darkened. "Faith, no wonder Molly was angry. You can't do business that way, sweetheart."

"I-I can't?" Jezebel asked weakly. His eyes were incredibly beautiful close up, fringed with long sable lashes. She breathed in quickly and the scent of him invaded her nostrils, sending a delightful shiver through her.

"Forget this Josh, he's a loose screw," the man said. "He should have paid you and you should have paid Molly. You certainly shouldn't have defended him to her."

"I-I was not defending him to Molly," Jezebel said, bemused. "And why should Josh pay me? He's my brother."

"Your brother!" The man's arms fell swiftly from Jezebel. He stepped back, shock writ upon his strong features. "Gads! Your brother."

Jezebel discovered his consternation bothered her. She shook herself firmly and said, "Yes, my brother! I know he is young and foolish, but Molly is unscrupulous. He could not see that, I'm sure. And ever since he's been . . . been squiring her, she's been bleeding him dry." Her chin lifted as the man continued to stare. "And yes, I would have paid Molly if it would have kept her from Josh."

"You would have paid her?" He made an odd sound. "You were going to pay Molly to keep her away from your brother Josh?"

"Yes."

"You are not a prostitute or actress?"

"No."

"Oh, Lord," he groaned, running his hands through his hair. "And I just paid my last money to Molly for you."

Jezebel looked hesitantly at him. "Because you th-thought you were buying me as an actress or a . . . a—"

"Prostitute," he said, nodding.

"Heavens," Jezebel breathed out. She shrugged helplessly. "Then you must get the money back from Molly because I—I am neither."

He cracked a laugh. "Do you think she'll give it back?"

Jezebel forced a smile. "Perhaps? If you explain to her it was a misunderstanding."

"You know she will not," he said, his gaze raking Jezebel. "She bloody well knew what she was doing—and what I was doing. There was no misunderstanding between us. It was only with you."

Jezebel flushed. "It is not my fault."

"Blast it, you should have stopped me," he said, turning to pace. "Why didn't you stop me?"

"How could I?" Jezebel asked. "I did not know why you gave Molly the money."

She watched him cover the small room in three strides. Suddenly he halted, studying her. She misliked the intent in his eyes. "But I did give her the money, did I not?"

"Yes," Jezebel said, suddenly wary.

"And she said she would leave Josh alone, right?"

"She did."

"Which is what you wanted, correct?"

"Well . . ." Jezebel hesitated.

"Correct?"

She glared at him. "Very well, correct."

A slow smile crossed his face. "Then I did pay Molly for you, did I not?"

"No!" Jezebel said quickly. "No, you did not!"

"I did," he declared, his eyes flaring in triumph. "You know I did."

Frustration stung Jezebel, and she looked at him with loathing. "All right, you did, but only in a manner of speaking."

He lifted a brow. "Do you have the four hundred and fifty to pay me back?"

Jezebel gritted her teeth. "It was only to be two hundred!"

"Do you have it?"

Jezebel looked down. "No, I do not." She lifted her head in defiance. "But I will find it . . . if you will give me some time."

He shook his head. "I don't have time. I need an actress now."

"I told you," Jezebel said, clenching her fists. "I am not an actress."

His eyes narrowed. "Then I will make you one. I just spent the last of this quarter's allowance on you, and by God, you are going to be my actress." He waved a hand. "I didn't really need a prostitute, so it is all right if you are not one."

"You are too kind," Jezebel said with a purr. The man only grinned at her. She stepped back. "I am not an actress, I tell you."

He stepped toward her, grinning. "But you shall be one."

"No!"

"It isn't that difficult," he said, his voice lowering to a soothing velvet.

It sent a chill down Jezebel's spine. "I am still not going t-to be your actress."

"Then pay me back," he said.

"You know I can't!" Jezebel protested.

"Yes." He nodded, his eyes sparkling. "I know you can't. Therefore, you will be my actress." He frowned suddenly. "You aren't married, are you?"

"No," Jezebel said, looking away.

"Engaged?"

Jezebel flushed. "No."

"No beau?" he persisted.

Jezebel looked at him, realizing the opportunity. "Yes, yes, I have a beau, and he's very jealous."

"What is his name?" he rapped out, snapping his fingers. "Quickly, his name?"

Jezebel jumped "His name? Ah, his name is . . . ahm."

"You do not have one," he said very positively. Jezebel felt a strong desire to hit him. "You have nothing to impede you. You'll have to make good and be my actress, won't you?"

She stared at the gloating man. Stifling a curse, she then turned smartly on her heel and stalked toward the door. "Molly, come back here!" she yelled. "Come back here this instant!"

Two

Jezebel paced the small parlor. She had been doing so since seven o'clock that morning. Upon every revolution she would veer to the door, stick her head out into the hall, and listen.

Perhaps he wasn't coming. He had said he would see her in the morning, and it was already well past ten o'clock. Perhaps it had been nothing but a bad dream last night, a nightmare of perverse proportions. Perhaps he had been castaway and did not remember. Perhaps only she remembered she had finally broken and promised to be his actress.

"You can't do it," she muttered to herself, gripping the door frame. " 'Twould be ridiculous, improper, insane." If she ever found Molly Flannigan again she would flay her alive. She had scoured the theater that evening and hadn't seen hide or tail of the deceiving, fast-footed hussy. "Drat, 'tis impossible!"

Jezebel turned, starting her fiftieth revolution across the parlor's threadbare carpet. Then she heard it. A sharp rapping upon the outside door. She halted, her heart sinking. Muttering an unfeminine curse, she picked up her skirts and bolted out into the foyer.

"I'll get it, Ruth!" she shouted as her hand clasped the doorknob. Drawing in a deep breath, she swung the door open.

The fiend of her nightmare stood upon the stoop, the devil's own grin upon his face. His hair tousled, his gray eyes bleary, he wore the same clothes as the night before. A huge, ominous black trunk rested beside him. "Good morning, Jezebel."

" 'Tis not morning," she said. " 'Tis already ten o'clock."

"That's morning to me," he said in a disgustingly cheery voice.

"And I am Miss Clinton, I hope you know," she said, her chin lifting.

His brow quirked. "And I am Terrence Vance, the Marquis of Haversham."

Jezebel's mouth fell open. "What?"

"Yes, my dear," he said. He leaned over and gently tapped her chin up. "No cit or Johnny raw for the actress Jezebel, only a marquis will do."

Jezebel's heart slithered to her toes. She had not asked one thing more of the man than she had to last night, not even his name. It was infelicitous to discover she had been 'bought' by a lord of the realm. "My Lord, I-I don't think—"

"Tsk, tsk," the Marquis said. "I am not My Lord to you, sweets. No standing upon ceremony for us. Not with the intimate relationship we enjoy. I am merely Terrence, Terry, darling, dear, or any other loving name you wish to call me."

No loving name came to Jezebel's mind, but she had a few others in full supply. Her eyes narrowed, and she said, "I see no reason to call you anything other than My Lord, and I do not see us as having an intimate relationship. All you need is an actress. You said you did not need a prostitute."

"And I don't." His brows rose. "But I do need a mistress."

"What?" Jezebel cried. "A mistress is a prostitute!"

"No," he said, shaking his head. "A prostitute is for one night, perhaps two, a mistress is for a respectable, long-term relationship."

"Respectable?" Jezebel wheezed. "Long term?" She did

not hesitate. She clutched the door and slammed it shut. An immediate pounding arose. Jezebel put her hands over her ears. The man was a deceiving, conniving libertine. He wanted a mistress, not an actress, and he had lured her in under false pretenses. The pounding became ear-splitting thuds. "Stop that!" Jezebel cried. The sounds were now booms. "Beast!" Jezebel muttered and jerked open the door. She almost received a fist in the face.

Terrence pulled it back just in time. "I'm sorry." Jezebel drew herself up to her fullest height and glared. He shook his head. "For shame, a lover's spat already."

" 'Tis no lover's spat," Jezebel said. "And it never will be!"

"Wait!" he exclaimed, before she could slam the door again. "What I meant when I said you must be my mistress is that you are supposed to act like one. That is part of your being my actress. It is not as if we have to actually go to bed together."

"I should hope not!" Jezebel said.

"Not unless you want to do so," Terrence said. Jezebel squeaked in protest and tried to slam the door again. Terrence's hand shot out and stopped her. "Jezebel, I was only teasing. Faith, but you are a sober one."

"Yes, I am," Jezebel said stiffly. "And that is why I cannot do this. I am not an actress. I-I am sorry about the money, but—"

"Oh, no," he said. "We shall rub along famously, I am sure. I shall refrain from teasing you, and the world can consider you my iron mistress." He grinned. "Besides, you have not yet seen what I have for you."

Jezebel's gaze roved with suspicion to the large trunk. "What is in it?"

"Your new attire," Terrence said, patting it. "I hope you know I've been hard at work all night long on your behalf."

"You really shouldn't have been," Jezebel said with deceptive sweetness.

"Nothing is too good for my Jezebel." He bent down and hauled up the trunk. "Now, we must get to work. Your acting coach is coming in an hour."

"An acting coach?" Jezebel asked.

"Yes." Terrence shoved past her, and Jezebel stumbled back, ducked, and barely avoided being smacked by the trunk. "He will teach you how to act . . . on stage that is, since you wish to forgo the other lessons. Now where shall we go?"

"To the parlor," Jezebel said. "And be quiet. I don't want Ruth to know you are here."

"Who is Ruth?" he asked as he followed her directions.

"My housekeeper," Jezebel said, lowering her voice.

Terrence entered the parlor. "She doesn't know?"

Jezebel swiftly closed the parlor door. "I haven't told her yet."

"You'd better, you know," he said, setting down the trunk. "Gads," he murmured, looking about. "What a depressing room."

Jezebel flushed, looking to the worn furniture and ragged carpet. "We . . . we are not rich."

"That is not what I meant," he said, turning suddenly serious eyes upon her. "Do you realize there is not one item which is not brown or black in here?"

Jezebel studied the room in surprise. The furniture was large, the heavy pieces of dark mahogany; the worn carpet was brown; and even the closed curtains were of a darker shade. "My father was a professor of history and favored these colors."

"Is the rest of the house like this?"

"Yes, I suppose it is," Jezebel said, walking swiftly to the beige settee and sitting upon it. She did not wish to mention that her room was done in soft champagnes and cream. "As I said, Father favored these colors."

"The iron mistress," Terrence said softly. He visibly shook himself "Well, we had best proceed, before your housekeeper discovers us. I gather she is the type to kick up a dust over this?"

Jezebel grimaced. "A veritable cloud. She is very proper."

"It sounds as if you go in dread of her." He strolled over to push open the curtains. Light flashed into the room, brightening and cheering it.

"She raised Josh and me since we were children," Jezebel said.

"Ah, yes, a family retainer." Terrence walked over to the trunk. "They are worse than family, aren't they? I had an old nurse who was just the same. Spouted fire and brimstone every other sentence."

Jezebel lifted a brow. "She didn't have much effect upon you I can see."

Terrence laughed. "No, I fear I was never one for hell and damnation."

"Don't be too sure," Jezebel murmured.

He snapped open the trunk, lifted the lid, and its contents spilled out. A jumbled mass of red, chartreuse, emerald, and purple silks assaulted the eye, a disconcerting splash of vibrancy in the dark room.

"Gracious!" she exclaimed.

Terrence withdrew a cherry-striped dress and studied her. "This should look fine upon you."

"Do you th-think so?" Jezebel fanned her slowly reddening face.

He cocked his head and surveyed her. "I believe you and Lucy are the same size, which will be good. We shouldn't have to take anything up." He tossed the dress to her.

"Lucy?" Jezebel said, catching an armful of silk. She looked down in consternation. "These are another woman's clothes?"

"Of course. I told you I have no money until next quarter. Your fee was rather steep."

"It was not *my* fee, and I cannot believe you wish me to wear another woman's clothing."

"Why not?" he said, frowning. "I assure you, Lucy has no need of these. She has a broken arm after all and won't be working for a while. Though it was a piece of work to turn her up, sweet, I assure you."

"Lucy!" Jezebel said, the puzzle piece falling into place. "She was the girl you were looking for last night."

"Yes," Terrence said, kneeling down and rummaging through the dresses. "I thought she'd be my actress for old time's sake, but when I heard she had broken her arm I knew it wouldn't fadge."

"For old time's sake?" Jezebel asked. "Oh, my goodness. She is your mistress, isn't she?"

Terrence paused. "No, she is not my mistress. If she still was, I wouldn't have been at the theater last night paying Molly four hundred and fifty pounds for you, now would I?" He shrugged. "Lucy and I parted company a few months ago, on good terms, of course."

"You—you are depraved," Jezebel gasped. She sprang up, tossing the cherry dress swiftly from her. "You libertine! You are forcing me to play at being an actress and forcing me to wear your ex-mistress's gowns."

Terrence stood slowly. His gray eyes flashed and his face turned cold. "I am not forcing you to do anything." Jezebel glared at him. "Am I forcing you? Really forcing you? If you would pay me back, I would be gone in a minute."

Jezebel flushed. "I . . . I cannot pay you."

"No, of course you can't," he said, stepping toward her. "And you don't really want Molly to give me the money back, do you? You wanted her paid off to protect your Josh, didn't you?" Jezebel remained silent. "Didn't you?"

"Yes," Jezebel snapped. "Yes!"

"And what does brother Josh think about his dear sister paying off his mistress?"

Jezebel flushed. "I . . . I don't know. He is out of town for another month."

"I see." Terrence's tone turned icy. "So you did this behind his back? Ever the conniving woman."

"I am not a conniving woman!"

He snorted. "Paying a man's mistress off while he is out of town isn't conniving?"

Jezebel lifted her chin. "I did it for his own good!"

"His own good?" His lip curled. "You mean you did it for what you thought was his own good. You wished to control his way of life and did it behind his back. Don't talk to me of morals, madame. I'll allow you your own, if you will keep out of mine, is that understood?"

"With pleasure." Jezebel was shaking with sudden rage. "I assure you, I do not wish to be anywhere near your 'morals.' "

"Fine!" he snapped. "Now if you will come and sit down again, we have work to do."

She stifled a growl, stomped over to the settee, and sat. "Just what is this work we must do? Why must I be an actress for you?"

"Because I have a meddling grandmother, very much like you," he said, kneeling down at the trunk once more. "She wishes to arrange my life, for my own good I assure you." He dragged out dress after dress, strewing them upon the floor. He tugged out a red feathered boa which looked like a dead snake. "Here, put this on." He tossed the limp thing at her.

Jezebel caught it with a start. She immediately sneezed. It still held a heavy, clinging perfume. She stared at it in disgust.

He glared. "It goes around your neck."

Frowning, she draped it inexpertly over her shoulders. "How is your grandmother wishing to arrange your life?"

"She is determined to arrange my marriage." He withdrew a red and gold corset, even its laces a tawdry gold. Jezebel choked, gawking at it. He noticed her gaze and looked down. When he looked up, his eyes were bright and speculative.

"I'm not putting that on!" Jezebel said. "I'm not!"

His eyes sparkled. "Come, darling, I think you would look charming in it."

"No," Jezebel said, mortified. She couldn't believe she was arguing over intimate apparel with a strange man who called her darling. "I will not."

"Very well." He sighed, dropping it to the floor. He looked up and frowned. "We must do something with your hair. Why are you wearing that frightful bun? It should be loose and flowing like it was last night."

"I didn't have time to fix it last night," Jezebel said. She had gone to see Molly on the spur of the moment. Her father had always admonished her for the besetting sin of impetuosity, and now she saw his reasons. "I had time to fix it this morning."

"That's not fixing it," he said, standing. "That's destroying it. Take it down."

Jezebel's hand flew to her hair. Terrence glowered at her in such a dark fashion she quickly attempted to find the offending pins. Her hands shook. Taking her hair down in front of a man was not common for her. "Why . . . uhm . . . why . . ." She couldn't seem to grasp one pin. "H-how is . . . is your grandmother arranging a marriage for you?"

"Here, let me do it," he said. He stalked over and brushed her hand away. "It's very simple. She has chosen the woman she deems perfect for me." His hand riffled through her hair and expertly found a pin. He plucked it and, with a flick of his wrist, sent it sailing. "Never considering to ask my opinion, dear grandmama has already approached this paragon's father for his permission to our union. I have no doubt they are drawing up the contracts this very minute." He unerringly found another pin and flipped it to the floor. "She has written me that Miss Arrowroot is very biddable, passable in looks, and since it is well past time for me to marry, she has seen to the arrangements. I, you see, have not been applying myself diligently enough to the endeavor."

Jezebel felt the weight of her hair fall. Terrence's hand did not leave the strands, but spread through them. She tried to ignore the tingling along her scalp. "But—but she can't force you into a marriage, can she?"

"Grandmother never forces anyone," Terrence said, sitting down next to her. "She merely arranges." He smoothed Jezebel's curls, playing with the tresses. He appeared distracted, not even seeming to notice the familiarity of this activity. Jezebel did. It felt far too divine and wicked. Terrence smiled slightly. "They call her the general, you know."

"I see," Jezebel said rather breathlessly. "And how do I come into this?"

"You?" His gaze returned to her, his eyes warming to gray velvet. He lightly brushed the hair at her temple. "You, my dear, are going to be my actress, with whom I shall create a scandal to upset London." He smiled. "It is easily capsized, I assure you. This scandal will be such that even the biddable Miss Arrowroot will be unable to stomach it, and it will be one that so enrages Grandmother she will finally wash her hands of me, as she has always promised to do, and will leave me to my justly deserved ruin."

"We are going to do that?" Jezebel whispered.

His gaze met hers and held it spellbound. "We are."

Jezebel shook her head. "I am no actress."

"You look like one," he said softly. "How did you get violet eyes?"

"Th-they are blue."

"They look violet."

"They aren't," Jezebel said, her throat constricting.

"And your hair." He entwined his fingers in it. "Grandmother will never believe it is actually this color."

"It . . . it's merely blond," Jezebel said, short of breath.

"Not merely," he replied. His eyes darkened. "You are indeed a woman a man can be disowned over."

"Disowned?" Jezebel's eyes widened. "Do you really wish that?"

" 'Tis better than wedding Miss Arrowroot," Terrence said. He slowly leaned into her. His breath was soft upon her face. "Far better." His lips descended. Jezebel's eyelids fluttered shut in trepidation and expectation.

A screech split the air. "Faith and begorra! What are you doing to my girl!"

Jezebel's eyes snapped open even as Terrence's head jerked back. She looked wildly about. Ruth stood in the doorway, arms akimbo, eyes ablaze.

"Miss Jezebel, shame upon ye," Ruth said, charging into the room. "Shame! Ye look a hussy!" The housekeeper suddenly stumbled. Righting herself, she glanced down. The laces of the gold and red corset entangled her foot. "Sweet Mary of God!"

"Oh, Lord," Terrence said. Leaning back, he roared with laughter.

"Stop that, you fiend!" Ruth cried, hopping up and down and shaking her entangled foot madly. The pernicious corset laces only wrapped about it all the more. She stomped her foot down and stumbled forward, the corset dragged behind her like a small tow. "Stop it, devil. What are you doing with my Jezebel?"

"She's not your Jezebel anymore, she's mine," Terrence said, his laughter subsiding to chuckles. He cast Jezebel a challenging look. "I think it's time for you to explain, my love."

"Your love!" Ruth shouted. "What be ye talking about, man?"

"Tell her, Jezebel," Terrence said, his lips twitching.

Jezebel's hand flew to her chest, only to be enveloped with feathers. "Um, Ruth, it's a very confusing story, but . . . but I'm going to be his actress."

"And mistress," Terrence said.

"Mistress!" Ruth shrieked. "Mistress!"

"I'll only be acting," Jezebel said quickly. "It won't be real."

"Acting?" Ruth cried. She jabbed a shaking finger toward Terrence. "A woman doesn't act at being a mistress with a man like him."

"Ruth, you wound me," Terrence said. "And here we've only just met."

"I can tell," Ruth said. "You're the devil's own, you are, with your fine looks and fine ways. I saw what you were going to do with my baby, and I'll not have it. She's but an innocent lamb for a wolf like you to fleece."

"No, I'm not," Jezebel said, stiffening. "I can take care of myself, Ruth. I am going to be his actress and nothing more."

"That's right," Terrence said. "You are talking to the great actress Jezebel now, and she's to be taken seriously." He put an arm about Jezebel and winked at her. "Isn't that so, lambchop?"

Ruth's bellow shook the rafters and rattled the window panes.

Terrence leaned back in the winged chair, wincing only slightly. Jezebel stood beside the piano singing a scale as Antonio Mazelli hammered out the notes. Her voice leaked out in breathless quivers, decidedly off-key.

Suddenly the piano disgorged five discordant notes.

"Impossible!" Antonio boomed in his deep voice, pounding three more times upon the keys. "Impossible." Terrence cringed and Jezebel clamped her hands to her ears, spinning to stare at the theater's manager. "Ah, ha!" he cried, shaking a finger at her. "You do not like that, do you? But that is what you sing!"

Terrence saw every line of Jezebel's body stiffen. "I beg your pardon?"

"It will not do!" Antonio threw up his hands, looking at

Terrence. "Terry, it will not do. She looks like an angel, but wails like a cat. A cat with its tail beneath ze hatchet. Chop, chop!"

"Well!" Jezebel said, her hands going to her hips. " 'Tis not true."

"Not true!" Antonio boomed, his dark eyes flashing.

"No, 'tis not true." She smiled widely to Antonio. "I do not look like an angel. I look like a hussy." She puffed out the sleeves of the yellow and grass green dress, with the low scooped neckline. "Surely if this is the fashion in heaven—"

"Then all actresses go to heaven," Terrence laughed, surprised by the impish smile upon Jezebel's face. "She has you there, Tony."

"Ah, *bella,*" Antonio said, his thick lips cracking into a grin. He held both hands out. "You are such a delight. But why must you torture me with such cruel notes. The singing, it should match you. Not be ugly and weak!"

"It's all in her breathing," Terrence said. "She is breathing wrong."

"You are right, Terry, you are right." Antonio sprang from the piano bench to his full five feet two. He walked swiftly to Jezebel. "The breathing must come from here," he said and placed his hand upon her stomach.

"Signore!" Jezebel slapped his hand soundly. Antonio jerked it back with a howl.

"Terry!" Antonio cried, looking very much like an enraged bull. "She slapped me. Me, *il direttore!*"

"Ma belle," Terry said, hiding his smile as he stood. "You must learn the director likes to think himself God. One does not slap God, does one?"

Jezebel did not look repentant. "If God is so familiar one does."

"I will not have her upon my stage!" Antonio cried. "I will not have such impertinence."

"Yes, you will," Terrence said calmly. "You owe me." He

looked at Jezebel. "Tony is right, Jezebel; you are not breathing correctly." He walked over to her and very slowly reached out his hand to place it gently upon her stomach. She watched him warily, but did not move.

"Yes, you show her, Terry." Antonio nodded vigorously. "You, she permits. But me, me she slaps, eh? Me, *il direttore!*"

"Breathe," Terrence said softly. Jezebel drew in air. His hand did not move. He pressed it closer. As his hand curved and defined the flatness of her stomach even beneath the corset and stays, he felt the lack of air himself. "You must breathe from deep down, not just from the chest. Your stomach must move, Jezebel."

"All right," she said. Her face serious, she breathed in again.

"No better."

"I'm breathing as deeply as I can."

"From here," Terry repeated, pushing against her stomach. "From here."

"Very well," she said. He saw her jaw clench. She took a great breath, and Terry finally felt her stomach move, but then Jezebel froze, her breath held. Her gaze flickered down before going to Terrence, consternation in her violet eyes. He glanced down. Her chest had also expanded, swelling her breasts well nigh over the tight-fitting green bodice. Raw heat flashed through Terrence. He could not tear his gaze away. "For mercy's sake, breathe out, Jezebel, breathe out."

She expelled her breath, and the bodice rose once more to hide those beautiful white curves. Terrence jerked his hand back quickly. "You'll have to loosen your corset stays."

"What!" Jezebel said, her hands rising to cover that which was already covered.

"You do not need a corset anyway," Terrence said curtly, stepping back.

"Yes, I do," Jezebel said, her face turning a delicate rose. " 'Tis only proper."

"Proper," Terrence murmured, running a hand briskly through his hair. He found he was sweating. He spun from her and strode to the chair and flung himself into it. "What is so proper about trussing up a woman's body and restricting it with so much whalebone that she cannot even breathe correctly?"

"I never had a problem with breathing until now," Jezebel protested, her eyes darkening.

"Me either," Terrence muttered. Then he looked at Jezebel, her hands still covering herself, the picture of affronted modesty. For some reason, it enraged him. "For God's sake, Jezebel, take your hands down. Act like a woman and not a lady."

"I am a lady," she said, dropping her hands to her sides, a militant look on her face. "And I cannot act any other way."

"Ah, Terry, Terry," Antonio said quickly. "Even I, *il direttore,* do not talk of the woman's corsets. They are determined to have them, we must live with it."

"Indeed, you must," Jezebel said, her eyes flashing. "I shall not give up my corset."

"Do you not understand?" Terrence said. "You cannot restrict yourself so. In acting all you have is your body. It is your tool."

"Tool?" Jezebel said. " 'Tis not my tool, but your tool." Their gazes met and locked in battle. Jezebel's fell first. When she looked up, her face was solemn. Traces of fear ran through her eyes. "I cannot do it, Terry. You must find another actress."

"I don't want another," Terrence said angrily. He saw her eyes widen, even as he felt his own surprise. "I mean . . . I cannot afford another actress."

"But—but must I go on stage?" she asked.

Terrence's jaw tightened. "Yes, you must. Grandmother is not easily fooled. If you don't appear on stage, for all of London to see and gossip about, she'll think you nothing more than another mistress of mine whom she can overlook. So will Miss Arrowroot, I assure you."

Jezebel's eyes darkened. "They would truly overlook that?"

"Of course, it would be nothing out of the ordinary," Terrence said. "You must be in the public eye to force them to reckon with you. And they must think I am totally enamored of you. So enamored that I'll not cast you off despite the scandal or their plans. If we were discreet, 'twould be too easy for them to sweep you under the carpet."

The slightest smile touched Jezebel's lips, and her eyes lightened. "You are never discreet."

He found himself answering that smile. "No, I suppose not." He experienced an uncomfortable hesitancy as he said, "Will you do it for me, Jezebel?"

"Yes," she said softly. Then her chin lifted. "But I am keeping my corset."

Terrence grinned. "Perhaps you could loosen it slightly?"

"I'll think upon it." Her lips twitching, she turned from him. "Mr. Mazelli, let us try again."

"Bene," Antonio said, crossing to the piano. "Let us try again."

Terrence leaned back in his chair. A warm relief flooded through him. Jezebel would be his actress. He did not know why it was so important to him. Perhaps it was because he knew that this time his grandmother was tightening the matrimonial net with a surety which frightened him. If he did not stop her soon, he might very well be lost. He had danced out of the Duchess's traps many times before, but one day he'd make a misstep and fall into one. He had to stop her now.

He looked to Jezebel as she began an awkward climb up the scales. She would be his salvation from his grandmother. He just knew it.

* * *

She was going to die. She just knew it. She stood offstage, in the dark, looking out at the actors upon it, not really seeing them. A flush ran through her, first hot, then cold. She twisted her hands together tightly. "I can't, I simply can't."

"Yes, you can," Terrence said, his voice soothing. He stood directly behind her. He had said he was there to lend her support. More likely he was there to ensure she didn't bolt. "It's only a song, Jezebel."

Jezebel swallowed hard. "Only?"

"It's not as if you have any lines to remember." His hand fell to her shoulder, squeezing it. "You don't even have to act."

"Just sing," Jezebel moaned. A numbness overtook her. She had trained two weeks for this, but it didn't matter now. She spun, plowing directly into Terrence. "I'm not doing this. I'm not."

He quickly enveloped her in a restraining hold. "Yes, you are. You must. Antonio has you on the playbill. You can't walk out."

Jezebel started. "I-I must. I cannot go out th-there."

Terrence frowned. "Jezebel?"

"Hmm?" She trembled so she couldn't speak.

He reached up and patted her face. "Jezebel?"

"Hmm, what?"

"Calm down. It's a small crowd out there."

She shook her head. "I don't care. I-I think I'm going to faint."

"Oh, Lord!" Terrence exclaimed. "You can't."

Jezebel nodded, a buzzing in her ears. "I can!"

Terrence looked hastily toward the stage. "You can't, sweetheart, they are almost finished. You have to go on."

"Not if I faint first," Jezebel said.

"The devil," Terrence muttered. Swiftly he reached into his vest pocket and pulled out a flask. He uncapped it. "Here, drink this, it will help."

"H-help?" Jezebel stammered. He lifted it to her lips. Since she couldn't breathe, she couldn't protest. She swallowed the liquid he poured into her mouth. "Ouch!" She wheezed as brandy burned down her throat and flamed in her stomach.

"It will calm you," Terrence said, withdrawing the flask from her.

"Calm me?" She harbored a conflagration in her stomach, and he thought it would be calming?

"Now breathe," Terrence muttered.

"Not that again," Jezebel said, yet breathe she did. Rapidly.

"Oh, Lord, they are finished," Terrence said as the actors exited the stage, milling past them. "It's your turn."

"My turn," Jezebel said in a jittery voice. She grabbed the flask from Terrence and swiftly gulped from it.

"Jezebel!" he cried.

The stage manager, Jake, rushed past. "You're on, Jezebel."

"On," she moaned. In a daze she handed the flask back to Terrence.

"You'll do just fine," he said. Then he twirled her about and pushed her toward the curtain's edge. She could hear the crowd talking—a rumbling as if a large beast awaited her.

She clung to the curtain. "No!"

"Yes," Terrence muttered. He swatted her hand from the cloth and pushed her forward.

Jezebel gasped. She was onstage, staring out at a sea of faces. And they stared back. Somewhere she heard the piano music begin. Still she stared. And still they stared. The music stopped all of a sudden.

"You missed your cue," Terrence hissed from offstage.

The music began again. Jezebel shook. The crowd began to mutter and hiss. The pianist banged heavily upon a set of chords, and Jezebel recognized her cue, being repeated over and over again. She opened her mouth and started singing, only from sheer desperation. Her voice came out in squeaks, horribly off-key.

A ripple of laughter rose. So did the brandy in Jezebel's veins, making a warming surge of rebellion pulse through her. She sucked in her breath and forced the words out in a bellow, hitting a higher octave but tonelessly.

"Move about," Terrence whispered from behind the curtain.

Jezebel sidled to the left, shouting out the words in an effort to drown the sound of the crowd. Unfortunately, she couldn't. She heard the loud boo of a man in the front row.

It was enough! Rebellion flared into liquored rage. She clamped her mouth shut, turned smartly on her heel, and headed toward the right wing.

She didn't get far. Terrence suddenly appeared, blocking her. He picked up the line of the song, singing in a deep baritone the words she was supposed to be trilling. " 'My true love is sweeter than the roses . . .' " The odious man was on key.

Intimidated, Jezebel attempted to brush past him. He snatched up her hand, dragging her to a halt. "Sing," he hissed. He squeezed her hand tightly.

Jezebel squealed into the song. "My true love is fairer than . . ." Terrence suddenly spun her in a pirouette. She came out of the spin so dizzy she held a strong vibrato upon her last words. Before she could regain her bearings enough to fathom which was stage right or left, Terrence stepped up to her and knelt upon one knee in the classic theater pose of a lover. He planted one foot firmly on the flounce of her dress, and grinning up at her, he clapped his hands to his chest as, with a moonling look, he yodeled out the next verse.

Jezebel, not daring to move lest she tear her flounce, glared daggers at him and bellowed along with him. When he held out one hand to her, batting his lashes madly, the audience roared with laughter.

"Give it to him, Jezebel," someone hollered.

Hard pressed, Jezebel ungraciously proffered her hand to Terrence. Whistles and catcalls arose. Terrence leaned over and kissed it in a grand display, then lifted his head to direct a satisfied smirk to the audience. Embarrassed, Jezebel tried to tug her hand away. He only gripped it more tightly and jerked her to him. Jezebel, off set, tumbled forward. She hit Terrence, and together they both fell back.

The audience hooted and laughed as Jezebel and Terrence, in a muddle, tried to right themselves. Jezebel, panting, was the first to rise. Hands on hips, she glared at Terrence who slowly made it to his feet.

The pianist hit the very last chords to the song.

"Make your bow, sweetheart," Terrence whispered through a wide smile.

Jezebel blinked, and realized the audience was actually applauding. Disconcerted, she performed a hasty curtsy and quickly ran offstage. Terrence bowed with a flourish and then strolled off the stage.

"How dare you," Jezebel said the minute he arrived behind the curtain. "How dare you!"

He grinned, his gray eyes bursting with amusement. "See, you did it."

"Only because you—"

"No need to thank me," Terrence said, chuckling.

"Th-thank you!" Jezebel gasped.

"I said there was no need." Terrence smiled quite innocently. "They are still applauding, best go and take another curtsy."

"Another one?" Jezebel asked. He waved her back to the stage. "Oh, very well." Jezebel glared at him, stomped out onto the stage, performed a brisk curtsy, and tromped back offstage to where Terrence stood, his arms crossed, a wicked look upon his face.

"Now, sirrah," Jezebel said, shaking a finger at him. "I—"

"Do you realize you just did your first performance?"

Jezebel stopped in midword. "What!"

"You just did your first performance."

She stared. The realization hit her like a team of horses. She had actually been out there in front of all those people. People who were still applauding. All her prior fears came back. She began to shake. Her stomach jolted. "You—you are right."

Terrence frowned. "What is the matter?"

Jezebel paled. "I think I'm going to be sick."

"Not now! You've already performed."

"It does not matter." Jezebel lifted a hand to her mouth. "I'm going to be sick."

She dashed past Terrence and ignored his calls as she ran.

Three

"The Marquis of H. has been known to be a patron of the arts, but his 'patronage' exceeded the general last night when he himself took to the stage! Bedamn! What is the boy about!" Lady Dorethea cried, pacing the Aubusson carpet.

Elizabeth Grenville clasped her teacup and watched her employer circle a small curio table, like a dervish. Lady Dorethea's small body was knotted energy. Her wide panniers, which she refused to set aside for those milk-toast modern fashions, rocked upon each turn.

"He appeared, in an unannounced performance, with the newest comer to the stage, the beauteous Jezebel!" The paper crackled in Lady Dorethea's hands as she gripped it. "Jezebel! What a foolish name for a woman to take! Atrocious!"

"Perhaps 'tis her real name," Elizabeth murmured and sipped her tea.

"Impossible!" Lady Dorethea slashed the air with the paper in her hand as if she wielded a hatchet. "And the woman cannot act! She cannot sing! 'The golden songbird trilled off-key in a voice which did not reach the first row!' Bah!" Lady Dorethea threw the paper down and ground a small foot into it. "She cannot act and Terry appeared onstage with her!"

"It said he saved the performance," Elizabeth said, controlling a twitching smile.

"Saved? Saved some little tart who cannot even hold her own onstage!" Lady Dorethea exclaimed. "I vow, I shall kill the boy! To dally with an actress is one thing, but to appear onstage for all the world to see, is another. And for a female who cannot sing at that!"

"Madame," a voice quivered from the door. Stilton, the butler, stood, stiff and correct. His elderly face paled as he held out a paper and missive. "Another paper has arrived."

Lady Dorethea put her hands to her hips. "Who is it this time?"

"The Countess Liven," the butler said, shoving his hands out, as if what he held was rancid.

"Ha!" Lady Dorethea stalked over and snatched the sealed envelope from him, leaving Stilton with the offending paper still in hand. After she ripped the missive open, her bright green eyes narrowed upon it. " 'In case, my dear Dorethea, you were not able to acquire a paper in the wilds of Devon, I thought you might need to read this!' The old cow!" Lady Dorethea tossed the letter over her shoulder. "Put it with the rest, Stilton."

The butler trod with stately decorum over to the settee, which was strewn with newspapers of every sort. Solemnly he laid the paper down upon the pile.

"I have so many dear, concerned friends," Lady Dorethea said. "We shall have a bloody bonfire tonight, Stilton."

"Yes, My Lady," the butler said, nodding. "I shall alert the staff." He trod from the room.

"What do you intend to do?" Elizabeth asked quietly.

"Do?" Lady Dorethea stalked over to the papers, and began swatting them from the couch. "I am going to town and—" She stopped. "No!" She turned and sat down upon the settee, her panniers all but covering the remaining sheets. "I shall not go to him. I summoned the boy here, and instead he takes to the stage with this Jezebel." A sweet smile crossed her face. "My Terry always did have mettle. How I love him for it." She shrugged and leaned back. "I overplayed my hand I fear, but I assure you, I will not do so again."

"Is there anything else I can do for you . . . ? Oh, My Lord," Jezebel said, hastily looking up from the script she held.

The stage she stood upon held a large armoire, which was behind her; a settee to the side, and a table and chair. She was supposed to be a "saucy maid" in the "great lord's" room. The "great lord" and leading man, Ralph, stood across from her. He frowned at her as the moment stretched into two. Jezebel looked back to her script, scanning the lines in a frenzy.

" 'Giggle,' " she read aloud. "Oh, yes!" She forced a smile and attempted a giggle. It sounded more like a horse's neigh. She saw Ralph shiver, and she trained her eyes back to the script. "Mistress said to make sure you are comfortable, My Lord Curtsy." Jezebel frowned. "That's not right." She looked up in confusion. Ralph rolled his eyes heavenward. "Oh, dear, I see." Fumbling with her script, she dipped a hasty curtsy.

"Hmmm, there is something you can do for me, sweetings," Ralph said, only glancing at his lines. He swaggered up to within an inch of her, bending close. What in heaven's name was the man doing? Jezebel nervously untangled her script from her skirts and found her place. She scanned the lines rapidly. The word "kiss" jumped out at her.

"Kiss!" she exclaimed. Her head snapped up in shock and cracked sharply into Ralph's face. He fell back, holding a hand to his lip. "Oh, I'm terribly sorry."

"My lip," Ralph cried out in a tenor voice far from the manly baritone he had been rendering. "It is bleeding."

"Stop! Stop!" Antonio cried from offstage. He flapped his arms and jumped up and down. "Jezebel, you were to kiss him, not maim him!"

"I-I am sorry," Jezebel said, looking at Ralph, who indeed had a fine stream of blood trickling down his jaw. "I . . . I lost my place."

"It will not do, Terry," Antonio cried to Terrence who stood beside him. "She cannot act. I have her on the bill for this week. Everyone is coming to see her, *your* actress, and she cannot act! I will be ruined."

"Calm yourself," Terry said. " 'Tis her first time. She was reading cold."

"Cold?" Jezebel squeaked. "It says I'm supposed to kiss him. That is not cold!"

"You do not have to kiss him," Terrence said. Antonio squawked, and Terrence lifted a staying hand. "He shall kiss you, Jezebel, all right?"

"Kiss her?" Ralph's voice was muffled behind his hand. "She broke my lip. I cannot kiss her."

"All she needs is practice," Terry said.

"Not with me she don't," Ralph said. He threw down his script and stalked from the stage.

"Ralph!" Antonio shouted. He threw up his hands. "He is my finest lead actor. Now I must go and do pamper heem." He glared at Terrence. "You, you see what you can do with her. Ralph," he cried once more. Jumping up to the stage, he chased after the departed actor.

"I am sorry," Jezebel said, shifting from foot to foot. "But Terry, I . . . I cannot k-kiss him—and in front of people."

"Yes, you can," Terry said, and he himself jumped up onto the stage. "All you need is practice."

"More practice than you know," Jezebel murmured.

"The first thing you must realize is that it's not a real kiss," Terrence said. "It is acting—portraying a semblance of things. But it's not a real kiss."

Jezebel nodded. "All right, it's not a real kiss."

"Good." Terrence smiled. "Now, we are going to rehearse this scene again." He walked over and picked up Ralph's script. He scanned it quickly. "Start with your line, 'Is there anything I can do, anything . . . ?"

"Yes." Jezebel nodded. She looked at her script. " 'Is there anything else I can do for you, My Lord?" Jezebel looked up and forced a giggle.

"No," Terrence said, shaking his head. "You are flirting with this chap. Haven't you ever seen a maid giving a man the come-hither, letting him know she's wanting to . . . er, well, wanting him?"

"No," Jezebel said, flushing. "My father was a professor of English, and we had no maids. Except Ruth, that is."

"God, no," Terrence said. "Don't use Ruth as an example, anything but Ruth. Don't think of the words themselves, they are nothing. You are trying to say with your eyes and voice that you want me."

Jezebel gazed at Terrence. His mahogany hair was disheveled, one lock slipping over his brow. His gray eyes were frowning and serious. His expression was rather endearing. A real giggle escaped her.

His eyes lighted. "That's it!"

Jezebel laughed, focusing upon the man before her. He was frightfully attractive with his tall, lithe body and broad shoulders. She softened her voice and said, "Is there anything else I can do for you, My Lord?" Terrence's eyes widened. Jezebel glanced quickly at her script and then back at him, smiling in what she hoped was an appealing way. "My mistress said to be sure and make you . . . comfortable, My Lord." She remembered to curtsy, but she did it low and deep this time.

Terrence, grinning, tossed down his script. "Hmmm . . ." he said, walking toward her slowly, his eyes never leaving hers. "There is something . . ." he murmured, gently taking Jezebel's script from her and dropping it, ". . . you can do for me." He bent his head, his lips just above hers. Jezebel instinctively closed her eyes, nervousness rising within her. It was in the script, she reminded herself. She was supposed to let him kiss her. "Sweetings," he breathed gently, and then his lips found hers.

His lips brushed hers, feather light and warm. Just a teasing touch. Yet it was Jezebel's first kiss, and it shot lightning through her. Suddenly she wanted more. She pressed her lips against Terrence's, moving her body to align it with his. The difference of his hard strength against her softness sent a shiver through her.

Those two little moves, suddenly changed everything. Terrence groaned, and his arms wrapped about her. His kiss hardened, deepened. Jezebel gasped as a new passion ignited within her. Terrence enveloped her very being; his scent, the bone and sinew of the arms about her, and the taste of his lips demanding and questing of her.

She reached up, placing her hands to his shoulders. New sensations developed as she could feel the strength of them. She let her fingers slip to his hair. It was silk. Terrence groaned, his hands sweeping the arch of her back, settling within the curve of her waist. Then he was pushing her back. Jezebel willingly moved with him, not thinking, only feeling.

They slammed up against the armoire. Its legs squeaked against the wood floor. Jezebel moaned as she felt the full weight of Terrence pressed against her. He lifted his hands and cupped her face, moving his lips across hers, finding a more perfect alignment. Heat, raw and glowing, pulsed through Jezebel.

Suddenly, Terrence pulled back. He stared at her. "My God!"

Jezebel stared at him. Cold reality doused the heat in her blood. She was pressed up against an armoire, kissing a man as if her life depended upon it. And it was supposed to be acting, not real!

"Terry," Antonio called.

"Lord," Terrence said. He whipped his hands from Jezebel and stepped back.

Mortification froze Jezebel as she lost the warmth of Terrence's body against hers. She looked down, unable to meet his gaze.

"Ralph, I have talked to," Antonio exclaimed, strolling onto the stage. "You must say I am great. Ralph is calmed. He will return, and he promises to kiss Jezebel."

"No," Terrence barked. He stepped farther away from Jezebel.

"What?" Antonio asked, halting.

"He cannot kiss Jezebel."

"But he can. His lip, it was but a small cut, a scratch. He will be able to kiss, yes."

"No!" Jezebel exclaimed.

"No!" Terrence shouted.

Antonio jumped. "Eh?"

"He is not going to kiss Jezebel," Terrence said, his voice a low growl.

"I don't want to k-kiss Ralph," Jezebel stammered. If she kissed Ralph the way she had Terrence it would be frightful. What had overcome her she couldn't say, but she didn't want to chance a second display of such wanton behavior, not with Ralph!

"Bella," Antonio said, his brown eyes turning apologetic. "Forgive me. I was too hard upon you. It's my temper. Do not listen to me. We shall practice the kiss—"

"She doesn't need practice, dammit!" Terrence said, running a quick hand through his hair. "And she's not doing the blasted scene with Ralph."

"I-I can't," Jezebel said, shaking her head. "I—I cannot act." She flushed. What was she saying? If she hadn't been acting, the scene with Terrence was far more reprehensible.

"She . . . cannot act," Terry said. "You cannot put her in this play."

Antonio's face fell. "Then what am I to do, heh? I have her on the playbill. They come to see her, to see her because she is your actress. This is what you wanted. Not me! Now

you tell me she cannot act and cannot do the scene. Terry"—
Antonio spread out his hands—"My boy, 'tis a small part,
the only small part for her."

"It's not small enough," Terry said.

"She must appear," Antonio said, his face reddening.
"She must. The public, he wants her."

"Then have her appear in something else," Terry said,
stalking up to Antonio and glaring down at him.

Antonio stepped back as he saw Terrence clench his fists.
"Very well, very well," Antonio went on. "But what are we
to do? We had her sing. She cannot. We were going to have
her act. Now you say she cannot act. What? What *can* she
do?"

Terrence's hand suddenly shot out and grabbed Antonio
by the collar. "Never mind what she can do, do you hear
me!"

"Y-yes," Antonio said in a strangled voice. "Yes."

Terrence dropped Antonio's collar, jerking back his arm.
"I'm sorry, Tony."

Antonio smiled weakly. He looked to Jezebel. "What a
couple you are. You, you slap *il direttore,* and he, he stran-
gles *il direttore.* There is no respect, no respect." He studied
them both silently. "Hmmm, yes," he said, suddenly smiling.

"What are you smiling about?" Terrence growled.

"Nothing," Antonio said quickly. "Nothing. But if you
permit, may I ask Jezebel if she can dance?"

"Why are you asking me?" Terrence snapped. "Ask her."

Antonio turned bright eyes to Jezebel. *"Bella,* can you
dance?"

Jezebel nodded. "Yes, I think I can dance. I will dance."

Antonio turned to Terrence, clapping his hands. *"Bene,*
we put her in the ladies' chorus, no? Perhaps she does a few
steps by herself? They come to see her only, not her performance, true?"

"Fine," Terrence said. "That's just fine." Then he stalked
from the stage.

Jezebel watched him go, a flush of embarrassment flooding over her. Antonio looked at her, his eyes softening. "Ah, *bella,* do not look so. If you cannot act, it must be accepted. Not everyone has the talent."

Jezebel bit her lip. The problem wasn't that she couldn't act. She apparently could act the wanton very well. It was a talent she did not wish to claim. She could only pray it would be a secret between Terrence and herself.

Jezebel sat at her vanity and gazed into the mirror. It was strange, how life suddenly walked into one's calm existence and spun one in a dizzying circle. Just like that! No invitation, no warning.

She eyed her tight bodice of purple and the blond hair flowing down her back with nary a proper pin or restraining influence. Suddenly she laughed in sheer excitement. Tonight would be her first party. Her father had never held parties, and she never knew if her mother had, for that woman had passed away when Jezebel was but five. Jezebel cocked her head to one side in contemplation. Perhaps her mother had given parties. It was she who had demanded the name Jezebel for her daughter, and she had stood firm on it until her father had agreed. It said much about her mother, for Roger Clinton was not a fanciful man.

"Mama," Jezebel murmured softly. A twinge of sadness passed through her. It would have been nice to be able to have shared her excitement with her mother at this moment. Then again, her mother might very well have disapproved of the notion. Jezebel did not need to think about her father. She knew he was rolling over in his grave this very minute.

Still, she would not change her course. She had entered this crazy, strange life to protect Josh, as she had always done. He was the center of her life. She knew she would do anything for him. Indeed, it had been that way since they were children. Her father had been a kind, but reticent, proper man, and the two motherless children had bonded together to offer the only true warmth and vitality within each other's life.

"Miss Jezebel" Ruth called as she entered the room. She halted upon crossing the threshold and stared. "Faith and begorra!" She crossed herself. "Ye look a proper heathen, you do!"

"Do I?" Jezebel laughed and rose. She spun around for inspection. "If you mean I look like an actress, then I am pleased."

"Pleased! How can ye be saying that?" Ruth said, her hands going to her hips. "Ye ought to be ashamed of yerself."

Jezebel knew she should be, but she wasn't. "Ruth, dear," she said, smiling, "do not badger me so. I am going to my first party."

"Aye, with a great lot of harlots and fancy men," the housekeeper retorted.

"Well, I suppose so." Jezebel ran a hand through her hair. "They are actors, after all."

"Tsk," Ruth said and steamed over to Jezebel. She swatted Jezebel's hand from her hair and proceeded to arrange the curls. "I didn't like that Marquis taking ye out driving and walking with his sort. Him showing you off to them like he owned you."

"It is important for the *ton* to see us together," Jezebel said, as Ruth tweaked a curl too vigorously. "We can't create a scandal if they never see us together."

"But now he's taking you to a party of actors and that is worse. 'Tis sinful."

Jezebel lifted her chin. "I must study how to be an actress. Besides, I'd rather go to this party than one of the *ton's*."

"Saints preserve us!"

"I would!" Jezebel said hotly. "You should but see them, Ruth! The women are quite beautiful, but one ensemble of theirs would equal what Father's portion was in a year. And they are wearing such in the park, or on the strut, as Terrence says. Heaven only knows what they wear in the evening. Why, 'twould most likely send Josh to Eton for years if he so chose."

"Aye," nodded Ruth, her hand reaching to smooth the satin of Jezebel's skirt, forcing it to fall into finer lines. " 'Tis the nobility. The higher orders."

"But they are not kind," Jezebel said, shaking her head. "They are cold and haughty."

" 'Tis because they think ye a strumpet," Ruth said, huffing as she straightened. "And could ye blame them for it?"

Jezebel frowned. "No, I suppose not."

Ruth shook her head. "Lord love us, I don't know what yer dear brother Josh will think of this when he returns."

"I'm doing it for him!" Jezebel said angrily. "I may appear the strumpet, but at least I saved him from a real one. He dare not say anything. I am doing it for him."

"Are ye, lass?" Ruth asked, her gruff voice suddenly softening. "Or are ye doing it fer yer fine lord's sake?"

Jezebel drew back, stunned. She thought of Terrence, of how his face grew set and angry when he mentioned his grandmother and her schemes. She thought of the women of the *ton* who surveyed her with narrow eyes from afar and lifted their shoulders and turned their backs upon her. She thought of the few men who did approach them, and their ribbing of Terrence for his appearance onstage, an appearance which was her fault. Jezebel shook her head slightly. "Perhaps."

"Dearie," Ruth said, putting her hands to Jezebel's shoulders. "The Marquis is not a marrying man."

"Of course he isn't," Jezebel said, frowning. " 'Tis why we are enacting this charade. He does not wish to be forced into marriage."

Ruth shook her slightly. "And what of you? How will ye ever marry after this?"

"Me?" Jezebel asked in astonishment. She had never

thought of herself and marriage. Indeed, sometimes she would dream of a hero, a loving husband to stand beside her; yet then the day would dawn and the worries of every-day life, such as how she was going to keep Josh and herself on their meager funds, would oversway such fantasies. "I had not thought."

"Well, think," Ruth said. "Ye are a woman and should be married."

"I promise I will think upon it," Jezebel said, reaching up to withdraw Ruth's hands from her shoulders and hold them. "Really I will, but at the moment I must do this. I owe Terrence the money, and I must help him. And it is my first party, Ruth. I plan to learn as much as I can about how to be an actress, but I hope to enjoy myself as well."

She was drinking too much, Terrence thought in concern as he glanced at Jezebel, who sat beside him upon an old settee. She had not said a word all evening, but her violet eyes sparkled like amethyst, and she watched the revelry in the green room avidly. It was a large, dull room, with mis-matched, dilapidated furniture strewn in the corners. The company, however, set it alight with their spirits and bawdy talk. Actors, actresses, and their consorts flirted and laughed.

And the blasted bottle was passed around far too often. Jezebel always smiled and held out her goblet, an old prop left from *Macbeth*. The few chunks of cheese and cold meats that served as food had long since disappeared.

"Jezebel," he whispered, as she lifted her goblet and smiled to the company at large. "You must cease."

"Cease?" She turned inquiring eyes upon him. "Cease what?"

"You are—"

"Jezebel," a red-headed actress named Tess called out at that moment. She strolled over, dragging young Lord Dar-lington, who was quite willing to live, and go about with her. "Do you think you'll be ready for the show Friday night?" Her blue eyes narrowed. "It's only two days from now, ye know, ducky."

Jezebel leaned over to Terrence and whispered, "She reminds me of Molly, don't you think?" Then she pulled back and smiled. "Oh, I believe I'll be ready."

"Ha, Jezzy!" A black-haired actress hooted from across the room. "That swan dive ye took into the curtains yesterday won't please the audience, I'll lay you odds."

"She don't care," Tess snorted. "They ain't coming to see her talent." She wrapped an arm about Lord Darlington, who straightened, puffed out his spavined chest, and cast upon everyone a proud and bleary eye. "They're coming to see her 'cause of him." Tess jabbed a finger toward Terrence.

Terrence stiffened. Suddenly he felt Jezebel's hand tight upon his arm. "And why not?" she said, flashing a brilliant smile. "Terry is a fine patron of the arts, ain't you, love?"

"Is he now?" Tess's eyes narrowed. "He ain't as fine as my Darlington." Her bosom rose and well nigh overpowered her low décolletage. "He bought me a prad and red carriage just t'other day." She turned her head and smacked her drunken lord upon the cheek. "Didn't you, lambkins?"

"Sure did," Lord Darlington nodded his head to and fro. "Anything fer my sweetmeats."

"Well now," Jezebel said. Terrence noticed her voice suddenly took on a harsher, almost cockney accent, a close imitation of Tess's. "I don't need a prad or such. My Terry gives me so-o-o-o much more," Jezebel cooed. Of a sudden she stood, only to plop herself firmly upon Terrence's lap. "S-o-o much more."

Terrence stiffened as she shifted to a comfortable position and wrapped her arms about him. "Jezebel!"

"Ah, ducky," Jezebel, her lips close to his ear, added, "I'm doing it correctly, am I not? They are all doing it like this," she murmured and nuzzled his ear. Heat flashed through Terrence. He strove to focus upon the room. Many had stilled to hear the conversation, but indeed, most of the women sat on their men's laps, and those standing had their arms draped about their mates. He watched as one woman nuzzled her lover, just as Jezebel was doing. Imitating them she might be, but it did nothing to quelch his rising passion.

"Stop it," he whispered.

Jezebel drew back obediently, but smiled smugly toward Tess. "My Terry, he ain't one for public display, but he is a fine protector."

"Not as good as my Darlington!" Tess cried.

"Think what you may," Jezebel said in her borrowed cockney accent, "But then you are older than he. We all know why an older lady likes a younger man, don't we?"

"What!" Tess screeched.

"Jezebel!" Terrence exclaimed. "You must be drunk!"

Jezebel dipped her head toward him and whispered, "No, I've been pouring it out behind us."

"You have?" Terrence asked as she drew back. She offered him a smirk and actually winked at him.

"Yer nothing but a bloody bitch," Tess said, apparently oblivious to the byplay and in a fine rage. "Ye think yer so much better than us all, with yer refined accent and ways. Hoity-toity and actin' like a duchess. Bet ye think ye got Terrence drinking out of yer slipper, don't ye?"

"Slipper?" Jezebel asked. She turned an inquiring look to Terrence.

He shrugged. "Men do that sometimes . . . as a toast to a woman, to signify they are at her feet with adoration."

"Oh, I see." Jezebel turned her gaze back to Tess. "I don't expect Terry to drink out of my slipper. He ain't at my feet." She suddenly leaned over and grabbed up Terrence's tophat that rested beside them. "In fact, I'll drink to him." Hat in hand, she said imperiously, "A bottle please."

One chuckling buck quickly stumbled over to hand one to her. Jezebel poured the wine into the hat. Then she stood and lifted it high. "I drink to my Terry. It's not his feet I like, but his head. And that's what I'm drinking to!"

Everyone gasped as Jezebel tipped the brim of the tophat and drank. She set it down and quickly plopped back down upon Terrence's lap.

Leaning over, she whispered, "Don't worry, I didn't drink much."

Terrence groaned as he put his arms about her. Jezebel looked around to find everyone was staring at them. "What is the matter?" she asked.

"Jezebel, I don't think you should have made that toast," Terrence said.

"Why not?" She wrapped her arms around his shoulders. "You are more intelligent than any of them. Even that silly Lord Darlington, and I don't care if they know it."

Thus spoke the professor's daughter.

Four

Jezebel drew in a deep breath and peered into the murky, smeared mirror. She rubbed at the red upon her cheeks, working it in more thoroughly. The other actresses had already left and were most likely waiting in the green room, ready for the show. She was glad to have a moment to herself.

She had never seen women so immodest in her entire life. Most of them had dashed around, borrowing stage paint from one another, in nothing but their petticoats. Tess hadn't even deigned to wear her petticoats, forswearing any covering. Myrtle, the youngest actress, only sixteen and already under the protection of Lord Sylvester, had giggled as Tess had flashed by and, leaning over, had whispered that Tess likened herself to a dancer and was vain about her body.

Jezebel had been glad to smear on the heavy greasepaint, if only to hide her burning blushes. Yet the women jabbered and elbowed each other good-naturedly as they moved about the cramped quarters with nary a consideration of the flesh they exposed. Talk of the shows—past, present, and future—streamed through their laughter and gossip, even supplanting the talk of their men. A feeling of excitement and electricity invaded the room, growing with each minute it became closer to curtain call. It caught Jezebel up.

She dusted the powder off her hands and rose. Perhaps tonight wouldn't be that frightening after all. It wouldn't be like when she sang. She would not be alone onstage. She would be but one in a group of women. Gratefully, she wouldn't be the center of attention.

It was going well! They were all forming a line for their last set of kicks. Jezebel sang loudly with the others, as she joined the line in the center between Mitzy and Tess. Now all she had to do was spin, then turn back, link arms with the others and perform the high kicks. Jezebel twirled with a flourish. Yet the minute her back was solidly to the audience she heard a roar of laughter. Oh, Lord! She wasn't supposed to have turned! They had taken that step out in rehearsal.

Hastily, Jezebel spun back to the front. Desperate to retrieve her error, she latched on to Tess's arm while she kicked her left leg out high and to the right. It was completely wrong. She hadn't grabbed Tess's arm after all, but her skirts. A rending sound and a curse let her know her mistake.

From Jezebel's other side a screech arose. The women hadn't been kicking right with their left leg, but kicking left with their right leg. Jezebel's leg was definitely out of line, and in the jumble of warring legs, her foot had contacted Mitzy's with forceful impact.

Mitzy, still screeching in pain, jolted to the side and rammed into Bess. Bess, caught off balance in the middle of a high kick, toppled completely back, her legs flying up in a wide vee. Since her arm was linked with Mable's, Mable promptly followed her to the floor. Katie went down next. It was a muddle of skirts, curses, and flailing stockinged legs, exposed to the very garters.

Appalled, Jezebel stepped back, only to come up against another body to the side of her. She heard a grunt and curse. As she twirled to her left, her eyes widened. The drastic chain effect to her right was now occurring to her left. The body she had hit was Tess's. Tess, with only half a skirt still on, had toppled and dragged Terese down. Terese, partnered with Melinda had brought her along to the floor. Jezebel groaned. It was more skirts, legs, and curses.

Then, and only then, did Jezebel become aware of the roaring in her ears. The roar of a theater full of people laughing and hooting. As she looked out to the audience, mortification engulfed her. She alone was left standing, the center of attention after all!

Jezebel heard Antonio bellowing, "Curtain! Curtain! Get the bloody curtain closed."

She stood frozen as the stage boys jerked and tugged the curtains shut, finally hiding her from the laughing and jeering people. Only then did she whirl about and dash from the stage, dodging the muddle of cursing women.

Terrence bolted from his seat in the audience. People in every chair and aisle hooted and hollered. Overpowering rage shot through him. They dared to laugh at Jezebel. There she had stood, all alone, an expression of such embarrassment and pain upon her face. He must go to her. She would be sobbing her eyes out by now.

He dashed up the aisle, slammed out of the doors to the lobby, and all but bounced two laughing stagehands out of his way. He made his way to the private door which would lead him to the dressing rooms backstage. He had to reach Jezebel. Soothe her. Calm her. She wasn't to blame. It was his own bloody fault for demanding she go onstage.

He sprinted toward the dressing rooms, knowing full well that was where Jezebel would be. As he approached them, he heard a terrible noise, women's voices raised in shrieks and screams. He ran up to the stage boy Jem, who merely stood outside a closed door, hands clasped and gaze turned toward heaven.

"What the devil is going on!" Terrence shouted, gripping Jem by the shoulder.

Jem's face was pale. "The ladies . . . they—they be, er, scrapping."

"Scrapping!" He shook Jem roughly. "Is Jezebel in there?"

Jem's eyes widened. " 'Course! That's why they're scrapping."

"Oh, God!" Terrence gasped. They would rend her to pieces!

He shoved Jem aside and rammed open the door. The scene that met him looked very similar to the one upon stage. Female bodies in a muddle, some on the floor, others standing, slapping and clawing at each other.

"Jezebel!" Terrence roared.

"Here!" A tousled, golden blond head appeared from the kaleidoscope of colors and bodies on the ground. He saw Jezebel lurch up. He also saw Tess spring up behind, her hair standing out like an enraged porcupine's quills, blood lust in her eyes, and her clawed hands reaching for Jezebel.

"Look out!" Terrence cried.

Jezebel spun around, but not fast enough. Tess successfully clamped her hands around Jezebel's throat. Terrence bolted forward, but three struggling bodies blocked him. He couldn't get through. My God, Tess would strangle her to death!

Suddenly he saw Jezebel's right hand shoot out and deliver an excellent jab to Tess's stomach. It was a fine bit of the home brewed.

Terrence froze, stunned himself at the fast action. Tess wheezed, her hands falling from Jezebel's throat to clutch her stomach. Jezebel turned and cast him a triumphant grin. "Good show!" he cried out, pride washing through him.

"There's her man!" a female voice screeched. "Get him." Brawling women rose in a harmonized effort and converged on him.

"Gads!" Terry exclaimed as pummeling hands hit him and fingernails scratched. He raised his arms, attempting to ward off the women. Honor stayed him from hitting the ladies, making him a sitting duck.

"No!" Jezebel cried out. He peered over his upraised arm to see her cutting a swath through the shrieking women. She clearly suffered none of his qualms. She belted some ladies with a fine balled fist, kicked at the others. Reaching him, she flung herself at him, her body a human shield.

Terrence wrapped one arm about Jezebel even as she diverted slaps and blows to herself. Honor be damned. He was holding the only lady in the room. The only one who mattered.

Tess shoved close and buried a fist in Jezebel's hair. Terrence reached out with his one free arm and popped Tess directly on the nose. The woman stumbled back, screeching curses even Terrence didn't recognize. Another woman surged to take her place. He swiftly leveled her, dragging Jezebel back with him toward the door. She swiveled in his arms to face the onslaught, and while he single-handedly boxed at the women, Jezebel kicked out with wicked precision.

They tumbled out the door, Jezebel grabbing hold of the knob and swinging it shut.

"Bejeezus!" Jem cried, hopping up and down as he stared at them.

"Hold this," Jezebel cried, clutching the knob as a volley of hammering came from the other side and the door bucked.

"I—I can't." Jem shook his head.

"You'd better!" Terrence growled, dropping his arm from Jezebel and covering her hands on the door to reinforce her hold.

"Terry!" a deep voice bellowed. Antonio appeared, charging down the corridor like a bull let out of his pen. "What is the matter?"

"Hold this, Tony!" Terrence shouted. "They want to kill Jezebel!"

Antonio halted immediately. "Me—I wish to kill her too!"

Terry's eyes narrowed as the doorknob turned and the baying of women rose even higher.

"We can't hold them," Jezebel cried.

"You won't have to have her onstage again," Terry said quickly, "if you only hold them off now."

"I won't?" Antonio's eyes lighted. *"Sì! Sì!"* He bolted forward and pushed their hands aside, clutching the knob with stocky, strong hands. "You go! You promise!"

Terry laughed and grabbed Jezebel's hand. "We'll go!" He turned and tugged her down the corridor. He did not have to strain, for she was as fleet as he was. "Goodbye, Antonio!" Terrence shouted.

"Is my debt paid?" Antonio's voice followed them as they dashed toward the backstage door.

Terrence stopped suddenly, raised his hands to his lips, and shouted, "Paid in full, Antonio, paid in full!"

"Aha!" Antonio's excited shout turned to one of pain.

"He couldn't hold them," Terrence said, grabbing Jezebel's hand again. "Come on, sweetheart!"

Not until they sat safely in the carriage did Terrence stop long enough to breathe. He turned his gaze to Jezebel, seated beside him. She waved her hands before her face and amazingly was laughing.

"You saved my life, Terry," she said, her voice breathless.

"And you mine." Terrence laughed.

"They were in quite a rage," Jezebel said. "It was Tess who incited it. She claimed I had ruined her career."

"She never had one." Terrence snorted.

"She thought this would be her big break." Jezebel giggled. "I think you broke her nose the last time you hit her."

He grinned. "I guess it was her big break after all."

"Heartless," Jezebel said, laughing.

"No," Terrence protested, "I thought she would strangle you."

"She almost did a few times. Luckily, Myrtle took up my side before you came." She chuckled. "Myrtle said it wasn't my fault if I was fiddle-footed and couldn't dance my way out of hell."

"Jezebel!" Terrence exclaimed.

"Well"—she looked at him with an impish grin—" 'Twas what she said. And since she took my side, I'm awfully grateful to her."

Terrence shook his head as he looked at the woman next to him. A jolt went through him. She had a blackening eye, and a cut lined her lip. Her costume vaunted rips and tears, the one at her bodice hinting at the white curves he remembered all too well. He coughed. "Um, yes." He quickly shrugged out of his coat.

"What are you doing?" Jezebel asked.

"Er, nothing," he said and swiftly handed it to her. "Here, put this on."

"Why?"

"Well," he said. "Someone rent your dress."

She looked down and gasped. Quickly she grabbed up the coat and struggled into it. Terrence politely looked away. When he returned his gaze to her, she sat, enshrouded in his jacket. He could see a flush of embarrassment upon her face, even in the dimness of the carriage. "You handled yourself very well back there," he said quickly, wishing to distract her.

She smiled, and he saw her eyes clear. "Thank you."

He shook his head. "Wherever did you learn such a punishing left?"

A smile tipped her lips. "From Josh. When we were young he was determined to learn fisticuffs, and since Father did not hold with such a violent, ill-bred sport, 'twas I who had to be his partner." She laughed. "Father thought we were merely enacting scenes from important battles. It was perfectly all right to study history."

Terrence barely listened. The softness in her eyes mesmerized him. It was so at odds with the harsh bruises upon her face. "You love him very much, don't you?"

Jezebel nodded. "Yes. He is my brother."

Terrence couldn't help himself. He lifted a hand to touch her lip. "You are cut there."

A stunned expression crossed Jezebel's face. She slowly raised her hand to his brow. "And you are there."

Terrence traced her lower lip. It trembled. He could neither take his gaze nor his finger from its softness.

"You . . . do you have any brothers?" Jezebel asked. Her voice was breathless. "Or . . . or sisters?"

"No," Terrence said, and with superhuman force he withdrew his hand. "I was the only child. My father and mother died when I was young. I was raised by my grandmother . . . and her sisters."

Jezebel's brows shot up. "All women?"

"All women." Terrence forced a laugh. " 'Twas more than enough." He could not help himself. He still needed to touch her. He reached over and picked up her hand. He saw her wince, and he looked down. Cuts marred her hand. "You hurt yourself."

Jezebel laughed. "Not as much as I did Tess, I hope."

Their eyes met and suddenly they both laughed in a union of amusement. "You are wicked, Jezebel," Terrence choked out.

She stopped laughing. Something like surprise flitted across her face. "I'm afraid I might be."

Terry shook his head and lifted her hand to his lips and gently kissed it. "No. You were a proper heroine."

She flushed and shook her head. "No, not proper at all. Ladies shouldn't hit other ladies."

"You mean other women," Terrence said. "They were not ladies."

"And I am even glad I . . ." She halted, worrying her lower lip. A flush stained her cheek.

"What?" Terrence asked, intrigued. She shook her head. "Come, we've been partners in battle, you can tell me."

"Well," Jezebel said, an embarrassed smile on her lips. "I am glad I loosened my corset stays. You were right. It helps ever so much in a fight."

Terrence stared and then barked a laugh. "The iron mistress unloosened her corset stays! And pleased to do it for a fight."

"I told you I was wicked," Jezebel said.

"No," Terrence said, wrapping a quick arm around her. "I am proud of you, Miss Jezebel Clinton. I'll gladly claim you as my mistress anytime."

"Even if you are made to be a laughing stock?" Jezebel asked, wincing. "And . . . and forced to fight the whole chorus line to save me?"

"Even then," Terrence said, but he could feel her body stiffening. "What is the matter?"

"Nothing," Jezebel said. "I . . . I have a few bruises, that's all."

Terrence whipped his arm from her. "I'm sorry, I was not thinking." Sudden regret filled him, and with it a driving concern. "And what of you, Jezebel?"

Her eyes flashed to his face and then lowered. "What of me?"

" 'Tis you who have been hurt far more than I," he said gently. " 'Twas you who had to face that audience, and it was I who forced you to do so. You are becoming notorious through no purpose of your own." He hesitated only a moment. "Do you wish to quit this, Jezebel?"

"Do you want me to?" she asked softly.

Terrence shook his head. "No, from the beginning it has always been what I have wanted. I want to know what you want."

She looked away, and instead of answering his question said, "Just what did Antonio owe you?"

He blinked. "What does that have to do with anything?"

"What did he owe you?" Jezebel asked again, her eyes turning to study him intently.

Terrence sighed. "I staked his theater in the beginning."

Her eyes widened. "That must have been a great sum of money."

Terrence shrugged. "Perhaps."

The cloud disappeared from Jezebel's face, and she smiled. "Then I owe you even more money than I did before, don't I?"

"The money be hanged," Terrence said quickly.

She shook her head. "No, I owe you a lot of money, and I am determined to pay my debt."

He gazed at her, and realized that though she wasn't answering his question, she was. The money didn't matter to him anymore, but if it was the key to her positive answer he would accept it. He had been as noble as he ever intended to be. "Well, come to think of it, it was a hefty sum, quite a hefty sum."

"Good," Jezebel said, and then added, "what I mean is, I'll just have to be your actress and pay you back, won't I?"

"Yes," Terrence said, relief settling warmly in his heart. "Yes, you will."

Her face clouded. "But I'm not sure Antonio will let me back on stage now."

"I doubt it." Terrence laughed. "That is, if he is still alive."

"I'm sorry."

"Don't be," Terrence said, grinning. "You may not have thought you succeeded, but you've gone beyond my wildest hopes in making a name for yourself. In fact, we are ahead in the game. It is time for me to take you home and introduce you to my dear grandmother, I believe."

"Introduce me t-to your grandmother?" Jezebel stammered.

He grinned. "We move into the enemy camp now. I've been waiting for this moment."

"You never told me," Jezebel squeaked, "that I would have to do that."

Terrence shook his head. "It was a hefty sum Antonio owed me."

She glared at him, but then a laugh escaped her. "And you say we women are conniving."

"I learned it at my grandmother's knee." Terrence grinned.

Jezebel's eyes turned dark. "I am not sure I can handle your grandmother."

"If you faced all those actresses, you can manage my grandmother."

"I'm not sure," she said, fear in her voice.

Terrence reached out and cupped her chin, forcing her to look at him. "I told you, Jezebel, I am glad to claim you as my mistress."

Her violet eyes lightened. "Then mistress I shall be."

"Thank you," he said softly, and forced a smile. "Now, I believe we need to go and get some beefsteaks."

Jezebel smiled. "Yes, I believe I am hungry."

"No," he said chuckling. "I meant for the bruise over your eye."

Jezebel looked downcast. "Oh."

"But we will get one for your stomach as well, how is that?"

Jezebel looked at him and her blue eyes gleamed. "Sounds like a famous proposal, Terry, my love, sounds like a famous proposal."

" 'The Actress Jezebel Brings Down The House,' " Elizabeth read from the paper she had picked up from the fresh pile before her.

"What? The gel finally learned to act?" Lady Dorethea asked, and took a swift drink from a brandy snifter. She claimed it was medicinal. When Elizabeth would mention that Doctor Tout did not see it as such, but claimed it dangerous for her spleen, Lady Dorethea would wave a hand and say that Doctor Tout was an old twiddlepoop and what would a sawbones know about fine brandy anyway?

Therefore Elizabeth held her tongue and scanned the article. She choked back a sudden gurgle of laughter. "Oh, my!"

"What? Read it!"

" 'Patrons of the arts that night were privileged to see Miss Jezebel Clinton kicking up her shapely legs—and also kicking her sister actresses. Miss Jezebel apparently swerved from the intended choreography and in so doing, caused the downfall of the entire chorus line. Actress after actress toppled, until Miss Jezebel alone remained standing. A novel way to take the stage, Miss Clinton!' "

"Oh, Lord," Lady Dorethea muttered.

" 'It was rumored,' " Elizabeth continued to read, fascinated, " 'that a brawl ensued in the female dressing room afterward. The actress, Jezebel, made good her escape only with the support of her well-known patron and sometime actor, the Marquis of H. It was noted that both possessed the science of fisticuffs to a fine degree. The actress, Tess Morgan, who many believe will certainly rise in the arts, will not be performing upon stage for a fortnight, she suffers a broken nose. Two other actresses were known to suffer sprained ankles.' "

"Forsooth, they left a bloody battlefield," Lady Dorethea said. Then she grinned. "But they gave those other actresses a proper drubbing, didn't they?"

"Yes," Elizabeth said, laughing. She set the paper down and reached for another newspaper, one that was known to be more scurrilous. " 'The actress, Jezebel, toasted her patron, the Marquis of H. in his own silk tophat. She was quoted to . . .' "

"Give me that!" Lady Dorethea said, springing up and spilling her brandy. She ripped the sheet from Elizabeth's fingers. "You don't want to know what the hussy toasted to, I assure you."

"What did she toast to?" Elizabeth asked, intrigued.

"Well, it wasn't his feet," Lady Dorethea muttered, crossing to toss that particular paper into the fire.

There was a slight knock on the door.

"Enter," Lady Dorethea said.

Stilton entered, his face very long. He bowed. "Your Grace . . ."

Without looking at him, but watching the flames devour the paper, Lady Dorethea said, "Just put them with the rest, Stilton."

"I am glad to say I do not bring another paper, Your Grace," Stilton said. "Miss Amelia Arrowroot awaits in the hall."

"Amelia!" Lady Dorethea exclaimed. "Show her in, Stilton, and do bring us tea." As Stilton bowed and departed, Lady Dorethea raced over to her brandy and quaffed it. Looking swiftly about, she buried the snifter in Elizabeth's sewing basket. When she turned and caught Elizabeth's eye upon her she said, "The dear child is quite innocent, you know."

Lady Dorethea had just made it back in time to sit and fan out her wide skirts, when Miss Arrowroot entered. Amelia was a petite girl, with large brown eyes and quick movements. Her hair was uncompromisingly brown. Unfortunately so was her complexion. As if that were not enough brown, Miss Amelia possessed a penchant for wearing the same color upon her person.

"Godmama," Amelia said and, with hands outstretched, moved quickly toward Lady Dorethea.

"My dear," Lady Dorethea said, rising graciously.

Amelia stumbled slightly. The women looked down to discover her foot resting upon one of the many papers littering the floor. "Oh, I am terribly sorry."

"Don't be, dear," Lady Dorethea said quickly and dragged the girl to the settee. "Elizabeth and I are . . . are merely . . . er, researching something. Do sit, dear child."

"Are you?" Amelia said. Her brown eyes brightened. "So am I. I am doing a study upon the brown-thatch wren." She leaned down to pick up the paper. "In fact, I heard there is to be a symposium by the Feathered Friends Society in London."

"No!" Lady Dorethea cried, and swiftly ripped the paper from Amelia's hands. She forced a smile as Amelia drew back in astonishment. "These are old papers . . . I am sure they would not have anything about . . . about birds in them."

Elizabeth stifled a giggle. At least not of the feathered variety. She noticed the large printed name of "Jezebel" slashed on the page as Lady Dorethea rolled it up and tossed it over the settee. Amelia only stared at Lady Dorethea.

"Well, now," Lady Dorethea said, smiling. " 'Tis a pleasure to see you, child. And how is your dear papa?"

"He is still at his hunting lodge," Amelia replied, frowning.

"Good, good." Lady Dorethea nodded.

"I miss him," Amelia said, with what appeared to be reproach in her eyes.

"Oh, er . . . yes." Lady Dorethea recovered her aplomb. "I did not mean to say I was glad he was not here. But you know men, they must get away to the wilds, away from civilization you know. The sport and all?"

"Indeed." Elizabeth smiled, knowing full well Lady Dorethea abhorred all manly sports. It took the men away from their rightful place, that of escorting women and seeing to the well-being and amusement of the fairer sex. "They must be permitted their escape . . . I mean, amusements."

Lady Dorethea glared at Elizabeth. However, Stilton once again entered, carrying but one silver tray. "Yes, Stilton? Where is the tea?"

He bowed. "Madame, Cook is still preparing it."

"Well then?"

"Another missive has arrived." He lifted a letter from the tray.

"Not now, Stilton," Lady Dorethea said, her jaw clearly tightening.

"I am sorry, but . . . but it is from Lady Theodora."

"Theo?" Lady Dorethea said. "Oh, very well, bring it here."

Stilton trod with dignity over to Lady Dorethea and offered the message. Lady Dorethea took it and waved the butler away. He quietly disappeared as Dorethea broke the seal and opened the missive. She scanned the lines. "Oh, Lud! Theo is coming to visit!"

"Auntie Theo?" Amelia said. "But she never leaves Warring's Crossing."

"She is now," Lady Dorethea said.

"But why?" Amelia asked.

Lady Dorethea met Elizabeth's eyes. "She feels there is a matter of importance she must attend to here."

"What kind of matter?" Amelia frowned.

" 'Tis nothing you should worry yourself over," Lady Dorethea said. Stilton appeared at the door again. This time he actually coughed. Lady Dorethea's eyes narrowed. "What now, Stilton? I do hope you mean to ask me if we should have the coconut macaroons or the scones."

"No, Your Grace." Under her daunting eye, he pulled out another missive. " 'Tis another one."

"From whom?"

"Lady Leticia," he said, his voice failing as Lady Dorethea threw up her hands.

"Leticia! Do not say she is coming to visit!"

"I would not know, Your Grace," Stilton said. "I did not

open your missive, and surely I never would. A good butler would never stoop to—"

"Oh, bring it here," snapped Dorethea. Stilton approached her with less dignity, and far more haste. She snatched the letter from him. He departed in a flash. She ripped open the seal, glanced at the missive, and tossed it down. "That's it! Letty is coming too! It is all tear stained, but I can decipher the most of it."

"Tear stained?" Amelia frowned. "Whatever is wrong with dear Auntie Leticia?"

"Nothing is wrong with her," Lady Dorethea snorted. "But you know Letty, she makes a chetleham tragedy over everything, the silly widgeon."

"Did she say when she would arrive?" Elizabeth asked.

"No, but you had best prepare. I have no doubt she'll bring her demn, precious cat with her." Lady Dorethea groaned. "And Theo will bring that beast Mordrid."

"Who is Mordrid?" Amelia asked.

"He is—" Lady Dorethea stopped in midsentence, and she stiffened as she glanced toward the door. "Stilton? Is that you?" The butler appeared again in the door frame. A twitch actually betrayed itself at the corner of his left eye. Dorethea's gaze narrowed. "Do say you bring the tea, Stilton. That is all I wish to hear from you, nothing more."

"Very well, Your Grace," Stilton said, bowing. He turned to leave.

"Where in blazes are you going?" Dorethea asked.

Stilton paused. "You said you wished to hear nothing more save about the tea, Your Grace. I regret to say, that was not my mission."

"Oh, very well," Dorethea conceded. "What is your mission?"

Stilton looked pained. "It—it is a letter from M-Master Terrence."

"For heaven's sake, bring it here!" Lady Dorethea

snapped and held out her hand. "I've been waiting for the boy to write me."

Stilton nodded and walked with dignity across the room to hand the missive to Lady Dorethea. He then departed with record haste. "I wonder what the rapscallion has to say for himself," Lady Dorethea said, opening the letter and reading it. "Good Lord, the devil! He is coming to visit."

"Oh my," Amelia said, her hand rising to her chest. "Is he coming to see me?"

Lady Dorethea looked up. A stern look crossed her face, but a tight smile replaced it. "Why yes, dear, he is." She lowered the letter. "And he is bringing a friend of his for you to meet."

"He is?" Amelia cried. "How nice."

"He is?" Elizabeth asked, stunned.

"Yes," Lady Dorethea said. "The lady is in the arts."

"The arts?" Amelia frowned.

Lady Dorethea reached out a hand and placed it upon Amelia's. "Yes, you know Terrence is a patron of the arts. The theater to be exact. He cares about it . . . much as your father likes his sports."

"I see," Amelia said, frowning.

"And the way you like birds," Lady Dorethea continued.

"Oh, yes." Amelia nodded. "I do so love birds."

"Therefore, you will understand if Terrence brings this . . . this thespian here. He is . . . is her patron."

"Of course I understand."

Lady Dorethea sighed and sat back. She appeared distracted, but then a little smile crossed her lips. She looked to Amelia, her green eyes bright. "Dearest, it appears this is going to be a house party. Why do you not come to visit us here? That way you will not be so very lonely while your father is gone."

"Oh, may I?" Amelia asked.

"Lady Dorethea!" Elizabeth exclaimed. "You shouldn't!"

Dorethea's smile turned positively wicked. "He thinks

he's going to outface me, the young scamp! Well, we'll see. Dear Theo and Leticia will be here as well. My, what a fine house party we shall have." She smiled to Amelia. "This will be worth missing your Feathered Friends Society for, I assure you."

"Does Terrence like birds?" Amelia asked, leaning forward. "As well as the arts, I mean?"

"My dear," Lady Dorethea said, "he absolutely loves birds. Birds of every plumage, I assure you!"

Five

It had been a strange, and wonderful day. Jezebel, lulled by the rocking of the carriage and the warm glow of the setting sun streaming through the window leaned her head back against the cushion and sighed. Terrence sat across from her, in very much the same relaxed attitude.

They had amused themselves through the long day with practicing Jezebel's actress voice and ways. They'd shared many a laugh and story. Terrence was a fount of hilarious and colorful tales about the denizens of the stage and their antics.

He now lifted his head as the carriage slowed and came to a stop. "We are here." He grinned at Jezebel when the driver came and opened the door. "Are you ready, my love?"

She returned the smile. "Ducky, ain't I just!"

He chuckled and crawled from the carriage first, turning and holding out his hand. Jezebel adjusted the low bodice of her cherry-striped dress, grabbed up the red boa, and swiftly wrapped it around her shoulder. Ruth would be horrified by her appearance. But then again, she had left the dear woman prostrate that morning, alternately crying and cursing that she would not permit Jezebel to go upon this journey alone. Jezebel couldn't count the times she had explained that actresses did not take chaperones when they traveled with their protectors.

Jezebel stretched out a hand to Terrence, and with a rustle and flourish of her satin skirts, she descended. The moment she alighted, she realized she was creating a stir. Postboys stopped and stared. Another couple, just alighting from a polished carriage, halted in their progress.

Jezebel drew in a deep breath, flipped her boa and said loudly, "Well, bust my stays, Haversham, didn't know there was anything like this outside of London."

Terrence smiled as he took her arm. "I told you, my pet, you'd enjoy it."

"Maybe meeting yer granny won't be the bloomin' bore I'd thought it," Jezebel said as she sashayed beside Terrence toward the inn's entrance. A young, tow-haired youth with ogling eyes stood frozen in their wake. Jezebel flashed him a large smile and whispered to him, "Heard she's got herself a real castle. The old gal's mighty warm in the pockets." She patted his arm as she went by. The lad colored beet red to his hair, and Jezebel stifled a giggle as they entered while the poor youth remained a frozen statue.

They strolled up to the desk, Jezebel twitching her skirts and swaying. She had learned from studying the actresses that one never remained truly still, but always performed some little trick of movement to draw attention to oneself.

The innkeeper, a short and round man, looked up. His face, once he spied Jezebel, turned as red as those of his postboys in the yard. Then his gaze turned to Terrence. He seemed to unstiffen, and his eyes lighted. "Ah, Lord Haversham, 'tis a pleasure to see you once more."

"And you, Bentwood," Terrence said, smiling.

"I haven't seen you since you brought that . . ." Bentwood halted as Jezebel's eyes narrowed upon him. He coughed. "Well, now, since some time. Will it be your usual room, My Lord?"

"Yes, please," Terrence said.

Jezebel's dark speculation upon just whom Terrence had previously brought here ground to a halt as the word "room," singular and not plural, sunk into her mind. "Room!" she exclaimed. "You mean rooms, don't you?"

Bentwood's eyes bulged. "Er . . ." He cast a nervous glance toward Terrence. "My Lord?"

"The usual, Bentwood," Terry said quietly and slipped out a note, which the innkeeper swiftly pocketed.

"But . . . but . . ." Jezebel clamped her mouth shut and forced a smile. "Here now, Terryberry, I thought you said I was suppose ter act proper this here trip, like a real lady." She turned a compelling gaze to Bentwood. "Ain't real ladies suppose ter have their own suite, or something. You ain't going ter think I'm a real lady now if'n we only take one room, are ye?"

The innkeeper cleared his throat. "Well, er, I couldn't say." His eyes suddenly flickered past her, then bulged alarmingly. "I'll be with you shortly, My Lord and Lady Kellair."

Jezebel whirled about quickly. She hadn't noticed the other couple's entrance. She flushed. Both were tall and thin, their faces as lean as the rest of them. They appeared to be well-bred horses in tandem, as their disapproving eyes rolled and their thin nostrils flared.

Terrence turned as well. "Good day, My Lord and Lady." The couple nodded shortly, their entire demeanor stiff. "Dearest," Terry said, with a warning note in his voice, "we are keeping My Lord and Lady waiting."

Jezebel flushed, yet the thought of one room goaded her. "Ah, we can keep them waiting, love," she said, cracking a grin. "You said I was supposed ter act like a proper lady, and proper ladies always keep them waiting, don't they now?" Surprisingly enough the man's stern face creaked into a smile. Not so, his good wife's. She reared back and snorted in offense. Jezebel turned back to the innkeeper. "Don't you have a suite with two rooms or something?"

Bentwood flushed. "I'm sorry, I only have one more . . . and . . . and with Lord and Lady Kellair here . . ."

"Oh," Jezebel said, nonplussed.

Terrence leaned over and whispered quietly, "Jezebel, I

don't have enough for two rooms." She looked at him quickly. He shrugged. "Well, in that case," she said. She forced a smile and looked to Bentwood. "Let Lady Kellair have the suite. After all, she's been a proper lady much longer than me." She winked at him. "Besides, ain't as if I can reform in one night now, can I?"

"Yes, madame," Bentwood said, his voice grateful and his gaze appreciative. He glanced to Lady Kellair then and flushed. "I mean . . . er, I don't know what I mean."

Jezebel turned. The woman looked so drawn up it seemed she would topple over with a good puff of air. Jezebel reached out and patted her chummily upon the arm. "You keep it, ducky, what's one room between us 'ladies,' heh? I lost the coin toss, but I ain't complaining. At least Haversham don't snore." She leaned even closer. "And you don't have ter thank me. Someday perhaps we can share a nip or two, what Lady Kellair?"

"Well, I never!" the woman said, drawing herself up.

"I'm sure you haven't," Jezebel cooed. "That's why I'm givin' you the suite, honey." She heard a snort from her husband. Jezebel looked at him. Borrowing a trick from Daisy, she winked slowly. "Now you all come and see me act when we're all back in London." She patted Lady Kellair's arm once more. "I'll get you in fer free. Slip ye in the backstage door—get you good proper seats too, see if I don't."

"Come, love," Terrence said quickly as Lady Kellair's face mottled to an amazing shade of purple and blue. Jezebel flashed a cheeky grin and allowed Terrence to lead her away.

"Gads," Terrence chuckled as he walked her down the corridor toward their room, tossing the key Bentwood had given them, "Tony wouldn't believe how well you did. 'Twas a performance of the first water."

Jezebel laughed. "I must admit, I surprised myself. I think

it's easier to act when——when you don't have a whole audience watching you."

"Stage fright," Terrence nodded, as he stopped before a door. He clearly knew this inn well. He unlocked the door and swung it open. "It's not easy to overcome," he said, entering and disappearing.

Jezebel suddenly stopped. Her heart migrated to her stomach as she gazed at the door to the one room she would share with Terrence.

"Jezebel?" Terrence called, and he appeared again. He frowned at her. "What is the matter?"

She drew in shaky breath. "Stage fright?"

He studied her and said in a gentle tone, "You don't need to be afraid, Jezebel. I know you are a lady." He smiled slightly. "A 'proper' one at that, and I promise you, I'll not do anything that would be considered forward."

"I-I know," Jezebel said. Except for that one time, Terrence had always treated her properly. It suddenly stunned her to discover how much she had come to trust this man. "I know."

His eyes darkened. "About that time onstage—"

"We don't need to discuss it," Jezebel said quickly.

"Yes we do," he said quickly. "I want you to know I will make sure that doesn't happen again."

"Of course," Jezebel said, flushing hotly. "And I will too, I promise you." They stared at each other a moment. Then she shook her head quickly. "It couldn't happen again, could it?"

"No!" Terrence said quickly. "No, of course not. We—we were caught up in the script."

"Yes," nodded Jezebel. "That was it."

"It was only acting," Terrence said.

"Yes," Jezebel said. "Only acting."

Terrence drew in a deep breath. "So . . . since we know that won't happen again, you'll come in?"

"Oh, yes" Jezebel said. "Of course."

He finally smiled. "Think of me as your brother, why don't you? It won't be as difficult then."

"Think of you as Josh?" Jezebel asked, stunned. She frowned and then nodded. Perhaps it would help. "Yes, yes I will think of you as my brother."

Terrence grinned and held out his hand. "It's a deal then?"

She laughed. "It's a deal." She put her hand in his. Immediately a bolt of electricity shot through her from his touch.

His hand tightened upon hers a moment, and then he jerked it back. "And I'll think of you as my sister," he said, a cord popping along his jaw. "That's it, you are my sister."

"And . . . and you are my brother," Jezebel nodded firmly. She stepped forward into the room with grim determination. She would treat Terrence like a brother if it killed her!

He was very much like her brother, Jezebel mused, as she sat on the floor and gazed at Terrence who sat on the floor across from her. It had been difficult going at first, for Terrence's "usual" room vaunted a decent-sized bed, a single chair, and nothing more. It appeared neither intended to sit upon the bed in the other's presence, and to take the only chair seemed impolite.

Jezebel had rambled about the room, attempting to feign savoir faire, until Terrence had grinned and said he didn't know about her, but he was famished. She had quickly agreed, but the thought of going down to the public rooms had weakened her hunger pangs. He had suggested they have a cold collation sent up so they didn't have to be on display.

Torn between propriety or the daunting experience of dining in the common rooms, Jezebel had turned craven and chosen to be alone with Terrence. In truth, it had seemed

the safer option. And when the boy had brought the platter
of cold meats, cheese, fruits, and wine, giving her the slyest
of grins and the most doltish of winks, Jezebel knew she
had chosen wisely.

Terrence had easily settled the lack of proper seating by
pulling the counterpane from the bed and spreading it upon
the floor, claiming they would have their own picnic. Jezebel, now quite full and comfortable, smiled at him. "I like
your notion of a picnic, Terry."

He looked up from the orange he was peeling and chuckled. "At least there are no ants or dirt to add grit to the
food." He grimaced. "And if it rains, which it invariably
does at picnics, we don't have to pack it in and make a mad
haul for cover."

"It is far more civilized," Jezebel agreed, reaching for the
last strawberry. She popped it into her mouth and munched
upon it. Terrence grinned widely at her. "What? What are
you grinning at?"

"You have juice trickling down your chin, Madame Civilized."

"Ooof," Jezebel said, quickly wiping at her face. He only
laughed all the more. "It is ungentlemanly, I hope you know,
to laugh at a lady."

"I'm not," Terrence said. "I'm laughing at a sister."

Jezebel grimaced. "Beast. You are as bad as Josh." Suddenly, a thought crossed her mind. She cocked her head and
said, "Why don't you want to get married?"

He stiffened slightly and looked at her. "What made you
ask that question?"

"I don't know," Jezebel said, shrugging. "It's just something I've always been curious about. I am sure there are
plenty of women, and women other than that Miss Arrowroot who would marry you."

"Faith," Terry said, leaning against the chair and stretching out his legs to the side. "Call the woman sister and she

starts acting like one immediately. Soon you'll be match-making just like all my other dear relatives."

"Well?" Jezebel frowned. "Don't you like women?"

"I like women," he retorted. "Just not marriage."

"Why?"

"Persistent, aren't you?"

"You've gone through so much trouble to ensure you won't marry, I only wonder why. And since I have been drawn into your machinations, I think it only fair you give me an explanation."

"Ha, machinations is the very word," Terrence said. "I truly love women . . ."

"And women love you," Jezebel said, nodding.

He cast her a quelling look. "You are all delightful, in-triguing creatures . . . and designing. If given half a chance, you start worming your way into getting whatever you want."

"What a disgusting way to put it," Jezebel said. "I never liked worms."

"Ah, yes," Terrence said, shaking a lazy finger at her. "But that is what you darlings do. You stoop to every con-nivance in order that you may control us men until we cannot call ourselves our own. You women do it so underhandedly that we men lose our freedom without even knowing it."

"I had not thought about it that way," Jezebel said. She considered a moment and then frowned. "But what are we to do?"

Terrence lifted a brow. "What do you mean, what are you to do?"

Jezebel shrugged. "You men can always get what you want without conniving. If you want land, you go out and fight for it; adventure, you can take off across the continent with nary a chaperone or bodyguard. Freedom, 'tis yours. You do not ask permission from father, husband, or brother. And if you wish to augment your fortunes, you can work for it if you are of the lower classes." She stared at him steadily. "Or if you are of the higher classes, you marry an heiress."

Terrence frowned. "I do not wish to marry an heiress."

"Yes." Jezebel nodded. "And because you do not wish it, you do not do it. Now if a woman does not wish to marry for money, but her family deems it fitting, she will marry for money. Unless she connives and in some manner circumvents it. Machinations, as you put it."

"Oh, Lord." Terrence rolled his eyes. "You sound like Aunt Theo."

"Do I?"

"She's one of those zanies. Never married. Lives by herself as a recluse. Beswears all men as foul barbarians meant to wreck women." His gray eyes darkened. "Is that why you never married? Are you bitter at men?"

"Oh, no," Jezebel said, shaking her head. "In truth, I believe I'm not married because I am not one of those women you talk about. I have not contrived." She frowned. "I have merely lived my life as it is, and as I should. Mother died when I was young, and that left me to raise Josh. Father was a dear in his own way, but very stern, and when not stating right and wrong, was lost in his scholarly pursuits. Someone had to run the household, see there were meals on the table, the green grocer was paid, and Josh taken care of." She shook her head. "And while I was doing all of that . . . I don't know . . . suddenly I became twenty, with nary a beau or prospect."

"Do you resent that?"

"No. I've never thought of it. Well, perhaps I've had my foolish dreams, like all women." She laughed. "I've envisioned my knight riding up on his white horse and carrying me off to his castle where we'd live happily ever after, madly and wildly in love." She smiled slightly at Terrence. "So much so that he couldn't even call himself his own."

Terrence tipped his head slightly. "Touché."

"But then, I didn't plan to call myself my own either,"

Jezebel said, shrugging. "I just didn't think of it as me and mine. I always thought of it as us." She drew up her knees and hugged them to her, resting her chin upon them. She chuckled slightly. "It was foolish, wasn't it? I see where your notion is more likely the truth. I suppose freedom and the word 'us' do not go together." Silence fell, and she lifted her gaze to Terrence. He studied her with an odd, closed expression upon his face. "What?"

He started, and then sprang to his feet. "It's time for us to go to bed."

Jezebel's head flew up. "Bed?"

"Yes," he said in a rough tone. "Bed."

Jezebel gazed at him, her heart catching. His face was unaccountably grim. "A-all, right."

He glared down at her. "Good Lord, don't look so frightened. I am going to leave you for a while. You may make your toilet and go to bed. And once you are settled, I intend to settle myself on the floor with a blanket." He stalked over to the bed and ripped a pillow from it. "And this."

"But the floor?" Jezebel asked.

"I can sleep anywhere," he said. "Now I will leave you. I assume a half-hour will suffice. Do hurry. We will both need our sleep tonight." Without another word he went to the door and opened it.

Jezebel started when he stepped out and slammed it shut. She blinked in confusion. She had clearly angered him in some manner, but how she could not fathom. She had finally agreed with him, and for that he had stalked from the room.

"Half an hour," she suddenly murmured. 'Twas no time to ponder the incompressible nature of the man. Springing up, Jezebel dashed to prepare for bed in the allotted time. She dove beneath the covers with a good fifteen minutes to spare. Leaning over, she went to blow out the candle, only to halt. If she blew it out, Terrence would not be able to see anything when he returned.

Deciding it was not right, Jezebel burrowed down under

the cover she had, making sure that not even the tip of her head could be seen. There she lay, waiting. An hour passed slowly before she finally heard the door open.

"Jezebel?" She heard Terrence's voice. She didn't want to say anything. Perhaps he would think she was sleeping. She burrowed deeper under the covers. "Jezebel? Are you asleep?" She heard him tread over. She held her breath. She was growing excessively warm, but determinedly she remained hidden. A pause ensued. "Very well," he said. "I'm extinguishing the candle." She sensed, rather than saw, the light being extinguished. Then she heard him rustle about. She heard a large thud and the bed shook.

"Damn," she heard Terrence mutter. More rustling followed, and she could only imagine that he'd settled down on the floor.

She lay there, eyes open to the dark. It felt so very odd to be sleeping in a room with a man in it. Or trying to sleep. Yet it felt odder, almost stupid, to have Terrence lying on the cold, hard floor while she wallowed in the large comfortable bed by herself. There was more than enough room in it.

Jezebel suddenly bit her lip. Just what was she thinking? That he should join her in bed? The thought burrowed into her mind, and she couldn't erase it. She wondered how it would be to have him, warm and masculine, beside her. She closed her eyes tightly, wishing to squeeze the thought from her consciousness. She forced herself to void her mind.

Unfortunately the word "us" suddenly whispered into the void. She could imagine "us" with Terrence beside her, not lying distant on the floor. The word kept tumbling through her mind, as if she could count that rather than sheep.

A tall blond-haired youth alighted from a hired hack and nimbly sidestepped the refuse in the gutter. The street lamps did very little to lighten the midnight darkness. In one hand he held a prettily wrapped package, and he whistled softly as he strode along the craggy street. He stopped at a door. Glancing at the small, grimy window which showed a light within, he smiled. Swiftly he rapped upon the door.

"Molly," he called in a loud whisper. "Open up!" At first there was no sound, and he called again. "Molly dear, it's me. Open up! I know you're awake."

Finally the door opened. Molly stood within, dressed in a red, faded silken wrapper. Her green eyes widened. "Why, Josh love. What ye doing here?"

The youth smiled. His arm shot out with the present. "Look what I brought you!"

Molly glanced down at the package. "Is it chocolates, ducky?"

He grinned. "I know you like them."

Molly snatched up the box and stepped back. Josh quickly ducked and entered the small flat. He halted as he spied a young girl sitting upon a chair. He bowed. "Excuse me, madame. I am sorry to intrude."

The girl, her face heavily painted, giggled. She rose with a litheness. "Madame? Coor, I like that!"

"Daisy," Molly said, her green eyes flashing. "Ye leave the cove alone."

The girl's eyes widened. "But—"

"No buts," Molly said. "Listen to me, I'll steer ye right."

"Aw," Daisy said. "Can't—"

"This here is Josh Clinton."

"Josh Clinton," she gasped. "You mean . . . he's . . ." She stepped back, looking at him. "Why, he's every bit as pretty as—"

"Daisy," Molly said, her tone rising, "get going. Josh here ain't been in town for a month, and he don't need you standing there gawking at him."

A flush rose to Daisy's face. " 'Gor. Sorry. I'll . . . I'll be leaving ye."

"Do that like a good girl," Molly said. "And don't ye

worry none. I've got a nice lord for ye. But first we've got to get you fancified. Proper acting."

"Yes, Molly," the girl nodded, her eyes brightening. She looked to Josh and sighed. "It was nice ter meet ye, Josh." Without another word, and only one sigh more, Daisy slipped out the door. Molly closed it firmly and turned to Josh. "What ye doing back here in London? Weren't ye suppose ter be over in France looking on your tour?"

Josh grinned and spread his arms out. "I couldn't stay away from you so long, my Molly." He stepped toward her, his blue eyes turning dark. "Come here, darling."

Molly raised the box to her bosom. "Now, Josh, ye behave yerself."

"I've been too long away from you for that." He grinned, a rather boyish, endearing grin. He swooped down upon her, crushing the box and her to him. He kissed her with a fervency.

"Mmmm, Josh, my boy," Molly sighed. "Ye shouldn't be kissing me."

He nuzzled her ear. "Why not, sweetheart?"

Molly groaned. "I promised ter leave you alone . . ." He kissed her earlobe. "Aw, what the hell!" Squirming, she pulled the box of chocolates from between them and tossed them to the side. "It'll be a free one. Yer sister can't mind that, can she?" She threw her arms about him, giving him a large, smacking kiss.

"My sister?" Josh said, the words muffled against Molly's lips.

"Hmmm," Molly murmured, her hands smoothing up to tug at Josh's cravat. "Darling boy, I've missed ye. How I've missed you!"

"Yes, yes," Josh murmured, drawing slightly back. "But what about Jezebel?"

"Jezebel?" Molly frowned as she tugged at Josh's cravat. "Wish there weren't so many damn knots."

Josh's hands instinctively went to perform the task. "My sister."

"Thank you," Molly said, tearing the buttons of his shirt open. "She's a smart one, your sister. Fly to everything." She chuckled and kissed Josh. "Had me bamboozled at first, but when she saw her opportunity, she didn't miss it." Her lips roved to Josh's ear. "Ye should be right proud of her."

"Proud?" Josh groaned as she nipped his lobe. "What . . . ? Stop that Molly, you know I can't think when you do that."

"I know." Molly chuckled. Her hands swept his bared chest and soon her lips followed.

Josh's hands went lightly to Molly's shoulders. He groaned. "Molly, why should I be proud of my sister?"

She chuckled, and her hand roved lower. "She nabbed the Marquis of Haversham." Chortling, Molly also nabbed Josh.

"What!" Josh shouted, slapping her hand away and hopping back. "What the devil do you mean?" He slapped Molly's hand again as she reached for him. "Stop that! What do you mean she nabbed the Marquis of Haversham?"

"Got him eating out of her hand," Molly said. Her gaze lowered and her green eyes flared. "Aw, darling, ye do want yer Molly, don't ye?"

Josh looked quickly down. "Zeus!" He crossed his hands in front of himself, his face reddening. "Now, y-you just stay there and tell me what you mean."

Molly stiffened slightly. "I means she's got the Marquis as a protector."

"What? What in blazes are you talking about?"

Molly looked confused, and then she smiled. "Ah, you're worried it wasn't done right and proper. That yer sister's giving it away for free." She moved toward him. "Don't you worry, it was done all right and tight. I made certain of that. Made the Marquis come down heavy, I did. He paid four hundred and fifty pounds for Jezebel."

"Paid . . . four hundred and fifty pounds . . ." Josh stumbled back. "For Jezebel."

Molly nodded. "That he did. So don't you worry none. He'll be treating her right. A man's got to put some money down for his mistress like, or he'll never respect her. But a man always respects ye when he's paid good money."

"I—I don't believe you." Josh shook his head. "I don't." Molly advanced once again upon him. He shook a finger at her. "You stay away from me! You—you took four hundred and fifty pounds for my sister!"

Molly stopped. "Josh, you mad because I ain't going to split it with you?" She shook her head. "I just can't. I've already spent it." Her chin lifted. "Yer Jezebel showed me the way. I ain't going to have to be an actress anymore. I'm going to be an abbess."

"An abbess?"

Molly nodded. "Mean, if I did so well by Jezebel, don't see why I can't do that for other girls." She frowned. " 'Course, your Jezebel's special. Mean, I can't take all the credit. I only got her the Marquis, but she'd done the rest. Best businesswoman I've ever seen." She laughed. "She's got him running through the paces fine like. Even got him to get her on the stage. Puffed her off real grand like."

"On the stage? Jezebel!" Josh shook his head. "Impossible. Not my sister!"

"Yes," Molly said. "That was a wrong turn, I must admit. She can't act. Should have seen the ruckus that last time she appeared. Old Tony had to shut down for a week 'cause the girls rebelled. But he's raised their pay, so they're back onstage now."

"I-I don't care," Josh said, his face darkening. "All I care about is Jezebel."

"Don't you worry none," Molly said, soothingly. "Rumor has it that she even has the Marquis taking her with him to see the Duchess."

"The Duchess?" Josh groaned and stumbled over to the settee to fall upon it. "A duchess!"

"She's the Marquis's grandmother!" Molly said. "Mean, yer sister's been under the protection of the Marquis for only a month now, and already she's gotten him to take her to see his granny. He must be plumb besotted. Bet she's thinkin' to get him to marry her. Now, I think she's flyin' a bit too high. Them grand swells never marry their mistresses. Think you should warn her about that, or she'll come a cropper."

"Marry!" Josh sprung up. "If he's touched Jezebel, he'll damn well marry her!"

Molly shook her head. "So's yer going to try that rig? Well, I hope ye succeed, but I thinks yer going to get burned at it."

"Bedamn I won't," Josh shouted, his fists clenching. "The man has defamed my sister. I'll kill him." He paced about the room. "I'll run him through."

"Now why'd you want to do that?" Molly asked in a flabbergasted tone. "He's paying the piper. You kill him and you won't get any more money. Mean, that's what yer sister's after. She wants you to get yer schooling."

Josh froze. "My schooling?"

Molly chuckled. "She seemed mighty determined about that. Said you all were run off your legs, and that she'd do anything so's you could get yer schooling." She broke out laughing. "Coor, love, the way she's leading the Marquis around by the nose, ye can go to any bloody school ye like."

Josh's face twisted in anguish. "She . . . she did this for me?" He stiffened, his hands clenching. "I'll kill the bloody bastard! I'll kill him!" He stormed past Molly. "I'll run him through!" he shouted as he yanked open the door. "Boil him in oil! Quarter him!"

"Josh, stop!" Molly cried, but he was already gone. She threw up her hands. "Now why'd he want to kill the man

who's paying the dibs?" She shook her head. "Thank God
he's got that sister watching out for him."

Terrence groaned slightly, striving to remain asleep. Yet
his neck cramped and complained of its position. In fact,
every part of his body complained. It didn't help that he
was fully clothed, except for his shirt. Pantaloons were not
meant to be comfortable sleep wear. Yet he hadn't wished
to try and change last night. When he had returned to the
room Jezebel was so burrowed under the covers that he was
frightened she'd suffocate if he had taken any time with his
own toilet.

Suddenly he heard a grating noise. His eyes snapped
open. They widened. The room was light. Lord, it must be
well past daybreak. He and Jezebel were supposed to be on
the road by now. He sat up swiftly, and just as swiftly cursed.

The grating noise persisted. It finally entered Terrence's
mind what it was. Someone was using a key at the door.
That someone, he had no doubt, was the maid. Muttering,
he sprung up. He'd be hanged if he'd let her discover him
sleeping on the floor. He scooped up the pillow and blanket
and dived toward the bed. He heard a mutter from Jezebel
as he scrabbled under the covers. Yet as he put a swift arm
around her she merely grumbled something indistinguish-
able and subsided. He turned her toward him just as the
door opened wide.

"Good morning," Terrence said, pretending sleepy surprise as the maid entered.

The little brunette froze immediately. Her eyes widened,
and the sheets she carried in her hands promptly fell out of
them. "Oh Lud!" she exclaimed. "I-I am sorry, My Lord.
Frightful sorry. But—"

"I know." Terrence nodded kindly. "I told Bentwood we'd
be leaving very early." At that moment Jezebel mumbled

something of sorts. "But I'm afraid Jezebel has overslept, and I am loath to wake her. She was worn out, I fear."

The brunette's eyes brightened as her gaze scanned his bared chest. She giggled. "I can believe that, My Lord."

"Minx." Terrence smiled and winked. His amusement faded, however, for he saw two figures walking past out in the hall. Unfortunately they both halted and had the brass to step closer to peer into the room from behind the maid. Terrence forced a grin. "Good morning, Lord and Lady Kellair. Did you sleep well?"

Lady Kellair's thin face sharpened to prudish lines, while Kellair's thin nose twitched. At that moment, Jezebel stirred. Sighing, she rolled over more fully onto Terrence, placing her head upon his chest and rubbing her cheek against it as if she were a kitten settling against its mother's fur. Terrence stiffened. He certainly wasn't her mother. He forced a grin to the onlookers, attempting to ignore the sudden tension coursing through him. "I know Jezebel did. In fact, she still is, as you can see."

"She's worn out." The maid giggled. "Plumb worn out."

"I see," Lord Kellair said, his widened eyes upon Jezebel, whose blond hair splayed out over Terrence's chest.

"Well, I never!" Lady Kellair said with a huff.

As if in subconscious answer, Jezebel raised a hand and wrapped it around Terrence's neck. Terrence could not help but chuckle. He looked roguishly toward the frowning Lady Kellair. "Never?" He then looked to Kellair. "I'm sorry for you, old chap."

"Clarence," spouted the enraged dame. "Are you going to let him speak to me like that!"

"Elspeth," Lord Kellair said. "It is time we go."

"Yes, please do," Terrence said, as he felt the light breaths of Jezebel against his heart. "You might waken Jezebel if you don't."

"Would we?" Clarence asked. His voice sounded hopeful, and his eyes remained riveted upon the slumbering Jezebel.

He raised his voice. "It would be a shame if we woke her, wouldn't it?"

Elspeth turned narrowed eyes upon her husband. "Lower your voice. We are leaving."

The poor fellow stiffened and the light evaporated from his eyes. He coughed. "Er, just what I said, dear."

Elspeth reached out and clamped a hand on his arm. She jerked him away. "How dare you! I saw the way you were looking at that hussy." She harangued him as they headed down the hall. "More infamous behavior, I've never seen. . . ."

The little maid giggled. "He's in for a rare trimming now."

Terrence chuckled. "I believe so. For a woman that's never, Lady Kellair does a lot of talking."

"Doesn't she just," the maid said. Jezebel mumbled something in her sleep. "Well now, I'd best leave." She winked at Terrence. "Before she wakes up."

"Yes," Terrence chuckled, then pulled a serious face. "She's a virago when she awakens, you know."

The maid watched as the sleeping Jezebel rubbed her head against Terrence's chest again. She giggled. "Poor chap." Grabbing the doorknob, she stepped back and closed the door upon them.

Terrence smiled, then frowned slightly, looking to the blond head upon his chest. "Jezebel?" Her fingers slid from his neck to pad against his chest. Terrence caught his breath sharply. "Jezebel?"

"Hmmm?"

"W-we have to be going, love," he murmured. Unable to resist, he lifted his hand and smoothed her blond hair. It was silken to his touch. Long, golden silk.

"No." She shook her head. "Am sleeping." She snuggled against him, her lips barely grazing his skin. "Mmm, sleeping. . . ."

Terrence shook his head, swallowing hard. "We have to leave."

"Don't want to," Jezebel mumbled, and curved her body close to his. "Want to stay."

"You want me to stay?" Terrence asked, confused, especially by the sensations clamoring through him.

"Mmm?" Jezebel's leg slipped across his. "Mmmm, yes."

"Are you certain?" Terrence whispered, smoothing her hair again.

She sighed.

"Jezebel." Terrence tangled his hand in her hair and tugged slightly, lifting Jezebel's face to his. Her eyes were closed, dark lashes fanning her cheeks. Her lips were petal pink, appealingly vulnerable with sleep. Terrence reached down and brushed those warm lips with his.

Jezebel made a sound like a purr, and even with eyes closed, she moved her lips against his. He was lost. Kissing her more deeply, he shifted, drawing her full warm body up against his. His hands roved her pliant curves, learning them with desire. Jezebel stretched, her body sliding against his. "Jezebel!" he muttered, his lips tracing the tender curve of her neck.

"Wh-what?" Jezebel asked. Terrence felt her stiffen, but his body was already so taut it didn't warn him. "What?" Suddenly she shifted to the side.

Terrence rolled with her, the movement inciting him all the more. Hazy confusion set in, however, when Jezebel pushed him back, curling up into a ball at the same time. Shock replaced the confusion when her two bare feet contacted his stomach. "Ooof!" The air wheezed out of him as Jezebel kicked him hard, rolling him right off the bed. He hit the floor with a crashing jolt.

"How dare you!" she cried. "How dare you!"

Terrence looked up in a daze. Jezebel knelt straight up in the bed, and her eyes shot violet, violent sparks. He hauled himself up to a sitting position, returning her glare. "How dare I?"

"You were kissing me!" Jezebel accused. "You were in my bed!"

"Yes, I was," Terrence said. "But only because you told me I could be."

Jezebel reared back, stunned. "I did no such thing."

Terrence waved a hand impatiently. "All right, you asked me to stay. I gathered it was the same thing."

This time Jezebel blinked. "I don't believe it."

"Believe it, Jezebel," Terrence said, his voice lowering in anger. "I asked you, and you said yes."

She shook her head, but her eyes showed doubt. "I was sleeping, I-I don't remember." Then her eyes narrowed. "Wait! Do not say I asked you into my bed, I couldn't have."

"No, you didn't," Terrence said, shifting irately. "I got into it because I heard the maid come in and I didn't want it all over town that my supposed mistress was making me sleep on the floor."

"The maid?" Jezebel glared at him. "You're lying."

"Lying?" Terrence stiffened. "No! Not only the bloody maid walked in, but Lord and Lady Kellair. But you don't remember, do you? You were too busy cuddling up to me and doing all but purring."

"I was?" She flushed. "I don't remember. I was sleeping, I tell you."

"Sleeping?" Terrence shifted. "Woman, if that's the way you sleep you're a menace to any poor unsuspecting man that gets near you."

"Well, you shouldn't have gotten near. You weren't supposed to be in my bed!" she yelled. "If I had been awake and conscious, I wouldn't have done that. But I wasn't, was I? When one is sleeping, one is not conscious!"

"And how was I supposed to know that?" Terrence asked. "I'm only a flesh-and-blood man, for God's sake. And when a woman acts like you did, I respond."

"You took advantage of me." Jezebel hopped up and down. "I was asleep, and you took advantage."

"No!" Terrence shouted. "You took advantage of me!"

She reared back and then blinked, lowered her eyes. "I didn't know, I tell you. I—I was only dreaming. I-I didn't know that . . . that I was actually doing anything like . . . like what you said I did."

"Dreaming? Just what were you dreaming?" Terrence's eyes narrowed, and he sprang up, stepping toward her; Jezebel screeched and sprang up on the bed herself. "No, rather, who were you dreaming about!"

Jezebel shook a finger at him, even as she rocked with her unsteady footing upon the feather tick. "You just stay away from me!"

Terrence saw green. "Who the hell were you dreaming about in that way?"

"It's none of your business," Jezebel retorted. Growling, he reached toward her. She squeaked and jumped back. Turning, she bounded off the bed. "Who I was dreaming about is none of your business. A woman's dreams should be private . . . and so should a woman's bed!"

"No proper lady would—"

Jezebel turned and glared at him. "What would you know about proper? At least I was unconscious, while you—you were doing it with full knowledge." She sped around the bed and snatched up the satchel resting on the floor. "You said you would act like my brother!"

"You weren't acting like my sister!"

"I was sleeping." Jezebel's chin jutted out. "A woman shouldn't have to be responsible for things she does while asleep." She hefted the satchel and shook it at him. "And a gentleman should not be so rude as to ask what she was dreaming either." She spun and charged toward the door.

"Where are you going?" Terrence yelled.

"I'm leaving!" Jezebel shouted back. She grabbed the doorknob and jerked the door open. "And don't try to stop me. I'm not going to—to remain around a . . . a dastard like you. I'd never be able to sleep safely again!" She charged out the door.

Terrence pelted across the room and out the door. Jezebel, satchel in hand, was marching down the hall in her voluminous night gown. "Jezebel!" She kept marching. "Dammit," he cried. "Look at what you are wearing!"

She suddenly halted. He could see her back stiffen as if someone had shot her. She glanced down, turned, and without looking at him, her face a deep red, she marched back. She wafted past him into the room and slammed the satchel down upon the floor, then turned and put her hands upon her hips. "I want you to leave!"

Terrence crossed his arms over his chest. "No!"

Her eyes widened. "You think I'm going to dress in front of you?"

"No," he snapped. "Not unless you are sleeping." He saw her flush more deeply. "I'm sorry," he said curtly. "But I'm not leaving until you promise you are going to go through with our plan."

"I am not going to promise!" Jezebel spat out. "I'll get you your money somehow, and then you can find some real floozy to do your bidding."

"I don't want any other floozy than you," Terrence bit out.

Jezebel reared back. "I am not a floozy!"

"No, only when you dream about some man," Terrence said, jealousy still goading him. "Some man you won't even talk about."

"Get out!"

"No," he said. "Not until you promise!"

"I'm not going to promise," Jezebel said, her eyes now slits.

He bowed and waved a hand. "Then, by all means, do go down to the taproom like that. Do go ask the stable boy for a hack. Or, better yet, do get dressed!"

"Very well," Jezebel said, gritting her teeth. She grabbed up the satchel. "I will get dressed. I refuse to remain around a scoundrel like you." She marched over to the bed. "After all, I've learned enough. All your actresses just dress anywhere, in front of anyone." She dumped out the satchel. Lacy petticoats and underclothing spewed out across the rumpled sheets. "I'm sure it doesn't matter to you. You're used to actresses."

Terrence's throat constricted as he gazed at the intimate clothing, clothing that would be so close to those soft curves he had felt. Slowly he gazed at Jezebel.

"So dressing in front of you sh-shouldn't matter," she said, her voice turning low. She raised a hand to the first small button of the twenty on her night rail and loosed it. "Does it?"

"No," Terrence said softly, his gaze riveted upon her hand.

"Of c-course not." She unbuttoned the next two buttons, laying bare her throat. He must have imagined it, but even from across the room, Terrence thought he could see the pulse at its hollow. Or was he only feeling his own pulse beating? Jezebel's hand froze, and he lifted his gaze to hers, willing her to continue, willing her to stop.

Her eyes were midnight dark, a confusion in them. "Please, Terrence, just leave."

He couldn't move. He wouldn't. She must remain in his life. He'd not let her return to find the man in her dreams. "No," he said softly. It seemed as if the entire room were wrapped about them with a heavy weight of need and desire. "You must promise . . . to stay. To be my actress. We . . ."—He drew in a breath—"We are too deep into it, for you to walk out now."

Jezebel shook her head slightly. "It can't be too late."

"It is," Terrence said softly. "Much too late."

Jezebel's hand fell from her throat, and she looked away. "Very well. If—if you will just leave and permit me to dress, I-I'll be ready to go to your grandmother's."

Guilt mingled with Terrence's satisfaction, and he said, "I promise, Jezebel, I'll behave. You'll never have to share a room with me again."

Jezebel only nodded. "Yes, I think that's best."

He wordlessly turned and walked out of the room, closing the door and then leaning against it, acting as sentinel. Terrence hadn't told her that he also intended to ensure no one else shared a room with her. He'd not let anyone else catch Jezebel sleeping. His blood heated again. Not the way she slept.

Six

Jezebel had never thought to be pleased to arrive at the Duchess's mansion, Haven Crest, yet she had decided Terrence's fear-inspiring grandmother might be an enviable exchange for her silent, scowling grandson who sat upon the other seat. The tension between them could have been cut with a knife, it seemed, though actually one would have required a broad ax to dent it.

Yet Jezebel had no intention of confessing to Terrence that it was he whom she had kissed in her dreams. Kissing a man in the privacy of one's dreams was a far cry from waking up and discovering that one was actually doing so. Reality presented a much too mortifying and dangerous equation to consider, so Jezebel kept her lips tightly shut and her eyes determinedly trained upon the hands clasped in her lap.

The carriage slowed to a halt, and a sigh of relief escaped Jezebel. When Terrence cast her a narrowed gaze, she flushed. He only said, "We are here. Are you ready?"

"Yes," she replied. "I believe I am."

"Good," he said briskly as the driver opened the door for them. Terrence alighted, then offered Jezebel his hand. She purposely ignored it and stepped down from the carriage, but she stumbled as Haven Crest filled her vision. Terrence put a supporting arm about her, and she didn't dispute it. Indeed, she clutched him for a moment as she gaped. Haven Crest was one of the largest, most imposing structures Jezebel had ever beheld. It seemed to stretch for miles in endless, daunting splendor.

"Go and announce us, Bootle," Terrence said. He released Jezebel and asked, "Are you all right?"

"Of course," she gritted out, fearful of standing alone on her wobbly knees. "Why shouldn't I be? If you've seen one Haven Crest, you've seen them all, right?"

Jezebel pinned her gaze upon Bootle who walked toward the mammoth structure with exceeding bravery and nonchalance. She never doubted the driver would be winded before he reached the front portico that lay a goodly ten yards away from the drive.

"Shall we?" Terrence said, waving his hand. Their gazes met, and both looked quickly away.

"Meowwwww!" A panicked feline yowl rent the air.

"What the devil?" Terrence muttered and turned to the right. An orange ball of howling fear charged at them. "Oh, no! Letty's here!" he exclaimed. The baying of a hound wafted upon the breeze. "Good God! Theo, too!"

"Who is . . . ?" Jezebel didn't finish, for the squalling cat had reached them. Indeed her eyes widened as the large, growling feline pelted around Terrence, who snatched at it and missed. "Oh, my!" Jezebel cried out in shock, as the cat ducked and disappeared under her broad, purple skirts. "Oh! Ouch! Ouch!" Jezebel's voice rose. The cat had circumvented her petticoats and was shimmying up her pantaloons. She felt every nail of the feline climber. "Terry! Help!"

"Good God!" Terrence bent swiftly.

"Get him," she cried as the cat got a death grip upon her thigh.

"But . . ." Terrence looked up at her from the ground.

"Get him!" Jezebel ground out the words.

"Sorry," Terrence muttered and lifting her hem, disappeared under her skirts.

Male curses and feline howls arose from beneath the pur-

ple satin. Jezebel closed her eyes tightly and strove to keep
her balance. Suddenly the baying of a dog deafened her, and
her eyes snapped open. A huge wolfhound with slathering
fangs bounded toward them. A group of women chased behind him, lamentably far behind.

"Terrence!" Jezebel cried. "A dog is coming!" Forgetting
all decorum, Jezebel hiked up her skirts to shed more light
upon Terrence's endeavor.

"Got her!" Terrence shouted. "Catch!"

Jezebel gasped as a wailing ball of fur flew up into the
air before her. She reached out and successfully clamped
her hands around the cat's middle. It dangled in her grasp
and raked its claws upon her hands. The Afghanistan hound,
sighting his quarry in such a vulnerable position, broke into
frenzied yaps and shortened the distance to it with long
strides.

"Oh, no," Jezebel gasped. Frantically she looked around.
The coach's open window drew her gaze. She twisted and
with superhuman force, threw the cat through the coach window. A heavy thud and an enraged meow followed.

Jezebel had no time to consider the feline's indignation.
Eighty pounds of rawboned hound rammed into her and
knocked her off her feet. She sputtered and choked as a
furry chest all but suffocated her. The dog scrabbled off her
with unkindly placed paws. Only then did Jezebel realize
another weight pinned her lower half. It was Terrence who
hadn't escaped her skirts before the beast hit them.

Jezebel lay there, exhausted, numb, and quite undone. She
started to choke, then giggle, and then laugh.

"Jezebel?" Terrence's concerned voice drifted through
her mirth. Still she giggled, even as Terrence unearthed himself from her skirts and inched his way along beside her to
study her face. "Are you all right?"

"Of course." She choked upon a laugh. "Other . . . other
than b-both beast and . . . and man having been b-beneath
my skirts, I-I am just f-fine!" She howled with laughter.

Terrence stared at her and then broke into roaring laughter. He put his arms about her, and both rocked with their amusement.

"Terrence, do stop making a spectacle of yourself," a firm voice demanded from above. Jezebel, tears streaming down her cheeks, looked past Terrence's head and discovered a tiny woman glaring down at them, her green eyes snapping, white hair astray.

"Grandmama," Terrence whispered into Jezebel's ear and then rolled off her to a sitting position. Jezebel also sat up, placing her hands upon the paving for support. She winced as gravel rubbed into the scratches upon her hands.

"Oh, thank heavens," another silver-haired woman, dressed in a youthful, frilly lavender dress breathed, coming to stand beside the Duchess. Faded blue eyes peered at Jezebel through tears, and her one hand pattered across her chest like the wings of a frantic humming bird. "You saved my poor Geselda."

"Damn fine toss you have there, gel," a gruff voice said. A stout woman with a mannish face and iron gray hair stepped up to join the ring around Jezebel and Terrence. "Thought you'd miss the window and old Geselda would have been a flat cake against the carriage."

"Don't! Don't say it!" cried the other woman, cringing, She turned to a slim, black-haired woman who stepped up behind her. "Oh, Elizabeth, Geselda could have been killed."

"But she wasn't," the girl said calmly and placed a comforting arm around the distraught woman.

"Hello, Terrence," another voice said. A brown-haired girl, with eager brown eyes, crowded through the throng of ladies. "I am so pleased to meet you finally."

"And I, too, I am sure," Terrence said, his face showing no recognition. He glanced to Jezebel, who shook her head, bemused at the onrush of strangers circling around them.

"Enough," the Duchess said. "We shall save the introductions for later. Terrence, cover your . . . your actress's legs!"

Jezebel, blinking, looked down to her legs. Her skirts were bunched up to her knees, her stockinged calves exposed. "Oh, dear!"

Terrence swiftly leaned over and tugged down her skirts.

"Thank you," she said.

He grinned and bounded up, but quickly reached down and offered his hand. Jezebel accepted and let him draw her to her feet. The circle of women about her gaped, politely of course, but they gaped nonetheless. The only one that did not consider her, she noted, was the wolfhound who had caused her plight. He sat calmly, back and wagging tail to them, head and snout pointed toward the carriage with anticipatory intent. Jezebel suddenly felt an urge to join the dog in his vigil and turn her back to the surrounding onlookers.

"Hello, Grandmama," Terrence said. "Do permit me to introduce Miss Jezebel Clinton." He turned and winked at Jezebel. "Jezebel, love, this is the Duchess of Devon."

Jezebel understood his silent command. She forced a breathless, wide grin to her face. Turning her gaze upon the Duchess she promptly stuck out her hand. "Pleased ter meet ye, Duchess! Heard lots about ye, I have." The Duchess stood rigid, so Jezebel reached over and grabbed her resisting hand, pumping it vigorously. "Been waiting to meet Terry's granny."

"Oh my," gasped the youthful woman.

"Gads hounds," exclaimed the stout one.

"I said to Terry, when he told me about you," Jezebel said, dropping her hand. "I said, Terryberry, now she sounds like my type of granny! Said I'd gladly swap my granny for his." Jezebel neighed a laugh. " 'Course, I can't. My gran's already stuck her spoon in the wall. We's all told her blue ruin would rot her gut, but she wouldn't listen. Drank a bucket of it every day afore she cocked up her toes and met her maker." She frowned. " 'Course, most likely she's with old horny toes instead. She was as mean as old Satan, that's fer sure."

"Indeed?" Dorethea said, her eyes narrowing. They raked Jezebel, settling upon her chest. A fine brow winged up.

Jezebel looked down to discover her adventures had pulled her low décolletage about indecently. "Gor, would you look at that!" She made a fine show of arranging her bodice, hoping to distract them from the red blush rising to singe her face. "I'm busting my stays, I am."

" 'Tis chilly this afternoon," the woman Elizabeth said quietly. She took her arms from around the older woman and withdrew her shawl. Her gray eyes sparkling, she stepped forward. "Don't you think so, Miss Jezebel?"

"Yes, yes," Jezebel said gratefully and accepted the offering, wrapping it quickly about her. "Thank you."

"Isn't Jezebel beautiful, Grandmother," Terrence said. He looked to the elderly lady in lavender. "Grand Aunt Letty, I'm pleased to see you. Permit me to introduce Jezebel."

"Oh, oh, yes," Letty said. Her faded blue eyes flickered to Jezebel. Looking as if she were taking medicine, she stuck out her hand. "I am pleased to meet you."

Jezebel, hiding her first true smile, reached out and took the proffered hand. "Pleased ter meet ye, Letty." She shook it very gently and released it.

Letty's face brightened, and she looked at her hand as if she were pleased it was still attached to her wrist. "I want to thank you for saving my dear Geselda."

Jezebel performed an expansive wave. "Aw, wasn't nothing. Couldn't have done anything else with the critter clawing through me skirts as it was."

"Oh, er, yes," Letty said, her parchment skin turning red. "I quite understand. Geselda is a naughty puss, but she didn't mean to misbehave I assure you. Only, with Mordrid chasing after her, well—"

"Letty," the mannish woman said. "Stop apologizing for your blasted cat. It's always underfoot."

"But, 'tis clear Geselda scratched her frightfully," Letty said. "Look at her poor hands. And though Geselda rarely scratches, when she does it is quite painful. I remember one time when she was still a kitten, just the sweetest little ball of fur in my hands—"

"Letty," the mannish woman said in exasperation, "we don't want to hear Geselda's life story at this moment. We'll be here until the moon rises."

"And this is Grand Aunt Theo," Terrence said, laughing. "Theo, permit me to introduce—"

"No need to," Theo grunted, directing a challenging eye to Jezebel. Jezebel didn't even tender the notion of shaking the woman's hand. Like Letty, she was afraid she'd lose the appendage if she did. "Been standing here, haven't I? Heard her name already. Heard it all too blasted often before this as it is."

Terrence's smile appeared quite innocent. "Why, Theo, you must have been following the theater news. And here I thought only Grandmother was an aficionado of the arts."

"Don't have to follow the theater," Theo said. "Everyone in England knows she's your—"

"Actress friend," the Duchess said quickly, shooting a dagger look toward Theo. "And that you are kind enough to support Jezebel in her craft."

"Oh, yes." Terrence grinned. "Jezebel is very, very talented."

"I have no doubt," Dorethea said, her tone stern. "Now, Terrence dear, I would like to make my own introduction." She walked over and put an arm around the petite brown-haired girl who had greeted Terrence before. "Permit me to introduce you to Amelia Arrowroot, my goddaughter."

"Hello, Terrence," the girl said, gazing at him with an eager look.

The Duchess smiled. "When I received your message that

you would be arriving, I suddenly had the splendid notion of making up a house party."

"You did?" Terrence said, his brow lifting.

"You did?" Letty said. "But, Dorethea, I never knew. I thought it was I who had written you. I came to discuss what we could possibly do about . . ." Suddenly she choked up. Her eyes widened and flew to Jezebel. She flushed. "Oh, I'm so sorry. I was . . . er, I was mistaken."

"Yes," Dorethea said with a bright, brittle smile. "I suddenly had this splendid notion of a house party. I did not want you or your . . . companion to be bored. And since Amelia was at loose ends, she was kind enough to join us."

"I see," Terrence said, his tone grim. He nodded his head toward Amelia. "Pleased to meet you, Miss Arrowroot." His smile did not reach his eyes. "Well, I am sure we shall have a jolly house party. Don't you think so, Jezebel?"

Jezebel gaped at the petite child the Duchess had chosen for Terrence's bride. She appeared . . . brown. Very much like Father's study.

Terrence reached over and pinched her arm. "Don't you think, Jezebel?"

Jezebel jumped and squeaked out, "Oh, yes. Just lovely, I'm sure."

It had been simply horrid. Jezebel had never known a dinner could be more torturous. They had dined in grand estate. So grand that the Duchess had seated Jezebel at the very end of the table, far away from Terrence. Clearly the Duchess understood the tactic of divide and conquer.

Yet, she had unwittingly done Jezebel a service, for she had seated Jezebel next to Elizabeth, whom Jezebel discovered was companion to the Duchess. Elizabeth had not only refrained from taxing conversation, but had proven a quiet, unobtrusive instructor on which of the myriad of forks Jezebel should employ. Having grown up in a house where three removes was sumptuous, the accounting of cutlery for six removes confused Jezebel mightily. She had never been so grateful as when the ordeal was over and she was permitted to escape to her room for the night.

Now dressed in her own nightgown, and feeling better for it, Jezebel shook her head and yawned. Pulling out a volume of poetry from her satchel, she padded over to the large ornate bed and settled into it. 'Twas sheer bliss.

A rap on the door unfortunately dispelled her pleasure. She sighed and set her book down. Knowing it could only be Terrence, she rose and grabbed up the worn wrapper, drawing it on as she crossed to the door. When she cracked it open, her jaw fell.

Lady Dorethea stood in the hall. She smiled and proffered a jar. "I brought ointment for your scratches."

"Ah, thank you," Jezebel said and reached a hand through the crack in the door to take the ointment. "That was right kind of you, Duchess."

Lady Dorethea's brow lifted. "I did hope you would invite me to enter."

Jezebel swallowed. "Of course, of course." She opened the door wide. "Do come in, please."

Lady Dorethea swept into the room. It seemed her small body swallowed the whole space with its energy. She turned, and her eyes widened. "Faith! Is that what you wear to bed?"

Jezebel stiffened. Feeling vulnerable in her shabby wrapper, she forced a laugh. "Well, now, some men likes it that way." To make a point, she pulled off her wrapper, displaying her white nightgown. "Likes to think of me as a proper lady, they do. All sweet and . . . and virginal."

"And Terrence prefers that?" A frown marred Dorethea's face. She shook her head. "I never would have guessed that of my grandson. But then, I never would have guessed he would have brought his mistress to my home either."

The Duchess apparently didn't care for roundaboutation.

Jezebel laughed, despite herself. "You don't hide yer teeth, do you, Duchess?"

"No." The Duchess smiled. "And you do not seem to hide much either, most definitely not your petticoats." She waved a hand. "But then, I far prefer it that way. I am not one of your namby-pamby misses that doesn't recognize a man's needs. Men always need mistresses. It does wonders for their conceits, and men must have their conceits, else they are the knock-knees of the world. I wouldn't have that of Terrence."

Jezebel stared a moment, offset. Then she forced a wide grin. "Well now, glad you approve. All the gals told me not to come, 'cause most you nobs are high in the instep about us ladies. Like you got a poker up your back. But Terry said you was a right one. If I said it once, I'll say it again, I wouldn't mind having you as my own granny."

The Duchess's gaze did not waver. "My dear, I hope you do not become too fond of that notion. I am not your granny, and I never shall be. I have enough upon my plate with Terrence as my grandson, I assure you."

Jezebel's eyes widened, and she stifled a laugh. "Right proud of him, ain't you?"

"In truth, yes," the Duchess said. "Though I cannot say I am pleased with his bringing you here. As your fellow, er, gels have told you, it is not done in proper households. However, if you will strive to practice discretion, I am sure we shall rub along quite well."

Jezebel lifted her chin. "Discretion?"

"Yes," the Duchess said, smiling kindly. "You do know what that is, do you not?"

"I do believe I do," Jezebel said. "It is where a woman like me acts in such a well-behaved manner a woman like you can ignore my existence."

The Duchess appeared stunned, and then she smiled. "I am so glad you have such a fine understanding of the word." She walked over and sat down upon Jezebel's bed. Suddenly she shifted, pulled from beneath her a volume of poetry. She looked at it, and her brow rose. "You read poetry?"

Jezebel flushed. "Er, I was under the wing of a professor. The old duck made me read poetry every night to him. Got me in the habit." She tossed her head. "Been thinkin' it's high time I be actin' in the finer shows. Like that there Shakespeare."

"I see," the Duchess said. Her brevity was commendable, yet she frowned as she set the book down. "As I was saying, I do not mind if you are Terrence's mistress, but I do expect you not to shock those here under my roof. Especially Miss Arrowroot."

Jezebel for once didn't have to pretend. Her eyes sparked. "You mean the one you have picked out to be my Terry's little wife, don't you?"

"Yes, I do." Dorethea nodded. "She will be perfect for him."

A sudden rage entered Jezebel. "I don't see that. She's . . . she's too quiet and—"

"Nondescript?" the Duchess quizzed. "My dear, that is why she will be perfect for Terry. I will not deny that Amelia is rather plain; she most certainly can not hold a candle to you." She studied Jezebel. "You are a very beautiful woman."

Jezebel shifted and waved a hand impatiently. "I'm not as beautiful as some of the women Terry's squired."

"Squired?" The Duchess laughed. "How quaint." Jezebel could have kicked herself for her mistake. "And no, you do not give yourself credit. You are a diamond of the first water. As is only right in a mistress. However, Terrence, no matter his peccadilloes, is a man of his class. He may enjoy your flamboyance and brash beauty, but when he settles he will be like every other Englishman of his generation. He will wish for a proper, biddable woman for wife."

Jezebel stiffened. "Oh, he will, will he?"

"Indeed." The Duchess smiled. "Terry does not care for

us women who take charge, you know. And you, my dear, must be one to take charge if you managed to finagle him into bringing you here."

Jezebel flushed. "At least I ain't trying to force him into a marriage he don't want."

"My dear," Dorethea said, "he is going to need to be forced into marriage, if he is ever going to marry. He does not know what is good for him, as most men do not. However, that is something I will handle." She smiled. "That is my arena. You as his mistress need not concern yourself with it."

"Oh, I don't?" Jezebel put her hands on her hips. "Well, I'll have you know, I'm partial to Terry, and he's fond of me. So if you excuse me, I will be watching out for his welfare, even if it ain't my arena."

The Duchess's face turned imperious, and she rose. "Do not meddle in what is not your concern, my young woman."

Jezebel stiffened and then drew herself up to as imperious a pose. "You said you would never be my granny, therefore I will never be your young woman, shall I? And as you noted, I am not one to sit back quietly. What Terrence wishes is what really matters to me, so if it requires daring to meddle in yours or anyone else's plans, then I beg your pardon, but I will not hesitate to do so."

The Duchess studied her. Jezebel refused to back down or look away. Dorethea cocked her head to one side and said, "You said that in quite a proper and correct manner."

A jolt went through Jezebel. She realized in her anger she had forgotten her accent. She shrugged a shoulder. "Told yer, I've been practicing that fancy talk." She directed a level gaze at the Duchess. "I even played a Duchess once, I'll have yer know."

"Then do, by all means, continue with your study," Dorethea said, walking toward her. "I far prefer that role." She stopped before Jezebel, green eyes narrowed. "But do not forget for one moment that I am the real Duchess."

Jezebel smiled sweetly. "How could I?"

Dorethea nodded and swept past Jezebel to the door. Suddenly she turned and said, "I know I need not ask, but you are practicing prevention of course."

Jezebel turned. "Prevention?"

"I would not have you become pregnant."

Jezebel turned a deep red hue. "Er, of course. I practice every kind of prevention."

"Indeed?" Dorethea said, curiosity in her voice. "Do you use the French letter?"

"Of course," Jezebel said nervously. "And every other kind, English, Italian, Greek! I know my translations, and . . . uhm . . . use them!"

The Duchess blinked. "I fear I am behindhand with the world." Shaking her head, she walked from the room, closing the door behind her.

Jezebel stood staring after her. A shiver ran through her. For all the appearance of civility, she had just entered into a catfight with the Duchess and she knew it. The gauntlet, no matter if it was of lace, had been thrown down, and she had accepted.

Jezebel walked slowly back to her bed in a brown study. Absently, she picked up the jar of ointment and opened it. She sniffed it and broke into a spate of coughs. It smelt horrendous. She capped it quickly, wondering if it didn't perhaps contain some poisonous components which could seep into the skin and kill one. She wouldn't put it past the Duchess one whit.

Another knock at the door interrupted her ghoulish reverie. "Drat. Who is it?" She quickly tossed the ointment down. Muffling an unladylike expletive, Jezebel walked over to the door and opened it.

Theo, in a frightful puce dressing gown and Leticia in a frilly pink one stood in the hall. Both held jars in their hands. Leticia, her eyes darting about the passage as if she expected a ghost to pop out at any moment, stuck hers out. Pink ribbons and bows bedecked it. "I . . . we, brought you some ointment for your scratches."

Theo jabbed her jar out as well. It was a large, black one. "Yes. Harrumph. Mean it was Mordrid's fault after all."

Jezebel's heart sank. "Thank you," she said and took both jars.

"You going to invite us in?" Theo asked, her brown eyes demanding.

Clearly Theo and Dorethea were sisters. "I suppose I shall have to," Jezebel said weakly. She turned and walked into the room. The two sisters quickly followed, and Theo closed the door with a resounding thud. Jezebel felt as if she had just been shut into the lions' den. She set the jars down upon the bed and turned, forcing a smile. "Well, it was very kind of you to bring these to me."

"Oh, no," Letty said, her fingers worrying one of the frills of her nightgown. "It was our pleasure. You saved poor Geselda's life, after all. And with such sufferance to yourself. I am truly indebted to you. I find that just one scratch from dear Geselda is frightfully painful, let alone many. But you need not fear, I have put Geselda in my room and have warned her that is where she will remain for the entirety of our stay here. She is not pleased, but I have explained it is for her own safety. After all, what if Mordrid finds her one day and you are not there to save—"

"Letty," Theo said. "You are dithering."

Letty jumped. "Oh, dear, so I am." She wafted over to a chair and sat in it. She smiled wanly to Jezebel. "I-I fear I dither. I've always been that way. Even as a child, I would—"

"Talk the ear off a sow," Theo finished. She stalked over to stand by Letty's chair, looking like a guard dog, a mastiff at that. Her eyes narrowed. "Is that what you wear to bed?"

Jezebel bit her lip. "Yes, yes it is."

"It's very nice," Letty said quickly. "Indeed, it reminds me of one I own myself. Isn't it nice, Theo?"

"No. If you ask me, it's damn disappointing," Theo said.

"Thought you'd have something more dashing on. Always wanted to see what you doxies wore. Thought it would be filmy, transparent stuff."

"In bright colors," nodded Letty, eyeing Jezebel's white cotton gown with sudden disfavor. "Black and red perhaps."

"Gold and purple," Theo took up. "With spangles!"

"Forgive me," snapped Jezebel, highly tired of being inquisitioned about her attire, "but it is my night off."

"Oh," Leticia said, nodding. Then she smiled to Theo. "Isn't that kind of Terrence? He truly is such a dear. He gives her a night off. He always has been a considerate employer. Why his staff even has—"

"Letty!" Theo said, her voice stern.

Letty flushed. "I know. I'm dithering."

"Yes," Theo nodded. "And that ain't why we came here."

Letty started, twisting her hands. "Oh, no, it isn't." She turned large eyes to Jezebel. "But I thought some pleasant conversation first, perhaps. I mean, it's only the polite thing to do."

"You're buying her off, Letty," Theo barked. "You ain't supposed to be polite."

Letty blinked. So did Jezebel. "Oh, I see." Letty nodded her head then and turned pale blue eyes to Jezebel. She drew in a deep breath, clearly nervous. Jezebel found herself shifting from foot to foot, Letty's nervousness transmitting itself to her.

"Well," Theo said, "do it! It was your notion."

"Miss Jezebel," Letty said. "Would you . . . would you . . . ?"

"Yes?" Jezebel asked.

"Would you . . . would you take five thousand pounds and leave Terry alone?"

"Five thousand pounds?" Jezebel exclaimed. Dazed, she walked over to the bed and sat quickly. "Five thousand pounds!"

"There! I did it!" Letty said. "I did it, Theo."

"Yes." Theo nodded. "You did it." As Jezebel looked up, stunned, she said, "Well, gel, will you take five thousand pounds and leave?"

Jezebel shook her head in wonderment. They were offering her money, just as she had Molly. The ante was raised, but it was the same transaction.

"Oh, dear," Letty said. "You are shaking your head. Do not shake your head, please don't. Theo, she is shaking her head."

"I see it," Theo replied. "Never say you won't take five thousand pounds."

"No," Jezebel said quickly. "No, of course not."

"Ain't no of course not," huffed Theo. "It's a good offer. A woman in your position should jump at it."

Jezebel gave a small laugh. "You have no idea what a woman in my position should do. No idea."

"It's my fault," Letty cried out. "I—I didn't ask right. I asked too quickly. Shocked you. I know when I am surprised, I do the same. Oh . . ." Huge tears welled in her eyes. "Oh, it's all my fault, and I so wanted to help Terry!"

"No!" Jezebel said quickly. "You asked it just perfectly." She sprang from the bed and dashed to Letty as the older woman broke into sobs. Kneeling, she automatically took up her hands. "Indeed, you did." She looked quickly to Theo. "Didn't she?"

"That she did," Theo said, and drew out a lace handkerchief. Jezebel took it swiftly and handed it to Letty.

Letty accepted it with a little sob. "No, I should have been more polite, not as rude."

"No," Jezebel said. "It was business and you did just as you ought. I assure you, I know! Buying a hussy off is very nerve-wracking. No matter how many times you practice it in the looking glass, it never comes out the way you want it to in actuality."

Letty looked up, a look of relief on her face. "You do understand, don't you?"

"Er, yes," Jezebel mumbled, suddenly realizing what she had said. "I-I understand."

"Then why aren't you taking the money?" Theo said, cutting to the nub of the matter.

"Because . . ."

Both women looked at Jezebel expectantly.

"Because . . . I'm powerful fond of Terry. That's why. He gives me all the money I need, and he's, um, a fine lover, I'll have you know."

"Oh, is he?" Letty asked, her tears disappearing.

"The best I've ever had," Jezebel nodded, pleased to see a smile come to the poor woman's face. Since she had never had a lover, it could not be considered a lie.

"Oh, I just knew it!" Letty said, her eyes shining with pride. "Our Terry is good at anything he sets his mind to."

"It's not his mind he sets to it." Theo rolled her eyes. "Should of known the boy would put a spoke in our wheel. Blast him, he's so damn good in bed we can't even buy his mistress off."

"Well"—Letty flushed—"it is a benefit that we cannot supply her. I mean, how can we compete? He even gives her a night off!"

"Then you won't take the money?" Theo asked curtly.

Jezebel stiffened. "No, I won't."

"What if we were to give you more?" Letty asked, leaning forward.

"Letty, stop it," Theo said. "You don't have any more to give. You are out of funds. You are always out of funds."

"I know," sighed Letty. "I simply have no head for business. Not like you, dear," she said to Jezebel and patted her hand. "My father always warned me to save for a rainy day . . . and now, now that rainy day has come." Her face crumpled. "I do not have enough to save my Terry fr-from your clutches."

Jezebel rose abruptly. "You do not have enough to save him from my clutches, so do not try."

"Very well," Theo said, her stolid face setting. "We've done all we can here, Letty!"

"I can find some more," Letty said, rising. "If you would only release my Terry."

Jezebel had had enough. "He is not your Terry. He is a full-grown man, and he is doing exactly what he wants."

"What he wants," Theo said, "is destroying his chances of ever contracting a decent marriage."

"Oh, no," Jezebel said. "I have it on the best of authority that a man can marry and have a mistress. 'Tis nothing uncommon in that."

"There is if he makes a cake out of himself over her," Theo said. "Everyone knows you're his actress. He even patroned you, and that's clear foolishness. You can't act two shillings worth."

"Or five thousand pounds worth?" Jezebel shot back. She put her hands upon her hips. "Don't be too certain I can't act!"

"Yes, Theo," Letty said. "That was unkind. Even if Miss Clinton's acting career has been an utter failure until now, it does not mean there is no hope. After all, I am sure acting is frightfully difficult."

"It's getting easier by the moment," Jezebel said, glaring at Theo.

"We will not let Terry make a bloody fool of himself," Theo thundered. "He's already dipped us in the scandal broth by bringing you here."

"And you were here to welcome me," Jezebel said. "Such an honor."

"Come, Letty," barked Theo. "We are not getting anywhere with this jade." She stomped toward the door and jerked it open.

"I think we should have been more polite," Letty said. She rose and drifted toward the door Theo held wide. "Indeed. You said we shouldn't be, but now we've set her back up."

"You can't set a woman's back up when it's always prone on a mattress, Letty," Theo said as her sister passed into the hall. She glared at Jezebel and, stepping out, slammed the door shut.

"Ooh!" Jezebel said, clenching her fists together. "Insufferable. Utterly insufferable!" She spun about and paced the carpet. "One asks me to be discreet and the others try to buy me off! Me! As if I am a tart!"

Once again a knock sounded at the door. Jezebel halted and glared. Cursing, she stomped across the room. "No, I told you," she shouted, ripping the door open. "Not even for ten thousand—" She froze and then flushed. "Oh, it's you."

Terrence stood in the hall, his gray eyes wide. He held a jar in his hand. "Jezebel?"

She looked down at the jar with loathing. "You've brought ointment, I see. How original." She turned and waved a hand. "Do come in. I know if I don't invite you to do so you'll ask to come in anyway." She stomped back into the room, crossing her arms. " 'Tis a family trait, no doubt."

Terrence entered slowly, his eyes wary. "What is the matter? And what is this about ten thousand?"

"Pounds," Jezebel said, refusing to look at him. She tapped her foot, and she jerked her head toward the bed. "Do put it with the rest."

Terrence tread softly over to the bed. His eyes widened. "I see you have a full supply."

"More than enough! Everyone is so solicitous."

His face darkened. Then he leaned forward and picked up a jar. "Grandmother's?"

"Yes." Jezebel nodded curtly.

He dropped it and picked up the one tied in pink ribbon. "Letty's, most definitely Letty's."

"Oh, yes."

"And Theo's," he nodded.

"Last, but not least," Jezebel said. "Most definitely not least!"

He dropped the jar onto the bed and turned with a sigh. "They were never ones to let grass grow under their feet. What did they say?"

"Say?" Jezebel lifted a brow. "Your grandmother was quite nice about it all, she understands a man has needs, you see." Unable to remain still, she started pacing. "I am quite welcome to stay, as long as I remain discreet."

"Indeed?"

"Yes." Jezebel spun quickly about, digging her heels into the plush carpet with a vengeance. "Whatever I do, I must not shock poor, sweet Miss Arrowroot. Who is just the perfect wife for you, mind you. She is not a managing female like I am."

Terrence coughed. "She called you managing?"

"Yes," Jezebel said, stopping to glare at Terrence, whose lips were twitching. "Me! Managing. You see, it was my notion to come here, and I finagled you into bringing me."

"You clever girl, you," Terrence said, his eyes dancing.

Jezebel narrowed her gaze. "Not so clever. She basically put me in my place. I am to remain sweet and discreet as your mistress while she handles the rest. The rest being to marry you to the biddable, Miss Arrowroot, that icon of English womanhood that all good Englishmen desire for wife."

Terrence's smile drained from his face, and Jezebel felt an unworthy pleasure. "So, that is the tack she is going to take. That is why Miss Arrowroot is here."

Jezebel nodded, clenching her teeth. "She intends to sweep me under the carpet despite what we've done."

"Damn!" Terrence said. "Blast and damn."

Jezebel laughed bitterly. "At least she didn't try to buy me off like Theo and Letty did."

Terrence stiffened. "They didn't."

"They did," Jezebel said. "For five thousand pounds, in

fact. And Letty would have offered more, but Theo reminded her she was out of funds."

Terrence studied her tensely. "What did you say?"

"Say? Say?" Jezebel's brows snapped down. "What was I supposed to say? I turned it down, of course."

"Good," Terrence said, softly. "Good."

Jezebel looked at him in surprise. Then sudden understanding knifed through her. "You thought I might accept it, didn't you?"

"No," he replied quickly. Yet she saw it in his eyes before he looked away.

The knife twisted further in her heart. "You really thought it!"

He looked up, his gray eyes implacable. "Very well, for a moment I did."

Rage saved Jezebel. Indeed, she shook with it. "You cad! You odious cad!"

"No," Terrence said, visibly stiffening. "What would you have me think? This morning you wanted to walk out on me. You said you'd find the money any way you could."

Jezebel's hands clenched. "Just because you bought me, you think I would let someone else do so? You thought I'd take your dear old auntie's money?"

"If you wanted to be shed of me bad enough," Terrence said.

Jezebel straightened, lifting her head high. "Do not mistake your creation with who I really am, Lord Haversham. You've drawn me into this scheme, and now you act as if I am the one conniving, as if I am the deceiver." She blew out her breath. "Well, I'm not. But you, my mighty lord, are going to find out who the real Jezebel Clinton is, and so is your family." She approached him in almost a stalk. "That I promise you. Your grandmother is going to see such indiscretion that she'll toss you out on your ear without a penny."

"She will?" Terrence asked.

She stopped before him, mere inches between them. "And your two aunts are going to find it would take an abbey to save you from my clutches."

"Indeed?" Terrence murmured.

"And you," Jezebel warned, anger thrumming through her, "will not be shed of me until you apologize for your insult."

An odd, slow smile crossed Terrence's face. "Then I will make certain I do not apologize too swiftly."

Jezebel froze, stunned. She glared at him. "Do you hear me? I'm going to make both you and them sorry!"

"Yes, my dear," Terrence said softly, nodding his head. "It is my fondest hope."

Jezebel stared at him, and he smiled back. Suddenly her anger melted away and humor took its place. She was threatening to do exactly what he wanted. A smile quivered upon her lips. "Cad," she murmured softly.

"Jade," he said. It was almost a caress. A scratch sounded at the door, and he grimaced. "Fiend seize it, who could it be now?"

"Go away," Jezebel called. "I am receiving no more insults tonight."

"Yes," Terrence said, his gray eyes soft upon her. "I've done the best."

Still, the scratching persisted, and something that sounded like a low mumble came to them. Jezebel, feeling oddly breathless, turned swiftly from Terrence. "All right, I am coming."

She walked to the door and jerked it open. She looked out, and then down. Mordrid stood before her. His brown eyes appeared hesitant, and he quickly hunkered down and whined.

Jezebel's brow winged up. "What do you want?" The beast rumbled deep in his throat and placed his head on his paws. Jezebel chuckled. "So, you're an outcast too tonight?" His tail thumped on the carpet. "Very well. From one outcast to another, you may come in." Mordrid jumped up, yapped, and dashed into the room. He totally ignored Terrence as he bounded onto the bed.

"Mordrid, get off!" Terrence said.

"No, do let him stay," Jezebel pleaded. "Those of us sunk beyond the pale will keep each other company." She walked over and sat down beside Mordrid, placing a hand upon his head. "Now, if you do not mind, Mordrid and I wish to go to bed."

"Jezebel," Terrence said, stepping toward her. "I . . ." A growl rumbled in Mordrid's throat, and Terrence halted. He stared at Mordrid. Mordrid stared back. "Well, I'll be." He stepped once more toward the bed. Mordrid cracked his canines open. Terrence threw up his hands. "Oh, very well, have it your own way." He stalked to the door and turned, then shook a finger at Mordrid. "But she's supposed to be my mistress, so don't think you're going to get to sleep with her every night." Mordrid only stood up on the bed, made a circle, and then plopped down.

"He's my protector," Jezebel said, biting back a smile.

Terrence's eyes darkened. "As I promise to be from here on out, Jez." He left without another word.

Jezebel stared at the door, and then she sighed. Deep in her heart, she hoped he would be. In this house, she would certainly need one.

Seven

"Sisters we are dealing with a hussy," Lady Dorethea said, her eyes narrowing as she watched the couple upon a blanket a few yards from them, while she and her sisters indulged in their picnic upon chairs. A footman stood behind them, awaiting their every wish. "An uncommon one, I own, but nevertheless a hussy."

"That she is," grunted Theo, her hand resting upon the collar of Mordrid. Rarely was Mordrid so confined, but today he was held, not nearly so much for his chasing of poor Geselda yesterday, as for the fact he had committed the sin of not only going over to the other camp, but sleeping with the enemy. "Can't believe Mordrid slept in that woman's room." Theo glared at her beloved companion. He lolled his tongue and wagged his tail. "Usually he ain't taken in by anyone, but that she-devil's seduced him as well as Terry."

"I do believe she-devil is too strong of word," Letty said. "She was very polite to us last evening when we visited her. Indeed, I thought—"

"You went to see her?" Dorethea asked.

"So did you," Theo said. "Beat us to the gate."

"Yes," Dorethea said, her lips tightening. "And it was a wasted visit. All I asked of her was to practice discretion, and look at her. She told me she understood the word, but I'll lay odds she's downed three glasses of champagne already. The way she is giggling and making up to Terrence is disgraceful."

"Oh, yes." Letty sighed, and her blue eyes began to tear. "Poor Amelia, how very mortifying it must be for her." The other two sisters fell silent while Letty sniffled. Neither wished to comment on the fact that at the moment Amelia chased after a blue bird of some long and tedious name and hadn't appeared at all distressed with the antics of Terrence and his lightskirt.

"Amelia will be perfect for Terrence," Dorethea said. "Edwin trained her well. She is looking the other way as a well-bred lady ought to do."

"Looking the other way?" Theo scanned the landscape and pointed. "You mean crawling the other way." Indeed, Amelia was at that moment on the outskirts of a cove of trees, down on her hands and knees while Elizabeth dutifully held up a branch from her progress. Theo snorted. "But you've got it right, Dorethea, she'll be perfect for Terry. Some other female would be throwing hysterics the way that tart is dallying with him in front of our eyes."

"Oh," sobbed Letty. "I do wish Jezebel had accepted our five thousand pounds."

"What!" Dorethea exclaimed. "Never say you offered her money!"

Letty's eyes widened and her tears dissipated. "Well, ah . . ."

"You have a tongue that runs on hinges," Theo said to Letty. She looked pugnaciously at Dorethea. "Yes, we offered her money, and you need not say anything."

"Yes I do," Dorethea said. "I cannot believe you were so doltish. Anyone reading her measure would have known it was a fool's errand."

"And asking her to be discreet wasn't?" Theo asked.

Dorethea threw up her hands. "You've weakened our position tremendously."

"Well, she didn't take it," Theo said. "So quit howling about it."

"Howling!" Dorethea glared frigidly at Theo.

"Don't give me that look," Theo protested. "Might frighten everyone else, but it don't me."

Dorethea glared, but it appeared to have no effect upon her sisters. "You offered her five thousand pounds. Just where did you expect to raise the funds?"

"Thought if we made the deal you'd have donated," Theo said.

"Donated!" Dorethea stiffened. "I'd not donate to such a toddy-headed scheme. That woman is a leech, and far smarter than the average doxy. Why, she knows far more about men than I had expected. Parading around in that demure nightgown, playing the innocent for them. She even reads poetry. And she knows more about . . ." She halted.

"About what?" Theo said.

Dorethea looked to Letty, whose eyes widened. "I'll tell you later."

"Oh, do tell me," Letty said. "After all, I am a full-grown woman. It isn't fair you keep it from me."

"You have never been married," Dorethea said.

"Well, neither has Theo," Letty said.

"I'm different," Theo said. "Don't have the tender heart you have. The facts of life don't upset me."

"It won't upset me," Letty claimed. "I promise. What does Jezebel know?"

Dorethea sighed. "It seems she knows more forms of prevention than I have ever heard."

"Prevention?" Letty asked.

"From getting with child," Theo said curtly. "What are they?"

Dorethea leaned over. "You know of the French leaf."

"The French . . ." Letty gasped. She stopped immediately as both sisters glared at her. "Oh, yes, I know. Do go on."

"It seems there is an Italian one as well," Dorethea said.

"Never heard there was," Theo said.

Dorethea shook her head. "I've been too isolated, I fear. I am behindhand with the newest inventions."

"Imagine," Letty said.

All three sisters stared at Jezebel and Terrence.

"We've got trouble," Theo said, gruffly.

"Yes," Dorethea said. "Grave trouble."

"Oh dear," sighed Letty, knowing full well she couldn't ask her sisters what the French leaf was, let alone the Italian one.

Jezebel dusted off her hands. "You are quite right. Your outdoor picnic is far less civilized. Dirt seems to appear everywhere."

Terrence chuckled and looked up to the sky. "And if I'm not mistaken, we will have the proper ending. It looks as if it shall rain soon."

Jezebel's look turned to one of concern. "Don't you think we should leave now? It surely wouldn't be good for your grandmother and her sisters to be caught in a deluge."

Terrence shrugged. "Why? 'Tis they who are inviting it with their sour, dark moods."

Jezebel giggled and lifted her glass of champagne to her lips. "They are rather displeased, are they not?"

He laughed, liking the way her violet eyes sparkled. "You are doing superbly, my love. But why not drink that glass, instead of tossing it out to the side as you've been doing?"

"I dare not," Jezebel said, shaking her head. "I have no notion of how I will react to spirits, and considering the fact your aunties would no doubt like to kill me, I believe I'd best keep my wits about me."

" 'Tis a waste of expensive champagne," Terrence said, knowing it was not right but thinking it would be delightful to see Jezebel tipsy. He'd like to be there when her ever-present wits weren't about her. It would be like when she was sleeping, perhaps. A surge of excitement shot through him, and he quelled it with difficulty.

"Fiddlesticks," Jezebel said, waving an airy hand. "If I can whistle five thousand pounds away, I certainly can pour out costly champagne."

Terrence frowned. "Jezebel, I am—"

"Don't say it." She set her glass down upon the blanket. "If you apologize so soon, you will have given me leave to go."

"Yes," Terrence said. "But I know I hurt you last night and . . ."

Suddenly Jezebel picked up one of the last grapes upon the small platter and held it temptingly before his mouth. "Do eat and be quiet! I do not wish to be serious today. I am playing a role, don't you know?"

Her eyes teased and challenged him. Returning that look of challenge, Terrence lifted his hand and cupped her wrist. Only then did he lean over and pull the grape from her fingers with his mouth. Her fingers curled and her wrist jerked slightly, but he held it firmly, swallowing the grape with a devilish smile. Jezebel's eyes widened with a delightfully stunned look. Unable to resist, Terrence bent and brushed a kiss over her knuckles. "I would not wish to bite the hand which feeds me."

"Indeed?" Jezebel said.

"Never," Terrence replied. Reaching with his other hand to unfurl her fist, he placed a slow kiss in her palm.

"I-I believe you know this role far better than I." Jezebel sounded breathless.

As breathless as Terrence felt. Even mere dalliance with this woman set his blood racing. "We must give them a good show," he whispered and moved to kiss the tender skin of her wrist, catching its pulse upon his lips. " 'Tis a hardened audience, my dear."

"I—I don't think so," Jezebel whispered, her eyes flickering nervously past him. "Your grandmother and aunts are well nigh falling out of their chairs. It looks as if Theo wishes to set Mordrid upon us."

"No," Terrence murmured. "I meant Amelia."

Suddenly Jezebel jerked her wrist away. A deep flush rose upon her face. "We most certainly are not going to do what it would take to shock *her!* We've been upstaged by a bird, I fear."

"What?" Terrence looked swiftly over toward Amelia. Or where Amelia should have been. Only Elizabeth stood as a marker now, Amelia apparently having crawled deeper into the thickets. He grinned after a moment and reached a hand out toward Jezebel. "That was dress rehearsal then. We shall have to do it again."

Jezebel slapped his wrist. "No, we shall not. We'll but incite your aunts, and by the time Amelia returns they will have mobbed us."

Terrence lifted a strawberry up between two fingers, challenging her. "Practice makes perfect, Jezebel."

She lifted a brow and then smiled. The softest, beckoning look entered her eyes. "Does it?" She did not lean over, but lifted her hand and, with one nail, ran it delicately down his upheld wrist to his cuff. Terrence felt a jolting sensation. Without a word, but still with that boudoir gaze, Jezebel flicked her nail and traced his fingers with it lightly. Terrence's hand shook. Courtesans had performed many tricks for him, even exotic dances, but just the tiniest movements of this woman drove him wild. She truly was a Jezebel.

He quickly dropped the strawberry and jerked his hand away. It did not help to know she could tease him far better than he had her. "Come, let us walk." He swiftly rolled to his feet and held out his hand.

"Very well," Jezebel said, smiling. She picked up the forsaken strawberry and popped it in her mouth. Even that incited Terrence, and he stifled a growl. She laughed and took his hand, permitting him to help her up. He kept her hand firmly in his, and they walked silently away from the group until they came to stand at the edge of the pond they picnicked beside. Desire still coursed through Terrence, yet a strange calm and peace filled him as he and Jezebel stood quietly, looking out over the water.

Suddenly she looked at him, a sadness in her eyes. "I do not understand, Terry."

"Understand what?" he asked softly.

"This is all so beautiful, and you will give it up, merely so you do not have to love."

Terrence shook his head, his fingers tightening upon Jezebel's. "I do not give this up so I do not have to love, I give this up so I do not have to marry."

"That isn't true," Jezebel said. "You said you do this so you will be disowned and never have to marry." Suddenly a cold raindrop fell and Terrence saw her shiver. "Amelia is but the moment. You do this so you will never have to love."

"No," Terrence said. "I may love, but I will not marry."

"But love and marriage go together."

"They do not," Terrence said, quickly releasing her hand. "Marriage is about land and money. A sanctioned form of destroying freedom and binding two people together so one cannot escape the other's control." A cold raindrop slashed his cheek and he winced.

"But should not love bind?" Jezebel asked. "Should not it be such that one desires to be committed to the other for life? Should not it be where both say to each other and the world that they will stand beside each other for always and let no other part them?"

"Good Lord, Jezebel," Terrence said in sudden, undefined anger. "How idealistic and naive can you be?"

Rain fell more heavily, setting a chill to his skin, matting Jezebel's golden hair to a dull sheen. Her eyes shimmered, the violet brightness drenched. "Apparently far too naive, I see."

She spun about to leave, but Terrence grabbed her shoulders, stopping her. "No, don't run away from me!"

"I am not running away from you," Jezebel said. "I am walking away from you."

"No!" he said, shaking her. "You will listen!"

"Listen to what?" Jezebel asked. No lightning lit the sky, but it flashed within her eyes. "Listen to you rant on about freedom with no commitment, no one controlling you. Well, as far as I know, love does control. It makes you better, bends you until you give more of your heart and spirit than you ever imagined. No, do not ask me to listen. You know nothing of love."

"And do you, Jezebel?" Terrence asked, fury shooting through him. "Have you ever loved a man?"

She glared up at him, rain streaming down her face, or perhaps tears. "Have you ever loved a woman?"

His fingers tightened upon the resisting cords of her shoulders. "Many times."

"No." She shook her head. "No, you've had prostitutes and mistresses. Exclusive rights for as long as the money holds." Her voice fell cold upon him, cold as the rain. "Now release me."

Terrence couldn't. A need drove through him. He wanted to kiss her, kiss the coldness from her eyes, kiss the cruel words from her lips. He bent toward her, drawing her against him.

"Don't," Jezebel said, struggling. "You shall not kiss me. Not for Amelia! Not for them!"

Terrence held her tightly, drawing the heat from her body which she herself would not give. "What if it is for me?" he asked hoarsely. "For me alone?"

Jezebel lifted her head, pain in her eyes. "Then I would remind you that you have no control over me. I have my freedom just as you do."

Terrence, feeling a sting as if she had slapped him, dropped his hands from her, stepping back. Something tor-

mented flashed deep within Jezebel's eyes, and then she
turned and ran. Terrence watched, a sheet of rain hazing her
figure. The rest of the party appeared a floating picture not
far from them, shifting and melting as they stood, waiting.

Terrence clenched his fists. The cold rain could not
quench the impotent rage within him. He could not control
it, just as he could not control Jezebel.

Elizabeth walked across the large hall, rearranging the
paisley shawl upon her shoulders. It felt good to be warm
and dry. In truth, she looked forward to dinner, for no matter
what one could say of Jezebel, she must admit the woman
added spice to the company. And she certainly had Lady
Dorethea in the boughs, something very few people were
able to do. Never in all the five years Elizabeth had worked
for the Duchess, had she seen anyone defy or irritate her in
such a fashion.

A sudden loud hammering at the entrance door startled
Elizabeth, so much so that she entangled her hands in the
fringe of her shawl. Frowning, she jerked them from the
threads. The hammering persisted. She looked swiftly about.
Stilton was nowhere to be seen. She had no doubt the worthy
butler was either in the kitchen striving with Pierre, the ex-
plosive Gallic cook or dealing with the demands of the
women above stairs, three of them elderly and in a sodden
miff.

She glanced toward the entrance. She could almost see
the massive oak door shake as the hammering persisted.
Whoever wished entrance seemed determined. She debated.
Deeming Stilton to have enough on his dish, she walked
over and opened the door. A fist shot toward her face. Gasping, she ducked.

"Oh, forgive me," a rough, male voice said. "I didn't
expect the door to open."

Elizabeth, blinking from the shock, peered into the night's

gloom. Another shock coursed through her. A tall, thin, golden-haired man stood before her. He might have appeared an angel come to visit, but for his blue eyes that shot fire and anger.

"Well, it did open," Elizabeth found herself saying through tightened vocal cords.

The man stiffened. "Is this the estate of the Duchess of Devon?"

"Yes, it is," Elizabeth said.

If his face could have darkened even more, it did. "Is Jezebel here?"

Elizabeth's heart sank. "Yes. Yes, she is."

"Damn! I knew it!" The man balled his fist and slammed it into his other hand. Suddenly he spun and paced away. "I'll kill him!" Elizabeth heard drift through the darkness.

"I beg pardon?" she said to empty air.

Suddenly the man was there before her again, breathing fire down upon her. "I must speak to Jezebel! I must! Let me in."

Elizabeth stiffened. The man might look like an angel, but he was clearly a bedlamite. "No, sir, I shall not. I do not know who you are, but you cannot just barge in here. This is the home of the Duchess of Devon, not a . . . well, I do not know what. But in polite houses one does not accept just anyone."

"You'll accept me," he said, his eyes flashing. "I'm going to see Jezebel." He moved to dodge past her right. Elizabeth feinted, blocking him. She heard him curse, and he lurched to the left. Again, Elizabeth barred his path.

"Step aside, madame," he cried. "I must see Jezebel."

"No!"

"You'll not keep me from her!" Suddenly, shockingly, he enveloped her in an iron hold and bustled her backward.

"Keep your hands off me," Elizabeth gasped, slapping futilely at him as her slippered feet skidded across the foyer's marble floor. "How dare you!"

"I must see Jezebel!" he said.

"You shan't!" Elizabeth cried. Freeing one hand, she delivered a blow to his chin.

His head snapped back. "Ow!"

Elizabeth drew her stinging hand back. "I'm sorry! I am, only . . ." Her voice trailed off under the unnerving intentness of the gaze he bent upon her. "Well, I am sorry."

"Who are you?" he asked softly. Though his arms tightened about her, his hold turned gentle, even intimate.

"I am . . ." Elizabeth blinked, suddenly forgetting her name. She was lost in the depths of the man's eyes and the warmth of his embrace.

"Josh!" a female voice exclaimed. "What on earth are you doing?"

Abruptly those arms dropped from Elizabeth, and the man's beautiful gaze left her. She felt oddly, ridiculously bereft as the stranger turned away from her.

"Jezebel!" he cried, shocked.

Shaking herself, Elizabeth turned as well. A golden goddess in a shockingly low-cut, blue brilliantine satin gown stood before them. Her lovely face showed every sign of stunned alarm.

"Begad, just what in blazes are you wearing?" the stranger asked.

"Never mind my attire," Jezebel said. "What were you doing with Elizabeth? And why are you here?"

"Why am I here? You ask *me* why?" the man asked, sputtering. He stepped toward her, his blue eyes flaming. "Did you not think I would follow, the minute I heard? How could you, Jez? How could you do such a terrible thing? Imagine my feelings when I returned to England to discover you gone. To discover . . ."—His voice cracked in anguish—"To discover you had run off with Haversham."

Jezebel's face turned to pale alabaster. "I-I didn't exactly run off with Terrence."

"You didn't?" His voice sounded pitifully hopeful. "But Molly said—"

Jezebel's eyes suddenly flared. "Oh, yes! Molly! If it wasn't for your Molly I wouldn't be here."

Josh lowered his head, looking conscience stricken. "You . . . you weren't to know about her."

"How could I not, Josh?" Jezebel cried. "You were spending everything on her! Everything!"

Elizabeth stifled a gasp. The man was a fiend. 'Twas clear he had shared an intimate relationship with Jezebel, yet had played her false with another woman.

That angelic devil straightened, and his fair skin flushed red. "What I do with my own money is my choice. I'm full grown and a man. It wasn't any of your business."

"Very well!" Jezebel lifted her chin. " 'Tis the same for me. What I do is my own business, not yours."

"No!" Josh strode to Jezebel and gripped her shoulders. "No! I won't let this damn Haversham have you! Do you hear me, Jezebel? I won't. I'll kill him first."

"My God, no!" Elizabeth gasped. The other two started, and both looked at her. She flushed. "I am sorry, but—"

"No, Elizabeth." The color drained from Jezebel's face. "No, it is I who am sorry. You must forgive us for . . . for fighting in front of you."

Elizabeth shook her head. "Th-that is understandable, but—"

"It is not right," Jezebel said. She turned dark, fulminating eyes to Josh. "We will discuss this matter in private, Josh."

He had the grace to look shamefaced. "Er, well, yes."

"Are you sure, Jezebel?" Elizabeth said, suddenly frightened for her. "I mean—"

"I'm sure." Jezebel nodded. "This—this discussion is better left in private."

Elizabeth cast a hesitant glance to Josh, who still gripped

Jezebel's shoulders. "But . . . but will you be safe w-with him?"

"What?" Josh exclaimed, his arms falling from Jezebel. "Of course she will. I'd never hurt Jezebel! I love her. She's my—"

"We will discuss it in private!" Jezebel shrilled.

Josh frowned. "But she needs to know—"

"No!" Jezebel exclaimed.

"No, indeed," Elizabeth said quickly. "I-I really don't wish to hear the details."

"But—" Josh protested.

"Come along," Jezebel ordered, grabbing his arm. "We will discuss this in private, I tell you!"

"But—"

"If you have any love for me," Jezebel said, "you will let me talk to you privately."

Josh stared down at her, looking bewildered. He turned to Elizabeth. "But I . . . well, I . . ."

"No, please," Elizabeth said quickly. "Do go, I quite understand."

Josh began to say something, but Jezebel dragged him away. Elizabeth stared after the two. Bethinking the danger of the man, who clearly was unstable, she raced to find Terrence.

"I can't believe it," Josh said, running a hand through his hair. "That Molly could have actually . . ."

"Sold me?" Jezebel asked, sitting upon the edge of her chair and watching Josh as he strode like a caged tiger about the elegant drawing room. "She did."

He turned. "But . . . but just because she did it didn't mean you had to honor it."

Jezebel lifted her chin. "Yes, I did. And I do not regret it one wit, if it has helped to break Molly's hold over you."

"Oh, it has. It has." He crossed to her and knelt, taking

up her hands. "But that you should—should ruin yourself for me, I cannot bear it."

"But I haven't ruined myself," Jezebel said quickly. "Not really."

"The whole town thinks you are the Marquis's mistress." Josh's face darkened.

"But I'm not," Jezebel said. "Surely that is what counts. What does it matter if a society I have no concern for thinks the worst of me?"

"What does it matter!" Josh's blue eyes widened. "Faith, Father must be rolling in his grave this very minute. Everyone thinks you a straw damsel, Jezebel. You, who are the most upright and virtuous woman in the world. And why? Because the Marquis of Haversham wishes to play games with his family." His eyes narrowed. "He hasn't played games with you as well, has he?"

Jezebel looked swiftly away. "What do you mean?"

"He hasn't been forward with you, has he?" Josh's hands tightened on hers. "Tell me. He hasn't dared to try and kiss you?"

"No, he hasn't tried," Jezebel said, flushing. Terrence had succeeded in kissing her, he hadn't merely tried.

Josh's eyes widened. "You're lying Jezebel. I can tell!"

"Jezebel."

It was Terrence's voice. Brother and sister jumped, then looked in unison to the room's entrance. Jezebel's heart sank. Terrence leaned against the closed door. She had not heard him enter, let alone close the door again.

Terrence smiled at her, though his gray eyes snapped with dangerous lights. "I heard you had company and decided to pop down to greet him."

"Oh, Terrence," Jezebel said. "I-I would like you to m-meet my brother."

"You bastard," Josh shouted. He sprung up and crossed the room before Jezebel could even speak. "You kissed her, damn you!" Josh drew back a fist and cracked it against Terrence's jaw.

Terrence received the punch with a controlled jerk. His eyes shot fury. "So, you act the enraged brother, when 'tis your fault Jezebel was even having to deal with the likes of Molly." His fist shot out and landed in Josh's stomach. Josh, doubled over, wheezing.

"Terry, no!" Jezebel cried, jumping up.

"She's done this for you, you young cawker," Terrence said, shaking his wrist. "And you dare call her a liar."

Josh caught his wind and charged Terrence. The two men came together like a thunderclap.

"Stop it!" Jezebel cried. "Stop it!"

"I've been waiting to do this for two days," Josh said, grappling with Terrence.

"And I since I've met Jezebel," Terrence said. Breaking Josh's stranglehold he delivered a lightning blow.

"Oh, in that case," Jezebel said, throwing up her hands in disgust. "Do proceed! If you two beasts wish to fight, far be it from me to stop you." Her words unfortunately fell further awry than the men's fists. "And if you two wish to kill each other, go right ahead. I'll not mourn you!"

Josh received a fine blow from Terrence and stumbled backward.

"No!" Jezebel cried, dashing forward and snatching the Ming vase from the table directly in Josh's path. She held the priceless vase high as Josh rammed into the empty table, sending it crashing to the floor. The men charged at each other again, and Jezebel performed some very fancy footwork to save herself and the vase from being milled down.

"Oh, no," she cried. Hugging the vase in one hand, she darted forward and snatched up a Dresden shepherdess with the other from another side table just before Terrence careened into it and sent it toppling. Without a moment to spare, she tossed her prizes to the settee's cushions and with a curse charged toward the men. They were dodging and swinging in a direct course for the ornate grandfather clock, the one set against the wall in a place of honor.

"Watch where you are going!" She circled the brawling men and threw herself in front of the clock, waving her hands wildly. "Stop it! You'll hit the . . . ooof." Terrence rammed into her, and Jezebel fell back smack into the ancient clock. Chimes clanged, glass cracked, and the old clock bonged out the wrong hour. Jezebel righted herself to the sound of outraged bongs and spun around to look. Splintered lines ran up the pane of glass, obscuring the golden wrought hands and tangled chains.

"That's it!" Jezebel turned back, eyes narrowed. Exhaling a breath of pure exasperation, she strode smartly up to the two men who at that moment had arms clenched about each other and appeared to be dancing. Jezebel thwacked her two hands against the nearest back, which was Terrence's, and shoved with all her might.

The men, never considering an outside force, capsized, entwined and cursing. Jezebel, wasting not a second, promptly sat down upon Terrence's back, Josh effectively trapped beneath. "I said enough," she declared, and bounced up and down for punctuation.

"Jez-Jez-e-bel," Terrence wheezed in a staccato. "S-stop it!"

"Only if you will," Jezebel said.

"Gads, Jez," Josh said. "I can't breathe."

"Do I care?" Jezebel said. "Now are you going to stop?"

Suddenly she heard a rumbling laugh from Terrence. "I don't know about you, old man, but I'll gladly stop. This isn't a position I wish to remain in."

"Zounds no," Josh said. "Jez, let us up for God's sake."

"You promise not to hit each other?" Jezebel persisted.

"I will if he does," Terrence grunted.

"I will," Josh said. "You've got a bruising punch there, you know."

"Yours is just as bad," Terrence returned.

"Josh," Jezebel said. "You promise not to do anything to upset our masquerade?"

"I'll try," Josh said. "Now will you let us up!"

Suddenly the door to the room burst open. All three occupants looked up, startled.

"Just what is going on in here?" Lady Dorethea asked as she entered, a tiny domino. Behind her crowded Elizabeth, Letty, and Theo.

"Nothing!" Jezebel said swiftly.

"Nothing?" Lady Dorethea stomped up to them. "You are sitting on my grandson and some other strange person. I do not consider that nothing."

"Faith," Theo said, her solid face darkening, " 'tis a bacchanalia."

"I hope not," Lady Dorethea snapped. "Considering 'tis Terrence embracing another man." Her eyes narrowed upon Josh. "Just who are you, sir?"

Jezebel sprung up, blushing. "Ah . . . he is . . . is . . ." She stopped, her mind refusing to come to her aid.

"We can explain," Terrence said, quickly rolling off of Josh and standing.

Josh, now lying supine on the floor with the women gaping down upon him, gurgled. "I am . . . well, I am . . ." He looked desperately to Jezebel. "Who am I, Jez?"

Elizabeth stepped close to Lady Dorethea and whispered into her ear. Lady Dorethea's face lit up, and she looked at Josh with a new respect. "So, you are Jezebel's ex-lover."

"Ex-lover!" Josh yelped. He jackknifed into a sitting position.

"Ex . . ." Letty's mouth formed a perfect O. "My, my!"

"Yes," Terrence said, grinning all of a sudden. "That is who the blighter is."

"Watch it," Josh growled.

Lady Dorethea smiled smugly. "Came chasing after her, didn't you?"

"Hot-blooded blade." Theo chuckled.

Josh, stumbled up, his face turning a deep shade of red. "Jezebel, help!"

Jezebel crossed her arms, smiling cruelly. "Do not look to me. You should have not barged in here." She tossed her head. "I have nothing to do with jealous ex-lovers, I'll have you know."

Josh's mouth fell open. "But . . . but . . . !"

Elizabeth once again leaned over and whispered something to Lady Dorethea.

"What's she saying?" Josh asked, all but hopping up and down. "What's she saying now?"

Lady Dorethea's eyes widened. "My goodness, you audacious scamp."

"Audacious?" Josh flushed, and he glared at Elizabeth. "What did you just tell her?"

"Only the truth," Elizabeth said.

Dorethea shook her head, though she smiled gleefully enough. "Fie, sir, to play poor Jezebel false and then come hotfooting it here as if you are the injured party."

"By gad!" Theo barked, her own eyes lighting. "Boy's got brass, damn if he don't."

"Amazing, isn't it?" Terrence said, his eyes twinkling. "And the chap attacked me the minute he saw me."

"That's because you kissed Jezebel," Josh sputtered to a halt. "Well, never mind."

"But if you played poor Jezebel false," Letty said, frowning. "Surely it shouldn't matter if Terrence kissed poor Jezebel. After all, you were kissing another woman."

"Her name was Molly," Elizabeth said, nodding. "And he spent everything on her!"

"Here now!" Josh cried. "Stop telling them that!"

Elizabeth stiffened. "Why? I'll not have Her Grace suffer under any delusions of what your character is like."

"Ain't nothing wrong with my character," Josh said, stepping toward her threateningly. "And if you keep telling tales—"

Elizabeth skittered behind Dorethea. "Do not come near me. I refuse to let you bully me as you have Jezebel."

"What?" Josh cried out.

"Yes, "Lady Dorethea said, chuckling. "Elizabeth is under my protection, and it seems young man that you have enough women to handle without taking her on." She grinned. "Though it appears as if Jezebel had you well in line herself when we interrupted . . . as well as my grandson." She shook her head. "Well, come along, it appears to me you both require attention." She glared at Terrence. "Else you'll be dripping blood on my carpet."

Terrence bowed. "Forgive me, my dear."

"You can't mean to let that man remain here?" Elizabeth exclaimed. "He is a . . . a philanderer."

"A scandalous man," Terrence said. "The whole town knows he's a Bluebeard."

"Who played me false," Jezebel added. Never had she seen her brother in such an uncomfortable position, and as angry as she was, she harbored not one merciful thought of assisting him.

Lady Dorethea looked speculatively at Josh, who turned a bright red. "Well now, I've always had a soft spot for philanderers and rakes."

"But he is dangerous!" Elizabeth gasped.

Lady Dorethea's smile widened. "Especially dangerous rakes." She walked up to Josh and placed a hand upon his arm. "If you are not doing anything for a while, young man, you are welcome to join our house party."

"What!" Elizabeth cried.

"Nothing like healthy competition," Lady Dorethea declared. "But I do not wish for you to come to fisticuffs with my grandson, again. Is that clear?"

"You can't mean to let him stay here," Elizabeth said again.

Lady Dorethea shrugged. "We certainly cannot send the poor boy away. He is injured, after all. You as a young lady, need to steer clear of him I own, but as an old lady I cannot help but like a rake; I can enjoy them without a threat to my well-being."

Josh cast Elizabeth a triumphant glance. He placed a hand upon Lady Dorethea's and smiled. "Madame, I am your rake, and I will be pleased to remain."

"Outrageous," Elizabeth cried. She spun on a heel and stalked from the room.

"Oh, dear," Letty said. "She is upset, and rightfully so I am sure. She has never come in contact with a rake before. Not that I have either." Her blue eyes brightened, but then turned regretful. "Oh, no, we haven't considered poor Jezebel's feelings." She looked hesitantly to Jezebel. "Dear, would you mind frightfully if he remained? I know it would be quite uncomfortable for you considering that—"

"I'm not leaving," Josh said quickly. "Got me an invitation and I'm staying."

Jezebel, recognizing the mulish set to her brother's chin, and realizing they'd goaded him as far as he would tolerate, sighed and tried for a weak smile. "No, Letty, I shall survive. I would not wish to ruin your entertainment."

"Oh, thank you, dear." Letty flushed. "I didn't mean . . . Well, ah, I shall go after Elizabeth and try to explain." She drifted toward the door. "He is injured after all, and we can't have that. Elizabeth should understand, she is a kindhearted child. . . ." She walked out still talking.

"Kindhearted?" Josh muttered. "Don't seem that way to me."

"You must forgive Elizabeth," Lady Dorethea said, chuckling. "Normally she does not fly up into the boughs like this. In fact, she is rarely ruffled."

"She ain't?" Josh's brows shot up. "From what I've seen, she's always ruffled."

"Perhaps she is not accustomed to rakes." Lady Dorethea's eyes twinkled.

"Or any other man, I'll lay odds," Josh muttered.

"Josh!" Jezebel exclaimed.

"Well," he retorted. "She's as prickly as a porcupine, Jez."

"Unlike dear Jez," Lady Dorethea said. "Now, come along Mr. . . . ? What is your full name, sir?"

"My full name?" Josh asked, alarm in his voice. "It's—"

"Villain," Terrence said, quickly. "Yes, that is it, Mr. Josh Rakesham."

Josh glared at him. "Thank you."

"Never consider it, old man," Terrence said, grinning.

Dorethea only blinked once. "Well, Mr. Rakesham, since Jezebel is under my grandson's protection for the moment, I believe you must suffer my ministrations. She can take care of Terrence."

"That she can," Terrence said, grinning. "She's the only woman I know that doesn't sit a fight out, but rather sits right on it."

"Humph," Theo said. "Don't think either of these fighting cocks should be pampered."

"I quite agree." Jezebel's eyes narrowed.

Theo stared suspiciously. "You do?"

"I do," Jezebel said. "They behaved like schoolboys."

"You're in her black books, old man," Josh said, sotto voce to Terrence. "Take it from me, best let her cool down first."

"I'll follow your advice," Terrence conceded. "After all, you've known her far longer than I have."

"Then you may come with me as well, Terrence," Lady Dorethea laughed. She led Josh and Terrence toward the door and out.

"Men," Theo said gruffly. "Who needs them?" She turned stern eyes to Jezebel. "I would have taken the five thousand we offered you and been shed of them both if I were you."

Jezebel glared after the trio. "Do not tempt me. At this moment, I'd probably even take a thousand."

"I can do that," Theo said, nodding.

Jezebel laughed, though her temper boiled beneath. "Oh, no, I fear I'd disappoint the Duchess if I did. She is enjoying this situation far too much."

Theo frowned. " 'Fraid you're right. Dorethea always was a ninny over rakes."

Josh wandered down the darkened hall with a slightly unsteady gait. The candle in his hand wavered, its light bouncing in the dark corridor and causing Josh to squint. He had drunk too much at dinner without a doubt. Yet every time he had looked at Jezebel, rigged out in a low-cut satin dress, pointedly ignoring him, his hand automatically went to his wine glass for another sip. That would turn into a gulp, however, when he looked to the man at the end of the table, the Marquis who had bought his sister for five hundred pounds. " 'Curst rum touch," he muttered.

He halted before a door and peered at it. Josh continued to peer, reciting to himself the directions the little maid Betty had given him. She had giggled and batted her lashes so much that Josh doubted he had understood them clearly.

After the third cantation, Josh nodded. "This is it." He tapped on the door and whispered, "Jezebel?" He received no answer. "You asleep? Jez, I need to talk to you." He tried the door and found it unlocked.

Opening it, he entered. He blinked, trying to define the room's contents, then spied the bed with Jezebel asleep in it. "Jez, must talk to you," he whispered and stumbled over to her. He sat down heavily and with an unsteady hand placed the candle on the bedside table. "I'm s-sorry about the fight." He received no answer, so he leaned over and shook the white-clad shoulder turned away from him. "Wake up, want to—bejeezus!" He cried as Jezebel suddenly jerked and twisted around. Alarmingly, she scrabbled up in bed with a scream. Josh clapped his hands over his ears. "Faith, Jez, don't screech so." Then his eyes widened and his mouth dropped. He stared, befuddled, at a tousled black-haired woman, her gray eyes dark with fright. "You're not Jezebel!"

"Of course not!" she snapped. "I'm Elizabeth."

"Oh, frightfully sorry." Josh sprung from the bed and stumbled back. "Didn't m-mean to wake you. Wanted to w-wake Jez."

She glared at him. "I don't believe it."

"S'true," Josh said. "W-wouldn't have come in to wake you. D-don't know you. Wouldn't be proper, not proper 'tall."

She stiffened. "And sneaking into Jezebel's room would be?"

"Y-yes," Josh said. "Ain't nothing wrong with that."

"How . . . how utterly dastardly!" Elizabeth exclaimed. "Not one night under our roof and already you are trying to sneak in to Jezebel, when she is Terrence's mistress now."

"She is not!" Josh clenched his fists and stepped toward her.

Elizabeth was cowed. "She isn't?"

Josh halted, remembering just in time. He shifted, and looked away. "Well, I guess she is."

"Which makes you a rake and rogue." Her tone was accusing.

"Yes, guess so," Josh gritted out. Then he glared at her. "But you don't have to keep reminding me, conf-found it. I r-remembered in time. D-don't need y-your help."

"I'm sure you don't," Elizabeth shot back, her gray eyes snapping in the candlelight.

The two combatants stared at each other. As they did so, Josh grew increasingly aware of Elizabeth's beautiful black hair, stark against her white night rail. He imagined the soft curves hidden beneath the white cotton. He flushed. "Er, well I-I best leave. Didn't mean to disturb you." He stumbled over and picked up the candle with shaking hands. "Th-thought that l-little blond maid B-Betty said . . . Well, never mind. Sh-she was giggling too much. C-confused me."

"The maid Betty?" Elizabeth said. "You've already set up a flirtation with her?"

"What? I . . ." Josh clamped his mouth shut. His head suddenly pounded as much as his heart did. Even in his drunken state, he knew he was losing ground. He stalked toward the door. "That's right. I'm a rake," he muttered. He turned and glowered. "D-dally with every fetching woman I see! Every bl-blasted one, mind you!"

He saw Elizabeth stiffen. A hurt, vulnerable look traced through her eyes. "Then I must be thankful I am not fetching."

"Not fetching?" Josh exclaimed, almost dropping his candle. "N-not fetching?"

The woman clearly lacked comprehension, and she wasn't even castaway like he was! The problem was she was too fetching. He wanted to kiss those trembling lips, and hold her close. Not only for her beauty, but to erase the elusive hurt he had glimpsed in her eyes. Then, through the turmoil, an exciting notion arose. Indeed, the thought struck him like a blinding light.

"Blast it, I'm supposed to be a rake, ain't I?" He straightened and walked back to the bed with an amazingly firm stride.

"Wh-what are you doing?" Elizabeth asked.

"I'm a rake," Josh said, thunking the candle down upon the table. "That's what I am!"

Without further ado, he sat down and jerked Elizabeth to him. He crushed his mouth to hers, muffling the screech upon her lips. She stiffened to stone, yet Josh held on tightly, kissing her with rakish abandon. Suddenly Elizabeth melted, turning to molten lava within his arms. Josh felt drowned, drowned by silken lips beneath his and warm flesh pressed sweetly to him. His entire world swirled. Groaning, he pulled back, shaken. Elizabeth's face was turned up to his, her lips still pursed, her eyes closed. It was a face of utter beauty. And innocence.

"Oh, God," Josh breathed, clutching her tightly, in direct opposition to his mental command to release her. "S-slap me!"

Elizabeth's eyes snapped open, dark with passion. "What?"

"Slap me," Josh gulped. "Quickly. That's wh-what you're supposed to do. I'm a rake."

"But . . ."—She shook her head—"I couldn't."

"Y-yes you c-can," he said, even as his hands, of their own wicked accord, smoothed over her back. "A-am a rake! It's o-only pr-proper."

He felt her stiffen. "Proper? You are telling me what is proper?"

Josh's gaze unwittingly fell to her lips, those soft lips that looked well kissed, but surely could be kissed some more. "N-not telling you. Only . . ." He swallowed hard. "Only warning you."

Elizabeth's eyes widened as he lowered his head. "Oh . . . oh no!"

A stinging slap halted Josh. His arms fell from Elizabeth as his head snapped back. He shook it, seeing stars and lights. He drew in a ragged breath, reality setting in, if not sanity. "There!" Josh said and jumped from the bed. He looked down at Elizabeth sternly, attempting to ignore her rumpled, bewitching state. "Now—now you remember I'm a rake. J-just slap me whenever you like." He flushed. "No, mean whenever you . . . you need to."

Elizabeth only stared at him. Josh grabbed up his candle and bolted from the room.

Terrence stood before the door, his candle glowing in the dark hall. He drew in a deep breath and regretted it. It only pulsed the brandy fumes to his head all the more. Faith, he had drunk too much at dinner. Yet, every time Josh Clinton looked at him, Terrence felt like a cad. And every time he glanced in Jezebel's direction to find her studiously ignoring him, he knew he was not only a cad, but a cad in very serious trouble.

"Jezebel?" Terrence called. He rapped more loudly on the door. "Jezebel, I wish to talk to you." Silence greeted him. He rapped again. "I'll keep knocking until you open the door, so you might as well do it now rather than later."

He finally heard sounds from within. He heard the key grate in the door, and it cracked open.

"What do you want?" Jezebel's voice said, low and cold.

Terrence leaned forward to peer through the crack. He could just barely define Jezebel's face, but the glitter in her violet eyes was unmistakable. "I want to talk to you."

"Well, I don't want to talk to you," she said. "I don't wish to talk to a man who brawled like a sailor with my brother."

"He attacked me," Terrence exclaimed.

He could have sworn he heard Jezebel growl, really growl.

"Yes, but you dived right in there quite readily. And you cracked your grandmother's clock."

"I apologize," Terrence said. Unfortunately the brandy fumes urged him to say, "But it felt good. Your brother had no reason to act self-righteous, 'twas he that spent all the money on his light-o'-love."

"And 'twas you that made me one," she retorted. "Your pretend one, I meant to say."

Terrence reared back slightly, for he heard another growl. He shook his head, stunned. He never knew a woman could growl like that.

"Theo was right," Jezebel hissed. " 'Tis better to have no man around."

Growling or not, Jezebel's statement caused anger to

surge within Terrence. "Don't listen to Theo. She hates men."

"And I can see why!"

"Open the door," Terrence ground out. "We are going to talk this out."

"No, we aren't."

"Oh, yes, we are." Terrence shoved his hand through the open crack. He heard a low rumble and then experienced a sharp bite. He jerked his hand back. Well-defined teeth marks ringed his thumb, and blood trickled down it. Dizzy and flabbergasted, Terrence said, "Jezebel, how could you?"

"It wasn't me, you clunch," Jezebel hissed. "It was Mordrid."

"M-Mordrid?" Terrence lifted his hand and peered at it. Yes, the teeth prints were canine, now that he noticed it. Unbelievable relief flooded him. It wasn't felicitous to think Jezebel had actually bitten him. "Thank God."

"But if you don't leave me alone," Jezebel said, "I'll follow suit."

Terrence nursed his hand at his chest, feeling embarrassed, enraged, and confused at the same time. "Blast and confound it!"

"Good night, My Lord!" The door slammed smartly shut.

Terrence glared at it. Even in his cups, he still possessed the sense to know when he was licked, or bit rather. He spun and stomped down the hall, cursing unreasonable females and rabid dogs.

He slowed, however, as he saw another light bobbing down the hall. Soon it merged with his, and he discovered Josh behind it. Josh weaved slightly, and one side of his face was red.

"Oh, it's you," Josh said, stopping.

"Yes." Terrence nodded. "It's me."

"I'm lost." Josh shook his head back and forth. "Damn lost."

"As am I." Terrence sighed.

"Devil a bit," Josh said and burped. "Then we'll never find our beds tonight. And I swear," he said quickly, "s'all I want is my own, you understand."

"Same here." Terrence nodded again.

"Good," Josh said, a drunken grin of relief crossing his blurry features. He blinked and pointed. "What happened to your hand?"

"I was bitten," Terrence muttered, quickly hiding it. "I went to try and apologize to Jezebel."

"And she bit you?" Josh exclaimed. "Bedamn. Never knew Jez to bite before."

"No, Mordrid bit me," Terrence said. "He was in the room with her."

"He!" Josh exclaimed, his blue eyes popping. "There was a he in the room with Jezebel!"

"Yes," Terrence said, growling a little himself. "Damn dog."

"And you left him there?" Josh's voice shook.

"Ill-mannered cur," Terrence murmured, his indignation swelling. "She lets him sleep with her, you know?"

"Let's him sleep with her? Fiend seize it, I'll call him out!" Josh shouted. "Blast! I'll run him through. He ain't going to sleep with my sister and get by with it!"

Terrence blinked, astonished. "He's a damn dog, you cloth head, you can't call him out."

"What? He's that good with the pistols?" Josh asked, blanching. "Is that why you let him sleep with Jez?"

"No," Terrence said. His head began to throb. "You don't understand. He's a real dog."

"I don't care if he's a real dog, that man ain't sleeping with my sister anymore. Not since I'm here. He can bite me all he wants, but I'll meet him on the dueling field, see if I don't."

"Josh," Terrence tried again. "Mordrid is a dog with four legs, hair, and the foulest breath imaginable."

"Oh!" Josh said. A sheepish expression washed his face.

"Sorry, went off half-cocked there. Just a little befuddled tonight." He raised a hand to his cheek and rubbed it. "Infernally befuddled."

"What happened to you?" Terrence asked.

"Oh, er, nothing," Josh muttered. "But I tell you, it ain't easy being a rake. Damn hard."

Terrence nodded. "S'all right, let me tell you, it ain't easy having your sister for a mistress either, even a pretend one."

Josh smiled. "I'll lay odds on that."

"Come on, old man." Terrence sighed. "I'll show you to your room."

Josh nodded. "I'd be forever grateful. Been afraid to try another door. Been wandering these blazing halls for an hour."

Eight

Terrence stifled a wince and raised the cup of tea to his lips. He sipped it gingerly, the hot liquid soothing as it trickled down his throat. It was the only soothing thing. His head pounded, his eyes burned, and the plate of eggs and bacon Stilton had placed before him appeared to be doing its level best to turn his stomach.

"Good morning," Lady Dorethea said, as she swept into the breakfast room. She proceeded, very noisily in Terrence's opinion, to sit down before him. She studied him with discerning eyes. "You shot the cat last night, didn't you?"

"Perhaps," Terrence muttered.

"No perhaps about it," Lady Dorethea said, reaching for the silver teapot. "I recognize the look well. I will have Stilton prepare a concoction. 'Tis clear you need the hair of the dog that bit you."

"I'd like to have every wiry one of them," Terrence muttered. Lowering his cup, he swiftly withdrew his hand and placed it in his lap. "But I'll not take a sip of one of your brews. They are lethal."

"Not as lethal as that head you are carrying, I'll lay odds," Lady Dorethea said, pouring herself some tea and picking up her cup. "Terrence, I wish to talk to you."

"You wish to talk to me?" Terrence asked. He snorted. "At least someone wishes to talk to me."

"I want to know what you think about Amelia," Dorethea said, studying him over the brim of her cup.

"Amelia?" Terrence asked. He looked at his grandmother and decided if she was unwise enough to ask him such a question when he suffered a hangover, she deserved the truth without the bark upon it. "I've never known you to come such a cropper, Grandmother. How you could ever imagine I'd be interested in that featherbrained bird chaser is beyond me."

"One does not consider personal interests when contracting a marriage," Dorethea said, and sipped daintily from her tea. "One considers lands and properties. Amelia's runs directly beside ours. 'Twould increase the holdings which someday will be yours."

"They never shall," Terrence said. "For I won't marry Amelia, ever. You might as well cast me off and have done with it."

"I won't." Dorethea set her teacup down with precision. "You aren't fooling me, Terrence. You brought that hussy Jezebel here just to try my patience, and I know it."

"Don't call her a hussy," Terrence said.

"Well, she is one," Dorethea snapped. "You are blatantly trying to destroy all my plans for your future!"

"Yes," Terrence said, gritting his teeth. "And I'll succeed, sooner or later."

"You shall not." Lady Dorethea's tiny fist pounded upon the table. "Amelia is the perfect wife for you, and you shall marry her."

"No, I won't," Terrence roared, goaded beyond endurance. "I'll not marry her or any other buffleheaded debutante you throw at my head, do you hear?"

Dorethea reared back. A fear darkened her green eyes. "Then who is it you intend to marry?"

Terrence shook his head and exhaled in sheer exasperation. "Just leave it be, Grandmother. This is not the time to brangle with me. I am in no mood to be polite."

Dorethea's face paled. "My God. You don't intend to marry that Jezebel, do you?"

"Marry Jezebel?" Terrence barked a bitter laugh. "I'd not marry a woman who kicks me out of bed, else sets a dog on me."

"She never did!" Dorethea exclaimed. "Impossible."

Terrence grimaced. He'd kick himself if he didn't already feel kicked. "Nothing's impossible with Jezebel, you'll discover."

"But she is your mistress," Dorethea said. "Surely you do not tolerate such behavior from her?"

"What I shall tolerate from Jezebel is not your affair," Terrence said stiffly.

"You should cast her off." Dorethea's eyes shot sparks. "I've never heard of a mistress doing such. You are the Marquis of Haversham, and the woman treats you as a—a commoner."

"One cannot condemn Jezebel as a toad eater, 'tis certain," Terrence said, his lips twisting. " 'Twas my fault. I made the mistake of telling her not to call me My Lord, and she took me at my word. She neither calls me Lord nor treats me as one."

Dorethea reached out a quick hand. "Terry, you aren't in love with the woman, are you?"

Terrence froze. He discovered he couldn't answer her question. He knew he surely couldn't be, but the words would not come out. He settled by saying, "I'm not going to cast her off, Grandmother, so you might as well cast me off instead."

"Good morning," a voice said from the entrance. Terrence and Dorethea looked up. Josh, bruises besmirching his face, stood within the door. "Er, that maid, Betty, directed me here."

"Do come in and have a seat, Mr. Rakesham," Dorethea said. "I most definitely am going to order Stilton to brew a concoction," she murmured lowly as Josh ambled with a dignified but clearly pained shuffle to the table and sat.

"Ah, Stilton," Dorethea said when that very worthy gentleman entered as if upon cue. "Do be so good as to prepare my remedy for a hangover."

"Forgive me, Your Grace," Stilton said, promenading over to the table and setting down a tray. A solitary glass with a murky, rusty red liquid rested upon it. "But I have already taken the liberty of doing so. Master Terrence's appearance suggested I should."

"Oh, Lord," Terrence said, stifling a shiver. "I'll not drink it. Josh may, if he so desires."

Josh blinked bloodshot eyes. "What is it?"

"Just something to make you feel better," Dorethea said, handing him the glass. "Do try it."

Josh appeared leery as he took the glass and lifted it to study it. "Like to know what's in it first, if you don't mind."

"Good morning," Jezebel's voice said.

"Saved, old man," Terrence murmured as both Jezebel and Elizabeth entered the room. "Toss it, if you can."

"Hmmm, what?" Josh asked, the glass frozen before him, but his eyes focused upon Elizabeth as she took up a chair across from him. A red stain flushed his fair complexion.

"Do drink it, son," Dorethea said. "It will help you."

"Hmmm, yes," Josh said dutifully. In an absentminded manner, he lifted the concoction to his lips and took a full swallow. His blue eyes popped wide. "Good God!" he shouted. Choking and coughing, he slammed the glass down. "Blast and damn!"

"Sir!" Elizabeth said. "There is no need to swear at the breakfast table!"

"Confound it, there is," Josh wheezed. "What the devil is in that?"

"Don't ask." Terrence chuckled, despite himself. "I've always thought Grandmother stole the recipe from a witch."

"I did not," Dorethea said, her chin lifting. "Lord Alvany gave it to me."

"Either way," Terrence said. " 'Tis poisonous."

"And you let Josh drink it?" Jezebel asked, her voice sharp. "You didn't warn him?"

"He's a grown man," Terrence said, nettled.

Jezebel's brow rose. "I see you did not drink it. I guess you are not that grown then."

Terrence stiffened at the insult. He reached for the glass. "Very well. I'll drink it to show I'd no intention of poisoning your dear . . . er, Josh."

"No," Josh exclaimed, snatching it from Terrence and shaking his head wildly. "Don't do it, old man. Dreadful stuff. Dreadful."

"I'll drink it," Terrence gritted out. "Jezebel deems it unfair you drank it and not I."

"Shouldn't do it." Josh sighed, but handed him the glass in obvious resignation. "Could kill you."

Terrence gripped the glass. His eyes steady upon Jezebel's, he downed its burning contents. A hushed silence fell over the room, as without a word Terrence slowly set the glass upon the table. Jezebel's gaze finally fell from his, even as Terrence's stomach rocked and roiled with the terrible brew.

"Hello, everyone," another voice said from the entrance. Amelia, dressed in a tan morning dress rushed in. She crackled with excitement. "Do you know there is a fair in the town today?" she breathed out as she sat down. "Do say we can go, Godmama." Her brown eyes turned to Terrence. "Wouldn't you like to go to the fair, My Lord?"

Terrence swallowed manfully, determined not to lose ground. "I am sure it will be enjoyable."

"I do love the fair," Amelia exclaimed. "I remember once when Papa took me; I was only seven, and I saw a two-headed cow. I couldn't believe it! Only imagine! And there was a man who ate fire. Can you believe it? He actually ate fire."

"Can believe it," Josh muttered. "Did just that a moment ago. What about you, Terrence?"

Terrence nodded. He looked pointedly at Jezebel who re-fused to meet his gaze. "I'd say we've already had all the fire-eaters we need this morning."

"And they had a talking bird," Amelia said, enthused.

"Well, we've got a talking birdwit," Josh whispered. "That should count."

"Young man," the Duchess whispered. "You go beyond the mark."

"And it knew the strangest calls," Amelia continued, never noticing. "It had one that started with a cocka-cocka cooo. It went like this." She lifted her voice and let out a shrill high call.

"Oh, God," Josh clutched his head. Terrence groaned and lowered his into his hands.

Amelia stopped and looked with wide eyes. "Is something the matter?"

"No, dear," the Duchess said. "The men are simply over-come with your fine rendition. They are looking forward to the fair tremendously, I assure you."

Elizabeth wandered amongst the crowd watching the peo-ple, stopping at some of the stalls. She had escaped her group without notice. Indeed, everyone was in such a tense mood, they barely saw her slip away. The only one in a merry mood was Amelia, who had been oohing and ahing over every little thing.

Elizabeth knew she had to find some time alone. The presence of Josh Rakesham had stretched her nerves taut. Every time she had peeked at him, a flush would rise within her. She couldn't help remembering his kiss, and the way she had melted into his arms.

"Excuse me," a male voice said from behind her. Eliza-beth turned to discover a tall, thin youth, standing there. He held her reticule in his hand. "Y-you dropped this."

"Why, so I did," Elizabeth said, surprised. She had been in such a brown study she hadn't even noticed.

He flushed and handed it to her. "H-here!"

"Thank you," she said, taking it. "I would have found myself in a terrible fix without it."

"Yes, ma'am." The youth shifted from right foot to left. "Must b-be careful at a fair. There are pickpockets and thieves. A lady sh-shouldn't be unchaperoned."

"Yes," Elizabeth said, looking down. "I'm afraid I wasn't thinking and wandered away from my party."

The youth cleared his throat. "I'll be glad to escort you back to them." He bowed quickly and offered his arm.

"Here now! Stop that!" another voice said angrily. Elizabeth turned about. Josh now stood behind her, his blue eyes shooting sparks. He glared down at the poor youth. "Be off with you, fellow! How dare you importune a lady!"

The youth's arm fell swiftly to his side. "I-I wasn't importuning her. She—she dropped her p-purse, I was returning it to her."

"A likely story," Josh said, snorting.

"No, I truly did drop it," Elizabeth said. "He was simply kind enough to return it."

"And then offer his arm?" Josh said. "I saw that."

"Yes," Elizabeth replied, indignation rising within her. "He was going to escort me back to my group."

"Well, he don't need to," Josh said. "I'm here to do that."

Elizabeth lifted her chin. "I far prefer this young gentleman's escort, sirrah."

"No you don't," Josh said and stuck out his arm. "He is a total stranger."

"And so are you." Elizabeth ignored his arm. She nodded to the youth whose face had washed out to ashen gray. "Sir, I accept your kind offer."

"No, she don't," Josh said, his brows snapping down. "She don't know you, she knows me."

"Well, ah . . ." The youth stammered, stepping back hastily. "I—in that case, h-he sh-should escort you b-back, madame."

"But I don't wish for him to escort me. . . ." Elizabeth's words petered to a halt. The youth had suddenly disappeared, sprinting through the crowd.

"Young puppy," Josh muttered. "The gall of him."

Elizabeth turned on him. "I cannot believe it, you frightened the poor boy off."

Josh stiffened. "Should be frightened off. No telling what kind of liberties he would have taken with you."

"While I know very well what type you will take," Elizabeth said, shaking with sudden fury. Picking up her skirts, she marched away from him.

"I ain't going to take liberties," Josh shouted. People stopped and looked. Elizabeth lowered her head and picked up her pace, mortified beyond endurance. "Stop, Elizabeth!"

A firm hand gripped her shoulder and dragged her to a halt. She was twirled about and Josh glared down at her. "I ain't going to do anything, but I am going to escort you back and that's that."

"Let me go," Elizabeth said, twisting in his hold.

"Here now," another voice called. Elizabeth and Josh froze as a tiny old man hobbled up, his watery gray eyes snapping, the one white strand of hair left upon his pate standing straight on end in the breeze. "Unhand the lady, I say."

"I beg pardon?" Josh said.

The older man looked to Elizabeth. "Is this young buck importuning you? If so, I'll—I'll cane him for you!" He raised a crooked, wooden cane and rattled it threateningly.

Elizabeth's eyes widened and she looked with bated breath toward Josh. His blue eyes had widened, but he dropped his hands swiftly from her. He bowed with an odd formality to the old man. "Forgive me, sir. I did not mean to importune the lady."

The little man glared up at Josh, appearing a small terrier just waiting to jump a Great Dane. "I'll level you, you young whippersnapper, if you've caused the young lady any harm."

"Er, no," Josh said. His lips twitched suspiciously, but his blue eyes were solemn. "I-I beg you will not. My, er . . . fiancée and I were merely having a small tiff."

"Fiancée? Harrumph," the old gentleman said. "Ain't no way to court a lass, you young cawker. You save the scrapping and brawling fer after the wedding, do you hear?" He cast Elizabeth a fierce look. "And ye best think before getting leg-shackled to this one, he's full of nip and vinegar." The small man jerked a nod and hobbled away.

Josh chuckled. "I'm full of nip and vinegar the man says."

A laugh bubbled from Elizabeth, so pleased was she Josh had displayed such kindness and respect toward the old man. "Let that be a lesson to you, sir. Else you'll be the same way when you grow old."

"Gads, best mend my ways," Josh said. He held out a hand, his blue eyes apologetic. "Let us cry a truce." Elizabeth, surprised, merely looked at it. "After all, I'd best reform upon the instant if I don't want to suffer a drubbing from your hero."

"Very well," Elizabeth said. Feeling suddenly shy, she hesitantly placed her hand in his. His larger one covered hers with a warmth which went straight to her heart.

Josh's eyes darkened and his clasp tightened. "The old chap was right. We should save the scrapping and fighting for after the wedding, don't you think?"

Elizabeth's breath caught. "Indeed. 'Tis no way to court a lady."

"I do apologize," he said. He lowered his golden head and placed a very courtly kiss upon her hand. "Let me make it up to you."

"Very well." Elizabeth was laughing and blushing at the

same time. She cocked her head and said, "You know, for a rake, you have very rough and ready ways."

Josh straightened. He looked rather embarrassed. "Ain't the typical rake, that's why."

"Oh." Elizabeth nodded. "I wouldn't know. I've never been around many men."

"Good!" he said, grinning boyishly. Then he coughed. "Mean, best if you don't know any rakes."

Elizabeth lifted a brow. "Other than you?"

"Other than me," he said, nodding. He seemed so full of male satisfaction Elizabeth hid her smile, amazed she was content to allow this devil his due. He grinned and, crooking his arm, tucked her hand into it. "You know, what I need is a proper lady to keep me in check."

"One with a cane." Elizabeth laughed as they turned, and in one accord, began to stroll along.

"Perhaps I'll be able to reform," Josh said.

"No," Elizabeth said, shaking her head and thinking of his wicked behavior of the night before. "I fear not."

"You'd be surprised," Josh said, an odd look upon his face. "Might be easier for me than you think. Much easier than you think."

"Letty, we really should not leave the group," Jezebel said as she trudged after the older woman. Since she did not wish to talk to Terrence, and Josh and Elizabeth had disappeared, she had chosen to accompany Letty when she had meandered away from the party.

"Oh, yes, you should go back," Letty said. "I am sure Terrence wishes you by his side."

"I doubt it," Jezebel murmured, feeling a twinge of guilt. Terrence was as cold as the North wind toward her presently, and she was forced to own to some of the blame.

"Oh, then this must be your day off." Letty nodded. "Terrence is such a considerate boy."

Jezebel refused to answer. "Letty? Just where are we going?"

"I want to see that cute little bear again," Letty said. "Did you see how the precious little fellow danced for us?"

"Yes, I saw," Jezebel said curtly. What she had seen was a poor creature prodded by its burly owner every time it dared to misstep in the dance.

"Imagine that, for a bear to be so clever," Letty commented as they circled around a makeshift tent. "One of the men said he'd be over here. Oh!" Letty cried, halting suddenly. "Oh, my stars!"

They had indeed found the cute little bear. Its owner was beating it with an iron rod, yelling and cursing for it to enter its cage. The cage was a rusty contraption, much too small for the bear's size and the poor creature balked at it, no matter the strikes he received.

"Oh no, no!" Letty's wail crescendoed with the bear's pained cries. She rushed toward them, waving her hands. "Oh, stop! Stop that you beast!"

"Huh?" The burly man looked up, his face mottled with rage. Within that one moment's pause, the bear gave a bleat like a baby's cry, and loped toward Letty.

"Gracious!" she exclaimed, as it raised on its hind legs and wrapped its paws about her waist, bawling and hugging her close. "Oh, you poor thing." Letty patted the bony head and a fountain of tears instantly streamed down her face.

"Get away from him," the man said, straightening. "He's dangerous, he is!"

"Dangerous?" Jezebel asked, anger propelling her forward. "Seems the only one dangerous here is you, sirrah!"

The man glared at her with beady eyes from his hulking head. "You stay out of this."

"I most certainly shall not," Jezebel said, moving to shield the sobbing Letty and the bleating bear. "You shall not strike that creature again."

The man's face twisted with rage. "I don't need no trollop

telling me what ter do! Now get away." He shoved her roughly from his path and grabbed at the bear. "It's my bloody bear, and I'll do whats I want!"

"No!" Letty cried, slapping wildly at the man's hands.

"Stop it, Gran!" the man bellowed. "Give me my bear!"

Try as he might, he couldn't cleave the bear from Letty's waist.

"Help!" Letty cried. "Help!"

Jezebel, shaking with fury, attacked the man from the rear and pummeled his back with balled fists. The man growled louder than the bear. He turned and broadhanded Jezebel with a beef fist. She flew back, crashing painfully into the iron cage. Wheezing, her legs giving out, she slithered to the ground, the rough iron behind her scraping her back.

"Stop!" a familiar voice shouted. Jezebel looked up through hazy, pained eyes. The world about her reeled and seemed to be cast in excruciatingly bright colors, but out of their patterns she could define Terrence and Dorethea charging toward them. The Duchess's panniers rocked like a boat on high seas. Jezebel giggled. "The Duchess sails. You're in for it now!"

"Duchess?" the burly man exclaimed.

"And the Marquis of Haversham," Jezebel grinned rather stupidly.

"Blind me! Ye can have the bloody bear," the man shouted and lumbered away. Jezebel blinked, as his large form disappeared from her fuzzy sight. He was moving fast for a large man, she mused, in a daze. Very fast.

"Jezebel," Terrence yelled, and then he was kneeling, taking her in his arms. "Are you all right, my dear?"

"Yes," Jezebel sighed and unconsciously cuddled close. "I am now."

"Just what in blazes happened?" Dorethea asked, her hands going to her hips, her eyes green fire. Letty stood sobbing, clutching her blathering bear. "Letty, stop that caterwauling this instant!" Letty hiccupped and halted instantly. "You too,"

Dorethea said to the cub. The bear bleated once more and silenced. "Now what happened? Why were you fighting with that hulking beast?"

"It's all my fault," Letty sniffled. "I-I wanted to see the cute little bear. When we came here . . . that man was . . . was beating the poor dear. I told him to stop and . . . and he attacked me." Her gaze turned toward Jezebel, tearstained but worshipful. "But Jezebel saved me."

"It was nothing," Jezebel said, blushing as the Duchess directed a stunned look at her. "Indeed, nothing at all."

"Nothing?" Terrence said, his voice rough. "I saw the brute hit you." He raised a hand to her face and touched it gently. "I should kill him."

"No," Jezebel said quickly, holding him tightly. "Stay here with me. He's gone after all."

"I'll find him," Terrence said, a cord in his jaw jumping.

"No, please don't," Jezebel said. "Promise me."

"He needs a good horsewhipping."

"Please," Jezebel said, fear invading her. "Please tell me you won't." Terrence's eyes were dark charcoal, his face stern. She lifted a hand to his cheek and smiled. "You already proved yourself by drinking poison for me this morning, I don't wish you to suffer more than that."

" 'Tis different," Terrence said.

"For me, Terry," Jezebel said softly. "Please."

He nodded curtly. "For you, then."

Jezebel smiled. "Thank you."

They suddenly heard a shout. Jezebel looked up to see Theo and Amelia busting toward them. Theo pulled in first, puffing and steaming. "What's going on here? Why is Terry hugging Jezebel in public . . . and why is Letty hugging that bear?"

Jezebel giggled slightly and her eyes caught the Duchess's. Her smile slipped. The Duchess was pale, and her green eyes studied Jezebel closely, a hidden emotion within them. Jezebel flushed deeply, feeling suddenly vulnerable, as if the Duchess had discovered a secret of hers, one she herself didn't even know. Jezebel looked swiftly away, fearing the man's blow had rattled her sanity.

"Terrence," Amelia asked, her brown eyes wide. "Why are you hugging Miss Clinton?"

"Jezebel was in a fight," Dorethea said with brevity.

"Oh, Dorethea, how could you say that?" Letty exclaimed. "It wasn't Jezebel's fault. She saved me!"

"Still don't explain why you're hugging that bear," Theo grunted.

"Jezebel saved him also," Letty said, patting the bear's head. "And I am forever grateful. That nasty man was going to strike me, just like he was hitting this poor creature." Tears swelled in her eyes. "He was trying to force it into that dreadful cage. The little bear didn't want to go, which anyone can understand for it is far too small for the dear . . . and the man was hitting h-him with a rod and yelling at him. I—I c-could not . . . not—"

"Don't start crying again," Dorethea said sternly. "The short of it is, Letty started an altercation with the owner of that bear and he attacked her. Then Jezebel stepped in and took the blows for her, is that not it, Letty?"

"Yes." Letty nodded. "Th-that is exactly it."

"Humph," Theo said. "Letty, you always were a tender-hearted fool. Look what a brouhaha you've created."

"Oh, oh," Letty wailed. The bear immediately set up a howl. "I-I am so s-sorry. I-I am s-sorry, Jezebel."

"Don't be," Jezebel said swiftly. "You did exactly what you ought. I'm proud of you."

Letty's face twisted. "You are?"

"Yes," Jezebel said. "One should always protect the weak."

"Like you did?" Terrence asked softly.

"That's fine and dandy," Theo exclaimed, throwing up her hands. "But what are ye going to do with the bear now?"

"We are not going to do anything," Dorethea said. "We

shall leave it here. I have no doubt the owner shall return shortly."

"Not the way he was running," Terrence said.

"Dorethea," Letty cried, hugging her bear. "We couldn't. We simply couldn't leave the poor baby here in that man's clutches."

"What are you expecting?" Dorethea asked. "That we take the bear home with us?"

"The man did say we could keep the bear," Letty said, her eyes lighting. " 'Twas the last thing he said, wasn't it, Jezebel?"

"Yes," Jezebel said cautiously. "But he said it out of fear, I believe. Once he knew he was dealing with a Duchess and a Marquis he decamped swiftly."

Terrence's brow shot up. "Do you hear, Grandmother, my title is worth something after all."

"As it should be," Dorethea said. "And others should remember." She pinned Jezebel with an accusatory look. Jezebel blinked, confused. The Duchess then turned her gaze to her sister. "But we are not keeping the bear, Letty."

"Gads, no," Theo said. "Don't be a ninny, Letty."

"Please," Letty pleaded. The little bear set up an imitation of mewling sounds.

"No," Dorethea said sharply. "I'll not have the beast added to the menagerie we already house."

"Faith, no," Terrence chuckled. He flicked Jezebel a teasing glance. "Else I'll find a bear in your bed as well as that dog."

"What?" Theo thundered. "So he slept in your bed again!"

"Who?" Amelia asked, her eyes showing confusion. "Who slept in Jezebel's bed?"

"I'm sorry, Theo," Jezebel said, flushing. "I know I should not have permitted him." She cast Terrence a challenging look. "But I found him a great solace to me."

"Solace?" Terrence laughed. "You mean he's a jealous cur."

"Who slept in Jezebel's bed?" Amelia asked again, her gaze skimming everyone's face for a clue.

"Enough!" the Duchess cried. "We shall not discuss who slept in Jezebel's bed."

"Or who did not," Terrence quipped.

"Gads no," Theo said. "Might be a long recounting."

"I said enough!" The Duchess stomped her foot. "Terrence, how dare you air your sleeping arrangements in public."

"But I wasn't," Terrence said reasonably. "I was talking about Jezebel's. And I only did so to put on record that I will take strong offense to Jezebel having the bear in bed with her as well."

" 'Tis reasonable," Letty nodded. "For then there wouldn't be any room for—"

"Letty!" Dorethea cried.

"Oh," Letty breathed out. "I—I am sorry."

"But those are my exact sentiments," Terrence said, chuckling. "Letty understands the difficulties. I'll accept being bitten, but heavens know what treatment I'll receive from a bear."

"Someone bit you?" Amelia gasped, and her eyes swung to Jezebel in shock. "And he was in Jezebel's bed?"

"What ho?" a male voice asked. Everyone started and turned. Josh and Elizabeth had apparently walked up without notice. "We talking about that blasted dog again?"

"Yes," Terrence said. "Amelia wishes to know the name of the dog in Jezebel's bed."

Josh's eyes lit, and he grinned. "Don't worry. Went through that all last night. He truly is a dog."

"Is he?" Amelia said.

"Worse," Terrence said, pointing. "If we don't watch it, the bear will be sleeping in Jezebel's bed as well."

Josh studied the bear still clutching Letty and shook his head. "Sorry, old chap. Looks like you're beside the bridge on that one." He winked at Jezebel. "It appears the bear ain't attracted to you, Jez. Has a tender for someone else. Looks like he'll be sleeping in her bed."

"He shall not sleep in Letty's bed!" Dorethea exclaimed.

"For shame, Grandmother," Terrence said. "Airing sleeping arrangements in public."

"That bear is not coming home with us," Dorethea said angrily.

"Oh, please." Letty hugged the bear more tightly. "Please let him come."

"You might as well let him, Grandmother." Terrence chuckled.

"Yes," Josh nodded. "Looks like they're attached at the hip. You don't want to leave your sister here as well do you?"

"Oh, very well," Dorethea cried, throwing up her hands. "He may come. But he'll stay in the barn and will not be permitted into the house."

"Wonder if the groom will let the poor cub sleep with him." Josh laughed.

"Enough!" Dorethea cracked. "Let us return home."

"Oh, thank you, thank you," Letty cried. "Do you hear that, little cub, you are coming home with us."

"Yes, do you hear that, sweetings?" Terrence said, hugging Jezebel close and imitating Letty's tones. "You are coming home with us. And you don't even have to sleep in the barn." Jezebel chuckled and then grimaced as Terrence shifted away from her. "You are hurt!"

"No," Jezebel said quickly. "Only bruised."

"Permit me," Terrence said. He quickly bent and lifted her into his arms with stunning alacrity.

Jezebel flushed deeply, though she was glad for his supporting arms. "I can walk."

"And I can carry you," Terrence retorted. He smiled pleasantly at the gaping group. "Well, are we ready?"

"Oh, let us go," the Duchess said, looking away. "Before we make even more of a spectacle of ourselves."

The Duchess's hopes were quite blasted. The fair attendees all stopped and stared at the sight. The Duchess, her head held high, stalked before the group, while her grandson, the Marquis, whistled and merrily carried his lightskirt in his arms, a very tousled and rumpled one at that. Next in the procession was the Duchess's one sister, a bear cub bleating and stumbling close by her skirts. The other sister trod heavily behind, clearly herding the two. The Duchess's companion strolled arm in arm with a tall, angelic-looking man, whose name everyone had already discovered was Mr. Rakesham. And last, trailing behind with a bewildered expression upon her face was the Lady Amelia, asking repeatedly and loudly just who had slept in Jezebel's bed last night?

A little boy was heard to cry to his mother that it was a better sight than even the two-headed cow he'd seen years ago.

Nine

Just how many birds did the girl know about? Terrence wondered as he allowed his horse to meander in the field. Amelia, astride a gentle mare beside him, meandered equally in her conversation.

"Then there is the owl," Amelia said. "The common man does not comprehend how many variations of the owl there are, or what a grand bird it is."

"Indeed?" Terrence murmured. He glanced to Josh and Elizabeth who rode ahead. They were laughing, and he felt a twinge of envy. It was impossible to laugh over the variations of the owl or the mating ritual of the raven. He heartily wished Jezebel were beside him instead, but he had given orders for no one to disturb her this morning, and he couldn't very well break his own command. He never doubted she'd need her rest after the fight yesterday.

"Wouldn't you agree?" Amelia said.

"Hmmm?" Terrence asked, turning his gaze back. A delicate flush painted the girl's cheeks, and she peered at him with shy brown eyes. He blinked, trying to decide what she was talking about. Most likely the call of the doodle bird.

"I said"—Amelia lowered her gaze—"That this is the first time we have truly been able to talk at length alone. It is nice, is it not?"

Terrence frowned, but said, "Yes, of course."

"We always have people about," Amelia said. "Like the Duchess or . . . or Jezebel."

"Yes, Jezebel." Terrence drew in a breath. Perhaps it would be the best time to take the gloves off and present the issue as scandalously as he could. If he could disgust Amelia here and now, things would be settled. "Let us talk about Jezebel."

"I wasn't taking you to task about her," Amelia said quickly. "I assure you."

"You weren't?" Terrence asked, nonplused.

"Oh, no," Amelia said. "I fully understand she requires much of your time. Godmama already told me actresses are notorious for their tempers and are quite demanding, and since you are Jezebel's patron, you must curry favor with her."

"I am more than Jezebel's patron," Terrence said, halting his horse. "I am—"

"Oh, look!" Amelia gasped, pointing. Irritated at the interruption, Terrence glanced in the ordered direction. A large bird was winging erratically toward them.

"What is it?" Terrence asked.

" 'Tis an owl," Amelia whispered.

The night bird, clearly very blind in the day, kept coming. Terrence, cursing, ducked as it skimmed his head. "Blast!" He stared after it as it continued its wayward progress. "I wonder what caused that poor bird to be flushed out in the day?"

" 'Tis fate," Amelia said, her voice breathless.

"What?" Terrence glanced at her. Her brown eyes gazed at him as if he were a god. A chill ran down his spine. "What do you mean?"

"It was a sign, don't you see?" Amelia said eagerly. "We are meant to be together."

"No, we are not," Terrence protested quickly.

"You were brushed by an owl," Amelia said. "Just after we were talking about it. And in daylight. You are a very special man."

"I am not," Terrence stated firmly. "I assure you, I am not."

"Our marriage will be blessed," Amelia said, her eyes shining.

"Our marriage?" Terrence swallowed.

"Oh, dear." Amelia flushed. "I know I've spoken out of turn. You—you have not discussed it yet with my father. Only the owl . . . it made me forget propriety."

"Let us talk about propriety," Terrence said. "Amelia, I must tell you, I am not only Jezebel's patron in the arts, I am also her protector."

"Yes." Amelia nodded and smiled sweetly.

"She is my mistress," Terrence said.

"Yes," Amelia responded, still with the Madonna smile. "I know."

"You know?" Terrence asked, stunned.

"Of course," Amelia said. Then she looked down and whispered, "But I am sure we shouldn't be having this discussion. It is not proper. I am to act as if you do not have a mistress. Only yesterday when everyone talked about Jezebel's sleeping arrangements, I knew for certain. I had a notion before, but I most certainly would not have said anything to anyone. Godmama is such a high-stickler and has been working very hard to maintain decorum."

"You know Jezebel is my mistress," Terrence asked, staring at her. "And you do not mind?"

"No, of course not. Why should I?" Amelia seemed sincerely concerned. "You need not fear I have not been raised properly. Mama explained it all to me, before she died, that is." She cast an adoring look at Terrence, one which sent another shiver down his spine. "You are so much like my papa. He always had actresses too, and Mama explained how we should behave in such instances."

"Good God," Terrence muttered, thunderstruck. "It does not matter my affections are engaged otherwise?"

"Affections?" Amelia frowned. She shook her head. "No,

they cannot be engaged otherwise. Jezebel is a woman of the lower order. Men do not fall in love with women like that. They are mistresses, while we ladies of the upper class are . . . well, ladies and wives."

A sudden, deep anger filled Terrence. He had indeed explained to Jezebel how marriages worked in the upper classes. He remembered her shock that a wife was to ignore a husband's inamoratas and behave as if they didn't exist. He had even laughed at her, chiding her for her bourgeois notions. He wasn't laughing now.

He looked at Amelia with mounting disgust. "You believe I cannot love Jezebel, merely because she is not of our class?"

"Of course you cannot," Amelia said calmly.

"Then why do you think I have brought her here?"

"Well," Amelia said, smiling a coy smile. "You know you shouldn't have done that. It wasn't discreet. But you are still single, and sowing your wild oats. Once we are married I am sure you will settle down."

"Just like your father?" Terrence asked.

"Yes," Amelia said. Once again she looked adoringly at him. "You are so very much like him. And now I know for certain since seeing the owl that our union is destined and will be blessed."

"With what?" Terrence asked. "Little owls?"

"No." Amelia giggled. "With children, of course."

"You can't be serious," Terrence protested. "Merely because a poor owl was spooked from his nest and winged past us, you will marry me?"

"You do not understand," Amelia said. "It is not common, not common at all."

"Good God." Terrence clenched his jaw. He jerked his horse's reins and turned his mount around.

"Where are you going?" Amelia cried.

"Home," Terrence called out.

He had to escape Amelia's insanity. He had to find Jezebel. He'd wake her up if necessary or shove Mordrid aside and crawl into bed beside them. Jezebel was the reality he wanted, and needed.

"Good morning, Stilton," Jezebel said weakly as she took up a lone place at the breakfast table. She winced, feeling the side effects of her tousle with the fair man. "Where is everyone?"

"Out, madame," Stilton said in calm tones as he walked over and poured her tea. Jezebel found Stilton's stately demeanor daunting. She kept reminding herself his behavior was proper for a fine butler, yet she could not help feeling he disapproved of her. She grimaced. It shouldn't be surprising, all things considered, but she still felt discomfited.

She reached for her cup. "Indeed?"

"Yes, Miss Clinton," Stilton said. "Master Terrence, Miss Amelia, Mr. Rakesham, and Miss Elizabeth are out riding. Master Terrence said he thought you should rest."

"Did he?" Jezebel murmured and quickly sipped from the tea.

"Yes," Stilton said. "Lady Dorethea is out visiting the curate, Miss Theo is taking her constitutional, and Miss Letty is still asleep, if I am not mistaken. She did not retire until very late, I fear."

"Really?" Jezebel asked. She herself had been grateful to find her bed very early last night.

"No, Miss Clinton," Stilton said. "Miss Letty appeared to have grave fears for the er . . . bear's comfort."

"Oh, dear." Jezebel bit back a smile. "Did she ever settle on a name for the cub?"

"Yes." Stilton nodded. "She has named him . . . Sir Drake."

"Sir Drake?" Jezebel laughed. "Oh, dear, how did she ever hit upon that name?"

"Miss Letty needs no logic, Miss Clinton," Stilton said.

He frowned. "She remained in the stables with Sir Drake until the late hours."

Jezebel stifled a giggle. "How roguish of her."

"Lady Dorethea was not pleased," Stilton said.

Jezebel quickly sobered. "No, I can understand."

"Will that be all, Miss Clinton?"

"Yes," Jezebel said, quickly looking down at her tea. Stilton bowed, and with that ever stately walk, took himself off. Jezebel sipped her tea, enjoying the solitude. In her present condition, it was the best medicine possible. That and the full supply of ointments she already possessed of course.

Jezebel had just finished her cup of tea and was finally eyeing the sideboard with some interest when she heard her name called, and called loudly. She tore her gaze from the pastry she had decided upon and looked toward the door. Her eyes widened in shock. Stilton stood within it. He appeared a completely different man. His fine apparel hung awry, and his dignified face worked with clear, mobile emotions.

"Miss Clinton!" he cried, sprinting into a room with an agility she'd never guess such a stately personage could possess. "Miss Clinton. Help!"

"What is it?" Instinctively Jezebel rose.

"Pierre the cook—I mean chef," wheezed Stilton, "he . . . he is going to kill Mordrid."

"What?" Jezebel gasped. "Has he gone mad?"

"Mordrid ate all the beefsteaks," Stilton said. "The kitchen staff has already fled."

"Good Lord!" Jezebel picked up her skirts and ran. Only at the door did she halt. "Stilton, where are the kitchens?"

"I will show you." Stilton buffeted her aside and took the lead. Jezebel made no objection, but chased after the butler. Both slowed upon approaching the kitchen entrance. Fierce, guttural Gallic curses rent the air amidst crashes and clatter. Over it all, the frightful howls of Mordrid rose, high and keening.

"Pierre has done him in," Stilton panted.

"He better have not," Jezebel said. Rage dispelled the chills coursing up her spine. She dropped her skirts and marched into the kitchen, fully prepared to do battle.

She did not have to look far. The kitchen was a war zone of overturned stools and benches. Pots and pans cluttered the floor. Flour and batter dripped from the walls and table.

Pierre, with a war cry like that of a red savage, swung a butcher's cleaver at a howling Mordrid. He barely missed Mordrid's tail. "I will kill you, you cur! Never, never, shall you touch my meat again!"

"Stop it!" Jezebel cried, aghast.

Pierre, never looking her way, swung the hatchet. Mordrid, yapped, vaulted over a stool more like a thoroughbred stallion than a canine, and charged toward Jezebel, his eyes dilated and desperate. Jezebel bent down, arms wide.

"I will kill you!" Pierre shouted. The deadly cleaver flashed.

Mordrid yelped and veered swiftly, ramming into Jezebel. She toppled back. A furry body cleared her as she blinked. Then, shockingly, the little French man also jumped over her, shouting invectives gratefully undecipherable.

"Beast!" Jezebel cried, and sat up, dusting off her hands the flour in which she had landed. She sprang up. Mordrid dove under the large, four-legged table. Pierre swung his cleaver. It thunked with force into the table's leg. He jerked at it, but the cleaver was well embedded. Mordrid, with a pitiful whine, crawled farther beneath the table.

"Enough," Jezebel cried, looking angrily about. A lone kitchen maid stood, clutching a broom and trembling, in the corner. Jezebel stalked over to her and grabbed the broom. "Give that to me!" The girl stared at her, in a daze, her grasp upon the broom frozen by fear. Jezebel tore the broom from her fingers, adding a few English curses to the din. Gripping the broom, she then spun about, eyes narrowed and furious.

Pierre at that moment successfully jerked the cleaver from the wood. He knelt and swiped again at Mordrid. Mordrid jumped back, and the table rumbled as his broad head cracked its top.

Jezebel charged. The bristles of the broom spanked Pierre smartly on his posterior.

"Owwee!" Pierre cried, scrabbling up. He turned, cleaver in hand.

"You deserve more than that," Jezebel panted as she gazed into angry, almost insane dark eyes. She poked the broom at him threateningly. "Now leave the dog alone."

"Putain!" Pierre cried and swung his cleaver. He lopped off the top bristles of the broom. "I'll not listen to the likes of you!"

Jezebel's eyes widened, but she bravely shoved the freshly shorn broom into the little man's chest. "Yes, you will!"

"Never!" Pierre cried. His cleaver thudded on the broom's stick, and Jezebel felt the weight she held lighten markedly as the broom's head toppled to the floor. She was left holding a pole.

"No English *putain* will stop me," Pierre said, his gaze fanatical. "That dog—he destroy my beefsteaks. Ha! I had them for two days in a marinade which was to be Pierre's best!" He swung again. Jezebel's grip rattled as she felt the reverberation of metal against wood. Another span of the broom handle clunked to the floor. "The sauce from it . . . ah, the sauce would have been so delicate, so superb, and now, now it lies in that dog's belly. He shall die, and no slut stops me!" His cleaver darted out and severed another length.

"No!" Jezebel stepped back, swinging up the short length of her pole. Pierre raised his cleaver.

"Move aside, Miss Clinton," Stilton suddenly roared from behind. Jezebel instinctively obeyed, not only at the force of the command, but because she was holding up what amounted to a baton against a mad chef with a cleaver.

She gasped as she heard a weird whizzing sound. A small cast-iron skillet magically flew past her, spinning and flipping. Cast iron clashed into steel blade. The cleaver flew as Pierre let out a howl of pain.

"My wrist!" Pierre cried, immediately clutching his hand to his chest. "My wrist, it is broken!"

"There's more where that came from," Stilton said, and stepped up to stand beside Jezebel, another pan in hand.

"Yes!" Jezebel said, shaking her baton.

A low rumble came from beneath the table, feral and dark.

The madness in Pierre's eyes disappeared, replaced with pain and fear. "I quit!" He darted toward the door, but turned to shout, "You, you will be sorry! Never, never shall you taste a fine morsel of Pierre's again!" Whirling, he sprinted out the door. The little kitchen maid, gurgling, scurried past them and followed.

"Why is she leaving?" Jezebel asked, dazed.

"She is Pierre's relation," Stilton said. "As is the rest of the kitchen staff who have fled."

"Oh." Jezebel turned to him and smiled with pleasure. "That was an excellent throw."

Stilton bowed. "Thank you, Miss Jezebel." A warm flush went through her. She was no longer Miss Clinton. "Pierre is not the only one that knows what to do with a skillet."

Jezebel's chuckle was cut short as a loud voice barked out, "What in blazes is going on!" She looked quickly to the open kitchen door. Theo stood within the frame, her face dark and belligerent. "I saw Pierre running across the yard. He was shouting those Frenchie words and that twit cousin of his was following."

"I fear," Stilton said, "that Pierre has quit our employ, Miss Theo."

"High time," Theo grunted. "Never did like that dandified, temperamental foreigner. He—" Her words were drowned out as a howl arose. Mordrid scurried out from under the table and crawled over to Theo. "Mordrid!" she exclaimed and knelt swiftly to hug the cringing and shivering dog. Her eyes blazed as she looked at Jezebel. "What did you do to him?"

"Miss Jezebel did not do anything," Stilton answered before Jezebel could speak. "Mordrid consumed Pierre's prized beefsteaks. Pierre then chased him with a meat cleaver, swearing to kill him. Miss Jezebel held him off with a broom, and Pierre turned his cleaver upon her." Stilton turned and bowed to Jezebel. "I apologize for Pierre's rude comments. I do not consider you a *putain,* madame." A jangling of a bell disturbed them. Stilton waited a moment and then nodded. "That will be Miss Letty. I fear she wishes her tea and breakfast in bed.". He looked about the room. "It will be difficult."

"Tell her to come down and get it herself," Theo said briskly as Mordrid whined and she hugged him close.

"Yes, madame," Stilton said, nodding. Jezebel thought she heard him sigh in relief as he left them.

"Are you all right, my darling," Theo said. Her voice was soft and gentle compared to her normal tones. Jezebel turned, slightly surprised, to look at woman and dog. Theo hugged the large dog, who rested his large jaw and head on her shoulder and stood quietly trembling.

"I am so sorry it happened," Jezebel said softly.

Theo looked up. Her eyes were slightly wet. "Is it true? You protected Mordrid?"

"I didn't do that much," Jezebel said, flushing. "Stilton had to save me in the end. I had taken a broom to Pierre, which was not wise. He made rather short shrift of it. Without Stilton's intervention with a frying pan I fear both Mordrid and I would have been luncheon."

"Thank you," Theo said, her voice low and gruff. "If anything had happened to Mordrid . . ."

"I know," Jezebel said quickly, feeling pain for Theo. "But it didn't."

Both women then looked at each other a moment. Theo

was the first to lower her eyes. With a sniff, she petted Mordrid's wiry fur. "Poor boy."

Jezebel quickly turned her gaze from them and forced a light voice as she looked about the kitchen and said, "My, what a mess."

Suddenly a screech rent the air, causing Jezebel to start. She spun around. Now Letty stood in the other door to the kitchen, hands to her mouth, blue eyes wide and already tearing. "Oh, my! Stilton told me what happened. This is terrible, terrible." She entered and tripped over a pot. "Oh, dear!" she exclaimed. "What are we to do? Oh, what are we to do?"

"What do you mean, what are we to do?" Theo asked angrily. "There is nothing to be done. Jezebel saved Mordrid and that's the end of it. Now don't start crying, for goodness' sake. Jezebel was attacked and you don't see her crying, so why are you crying?"

"I don't know," Letty said, tears running down her cheeks. " 'Tis my nerves I fear. Only think of it. First it was Sir Drake, and now it is Mordrid. Poor Jezebel."

Jezebel blinked and suddenly laughed. "I do believe I'd best stay away from animals from now on."

Theo cracked a wry grin. "Seems that's all you been doing since you came here, is saving our pets." A shrewd light entered Theo's brown eyes, and she said, "You intending to save any other pet of ours, a human one perhaps?"

Jezebel flushed. "I-I don't know what you mean."

"You got a tender heart, gel," Theo said, hugging Mordrid close. "And I'm telling you now, Letty and I withdraw our offer."

"We do?" Letty asked, her look as bewildered as Jezebel felt. "What offer is that?"

"We ain't going to pay her five thousand to leave Terrence," Theo said. "We ain't even going to pay a shilling."

Jezebel blushed, but said, "Drat. And here I was thinking

about taking you up on it, if I wasn't chopped up before that."

"Oh, no," Letty cried. "You cannot believe we meant to kill you. Are you going to leave us?" Tears welled in her eyes. "We'll strive to keep our pets away from you."

"All but one," Theo said.

"But . . . but . . ." Letty halted. "Oh, dear, what will Terrence say if he finds we've frightened you off."

"You haven't," soothed Jezebel quickly. Desperate to turn the subject, she looked about the kitchen and then laughed. "But we may all want to turn tail once the Duchess sees this."

"Oh," Letty gasped. "Dorethea. She will be in such a rage when she comes home to discover Pierre is g-gone and—and there is n-no luncheon."

"The devil," Theo cursed. "I never thought about that. I know she'll blame Mordrid."

"Or me," Jezebel said dryly.

Letty chewed her lip. "Dorethea's temper is always worse on an empty stomach. Whatever shall we do?"

Jezebel said hesitantly, "I do know how to cook."

Letty's eyes widened. "Do you?"

Jezebel laughed. "Of course. I shall get a meal prepared for luncheon. We shall feed Lady Dorethea before we tell her Pierre has taken French leave." She grimaced. "Sorry."

"I know how to make scones," Letty said, brightening. "I could do that!"

"I don't know how to cook," Theo said, "but I can clean this place up."

The three women stared at each other and suddenly bolted into action. Jezebel bent to pick up a pot, Letty turned a stool upright, and Theo rose and picked up a kettle.

"Jezebel," a voice cried from the door.

She looked up. Terrence stood in the opening, as did Amelia, Josh, and Elizabeth. He studied her, his face pale, his eyes darkened with concern. "Stilton told me what happened."

Wishing to erase his look of concern, Jezebel winked at him and said, "Hello, ducky. You missed it. I had another man chasing me this morning."

Terrence's expression lightened and he strolled over to her. "Tsk, tsk, first the man at the fair and now the chef." He took her hand and held it tightly. "Really, love, I'm not sure I can handle the competition."

"Oh, Terry," Letty cried, "surely you cannot believe Jezebel would have a tendre for either of them. They were dreadful and had the meanest of intentions toward her. I am quite glad you have taken Jezebel under your protection."

"Letty!" Theo barked.

"Er . . ." Letty froze and her eyes flew quickly to Amelia. "Er . . . wing. That is what I meant. Yes, I meant wing." Behind Terrence, Josh sniggered, making Letty flush. "Oh, no. I didn't mean that word either. I meant—"

"I know," Terrence said. "But 'protection' is the word. Though how I'm to do it is beyond me, since Jezebel is so busy protecting everyone else."

Jezebel narrowed her eyes and withdrew her hand. She bent down and picked up a skillet, raised it high. "Terry, dearest."

His eyes sparkled. "Yes, my chick?"

"Get an apron on," she cooed. "We need to cook."

"Cook?" Amelia gasped. "But—but we can't cook!"

"I can." Jezebel grinned. "Ruth saw to that."

"Who's Ruth?" Letty asked.

"She is"—Jezebel stopped momentarily—"Someone from my past life . . . before I fell upon hard times."

Josh hooted. Letty turned a darkling gaze upon him. "You, sir, are rude. You should not laugh at poor Jezebel's misfortune." She turned sympathetic eyes to Jezebel. "Go on, dearest, what was your prior life like, before you . . . before you . . ."

"Before she met me?" Terrence asked, his lips twitching.

"I . . . I . . ." Jezebel hesitated, then said with a sigh, "I wouldn't want to shock you. And we have cooking to do. Let us get started."

Lady Dorethea entered the foyer and halted. Stilton was not there to meet her. "Stilton?" She received no answer. She called for him and again received no answer. She then began to take off her wrap, looking about. "Stilton?"

She walked across the foyer. She thought she saw a footman approaching, but for some odd reason, when he saw her, he skidded to a halt and ducked through a door. She walked through the strangely quiet house, but finally, hearing voices in the breakfast room, she stepped into it.

Betty, the maid, was holding a dish, while Thomas, the footman, wrapped his arms around her from behind.

"Stop that," Betty giggled. "I have things to do."

"Betty," Lady Dorethea said sternly, "what are you two doing in here?" Betty screeched and dropped her dish. Thomas quickly unwound himself from the buxom maid and stood at attention.

"Sorry, Your Grace," Betty stammered. "I-I was cleaning up in here."

Dorethea frowned. "You are an upstairs maid, what are you doing clearing dishes?"

"Um, er . . ." Betty blushed. "We are short of help this morning."

"Indeed?" Lady Dorethea lifted a brow. "Is that why Thomas, who is a footman, is helping you?"

"I . . . I . . ." Thomas came to a halt.

"You need not explain," Dorethea said. "I know exactly what kind of service you were offering Betty. Now where is Stilton?"

"St-Stilton?" Betty squeaked.

"Yes," Lady Dorethea said in a low, dulcet tone. "You know, our butler?"

"I-I know," Betty replied. "Ah . . . Thomas, where is Stilton?"

"He's . . . he's . . . he's gone out!" Thomas rose to a falsetto.

"Yes." Betty nodded. "That's what he's done."

Dorethea pinned Betty with a sharp eye. "Betty, where is Stilton?"

Betty flushed. "He's in the kitchen, Your Grace. But please . . . please don't say I told you."

"The kitchen?" Dorethea frowned. "You totty-headed girl, there is nothing wrong with Stilton being in the kitchen."

Betty's eyes widened and then she laughed nervously. "That's right. There ain't . . . er, isn't anything wrong with that. Is there, Thomas?"

"No." Thomas shook his head. "Nothing wrong with that at all."

Dorethea rolled her eyes to heaven. "Return to your normal posts. Especially you, Thomas." She turned and walked out of the room. "Faith, I have imbeciles for servants. There is nothing wrong with Stilton being in the kitchen." She halted abruptly, her eyes narrowing. "Or is there?"

Lady Dorethea's pace picked up mightily as she marched through the halls and to the kitchen. Once again she heard laughter coming from it. Everyone in the house seemed merry today. She pushed open the door and came to a standstill.

Indeed, Stilton was there, but a cook's apron enveloped him, greatly deflating his dignity, and he stood at the fire, diligently stirring something in a large pot. As for the other inhabitants of the kitchen, they were clearly not who they should be. Rather than the kitchen maids, Elizabeth and Josh sat on stools, paring potatoes. Amelia sat beside them on the scullery maid's bench, her fists to her mouth, watching them with wide eyes. At the table where the two chefs apprentices should be stood Theo and Letty. Theo held a dripping, cracked egg in her hand, while Letty held a glass in one hand and with the other poked at a large, frightening lump of what could be dough, though the popping craters and bubbles made it look more like a living mass. At the chef's table stood Jezebel, powdered with flour and stirring a batter. Terrence stood close behind her. He reached around and swiped a finger through the batter.

"Stay out," Jezebel laughed and slapped his hand away.

"Just being the royal taste tester," Terrence said.

Dorethea drew in a breath. Their closeness looked too natural, even in a kitchen. "What in blazes is going on in here?"

Everyone looked up from his or her task.

"Hello, Grandmother," Terry said, a clearly devilish look in his eyes. "We are cooking, cannot you see? But we hoped to surprise you."

"Surprise me?" Dorethea put her hands to her hips. "Have you gone mad?"

"No." Terrence grinned. "But Pierre did."

"Yesh, Dorethea," Letty said and hiccuped. "Oops. He almost killed Mordrid and Jez-zebel. T-took a meat cleaver t-to them." She plowed one fist into the dough before her. "Fiend! But Jezebel f-foiled him."

"And Stilton," Jezebel said. "Don't forget Stilton."

"Stilton?" Dorethea asked.

Stilton, ladle in hand over his steaming brew, bowed. "It was nothing, Your Grace."

"Nothing?" Jezebel exclaimed. "If you hadn't used that skillet so readily, I would have been carved meat."

"Rather than the beefsteaks," Terrence murmured, putting his arms around her.

"But then he ran-n-n off," Letty cried enthusiastically. "Took French leave." She began to giggle, and giggle. "Oh, my, oh, dear!" She slapped at the dough with the one hand, while she took a sip from the glass she held with the other.

"Letty? What is the matter with you?" Dorethea asked, frowning.

"You must excuse her," Josh said, tossing a cleaned potato into a bowl. "She didn't believe it was cooking sherry."

"We did tell her, Your Grace," Elizabeth said. "But she would not listen."

" 'Tis too fine to be jush cooking sherry," Letty said, shaking her head to and fro. Then she unaccountably dipped under the table. Dorethea heard her muffled voice. "Here, Mordrid. Have some. It will make you feel better." A low grumble sounded, and then a pitiful whine. Letty popped up. "He d-doesn't want any, poor doggy."

" 'Course he don't want any," Theo said. "He almost got killed today. Let him stay there. He'll come out when he wants to." She dropped the egg into a bowl. "Just can't get the hang of this."

"Try another one," Jezebel told her. "We cannot use it with shells in it."

"Can't we pick them out?" Theo asked, peering into the bowl and stabbing her fingers into it, coming up with a large white, dripping shell.

"No," Jezebel said. "I assure you. I've tried. One always slips by. Just treat it lightly the next time."

"Not my fashion," Theo muttered, picking up another egg. She turned and held it out. "Amelia, you try it. You're good with birds . . . should be good with eggs too."

Amelia stiffened on her stool. "I do not cook. A lady—"

"I know," Theo grunted. "Never cooks. You've told us."

"Yes," Josh said and grinned at Dorethea. "We told her to go kill a chicken for us, but she wouldn't. And then she squawked all over when I said I'd do it. So you'll have no chicken today. Pity." He shook his head. "Jezebel is famous with chicken."

"Jezebel is . . . ?" Dorethea began, and then bit her lip. Her eyes narrowed. "I do not care what Jezebel is, I want to know what is going on here?"

"I told you," Letty said, pulling a long face and twirling her glass. "D-do try and l-listen. Jezebel saved Mordrid from Pierre."

"Might as well confess the whole, Letty," Theo said. She looked defiantly at Dorethea. "Mordrid ate Pierre's beef-steaks."

"Beefsteaks he had marinated for two days in his own special sauce," Jezebel nodded.

"Pierre lost his temper, Your Grace," Stilton said. "He was in a rage like I've never seen, and I am glad to say shall never see again. He started chasing after Mordrid. That was when the kitchen staff departed."

"They did?" Dorethea asked, anger rising within her.

"Yes, Your Grace," Stilton said. "I could not stop them. Just as I could not stop Pierre, not single-handedly. You were not here, Your Grace, and everyone else was unavailable. 'Twas fortunate Miss Jezebel was here."

"Was it?" Dorethea said, eyes narrowing.

"Oh, yes." Letty nodded. "She saved Mordrid, just like she did my d-darling Sir Drake."

"Did she?" Dorethea said frigidly.

"Am mighty grateful." Theo coughed. "Wouldn't have known what to do if that Frenchie had killed my Mordrid."

"Grateful!" It fueled Dorethea's rage.

"Glad you brought her here, Terry," Theo said, looking to Terrence.

"It was my pleasure." Terrence's eyes glinted. "All my pleasure I assure you."

"Ridiculous!" Dorethea cried. "Theo, how could you say that! You are glad that Terrence brought his . . . his . . ."

"Inamorata," Terrence filled in. "Ladybird? Mistress?"
Dorethea gasped.

"Oh, don't worry, Amelia understands," Terrence finished.

"I do," Amelia said, frowning severely. "But we should

not speak of it. One does not mention such things. We are ladies and must overlook that Miss Clinton is . . . is not."

"Well, we may be ladies," Theo snorted, "but we'd be in the devil's own scrape without Jezebel. Mordrid would be dead, and we wouldn't have anything to eat to boot."

"Huzzah!" Terrence said.

"And Sir Drake would still be with that nasty man," Letty put in as her tears began to flow. "So what if Jezebel has fallen on hard times, and has a past life she cannot talk about, what does it matter?"

"What does it matter?" Lady Dorethea cried.

"What does it matter?" Theo snapped, looking pugnaciously at Dorethea. "Don't be so top-lofty, Dorethea."

"She's been everything that has been kind." Letty openly wept now.

"Kind! Bah!" Dorethea threw up her hands and spun out of the kitchen. No one followed, which only fueled her rage. She'd had enough of Jezebel. The strumpet had turned her house into bedlam. There was a damn bear in the stables, and her sisters were in the kitchen, cooking as if they were common wenches. Terrence openly admitted Jezebel was his mistress, and in front of the very lady who should be his wife. The jade had won everyone over, but not her.

Dorethea charged through the house, took the stairs, and slammed into her room. She crossed to her escritoire and sat down. Unlocking a drawer, she pulled out a document. She hastily scratched out a sum, then increased it twofold. At last slowly, adroitly, she placed Terrence's signature to the marriage contract between him and Miss Amelia Arrowroot.

Ten

"He likes them," Jezebel laughed as she held out a flat, misshapen scone to Sir Drake. The bear wrapped his paw around it and immediately lifted it to his snout.

" 'Tis fortunate someone does," Terrence said, sitting upon the old stool in the stables, watching woman and bear. He enjoyed the way Jezebel's hair escaped its pins in silken strands, how her blue eyes glinted as she fed the bear cub. Sir Drake, after snuffling and devouring the lumpy wad, bleated and held out a paw.

"Oh, you greedy bear," Jezebel chuckled. She held the last one high as Sir Drake began an odd, shuffling dance. "I'm not sure you should have it, else you'll need a posset or powder this evening."

"I'm not sure we all won't," Terrence murmured.

"Come," Jezebel said, casting him a teasing glance. "It was a grand meal."

"Your courses and Stilton's stew were excellent," Terrence admitted. "But Letty's scones left something to be desired."

At that moment Sir Drake bleated and clapped his paws together, his brown eyes trained upon the scone Jezebel held high.

"Sir Drake appreciates it," Jezebel said. "He thinks it a rare treat. 'Tis too bad the Duchess did not choose to come to our feast."

Sir Drake, apparently noting the lack of attention, suddenly let out a bearish howl. Standing on two legs he walked toward her, paws and arms out. He embraced Jezebel around the waist and cried out.

"Oh, my goodness!" she exclaimed.

"Here now," Terrence said, standing. "Keep your paws off my woman." Sir Drake leaned his snout against Jezebel's bodice and drooled.

"Toad eater," Jezebel laughed. "Do let go."

Terrence chuckling, walked over and lightly thunked Sir Drake on the head. "Unhand her, sir. She is mine, I said." Sir Drake bleated and slobbered all the more.

"He appears to contend your claims," Jezebel said, giggling.

"That I'll not have," Terrence said. He snatched the doughy scone from Jezebel's clasp and almost shoved it into the jaw of the howling cub. Sir Drake immediately stopped his complaint, left off his bear hug of Jezebel and prodded the scone more securely into his mouth.

"You fickle love," Jezebel cried in mock consternation.

"Do not be disconsolate," Terrence said, and quickly put his arms about her. It seemed as if it had been too long since he'd touched her. He'd not thought of it, yet holding her now, made him aware of that.

"Terry?" Jezebel looked at him with wide eyes. She made the slightest movement of pulling back.

Terrence held her, and forced a grin. "Never say you care for that cub's embrace more than mine. I will be cut to the quick. Soon Sir Drake will be moving from the stables and will supplant poor Mordrid in your bed."

A deep flush rose to her cheeks. Terrence knew he was unconscionable to tease her, but could not help himself.

Jezebel looked down. "I wish you would stop t-talking about my bed or who . . . I mean what sleeps in it."

"I cannot help it," Terrence said, his eyes fixed on her lips and the way she licked them in nervousness. They needed kissing, his kissing. "You are my mistress after all."

Jezebel shook her head. "I am not your mistress. I am no one's mistress!"

"No one's mistress," Terrence said softly. The warmth of her body drew him, yet her words caused an anger to seep through him. He tensed and asked softly, "And will you ever be?"

"What?" Jezebel's violet eyes flew to his, wide and almost frightened. "What do you mean?"

He gazed at her, wishing suddenly he was able to see to her very soul. "When will you share your bed with a man?"

Jezebel drew back, her eyes shuttering. " 'Tis none of your business."

"And it is no one else's, of course," Terrence suddenly snapped. Her innocence drove his anger, he knew, but it did not matter. "Good Lord, you have so much love to give, Jezebel. Faith, you take a hammering from a Gypsy to save Letty and that bear, you stand off a mad Frenchman for a mere dog. You wouldn't even be here if you hadn't been out rescuing Josh from the clutches of his strumpet. But when," he asked, shaking her slightly, "when will you allow that love to be a woman's love for a man? When will it be a love with something for yourself in it?"

Jezebel's eyes became dark, almost lost. She shoved at his chest. "Why are you asking me this? Must I become your mistress in actuality as well as pretend?"

Terrence stiffened as if she'd slapped him. He dropped his hands from her shoulders and stepped back. "Must you? Be my mistress? No, that's not what I want! That is not what I meant."

He saw her shake her head. "Of course not! You enter my life and force me to play the role in your grand scheme. A scheme that's only purpose is to ensure you never need to marry, you never need to commit to love. And then you dare to ask me why I have not done the very thing you fight to ensure you will not do."

"Being a woman and sharing love with a man is not the same thing!" Terrence said.

Her eyes flashed and her chin lifted. "Once again, are you asking that I become a mistress?"

Terrence stared, balked rage making him clench his fist. "Dammit no!" He turned from her, unwilling to see the challenge and hurt dignity in her eyes.

"Then I will answer you." Her voice came to him soft and low. "When this is all through, and you have your freedom, then I will find a man who loves me and wishes to marry me, and I will take him to my bed and love him as a woman loves a man."

The vision, sharp and cutting, swam before Terrence's sight. Jezebel in the arms of another man, her blond hair spilling over them both. He whirled, and the word was ripped from him. "Jezebel!"

She stared at him with a coldness, almost a deadness. "I believe I have learned how to catch a man now. I have had enough lessons in how to get what I want no matter whom I use or coerce."

"If you mean me," Terrence gritted out, stalking to her, "I have not—"

"What?" a voice said from the stables' door. Terrence halted and then spun about. Lady Dorethea stood within the frame, her brow arched. "Have I interrupted a lovers' tiff?"

"No," Terrence gritted. "Of course not."

"Pity," Lady Dorethea said in a brisk tone.

In her wide skirts and expensive silk Lady Dorethea looked completely out of place. Terrence asked curtly, "What brings you here?"

"Tsk," Lady Dorethea said. "So curt. I do believe I've interrupted a quarrel after all. Then perhaps I come as an angel of mercy." Her eyes narrowed. "I came to tell you that Edgar Arrowroot will be arriving by the end of the week."

Terrence stiffened. "Indeed?"

"He will be expecting you to discuss matters of importance and business with him."

"Why would he do that?" Terrence asked, his eyes narrowing.

Lady Dorethea lifted her chin. "Because I told him you would. Then, in another week, I will hold a ball." She turned her gaze to Jezebel and her smile was tight. "I am sure, my dear, you would not care to remain for it."

Jezebel's chin lifted. "I wouldn't?"

"No, only the finest of the aristocracy will be there and the dress"—her eyes roved over Jezebel—"will be very formal." Once again she smiled a brittle smile. "Therefore, I am sure you will wish to return to London. One should not remain out of the spotlight for too long, else one's fans might forget one. And your 'career' on the stage is important. It is your bread and butter, after all." Lady Dorethea lifted her skirts and turned. She cast a look over her shoulder. "And you may take the bear with you, he might help in your act."

She departed and Terrence looked to Jezebel, who was stunned. "I am sorry. She had no right."

A bitter smile tipped her lips. "At least she does not wish me to become your mistress." She shook her head. " 'Tis of no significance; it is only one more lesson I am learning from your family on how to get what I want."

"And is that all you've learned?" Terrence asked lowly, his voice hoarse. "Is that all you will remember of us, of me?"

Jezebel shook her head slightly. "No, it's not all I'll remember. You taught me how to act, remember?"

"Oh, yes," Terrence said, remembering her torturous time upon stage, which he had orchestrated. "I'm sure you will be forever grateful to me for that." He looked at her, blanking all the emotion from his face. "You are going to leave, then?"

"No," Jezebel said. A different smile crossed her lips. "You do not understand. You taught me to act."

Terrence's hand slashed the air, his emotions slipping through. "Why remind me!"

"Because," Jezebel said. "I'm not leaving."

Terrence froze. "Why not?"

Jezebel looked away. "Because I am who you said I am. I've come to care for Letty and Theo—and all their . . . their pets."

They gazed at each other. Terrence would not ask the question that lay between them. Would not ask if she cared for him. "You will stay?"

"Yes," she said slowly. Then, in a whimsical tone of voice she added, "You know, Theo and Letty withdrew their offer today, they'll not give me five thousand to leave."

Terrence shook his head, but could not move. "No, I didn't know. It seems rather unkind since you saved their pets."

"No," Jezebel said, that strange smile upon her lips. "Not all of them." She lifted her chin. "My Lord, I believe we have a few scenes which still need to be played out."

Terrence smiled, grateful his foolish anger had not frightened her off, nor had the Duchess's cruel behavior. "Yes, I believe so. I can tell by your look, you've already written the script for one of them."

Jezebel nodded. "Yes, I believe it only fair the local people experience a taste of my talents."

"Indeed?" Terrence asked.

A delightful grin transformed her face. "If Father Arrowroot is coming to discuss wedding plans with you at the end of the week, I believe he should hear of your fame and mine in advance, don't you think?"

Terrence stared, stunned. He cracked a laugh. "I don't know exactly what you propose, my Jezebel, but I'm sure it will be interesting."

Jezebel strode to the barn's door. She looked over her shoulder and smiled in a way that Terrence thought would bring a house down if an audience ever saw it. He knew it brought him down. "The Duchess is wrong. Why go to London to further my career, when here will be just fine?"

"Gentlemen," Terrence said, standing at the old battered piano which Jake, his friend and the proud owner of the Fighting Cock tavern, had commandeered, "straight from the stage of London, here to perform for you, is the beauteous Jezebel Clinton."

"That's you," Josh whispered, holding tight to a small shot of whisky.

"I know it's me," Jezebel hissed and stood up from the rickety chair. She stared at the sea of rough, dirty faces turned toward her. "G-good afternoon, gentlemen," she said, smiling. Still they stared. She swallowed hard.

"Go on," whispered Josh.

"I will." Jezebel swiftly reached over and snatched the shot glass from him. She downed its contents in one gulp.

"Here now," Josh cried.

Jezebel wheezed and slapped it upon the table. "Here it goes, boys," she said and waved a hand. "Terry, love, let's have some music."

Terry crashed into the chords of the first stanza. Jezebel glimpsed a tiny, wizened man gaping at her from amidst the throng. His eyes were wide and adoring as he withdrew his hat with respect. That one movement fueled Jezebel's courage, far more than the whisky burning her insides did. She opened her mouth and thankfully began upon the right chord.

Grins instantly split the features of the men and Jezebel discovered a strong desire to give them the best show she could. Flapping her boa, she began to stroll around the room, singing the song as loudly as she could. By their attentiveness, it was clear this crowd was as tone deaf as she. She had found her proper milieu.

As Jezebel swished and sashayed through the tavern of

men, her voice became stronger and louder. She circled a table and came close to the little man she'd noticed. His hat still gripped in his hand, he goggled at her. Impulsively, Jezebel blew him a kiss. He stiffened and reared back, suddenly toppling off his stool. A roar of laughter arose.

"Petey's bowled over," a voice shouted.

"Sweetings, throw me one!" another rough voice shouted. Jezebel turned. A large, bovine-faced man sat at another table, grinning like a schoolboy. Jezebel winked at him and blew him a kiss as well.

He slapped beefy hands to his chest, crying, "Smitten, I is!"

The men laughed and good-natured cries arose for kisses. By the time the end of the song came, Jezebel had blown more kisses than she had hit correct notes. Terrence pounded out the final chords loudly. Laughing, Jezebel curtsied. Chairs toppled back and rough voices shouted for more as the men rose in uproarious applause.

A thrill shot through Jezebel, and she understood, in that one moment, what drove actors to perform night after night. She heard Terrence strike the chords of a new song and promptly began singing. They wanted more, and Jezebel wanted to continue. The men refused to sit down, all still standing, watching her as if she were the great Sarah Siddons.

"I can't see," a voice shrilled out. Jezebel noticed Petey's face bobbing up and down over the broad shoulders of the men before him. "I can't see!"

"Jez, over here," Josh shouted.

Josh stood at the bar, patting it, a proud expression on his face. Flipping her boa, Jezebel strolled over and sang to Josh. The bartender stood beside Josh at the ready.

"You're doing grand," Josh whispered, and then both men grabbed hold of her and lifted her onto the bar. Jezebel's voice jiggled alarmingly, but the men only applauded as she swung her legs over and stood atop the bar. As other men dashed to clear it of tankards and bottles, Jezebel began to mince along upon it, as she had seen an actress do, waving her hands and batting her lashes.

Her glance suddenly caught that of a tall, dark-haired man who stood at the entrance of the tavern. A qualm whispered through her. He was clearly an aristocrat, and the considering, preying look in his eyes did not please her one wit. Jezebel turned her gaze away from him, to the more open and honest looks of the common men in the tavern.

She belted out the words with fervor, and took the bar for her stage. Yet, as Terrence went into another round, she noticed she grew more breathy, her voice squeaking. She was not breathing correctly, apparently. Realizing her limits, Jezebel quickly finished the song and flourished a deep curtsy to more applause and cries for more.

"No, no, that's all, gents," she said, panting. She sat down quickly on the bar.

"Allow me," a voice said. She glanced up. The dark-haired man had somehow transversed the room without her knowing and stood before her. Before Jezebel could say a word he cinched her waist and hauled her from the bar. Quickly, fluidly, he dipped Jezebel and kissed her fully upon the lips. Jezebel struggled, scrunching her eyes closed in strong distaste.

A bellow arose. The man's lips were suddenly torn from hers. So were his arms. Jezebel crashed to the sawdust floor. Dazed, she pulled herself to a sitting position and peered up. Three men hovered above her; the dark-haired stranger, Terrence, and Josh.

"I am sorry, *ma chère,*" the stranger said, offering her his hand. "It is not my habit to drop women, but this rude oaf ran into me." He jerked his head toward Terrence.

"He's not an oaf," Jezebel said, angrily dusting off her hands.

"Don't dare to touch her again," Terrence said quietly. Jezebel froze. The anger snapping from Terrence was tangible.

The stranger stiffened, raising a dark brow. "I beg your pardon?"

"No, you shall beg Jezebel's pardon." Terrence nodded toward her.

"Terry, it's all right," Jezebel said quickly.

"No, it ain't. Blighter dared to kiss you," Josh said. He glared at the stranger. "You'll apologize to Jezebel and do it damn fast, sirrah."

The stranger's eyes flashed, and a cold smile crossed his lips. "Shall I, my pretty bantling?"

"Pretty!" Josh yelped. "I ain't pretty!"

"You shall apologize to the lady," Terrence said softly. "And do it quickly."

"Lady?" The man's brow rose with arrogance. "Dominic St. John does not apologize for kissing a woman. And most certainly not a—"

"Don't say it," Terrence said.

"A strumpet." Dominic smiled. "That is the English word, no?"

Terrence's hand shot out and slapped the man's face. "I told you not to say it."

Murder flared in the man's eyes. "You dare to strike me? You wish to die for a strumpet—"

He never finished. Josh lunged forward and slapped him again.

"Josh, no!" Jezebel cried out.

Josh shook his hand, glowering. "He said that damn word again."

Dominic lifted a hand to his lip, wiping a trickle of blood from it. "I demand satisfaction, sir!"

"You can have it," Josh snapped. "And with pleasure."

"I believe he means from me," Terrence said. "And I gladly accept."

"No." Josh shook his head vehemently. "He meant from me." He looked to Dominic. "Didn't you?"

Dominic stared, and then gave a very Gallic shrug. "It

does not matter. I will not tolerate being slapped by any man."

"Then I will give you satisfaction," Terrence said, bowing.

"So will I," Josh said quickly.

"No," Jezebel cried, bolting up to stand in the middle of the three men. "Terrence, you shall not fight over this, do you hear?"

"Stay out of this, Jezebel," Terrence said, and swiftly grabbed her, swinging her behind him.

"Yes, Jez." Josh caught her shoulders and pulled her to the side. "We've got to settle this. I think I should get to fight him first."

"No," Terrence said. "I claim the right first."

Dominic's eyes lit and he shook his head. "You two should not be so fast to rush to your deaths. I have had many duels, and alas, every man who meets me has met his maker."

"It's my right, blast it," Josh protested. "I get to fight him first."

"You mean die first," Dominic said.

"No!" Jezebel exclaimed. "No one shall die."

"Be quiet," Josh and Terrence said to her as one.

"I shall not," Jezebel retorted, impotent rage flaring within her.

Josh immediately clamped a hand over her mouth, and muffled her objection. He frowned at Dominic. "I think I ought to be able to fight you first."

Dominic's face showed his confusion and then he glanced to Terrence. "We have a matter of protocol, I believe. Just who are you in relation to—"

"Don't say it," Terrence growled.

"This woman," Dominic said.

"She is . . . my mistress," Terrence proclaimed. Jezebel tried to object, but Josh tightened his hand over her mouth.

"I see." Dominic's brow shot down. He studied Josh. "And who are you, sir?"

"I am . . ." Josh stopped and blushed. "I am . . . er . . . her ex-lover."

"Her ex-lover?" Dominic's eyes widened and he stared at Jezebel. "Madame, you are most uncommon. I did not know that an English woman had such ability; I thought only the women of France could demand such devotion from men."

"You insulting her again?" Josh cried, even as Jezebel retorted a muffled curse.

"No, no," Dominic said. "Most certainly not. But since you are but the ex-lover, the present lover has the right, eh?"

"Don't see that," Josh said, frowning severely. "I've known Jez longer, I ought to have prior claim."

"I have first right," Terrence insisted.

"Very well." Josh sighed. "I'll second you then. And after you're done, I'll get my turn."

Dominic bowed, a smile twitching at his lips. "But of course. But who shall be your second, for this man will be dead."

"I'll be his second," a high voice cried out. Petey elbowed his way through the crowd.

"Very well," Dominic said, nodding. "Let us meet tomorrow in the morning. Choose your weapons."

"It will be pistols," Terrence said curtly.

"Yes," Josh agreed.

Pistols, thought Jezebel. Josh couldn't hit the side of the barn with a pistol. She bit down angrily upon Josh's hand.

"Blast it, Jez!" he yelped. His hand fell quickly from her mouth.

"Stop this, all of you," she cried. Struggling out of Josh's arms, she stomped up to Terrence. "Terry, you shall not fight."

"I shall," he said, rage glowing in his eyes. "He dared to kiss you."

"Oh!" Jezebel cried, throwing up her hands. The expression in Terrence's eyes was that of a mule who wouldn't budge. She whirled angrily upon Dominic. "You, sir, you started this all. You know you should not have kissed me. Now simply apologize and have done with it."

"I am sorry, mademoiselle," Dominic said. "But I shall not apologize. They hit me."

"Did they?" Jezebel narrowed her eyes. With a swift movement she kicked Dominic in the shins. He stiffened, even as Josh cried out. "There, I kicked you. Shall you duel with me as well?"

Dominic grimaced, but shook his head. "I am sorry, *chérie*, my schedule, it is already full. Besides, I do not duel with women."

"Why not?" Jezebel asked, placing her hands upon her hips and glaring. " 'Tis my honor you impugned, not theirs."

"Madame," Dominic said, giving the other two men a hapless shrug, "it does not matter, a man does not duel with a woman."

"No, he only kisses her without her permission," Jezebel snapped. He offered her a blank expression and said nothing, so she spun about and raked Terrence and Josh with a scathing eye. They, too, had the same blank look. She threw up her hands. "I see that I am most certainly not involved with this, but if any of you dares to kill the other, you will have to answer to me. Do you hear?" Shaking, Jezebel stalked from the tavern. The silent men stepped aside as if she were the queen, that or a pariah.

"I believe she means it," Dominic breathed out, appearing stunned.

"Jez never did understand about honor with us men," Josh said, coughing. "Has a temper, she does."

"I'll take care of Jezebel later," Terrence said. "Now when shall we meet?"

The other two men looked at Terrence with clear respect. Then they fell to making their plans for the morrow.

* * *

Josh sat quietly in the large chair, his hand wrapped about a bottle. One lone candle lit his bedroom. He lifted the bottle and drank deeply from it.

Tomorrow he would engage in his first duel, and most likely his last. Every man in the tavern had made certain he knew that Dominic St. John was a devil with the pistols and had not boasted when he'd said he always killed his man. Josh closed his eyes. He couldn't hit the side of a barn with pistols, and he had called out a devil with them. Not that swords would have been better. He knew even less about those.

Fear hollowed out his heart when he thought of what would happen to Jezebel if he were killed. Her life was in such a tangle, and it was all due to him. Worse, he had spent most of his funds upon Molly. If he died Jezebel would have little to support her. He shook his head, wondering how he had been such a fool. He realized now he couldn't even say he had loved Molly, not one jot. It had merely been heady to be able to have an older woman attracted to him. Josh clenched one arm of the chair and closed his eyes tightly. He couldn't die. He must be there for Jezebel, as she had always been for him.

A soft knock at the door interrupted his tortured thoughts. He sighed, having fully expected it. Indeed, he had only been waiting.

"Come in," he said, without even opening his eyes. He heard the door open, heard the rustle of skirts. "It's no use, Jez, you can't talk me out of it."

"I'm not Jezebel," a voice said quietly.

Josh's eyes snapped open and he sat up. "Elizabeth! What are you doing here?"

She walked slowly toward him. Her black glossy hair fell about her shoulders, and she wore a soft white night rail. Her gray eyes were dark. "Betty told me."

"B-Betty told you what?" Josh asked, bemused. She appeared an angel come to visit him in his last moments on earth.

"That you will fight a duel tomorrow," Elizabeth said softly. "Over Jezebel."

Josh gripped the bottle tightly and looked away from her. "Blast, does everyone know about it?"

"Yes," Elizabeth said. " 'Tis a small town. We are not accustomed to duels here."

" 'Tis clear," Josh said gruffly. "Else Betty would have known better than to tell you. Maids ain't suppose to tell the ladies about these matters."

"Why not?" Elizabeth said. She seemed to float across the floor, and then, with a graceful movement, she sat down upon Josh's lap. "If it is the truth."

"Elizabeth!" Josh cried, shocked.

She wrapped soft, silken arms about him. Her light perfume teased his nostrils. "Is it the truth?" she whispered. "You will duel with Dominic St. John?"

"Y-yes," Josh stammered, his heart pounding alarmingly.

"He will kill you," she said lowly.

"P-perhaps."

Elizabeth's gray eyes darkened to charcoal. "Kiss me."

Josh tensed. "Wh-what?"

"Kiss me," Elizabeth whispered, moving her lips to within a breath of his.

"Oh, er—" Josh swallowed—"If . . . if you want me to . . ."

"Yes," she said. "Yes."

Josh was lost. He lowered his lips to Elizabeth's. She met him with a warmth and passion which ignited Josh. He dropped the bottle as his arms enveloped her soft, pliant body. "Gads," Josh muttered, tearing away from her sweet lips and burying his head in her hair. He drew in deep breaths; her scent sending him reeling with each gasp. "Elizabeth!"

"Don't do it," she pleaded, pressing her body tightly against his. "Don't meet St. John. You will be killed."

Josh gripped the live vibrant woman in his arms. She was no angel, she was Elizabeth, and he swore to himself that these would not be his last moments upon the earth. "No," he whispered, turning to kiss the curve of her neck. "I won't."

He felt her body relax. "You won't?"

"No. I swear I won't die. I will kill him, and I will come back to you."

"What!" Suddenly Elizabeth reared back and slapped him resoundingly.

Josh blinked, his arms falling from her in shock. "What was that for?"

"You cad!" Elizabeth scrabbled from his lap. "You dare to kiss me—"

"You told me I could," Josh said, befuddled. "You even sat on my lap."

"You kiss me and then say you will kill that man and return to me?"

"What do you want me to do?" Josh asked, blinking. "Do you want him to kill me?"

"No!" Elizabeth stomped her foot. "I don't want you to duel."

Josh flushed. "Oh. Er, I didn't understand."

"And if you do meet St. John, you needn't worry about returning to me," Elizabeth said, "because I won't want you." Josh thought he saw a tear gleam in her eyes, but she ran from the room before he was certain.

"Damn," he muttered. "Blast and damn." He looked hastily around for his bottle. He discovered it on the carpet, spilt out. "Blast and double damn!"

Terrence stood, gazing out the window of his bedroom into the dark courtyard beyond. He couldn't erase from his mind the picture of Dominic St. John bending Jezebel over his arm and kissing her as if she were a common doxy. A jealousy shot through him. And a guilt. If it wasn't for him, no man would have ever dared to treat Jezebel so. No man would ever have mistaken her for a lightskirt. No matter that he himself had done so upon their first meeting, Terrence realized he must have been mad that night, or else, his conscience whispered, he had wished for Jezebel to be one. Worse, in a way, he had made her one.

His jaw clenched. It did not matter. Tomorrow he would kill Dominic St. John and no man would ever again think to touch Jezebel Clinton without respect. Terrence had claimed to be her protector and so he would be.

He heard a rap at the door and knew it opened even as he turned around. Jezebel stood upon the threshold, her violet eyes dark. Terrence smiled wryly. "Now here's a turn, you visiting my bedroom."

Jezebel did not flush, or falter. She walked directly up to him and looked him in the eye. "You are going to go through with the duel?"

He chuckled. "Full frontal attack. Yes, I am going through with the duel."

"Why?" Jezebel asked.

"Because St. John dared to kiss you," Terrence said, his voice roughening. "He treated you like a whore."

"And what did you expect?" Jezebel asked. "I was dancing and singing in a tavern. It was a reasonable mistake."

"I know, damn it," Terrence said, spinning from her. "I know."

"Then why do you wish to fight this man?"

"Because I am your protector now," Terrence said, turning to her. "He mistook you for a common doxy because of me, and by God I'm going to rectify it. No man is going to touch you."

"They will if you die," Jezebel said, her voice low.

"Then Josh will protect you," Terrence muttered.

Jezebel's eyes flared. "You think I want Josh killed over this?"

"I didn't mean that! You know I didn't."

He saw her tremble. "I don't want you doing this. I don't want you to get killed. I don't want Josh to get killed. Don't ruin my life!"

Terrence chuckled bitterly. "I've already ruined it, I believe."

Jezebel's eyes widened and she turned from him. Shaking her head, she walked away.

"Jezebel," Terrence called softly. She stopped. "Don't leave me in anger."

She turned, her back straight, her head regal. "What am I to do? Should I be all sweetness and docility? Kiss you goodbye and wave merrily while you go off to get yourself killed?"

"No," Terrence said, walking slowly up to her. She glared at him with shimmering eyes. He saw her tremble, tremble as he did. He groaned and said hoarsely, "Yes, damn you, yes." He grasped her shoulders and jerked her to him. He needed her, needed to feel her softness against him. His lips met hers harshly, demanding the comfort she swore she would not give.

Yet Jezebel did not pull back, rather Terrence felt her body surge, strong against his, her arms wrapping about his shoulders. Terrence groaned deep in his throat as Jezebel kissed him wildly back, turning his demand into hers. Both clung to each other in a clasp of passion and need.

Jezebel turned her lips from his, burying her head against his shoulder. "I shall not forgive you if you go to this duel."

Terrence breathed out a rasping breath. "I will not forgive myself if I do not."

He felt her hold loosen and released her, knowing he must. Jezebel did not look at him as she stepped from his arms. Neither did he look at her as she left. He heard the door close softly.

When Terrence closed his eyes he could still feel Jezebel in his arms. She had not offered him comfort, but she had given him strength.

Jezebel walked down the darkened hall, blinking back tears. Terrence was wrong, so very wrong. She had thrown it at his head that he had coerced her into a life she did not wish, that he had done it for selfish purposes. Yet now, when he might die on the morrow, she could no longer lie to herself. She had secretly enjoyed the life he had orchestrated for her. She had seen and lived more in the farce he had created than she had ever done in her own, dull existence.

Hot shame, mingled with fear, singed Jezebel. Terrence should not sacrifice himself for her. He should not have to make restitution for the very times she cherished within her heart. He had given more to her than he had ever taken.

So deep was she in thought, she never noticed until she ran into another body in the hall. Jezebel stifled a cry. "Who is there?"

" 'Tis me, Elizabeth," a weak, watery voice said.

"Elizabeth?" Jezebel peered into the darkness and her gaze defined the other woman. "Are you all right?"

"Y-yes," Elizabeth said. "Yes, of course."

A silence fell.

"I must confess," Elizabeth said, "I-I went to see Josh."

Understanding struck Jezebel. "You know then."

Elizabeth sighed. "Yes, I do."

Jezebel sighed as well. "I went to see Terrence. He will not withdraw from the duel."

"Neither will Josh," Elizabeth revealed.

"I c-cannot bear the thought," Jezebel said.

"You love him, don't you?" Elizabeth asked softly in the dark.

Jezebel paused. She had not expected the question. But

at this moment, she could not lie. "Yes, yes I do. But please, do not tell him."

"Not tell him?" Elizabeth was stunned. "Why not? He loves you very much."

"He does?" Jezebel asked, her heart suddenly pounding.

"Of course," Elizabeth returned strongly, almost angrily. "I just came from his room."

Jezebel's heart sank. "You mean Josh."

"Of course I mean Josh." Elizabeth was indignant. "Who did you think I meant?" Jezebel could not bring herself to answer. "Oh, I see. But Josh loves you so very much, he is willing to die for you."

"And I love him," Jezebel said.

"Him as well?"

Jezebel heard the disapproval in Elizabeth's voice. She laughed suddenly. "I love Josh as a sister would. I consider him a brother."

"I see," Elizabeth said.

"No, I don't think you do." Jezebel was smiling slightly. Then pain rose in her again. "But I cannot let Josh be killed. I cannot let Terrence be hurt. I . . . I cannot. They wish to protect me, when 'tis they who need protection."

"Yes," Elizabeth said. "They do."

A pregnant silence fell.

Jezebel asked, "Are you thinking what I am thinking?"

"Yes," Elizabeth said. "But I cannot think how."

"Come to my room," Jezebel said. "There must be a way."

Two shadows drifted down the hall.

"Are you sure this is his house?" Jezebel whispered, peering at what appeared to be a library in the glow of the moonlight.

"Yes," Elizabeth said. "But are you sure you know how to use that pistol?"

"Yes." Jezebel gripped the large old pistol and crunched glass as she stepped forward. "But I do not wish to have broken someone else's window, and I certainly don't wish to shoot anyone but St. John."

"He leased this house a year ago. The Duchess and I visited him once," Elizabeth whispered, falling in behind Jezebel as they slowly circumvented dark objects and made their way to the door. "But you aren't really going to shoot him?"

Jezebel swallowed. "Only if he is recalcitrant." She reached the door and taking a deep breath, opened it. It appeared to lead into the great hall. "Thank heaven, you were right."

Both ladies slipped into the marble hall, then promptly froze in the middle of it when the sounds of voices came to them.

"Oh, no," Jezebel whispered, pointing to a closed door to the right, beneath which a crack of light shone. "He is still entertaining."

"At this time of night?" Elizabeth gasped. "And with two duels tomorrow. Does the man have no delicacy?"

"Apparently not," Jezebel said. "How very unaccommodating."

A sudden, shocking scream rent the air. Then a shot rang out.

"Good Lord," Jezebel breathed.

Both women dashed across the hall. Elizabeth reached the door first and shoved it open. Jezebel charged in, holding her pistol high. She skidded to a halt. "Oh my!"

The Duchess of Devon looked up from where she stood over the fallen body of a man, her cane rammed into the small of his back. "Why Jezebel . . . and Elizabeth. Do come in and close the door. We are sure to have company soon, since Letty was such a ninny as to discharge that pistol."

"I-I only meant to frighten him." Letty stood a few feet

back, her face pale as she waved a small pistol. "I—I didn't mean for it to go off."

"Birdwit," Theo said, standing on the other side of the fallen man. "Told you I should carry it."

"Is he dead?" Jezebel asked, juggling her gun and going to close the door.

"No, I'm not." It was St. John's voice and his body stirred. Dorethea jabbed in the cane more firmly. "Ouch!"

"Letty merely winged that ugly picture over there," Theo said.

"I'm so sorry, Lord St. John," Letty said, tearing up. "I will buy you another picture. If you tell me who the artist is—"

"Letty," Dorethea snapped. "We are not art collecting. We have business to attend."

"Ugly?" Dominic objected from the ground. "I paid a fortune for it."

"It's still ugly," Theo said.

"Oh, then I won't get you another," Letty said. "I am on a limited income, you see."

A sudden battering at the door sounded. Jezebel swiftly rammed all her weight against it as someone on the other side tried to open it. As Elizabeth joined her, the doorknob rattled.

"My Lord," a frightened voice called. "Are you all right?"

"Of course I am," Dominic called out. "Just go back to bed."

"We heard a shot," the voice called.

"I was cleaning my gun," Dominic shouted from the floor, "and it went off. Now go to bed."

"But we heard a scream," the voice persisted.

"It was . . ." Dominic halted. Dorethea rapped him with her cane. "Ah . . . it was me!"

A silence fell.

"You, My Lord?" The man behind the door sounded flabbergasted.

"Me," Dominic gritted out. "Now go back to bed before I dismiss you from my services."

"Very well, My Lord." Mutters and mumbles seethed through the door, and then silence reigned.

"Now, Your Grace," Dominic said. "Would you permit me to rise? It is very difficult to discuss matters in this position."

"I think it a very good position for you," Jezebel said.

Dorethea sighed. "No, Jezebel. You of all women should know a man loses all concentration when in an embarrassing position." She pulled her cane back. "You may rise, St. John, but any ungracious move and I'll let Jezebel shoot you."

"And I know how to fire a pistol," Jezebel warned as St. John crawled to a standing position.

He bowed, his dark eyes glinting. "As I said this afternoon, you are an uncommon woman." He turned, looking at the three elderly women surrounding him. "Ladies, let us have a seat. There is no reason to stand for the discussion." He smiled. "I'd ring for tea, but I do not believe it would be wise."

"Very well," Dorethea said and marched over to sit upon a settee.

"Yes." Letty sighed and squeezed into a small, dainty chair. "I feel rather faint."

Everyone promptly took up chairs. Dorethea lifted her brow and looked at Dominic as he seated himself across from her. "Well, have you become reasonable and decided to withdraw from the duel?"

Dominic smiled. "Of course, madame. Meeting two men upon a green is one thing, but fighting five women? I am a brave man, not a stupid one."

"Pity," Theo said. "Was hoping to kill you."

"No," Jezebel said. "I believe that would have been my right."

Dominic stared and then laughed. "What a group you

are. Everyone so bloodthirsty and claiming the right to kill me."

"You shouldn't have kissed me," Jezebel said.

"I am coming to comprehend that," Dominic said. "You appear to be more protected than the finest lady."

Jezebel flushed. "I'm no lady."

"But she's got friends," Theo said. "Which is more than I can say for you."

"And," Dorethea said, "since she is the mistress of my grandson the Marquis, you should never have dared to touch her. What belongs to our family should be respected." Jezebel's mouth dropped open, and in truth a warmth flushed through her.

"I understand," Dominic said. "But I did not know she was your grandson's mistress. I but saw her singing in the Fighting Cock, on top of the bar, and did not stop to ask."

"Yes." Dorethea lifted a brow toward Jezebel. "Jezebel has a difficulty with discretion."

"On top of the bar?" Letty breathed out, leaning forward eagerly. "Really? Was Jezebel giving a good performance, then?"

"Good enough to make me kiss her," Dominic smiled.

"Really?" Letty smiled to Jezebel. "You must be improving, dear."

"I was still off-key," Jezebel admitted, flushing.

"Men don't care about key," Lady Dorethea said. She leveled a stern gaze upon Dominic. "I own I am displeased with Jezebel for her want of discretion, but what is your excuse, sirrah?"

Dominic shrugged. "I have the same besetting sin, I fear."

"Very well." Dorethea nodded. "But you should have apologized for it rather than accepting the challenges of Terrence and Josh."

"They struck me, Your Grace," Dominic said. "A man of honor cannot accept that."

"That you are a man of honor is still to be seen," Dorethea said.

Dominic nodded. "What would you suggest I do to prove it? Other than submitting to your killing me, that is?"

"Withdraw from the duel, send round an apology."

"No," Dominic said. "That I will not do."

"We can truss him up and ship him to London," Theo suggested. "There are plenty of press gangs that would have him."

"No," Dominic said quickly, for the first time appearing nervous. "I promise you that is not necessary. But you do have something there. I will merely disappear for a month or so. By the time I return, I imagine I shall have devised a plausible story. I may even use your story, madame, but I hope not to have to actually live it."

"Very well," Dorethea said. She pinned him with a gimlet eye. "But how do we know you will keep your promise, and not meet with Terrence and Josh in the morning?"

"Madame," Dominic laughed, "if I were to do that, I would only have two infelicitous choices. First, I could permit them both to put bullets through me, or else I could kill them, but then I would have five women certain to kill me, and the odds are not such that I wish to take them. I have found women far more dangerous than men, since your sex does not cavil at killing a man secretly."

"Of course not." The Duchess rose. "You do not think we would care to make cakes of ourselves like you men do, trudging out to a field and shooting at each other point-blank for all the world to see, including the authorities. We women understand delicacy."

"Of course," Dominic said, a wry tone to his voice.

"Let us go, ladies," Dorethea said. "This man has to pack, and we must return before we are missed." Everyone rose and moved toward the door. Lady Dorethea stopped to look at Dominic who was still sitting. "I assume that never a word of our visit shall get out?"

"Oh no." Dominic chuckled. "It would not do my consequence any good for the world to know I was done in by five women." He smiled. "I believe I have that much discretion."

"Good." Dorethea turned to Jezebel. "How did you two arrive?"

"We stole a horse from the stables," Jezebel said.

Dorethea grinned. "Well, we stole the carriage. You might as well return with us in comfort, my dear. Now do come along."

Eleven

Only the faintest of morning rays shone into the breakfast room, yet all the ladies in the house were already fully dressed and breaking their fast at the table. Stilton found himself busy, for the ladies appeared ravenous, all ordering up their favorite specialties from the new cook, a good stolid English woman from the local town, who by the by adored children and dogs. The Duchess had deemed the cook's penchant for both would work well within the household.

Only Amelia said she did not wish to eat. Indeed, she appeared wan, and she clutched her cup with white fingers.

"Amelia, dear," Dorethea said, mounding a spoonful of marmalade upon an already lavishly buttered muffin. "You do not appear well this morning."

"Oh!" Amelia's teacup shook, and she set it down with a clatter. She turned nervous brown eyes to Dorethea. "Oh!"

"What is it dear?" Letty asked. "Do you suffer the migraine? They can be dreadful. Why some days, and especially the days when I wish to feel well and have so much to attend, I will contract the most dreadful migraine and must lie down upon a bed, in a darkened room. 'Tis the only thing which will help. Also, rose water and perhaps a small amount of laudanum seem beneficial." Her face fell. "I am sorry, but I fear I forgot to bring my laudanum."

"I have a supply," Dorethea said. "Would you care for a dose Amelia? Perhaps you did not get your sleep last night."

"No, no I didn't," Amelia admitted. She looked hastily

about the table. "Oh, I cannot bear it. Godmama, I-I fear I must tell you something. Something dreadful."

"Oh?" Dorethea asked. She laid down her muffin and delicately licked her finger. "Do go on."

Amelia looked harriedly to all three elderly women. "I-I am not certain I should tell. I fear it might cause you great distress; indeed it might cause you to faint. I-I know when I heard it from Betty I nearly did."

"We shall try to be brave," Dorethea said.

"You must be very brave," Amelia warned. "It might be a frightful strain upon your heart."

"We'll try to keep the old organs in line," Theo said.

"Very well." Amelia drew in a deep breath. "At this very moment your grandson and . . . and Miss Jezebel's, er, friend are meeting for a duel with Dominic St. John. Father says Dominic St. John is a crack shot."

"I know dear," Dorethea said, picking up her tea and sipping. "In fact, we all know."

"What!" Amelia looked in shock to them all.

"Betty is a very busy maid," Elizabeth said apologetically.

"I did not hear it from Betty." Dorethea sniffed. "I never listen to backstairs gossip."

"Then who told you?" Amelia's gaze flew to Jezebel. "Surely you did not."

Jezebel shook her head. "Of course not, though now I realize I should have. I far prefer traveling in a carriage than by horseback."

Amelia blinked. "I beg your pardon?"

Dorethea laughed. "You must learn the aristocratic way, Jezebel. No matter what transpires, do look to your comfort as well." She turned her gaze to Amelia. "I heard it from Stilton, Amelia. He informed me as a proper butler should."

"You know!" Amelia cried. "But . . . but how can you be so . . . so calm?"

"Why shouldn't I be? After all, there is nothing I can do

about it." Dorethea said. "Men do hate it if we interfere with their affairs."

"Indeed." Jezebel nodded. "A man's honor is something we poor females can never understand."

" 'Sright," Theo said. "If they want to shoot holes in each other, then we got to let them. That's why I say don't get too attached to the creatures, and certainly don't marry one. Never know when one will trip over the other, get in a rip, and call him out. Then we are left wearing the widow weeds, and for a year at that."

"Oh, how can you?" Amelia cried. "I could not sleep a wink last night, dreading what will happen this morning."

"So what did you do?" Jezebel asked.

"Do?" Amelia looked at Jezebel as if she were insane. "Why I prayed, I prayed all night."

"Then you did not see Terry?" Jezebel asked.

"No, of course not." Amelia gasped. "A lady does not visit a gentleman's room."

"Well, I'm no lady," Jezebel said.

"And I'm but a companion." Elizabeth shrugged.

"I own, however, I was too tired to worry over it," Jezebel said. "Me, I fell into bed and was out to the world."

"You just fell asleep?" Amelia cried. "How could you? Terry would not have been in the duel except for you. Neither would Mr. Rakesham."

"You must understand," Jezebel said. "We common folk don't suffer the excesses of emotion you toffs do."

Amelia gasped. "But . . . but he is . . . is your, well, you know."

"Yes, I know." Jezebel grinned. "And a mighty fine one at that."

"Jezebel," Dorethea warned. "Do stop upsetting Amelia. Amelia has shown just the proper feelings she ought. Why she didn't get a wink of sleep last night. She contributed mightily to Terrence's cause."

"And prayed to boot," Theo said, nodding. "Sounds to me like she had the roughest job."

At that moment Stilton entered the room and the ladies fell quiet. "Yes, Stilton?" Dorethea asked.

"The gentlemen have arrived, Your Grace," Stilton said, bowing.

"Oh, they are alive," Amelia cried. "Praise be!"

"To be sure," Dorethea said. "And how do they look, Stilton?"

"Oh, yes," Amelia pressed on, "they are not . . . not wounded, are they?"

"No, Miss Amelia," Stilton said solemnly. "At least I see no physical wounds. They do appear to be rather testy, however, Your Grace."

"Cross as crabs no doubt," Theo speculated.

"Do bring them to us, Stilton," Dorethea said. As the butler disappeared she cast a minatory look about the table. "Now remember ladies, we are not to know anything about their activities. Well, Jezebel is supposed to know, but not the rest of us."

"Good morning, Terrence," Dorethea greeted the men as they entered. "And Mr. Rakesham."

Both men halted upon the threshold, their faces rather grim.

"Good morning," Terrence said. "You are all up rather early, are you not?"

"Yes, we are," Dorethea replied blandly. "But we have a full day ahead of us. We ladies intend to go shopping later on and wished to make an early start."

"Shopping!" Josh exclaimed.

"Why indeed," Dorethea said. "There is a ball within two weeks, and it is never too early to plan one's wardrobe." She smiled. "But you two are up early as well. Out riding?"

"No," Terrence said, walking over and finally taking up a chair. "We had business to attend."

"And was it successful?" Jezebel asked, fluttering her lashes.

Terrence turned a dark look to her. "I am here, am I not?"

"Then do have some breakfast." Jezebel smiled sweetly. "I am sure you are sharp set. Or do you have to depart somewhere rather hastily?"

"No, confound it," Josh exclaimed, flinging himself into a chair. "Didn't have the meeting at all, Jez. The loose fish . . . er, gentleman . . . never showed."

"He didn't?" Jezebel widened her eyes.

"Terrence," Dorethea said. "Whoever your business associate is, I advise you not to enter into any more enterprises with him if he cannot show on time." Terrence turned a penetrating look upon Dorethea. "Reliability is important in all business ventures."

Terrence almost growled. "I assure you, I still intend to do business with the gentleman."

"Oh, you shouldn't," Letty cried. Then she gulped. "I mean, Papa always said if a man even proved ten minutes late, one should not have anything to do with him. He had a partner who was always late, and in the end, the man took off with Papa's money. So that proved the matter, without a doubt. Now as for women, it is a different story. It is perfectly reasonable for us to be late and does not show a disposition to steal, not one whit."

"Letty," Theo said. "You are rambling again."

"Yes," Dorethea agreed. "And we were discussing dresses before the gentlemen came in."

"Dresses?" Josh sputtered. "Well if that ain't cool. Here we are out and about to, er, do business and you ladies are talking about folderols."

"Being well dressed," Dorethea said witheringly, "is of the utmost importance."

"Oh!" Amelia's hand went to her mouth. "If—if you will excuse me." She stood and dashed hastily from the room.

"I'll go after her," Letty said, rising quickly. "The poor dear, she—"

"She suffers a migraine," Dorethea said. "Yes, do go, Letty. I will come with the laudanum in the nonce." They watched as Letty dashed after Amelia. "I do hope Amelia will feel better, but an afternoon of shopping shall do the trick I am sure."

"Yes, a new dress fixes all," Terrence said. He turned his look to Jezebel. "I hope you will ride with me, before the shopping expedition that is."

Jezebel lowered her eyes. "That would be pleasant."

"I say," Josh exclaimed, his face brightening. "Would you care to go riding with me, Elizabeth?"

"No, Mr. Rakesham," Elizabeth said with cold formality. "I do not wish to go. I believe I have far more important matters to attend to this morning."

"More important matters?" Josh's blue eyes appeared stunned.

"Indeed," Elizabeth said, rising. "Perhaps you would care to ride with Jezebel."

"I want to ride with you," Josh said, his face flushing.

"No, sir, I assure you, you do not." Elizabeth's tone was crisp. "But it is of no significance, for I most certainly do not care to ride with you." She nodded and walked swiftly from the room.

"Tea anyone?" Dorethea asked.

"Faith," Josh said, staring after Elizabeth. "Wish that blasted chap would have showed. Could have done a service for me and put me out of my misery."

"Jezebel, slow down," Terrence called, his horse thundering along behind hers. Jezebel grimaced, but pulled in the reins of her mount and brought it to a halt. They rode beside the ornamental pond, and in the distance the Duchess's estate lay before them. She had almost succeeded in returning to it without having a private discussion with Terrence.

Jezebel forced a laugh. "You said you wished for a ride."

"I said a ride," Terrence said, bringing his horse up to hers. "Not a steeplechase. Let us dismount and walk for a while, unless you intend to run as well, versus walking." He quickly dismounted.

Jezebel attempted to hide her flush. "I'll try for a more sedate pace," she said as he reached to help her from her horse.

"One would have thought the devil was after you," Terrence said, still holding firmly to her waist and gazing intently at her.

Jezebel looked quickly up. Then she smiled. "No, just you."

He cracked a laugh. "Cruel, Jezebel, cruel. Today I almost faced death for you, and you treat me thus."

"A death I did not wish you to face, remember?" Jezebel forced herself to step from his hold. "Let us walk. Or is taking even one step too fast a pace for you?"

"I don't know, perhaps it is," Terrence said, shaking his head. He took the reins of both horses and leading them over to a tree, tied the beasts off. Jezebel stood watching him, hoping her heart wasn't in her eyes, or the lie within her gaze. He turned and walked toward her. "Would you be so cavalier if I had met with St. John this morning, I wonder."

"But you did not," Jezebel said swiftly, and walked just as quickly from him.

"But if I had, Jezebel," Terrence called. His tone was such that she felt forced to stop and turn. "Would you be as cool about it as you are now?"

Jezebel tensed, but smiled. "Seeking sympathy, My Lord? You'll not receive it from me."

"Oh no?" His eyes darkened. "Imagine it, Jezebel. I raise my pistol to fire at St. John." He pantomimed the motion.

"But alas, St. John shoots first." His arms flung out, and then he grasped his chest and wheezed. "I am wounded, mortally wounded."

"Stop that," she said, though a bubble of laughter rose within her.

"I'm dying." Terrence began to reel. "Goodbye, cruel world!" He staggered. "Dying!" He careened. "Goodbye, cruel Jezebel!" He toppled to the ground.

"Terrence!" Jezebel laughed. "Do get up, you'll get wet."

He lay still, but said, "What does wet mean to a dead man, as his blood spills into the ground."

Jezebel stopped laughing. A chill chased down her spine. "Do get up," she said, walking swiftly over to stand above him. "Get up this instant."

Terrence peeked at her from one eye. "Would you cry at my funeral, Jez? What would you do?"

"Do?" Jezebel put her hands upon her hips. "Why I'd come to it dressed in . . . purple, bright purple with pink trim!"

"Ouch!" Terrence blinked his eye shut and slapped his hand to his chest. "No black?"

"Perhaps an armband," Jezebel conceded. "With pink trim, mind you."

"And would you cry?" Terrence asked, his eyes still shut.

"Of course," Jezebel said. "And very affectingly, to be sure. I'd kneel at your casket," she said, kneeling down beside him. "Like this."

"Be careful," he whispered from the side of his mouth. "You'll get wet."

"I am an actress," Jezebel said. "What does wet mean when I am performing a grand, deathbed scene? For I would be crying copious tears. Fake, mind you."

"Fake?" Terrence suddenly sat up, and before she could move gripped her shoulders. His eyes were warm, almost challenging. "Would they truly be fake?"

"Of course," Jezebel said, lifting her chin to counteract

the sudden vulnerability she felt. "For how could one cry for someone who had wantonly gone to meet his death?"

"Ah, 'tis that which displeases you." He lifted one hand to trace her cheek. "I did not do what you wished and you are miffed."

"Miffed?" Jezebel stared at him, even as a tingle raced after his touch. "We are talking about you getting killed. Y-you make . . . make it sound as if . . ." Terrence traced her lips with his thumb and her concentration slipped. "As if I w-were upset over y-you not taking me t-to a ball or something rather than you d-dueling." Jezebel halted, for her heart was racing.

"Go on," Terrence said, and his hand slid to cup the back of her neck.

"Go on?" Jezebel asked, blinking.

"Yes," Terrence nodded. "The deathbed scene. You are crying over me, copious fake tears." He leaned over, his face close to hers. "And would you, in the grand style, lean down and give me one last kiss goodbye."

Jezebel shivered. "No."

"Why not?" Terrence whispered.

"Y-you would be dead," she whispered. Helplessly her gaze focused on his lips, soft sensual lips tipped in a light smile. "Your . . . your lips would be cold."

"Then I am glad I am alive," Terrence said. He moved slightly and softly brushed her lips. "They are not too cold, are they?"

"No," Jezebel whispered. "Not at all."

"Neither are yours," he said and kissed her again.

Jezebel moaned slightly, gladly melting into Terrence as he wrapped his arms around her. If he had met St. John and been killed, he wouldn't be doing this. She'd never be able to feel what she did now, ever. She shivered at the frightening truth and the knowledge of it. "Don't ever duel again," she said, holding him tightly.

"I shan't." Terrence chuckled, shifting her in his arms.

"Since you refuse to kiss me if I'm dead." Jezebel hid her face against his shoulder. Then his voice changed. "Though it is very hard to duel when the challenger does not arrive."

Jezebel tried not to stiffen. "I am glad he did not."

"Tell me," Terrence said, drawing slightly away. Jezebel sat up slightly, preparing herself for what she knew would come. "Did Grandmother and my aunts know I was going to duel this morning?"

Jezebel stared, and tension drained from her. He was thinking about his grandmother and aunts. "I do not know." She frowned, trying to decide the best course. "Though I would not be surprised if they knew."

"I wonder," Terrence said, his eyes narrowing. "If they had anything to do with St. John not appearing."

"Why would you think that?"

"Because," Terrence said, his lips tightening, "they have interfered and contrived in my life since I was a little boy."

"And is that so wrong?" Jezebel asked with a tremor.

His face turned grim. "A man must be permitted to fight his own battles."

"But you did not let me fight mine," Jezebel pointed out. "You wished to duel St. John, when he had insulted me, and it should have been my battle."

"That is different," Terrence said. "You are a woman and I, as a man, should protect you."

"I do not see why it should matter—our genders," Jezebel said, frowning. "If one cares for another, then it is only natural to protect them."

Terrence stilled. "Then my grandmother and aunts did do something to make St. John withdraw?"

"No!" Jezebel flushed. "I can tell you truthfully that . . . not one of them forced St. John to withdraw."

"In truth?" Terrence said.

"In truth," Jezebel replied. Now if he asked if they all had done so, she would be in the suds.

"I am not sure I believe you," Terrence said. "But sooner or later I will find out, I always do."

"Do you?" Jezebel swallowed hard. "And what if you do find out they did something—not that they did, but if they did?"

Terrence studied her and then smiled. "I will do what I always do. I grow very angry and then forgive them. They are family after all, and one cannot help but love them."

Suddenly Jezebel wished she were family, wished with all her heart that Terrence would love her in this way as well. She leaned over and kissed him hard upon the lips.

"What was that for?" Terrence asked, drawing back, a stunned look on his face.

"Because you love your family." Jezebel smiled.

Terrence grinned. "Hmmm, you know I love them greatly."

Jezebel raised her brows. "You do?"

"Yes," Terrence said, nodding. "Even more than that."

"Well, in that case . . ." Jezebel murmured. Chuckling, she leaned over and kissed him once more. Her laughter stilled, however, as the warmth of Terrence's lips stole every thought away, and his arms slipped about her. There was no hesitancy or lightness as he pulled her body to him. It seemed the most natural curve and fit, Jezebel thought hazily as they twisted about and both fell to the ground. The earth didn't feel damp one whit as heat surged through Jezebel. In fact, the crispness of the air mingling with the elusive scent of Terrence was a powerful elixir.

Jezebel moaned as her world spun. She swore she could even hear horns blasting. She kissed Terrence wildly. The horns still blasted. In truth, they came closer, sounding more and more real.

Terrence tore his lips from Jezebel's. "What the devil?"

Jezebel stared up into his perfectly chiseled face. Horns still blared. She blinked. "They're real."

Both sat up, looking around. Jezebel was still passion dazed.

"Oh, Lord," Terrence muttered. Jezebel found herself swiftly and unhappily free of his embrace as he bounded up and shielded his eyes, looking toward the house. "Blast!"

"What?" she stood up unsteadily. A huge coach was bowling down the paved way, coming to a halt with a flourish. A string of magnificent horses, all huge and shiny were in tow, outriders accompanying them. "Heavens."

"Sir Edgar," Terrence muttered. "He's arrived early."

"Sir Edgar?"

"Amelia's father."

"Oh," Jezebel said. Her heart sank to the pit of her stomach.

Terrence took hold of her hand. "He cut his hunting short apparently."

"That or he has a new quarry," Jezebel said softly, glad for Terrence's firm clasp.

"Bedamn, Dorethea," Edgar said as he lowered his weight into a chair. He was a large, blustery man, still with the remnants of bold good looks. His black hair showed only a distinguished amount of graying in it, and his brown eyes held a sportsman's vitality. "Do you know you have a bear in your stables?"

"He's merely a cub," Dorethea said mildly, signaling Stilton to pour a brandy for Edgar and a sherry for her. "So don't think to add him to your trophies."

"Ha," Edgar snorted. "Wouldn't add such a puny specimen to my collection. Thought he would have spooked my cattle, but the little bugger was dancing and making up to them like an Orange Street trollop."

"Letty says he's had a blighted life," Dorethea murmured, taking a sip of her sherry.

"He's an animal for God's sake," Edgar said. "They don't have lives one way or t'other." He smiled to her. "Now, on to business. Your boy Terrence came down heavy in the settlement. Was quite pleased. Quite pleased."

"I am so glad," Dorethea said, and suddenly set her glass down.

Edgar's black brows snapped down. "But I ain't pleased to hear about this here tart he's got in tow. Making a cake out of himself. Even dueling over the trollop."

"So you already heard?"

"News like that travels fast," Edgar rumbled. "Heard it when I racked up for the evening last night." Then he started. "Did the boy come out right this morning? He ain't maimed or dead, is he?"

"No," Dorethea said. "And I thank you for your concern. But no, St. John never showed."

"What!" Edgar's glass almost capsized. "Impossible! St. John's a man of honor for God's sake, man of mettle. Has never withdrawn from a duel in his life. Don't have to, hit his mark in the four he's had."

"It's a mystery," Dorethea said, shaking her head, her eyes wide. "He never showed. And from what I've heard, his servants don't know where he went."

"Too smoky by half," Edgar said, frowning.

"We'll just wait and see," Dorethea said, smiling. "Won't we?"

"Hmmm, yes." Edgar took a long pull of his drink. "But what are we going to do about your grandson's ladybird? He ain't practicing discretion. Heard she and he had London set on its ear."

"Jezebel is an actress," Lady Dorethea said. "She can't help but draw attention."

"Actress, ha." Edgar snorted. "Heard the reviews. She ain't an actress by their account."

"You heard that even at your hunting box?" Lady Dorethea asked. "I did not know you had the amenities of the newspaper there."

Edgar grinned. "Had me a bit of fluff visiting. Now she's

a right fine little actress herself." He frowned. "Strange, said she'd never heard of Jezebel before all this huzzah, and she's been round the theater all her life. But it don't matter. What matters is how we are going to get rid of this Jezebel."

"That is a problem," Dorethea said. "I fear Terrence has developed an attachment to her. A fondness, as it were."

"For a doxy?" Edgar shook his head. "You mean she's a good tumble, ain't nothing more. A noble man don't have feelings for his light-o'-love. You know better than that."

"It is what I thought," Dorethea said, frowning. "But Jezebel is rather . . . uncommon for a common jade."

"Buy her off," Edgar said. "We've got to get rid of her."

"We tried," Dorethea said. "It didn't work."

"Bedamn," Edgar said, a look of shock on his face. "You mean the trollop wouldn't take your money?"

"That is what I mean," Dorethea conceded. "And we offered her a healthy sum."

"Never heard of such," Edgar said, looking appalled. "What's the world coming to when a straw damsel can't be bought off? Don't she have any decency?"

"I fear not." Dorethea's lips twitched. "I fear she may have a tendre for Terrence."

"Well, we've got to do something," Edgar blustered. "It ain't decent, the boy carrying on with her on the eve of his engagement. Mean, he signed the papers right and tight."

"I must confess," Lady Dorethea said. "They were signed in a fit of temper."

"What?"

"I mean," Dorethea said, lowering her gaze. "That Terrence signed them when he was angry at Jezebel and planned to cast her off. Yet he has weakened in his resolve."

"A fine state of affairs," Edgar roared, and rose. He began striding about the room. "I'll have a talk with the boy."

"No!" Lady Dorethea exclaimed. Edgar halted to stare at her. "I mean, Terrence is an honorable man, he will do what is correct. After all, you and I both know this liaison of his with Jezebel will end, while a marriage between Amelia and Terrence will last. He'll come to his senses, but to discuss it with him at this moment, would be unwise—very unwise. In fact, I wouldn't be surprised if he acted like he never even signed the contract."

"Good God!" Edgar exclaimed. "I can't believe it."

"You know how young men are," Dorethea said in soothing tones. "They bolt at the thought of marriage. I am sure Jezebel is a diversion, but if we push the lad before he is ready, we may very well lose him." She looked away. "I can vow that with a certainty."

"You mean we are to stand by while he makes a fool of my little Amelia?" Edgar roared.

Dorethea turned her gaze back on him, her green eyes displaying sympathy. "I fully understand your outrage, Edgar. If you wish to withdraw from the marriage contract I would agree." Silence fell in the room. "In truth, Edgar, it might be for the best after all. I myself can no longer countenance Terrence's cavalier treatment of Amelia, and I can see that it can only cause you outrage, as her father. I am sure we could see Amelia settled with a far better man than Terrence."

"No," Edgar said after another moment. He walked back to his chair and sat down on it. "Let us not be hasty. I mean, after all, the boy is just having his last fling before settling down to his responsibilities."

"I am not sure," Dorethea said. "Jezebel seems very attached to Terrence."

"Well then," Edgar said, frowning, "we'll have to get her unattached. A woman like that can always be bought, one way or another. If she don't have sense enough to take the money, then we'll find another way."

Dorethea raised her brows. "What do you have in mind?"

Edgar suddenly grinned. "It appears the bit has a romantical part to her. All she needs is for her attentions to be drawn away from Terrence to cut him out. Can understand that, the chit won't want to give up a protector without having another in the wings."

"Cut Terrence out?" Dorethea asked, her eyes widening.

"Course." Edgar puffed out his chest. "I have a way with the ladies, don't mind telling you."

The oddest gurgle came from Dorethea. "You mean, you intend to cut Terrence out with Jezebel?"

Edgar glared at her. " 'Course. I ain't going to lose that settlement. Mean, ain't going to have my puss outrun by a fancy piece, no matter how uncommon she is."

Dorethea stared, and then she said in a weak tone, "Very well, Edgar, if that is what you wish. But at any time you wish to withdraw from this contract, you may."

He grinned. "Won't need to withdraw."

"But you must promise me," Dorethea said, eyes narrowing. "That you'll not raise the issue of the contract with Terrence."

"No, of course not," Edgar said, ruffling. "Would be a fool thing to do. Have to free him from his ladybird before he'll come to reason."

"You are so right." Lady Dorethea was smiling. "I always thought you one of the most intelligent of men, Edgar."

" 'Course, 'course," Edgar nodded and stood. "Now don't you worry your little head over all this. I'll take care of it." He walked toward the door.

"Where are you going?" Dorethea asked.

Edgar turned and grinned. "Going to get spruced up. Meet this little Jezebel." He winked and left the room.

"You are a fool, Dorethea," the Duchess muttered, staring after Edgar. "He wants the damn money too much." Then suddenly she grinned and chuckled. "But seeing him try and cut Terrence out should be amusing." She rose and shook her skirts out. "Terrence is by far too complacent about Jezebel. Tsk, why didn't I think about it myself?"

Twelve

"Only two more days until the ball," Letty sighed as she sat in the morning parlor with Dorethea and Theo. Geselda, let from her room since Letty was feeling guilty about her neglect of her dear kitty, rested upon her lap. Letty's fingers stroked the creature's fur furiously. "I am so excited, I can barely contain myself!" Geselda, experiencing that excitement with a pulled hair, yowled an objection. "Oh, I'm sorry, dearest."

"Fear Terrence is a nipfarthing," Theo said gruffly from the other chair. "Mean, the dress Jezebel chose for the ball was cheap. We should talk to the boy."

"No," Dorethea said, smiling "I believe he has enough to contend with at the moment. Therefore I took it upon myself to order a more appropriate gown for Jezebel. It shall be arriving from London this morning."

"Oh, how wonderful!" Letty cried, starting eagerly and upsetting Geselda so much the cat hissed and jumped down from her lap, stalking away stiffly. "I am sure it will far outshine Miss Durham's. Not that Miss Durham isn't a fine seamstress, but she is not aware of the height of fashion as a London seamstress would be."

"To say the least." Dorethea's tone was dry. "I also ordered Elizabeth a gown."

"Best watch that, Dorethea," Theo said. "You'll be sending young Josh farther into the dumps."

Dorethea smiled. "I mean to."

At that moment the door opened and Betty, laden with a large tea service, entered. She brought it over and set it upon the table.

"I fear that young Josh is drinking too much lately." Letty shook her head sadly. " 'Tis not good for the poor boy, I am sure. Even if he is a rake."

"Doubt he's arisen yet this morning." Theo chuckled.

"Thank you, Betty," Dorethea said. "We will serve ourselves."

"Yes, Your Grace." Betty dipped her a quick curtsy. Her blue eyes glowed as she bustled from the room. Dorethea followed her exit contemplatively. "I wonder what the little hussy is up to."

"Hussy?" Letty asked. "Are you talking about Jezebel that way again? For shame. And here I had thought you had grown to like her. You know, I believe our company has been tremendously beneficial to Jezebel. If you notice, her speech has improved and she can upon occasion act like a lady."

"I noticed," Dorethea said. "I was not talking about Jezebel but Betty."

"Betty?" Letty frowned. "Why ever would you talk about Betty?"

"Why?" Theo asked. "Haven't you noticed her twitching her skirts around that boy Josh? Problem is, the boy looks like an angel and the gels can't help themselves."

The door burst open once more, and Edgar Arrowroot, resplendent in yellow jacket and belcher tie, entered.

"Ah, Sir Edgar," Letty said, smiling. "You are just in time for tea."

"No, no," Sir Edgar responded. "Sorry I don't have time. Do any of you know where Jezebel is?"

"I believe," Dorethea said, her eyes twinkling. "She is helping Elizabeth today with the flower arrangements. You might find her in the conservatory. The plants from London have just arrived."

"Ah ha." Sir Edgar rubbed his hands together. "Excellent.

Excellent. I will see you, ladies." He spun on his heel and bolted from the room.

"Might have given Jezebel a breather," Theo grunted. "He's been after her like a hound from hell."

Dorethea laughed. "Edgar always was a sporting man. His tenacity is to be admired."

"Tenacity?" Theo asked. "He's a damn barnacle clinging to Jezebel's hull."

"He intends to replace Terry in Jezebel's affections," Dorethea said.

"Oh, no!" Letty exclaimed, and her nose wrinkled. "Edgar would never suit Jezebel."

"Wonder Terry permits it," Theo grumped. "Best tend to his garden."

"Yes," Dorethea said, with a complacent smile. "But Terry is determined not to be a gardener. Tell me, does Mordrid sleep in Jezebel's room still."

Theo flushed. "He does. But it's understandable now. She saved his life. The dog should be beholden."

"Excellent," Dorethea said, smiling.

"Godmama," a sweet voice called, and Amelia appeared at the door. "Have you seen Terrence?"

"No," Dorethea said. "But I would imagine he is in the stables; I heard he intended to ride this morning."

"Oh?" Amelia frowned. "I asked him last night if he meant to ride, and he said he did not intend to do so."

"He must have changed his mind," Dorethea said with a sweetness.

"Very well," Amelia said, nodding. "I will see." She departed from the room.

"Ha, little Amelia seems to be as tenacious as her father," Theo observed.

Dorethea leaned back with a sigh, a very pleased one. "Yes, I swear I can hear the baying of the hounds."

"Hounds!" Letty squeaked. "Never say so. I do not hear them. Oh, kitty, where are you?"

"Ain't sporting of you, Dorethea," Theo said, frowning, "Ain't sporting of you a'tall."

"I think it is," Dorethea said, laughing. "What a delightful day this should prove to be."

Josh tossed and turned in his bed. Over and over again, Elizabeth slapped him in his dreams.

"No," he muttered. "No."

"Is there anything I can do for you, sir?" a warm, female voice cooed.

Josh frowned. It wasn't Elizabeth's voice. Besides, in his dream, she was just swinging her hand back to deliver another slap.

Josh opened his eyes in confusion. A groan gurgled from him as the brightness of the day blinded his eyes.

"Sir?" that soothing voice murmured again.

Josh's eyes widened. The shapely form of the maid Betty stood very close to the bed.

"What?" Josh scrabbled up. He moaned as his world rocked. "B-Betty, what you doing here?"

"I'm here for your pleasure," Betty said, and she sat down upon the bed, very close to him. "Her Grace said to make you comfortable."

"S-she did?" Josh stammered. Betty was leaning over, her bountiful bosom even closer to him. Alarms shrilled in Josh's aching head, and he scrabbled out of bed. He swayed, his equilibrium objecting, and raised a shaky hand to his eyes. "Ouch!"

"Mr. Rakesham?" Betty asked. "Are you all right? Can I not help you?"

"Er . . . no," Josh said, swallowing hard. "Don't think I need anything right now."

"Are you sure?" Betty rose with a feline litheness. "Perhaps I could help you dress. I see you have no valet."

"No," Josh mumbled. "Don't ah . . . bring one into the country with me."

"Let's see. What would you like to wear?" Betty giggled, and she sashayed over to the wardrobe and swung the door wide. "Which outfit would you like, sir?"

"Don't know," mumbled Josh, trying not to flush.

"I like you in this one," Betty said and pulled out a jacket. "And these." She snatched up his pantaloons. Hugging them close against her chest, Betty strolled over to Josh. She stopped an inch from him and smiled up at him, batting her lashes.

"There you go again," Josh complained, her rapid eye movement befuddling his already fogged brain. "Stop that!"

"Stop what?" Betty breathed out. She diminished the last inch, pressing her full body against his.

"Never mind," Josh gurgled. He stepped back and grabbed the clothes. "Thanks. I can dress from here."

Betty advanced once more. "But you should let me help you." Her hand grabbed his nightshirt at the waist, tugging it up.

"Here now," Josh cried, slapping at her hand. "Stop that. That ain't proper."

Betty giggled. "Do you really want ter be proper?"

"Yes," Josh muttered, pulling his nightshirt down so firmly it snapped his collar buttons. "Elizabeth ain't going to look at me while she thinks me a r-rake." His eyes suddenly bulged. "Elizabeth! Gads! You got to get out of here. If she finds you here—not that she would—won't come near me, but . . . but"—He shook his head—"It still ain't proper." Clutching his clothes as a shield, he pushed Betty away. "You got to go!"

"Here now!" Betty exclaimed.

"You can't be here," Josh said.

Betty began to object. "But—"

"You can't!" Josh shoved his clothes into Betty's hands

and, with his arms free, enveloped her in an encompassing hold.

"Coor," Betty giggled, wiggling. "That's more like it."

"No, it ain't," Josh muttered, and lifting her from her feet, bustled the maid to the door despite her shrieks. "Got to get you out of here." Her feet barely touched the ground as Josh swung her to one arm and jerked open the door. Then he hauled her bodily into the hall. "Before Elizabeth sees—"

"Before Elizabeth sees what?" an angry voice asked.

Josh froze, his arms wrapped around Betty, his clothes a damning muddle in Betty's own grasp. Elizabeth stood before him, outrage in every line of her body. "Ah, Elizabeth. What are you doing here?"

"Certainly not coming to see you," Elizabeth said, her eyes shooting daggers. "I was going to see Jezebel in the conservatory."

Josh blinked and said, "This ain't the conservatory."

"No." Elizabeth's voice was low and furious. "It is merely the hall that I use to go to the conservatory. I am sorry, I was under the impression it was a public hall. Not a private one where you dally with . . . with the maid."

"I ain't dallying with her," Josh yelped. "Betty only wanted to help me dress. But I told her I didn't want her help." He looked desperately to Betty. "Didn't I?"

Betty glared at him and remained silent.

"Didn't I?"

"Of course not," Elizabeth said in a tart voice. "Why should she help you dress, when she evidently helped you undress? The process would be quite redundant."

"She didn't help me undress," Josh cried. "Tell her Betty! We didn't do anything, did we?"

"No, we didn't," Betty spat out.

"See!" Josh said quickly. "Elizabeth, you've got to believe me. I wouldn't do anything with Betty, I swear. Betty, tell her. I wouldn't touch you for the world."

"You bleeding cove," Betty cried, her voice rising to a

shrill pitch. "Why wouldn't you touch me? Ain't I good enough for you?"

" 'Course you're good enough for me," Josh said. "Didn't mean that."

"Then you did touch her!" Elizabeth cried.

"No," Josh exclaimed, frustrated. "I just told you, I didn't."

"And he ain't going to," Betty snapped. She struggled out of his arms and, with one hand, slapped him smartly.

"Blast it," Josh groaned, shaking his head as stars shot before his vision. "Now everyone's slapping me."

"No one treats me that way," Betty said. "Flash cove or not!" Putting her nose into the air, she stomped down the hall, the cuff of his shirt flapping over her arm as if in farewell.

"Betty, come back," Josh cried out in alarm. "You've got my clothes."

"Which you have no need of, I'm sure," Elizabeth said in a silky, lethal tone. "Besides, she should have them by rights."

Josh turned a stunned gaze back to Elizabeth. "Now why should she have my clothes? She ain't going to wear them."

"I meant as a prize," Elizabeth retorted, her hands clenching. "A sweet remembrance of you, you cad."

"I ain't a cad," Josh said, his face clouding. He stepped toward her, gripping her shoulders. "I told you, I didn't touch her."

"And you're not going to touch me," Elizabeth said. She then hauled off and slapped him.

Josh shook his head the second time. "Confound it. You've got to stop slapping me."

"No I don't." Elizabeth pushed past him and stalked down the hall.

"Elizabeth, come back here," Josh ordered, striding after her, rage surging through him with every step. "I want to talk to you."

"Well, I don't want to talk to you," she called over her shoulder and picked up her pace.

"You bloody well are going to talk to me," Josh growled, speeding up his own pace.

Elizabeth glanced hastily over her shoulder. "Stop following me. You're not dressed."

"You said I didn't need to be," Josh said angrily. "Now stop and talk to me."

"No!" Elizabeth broke into a run.

"Yes!" Josh cried out, falling into a lope. "You are going to talk to me and that's that!"

"Terrence, there you are," Amelia called.

Terrence's hand froze as he brushed the horse, and he shivered. Amelia had found him again. It seemed he couldn't escape her these days. He had now fully learned the difference between a thrush, a lark, a swallow, and every other damnable feathered creature in the sky. And Jezebel was no help. She was supposed to be his mistress, but when he saw her she was always accompanied by Edgar. He was growing to abhor the Arrowroot family.

"Yes, here I am," Terrence sighed, turning.

"Godmama said you might be here," Amelia said, smiling and walking into the stables.

"She would," Terrence muttered under his breath.

"Isn't it exciting?" Amelia said. Her brown eyes took on a glow.

"What? Finding me here?" Terrence asked, frowning.

"No, the ball," Amelia said. "It is only two days away." She looked down. "I have a new gown, you know?"

"You do?"

"It was very expensive and is very fine," Amelia said.

"Indeed?" Terrence was rather surprised to hear Amelia be excited over anything but birds.

"Yes." Amelia nodded. "It has embroidered peacocks

upon it, and it is quite dashing. Father said it was far too bright. But the peacocks—"

"Decided you upon it," Terrence said. He should have known better. It was the birds on the gown and not the ball.

Amelia stepped closer, looking up at him with anticipation. "Are you going to ask me to marry you at the ball?"

"What?" Terrence asked, shock coursing through him.

"It would be the perfect time," Amelia said. "And I just know Godmama set the ball for it."

Terrence reined in his temper and said as gently as he could, "No, Amelia, I am not going to ask you to marry me at the ball. I am sorry, but I am not."

"Oh," she said. Then she smiled. "You are waiting for a better time?"

"No," Terrence said. "I am not."

"I'll just wait for you to surprise me then," Amelia said.

"Surprise you?" Terrence asked, drawing out his breath. "I fear I might surprise you, but not in the way you think."

"I do think it would be nice if you would ask me at the ball." Amelia sighed. Oddly enough, she stepped even closer. Unaccountably she turned up her face, closed her eyes, and pursed her lips.

Terrence stared. "What . . . what are you doing?"

Amelia opened her eyes a bit. "I am inviting you to kiss me."

Terrence's heart sank. "I see. I am sorry, but that would not be proper."

Amelia frowned. "Father said I should let you kiss me; it will make you ask me to marry you faster. All you need is a little encouragement."

"I don't need encouragement," Terrence said, with growing irritation. "I am simply not going to marry you."

"Father said you'd say that." Amelia nodded. "But you know you—" She halted suddenly. "Oh, I wasn't supposed to say that."

"Say what?" Terrence asked.

"Nothing," Amelia said, shaking her head. "I am sorry. I know you do not want to talk about it."

"Talk about what?" Terrence asked, exasperated.

"About our marriage and the contract," Amelia said.

"There is no contract, and I am not going to marry you," Terrence said, his temper finally slipping its leash. "That is what I've been trying to tell you all along."

"Yes, of course," Amelia said in a rather unbelieving tone. "Now will you kiss me?"

Terrence stared at Amelia. She looked so very complacent and sure of herself. He narrowed his eyes. The girl clearly needed a lesson in reality.

"You want to be kissed?" Terrence said, smiling grimly. "Very well."

He reached out and hauled Amelia to him. She felt odd in his arms, all bones and stiff angles. He lowered his lips to hers and kissed her. Her lips remained still, cool, and unresponsive. Terrence drew away, stepping hastily back, controlling a sudden chill. "There."

Amelia opened her eyes and blinked. "That was not unpleasant."

"But was it pleasant, Amelia?" Terrence asked sharply. "Did you feel any passion, any warmth?"

"No," Amelia said calmly. "But a lady does not feel those things."

"Some ladies I know do," Terrence protested. He narrowed his eyes. "Do you still want to marry me now?"

"Of course," Amelia said, nodding.

"Why, for God's sake?"

"Because we will be a perfect match." Amelia looked at him as if he were dense. "Our lands march next to each other, our families will benefit from our joining."

"Don't use the word family," Terrence said, shivering at the thought of this female in his bed. "You do not know what it means, so do not use it."

"And we are destined," Amelia continued. "The owl—"

"I don't care about the damn owl," Terrence said. He stared at Amelia. She stood sweetly, looking very much like a true flesh and blood woman. Yet she was but a parody, more calculating and coldhearted than the most hardened jade. Their kiss had sent a fear through him. It had belittled him, making him nothing, for it held no passion or humanity within it and drained him of his.

"I'm going," Terrence said quickly, walking past her.

"Where are you going?" Amelia called.

"To see a lady," Terrence said, having recalled violet eyes that sparked with spirit and lips that, no matter the words or denials upon them, made him feel real and whole.

Jezebel stood, breathing in deeply of the wonderful scent of flowers. The smell was overpowering. The flowers the Duchess had brought in were not only abundant enough to fill one ballroom but two, in Jezebel's opinion. Rosebushes stood in rows, bright with blooms. Smaller potted plants rested upon benches and tables, and large ferns were ranked behind them. She clipped the roses from one bush, placing them in a basket.

"Jezebel, my love," Edgar's voice called. She turned to find him gazing at her with the expression she had come to hate, one of familiarity and disrespect. "Ah, a nymph in the gardens."

Jezebel turned back to the rosebush. "Good morning, Sir Edgar."

"You are the fairest rose here," he said, strolling up to her.

Jezebel swiftly moved away to another bush. "Please do not try to flatter me. I told you, I do not care for your compliments."

"Every woman cares for compliments," Sir Edgar said, grinning.

"Perhaps," Jezebel said in exasperation. "But I do not care to receive them from you."

Sir Edgar frowned. "No, you care for those made to you by Terrence who is betrothed to my daughter."

"He is not betrothed," exclaimed Jezebel.

Edgar waved a hand. "As good as betrothed. He just hasn't announced it. I'm giving the boy time, but I grow impatient."

"You'll grow more impatient," Jezebel said. "Terrence is not going to marry Amelia."

A smug look crossed Edgar's face. "Don't be too certain about that. He's diddling you, my dear."

"Diddling me?" Jezebel asked, enraged.

" 'Course." Edgar nodded. "He's going to marry Amelia, all right, but is holding back on it until he knows he's got you wrapped up all right and tight. Wants you both. Can understand that. But you'd best think. Being a mistress of a married man ain't as good as being mistress to a single man. A married man will neglect you more often. Won't be able to pay as much attention as a sweet morsel like you deserves." He shook his head. "You'd better cut your losses and throw in with me. I'll take care of you."

Jezebel stared, amazed. "Take care of me?"

Edgar nodded. "I'll be a much richer man after Amelia and Terrence are married. I'll be able to buy you anything your little heart desires."

Oddly, Jezebel began to shake. Edgar said it with such certainty it frightened her. "No, I . . . I would never let you take care of me."

Edgar's face darkened. "Why? Terrence is hot for you now, doesn't think he has you under enough control yet, but once he does, he'll marry Amelia like he ought."

Rage suffused Jezebel. "He's not hot for me, but he won't marry Amelia."

"Yes, he will," Edgar said. "But he's got to get weaned from you first. And you've got to get weaned from him."

Lust emboldened him and he stepped quickly toward her. "And I'm just the man to do it."

"Stay back." Jezebel scurried away accidentally knocking into a bench.

"I want you Jezebel," Edgar said, his voice deepening as he advanced. "Leave the boy, it's a losing game. Be sensible."

"S-sensible?" Jezebel snatched up a potted ivy from the bench and held it up in warning. "I won't be sensible if you come near me one more time."

"You'll like my bed better than Terrence's," Edgar said, stretching out his arms invitingly. "Especially when Amelia comes on board."

"No." Red hot rage at his crudity, fueled by a green flame of jealousy, flared through Jezebel, and the pot flew from her fingers.

Edgar ducked and it sailed past him, merely spraying dirt upon him. His eyes glowed, and a disgusting rumble, sounding of passion, came from him. "Gads you're a spirited filly."

"Aren't I?" Jezebel muttered. She grabbed up a geranium pot and sent it sailing. It smacked Edgar in the chest. He roared, but Jezebel didn't halt. She snatched up a good-sized fern and chunked it at him. Edgar, his eyes widening, attempted to catch it, rather than have it hit him undeterred. He succeeded, but the momentum sent him teetering back. He tripped over a rosebush and bellowed a curse as he went crashing down. Jezebel armed herself with another small pot, preparing for Edgar if he should succeed in untangling himself from the shrubberies.

"Jezebel, what are you doing?" Elizabeth cried.

Pot in hand, Jezebel spun around. Elizabeth stood not a foot from her, gazing at her with shocked eyes.

"I'm being a spirited filly," Jezebel said, shaking with rage.

"Elizabeth," Josh roared as he emerged through two large

ferns, his fair face flushed and furious. "I told you we are going to talk."

"We are not," Elizabeth said, her face darkening. "Excuse me, Jezebel." She snatched the pot out of Jezebel's hand before Jezebel could object.

"What ho!" Josh exclaimed as Elizabeth shied it at him. He hopped and ducked looking terribly ridiculous in his nightshirt.

"Josh," Jezebel cried as she noted his attire. "You aren't dressed."

"No," Elizabeth said, snatching up another pot from the bench. "Betty has his clothes!" She sent the pot flying.

"Betty?" Jezebel asked in astonishment, but was distracted when Edgar lumbered up from the rosebushes, twigs and thorns clinging to him.

"You she-devil!" Edgar roared.

"Stop throwing those things!" Josh blasted.

Jezebel turned and grabbed the next pot of zinnias at the same time as Elizabeth.

"Mine I think," Jezebel gasped, for Edgar was charging down upon them, a snorting bull.

"Yes," Elizabeth said and released the pot, grabbing up the daffodils next to it.

"I told you to stay away." Jezebel swiveled and flung the pot at Edgar.

"And I'm not talking to you," Elizabeth said, shooting off her volley.

The zinnias hit Edgar smack in the face, the blooms and pot bouncing off, but the dirt caking on his face, a gloomy mask. "My eyes," Edgar bellowed. "I can't see!"

The daffodils unfortunately hit Josh in a much lower and far more vulnerable place. Shock and pain twisted his face, and he doubled over. "Gads," he wheezed and crumpled to his knees.

"Josh!" Elizabeth cried, stunned.

"Papa!" a new voice called out as Amelia charged through the greenery.

"Jezebel!" Terrence exclaimed as he appeared.

"Oh, Josh, I'm sorry," Elizabeth said, rushing over to him.

"Papa, you're bleeding," Amelia cried, dashing up to him. "And dirty!"

"Jezebel," Terrence said, approaching with a slower pace. "What on earth have you been doing?"

"Practicing my aim," Jezebel wheezed out and stumbled over to him.

"Is that all?" he asked, and enfolded her in a warm embrace. As his chuckle rumbled forth, the tension drained from her.

"Is that all!" roared Edgar, rubbing at his face. "She damn near blinded me!"

"Yes, her beauty can often do that," Terrence said quite calmly.

"Papa," Amelia gasped. "Your nose is bleeding."

"Bedamn!" Edgar growled.

"Josh," Elizabeth cried, kneeling down. "Speak to me."

"S-sorry." Josh was still doubled over and rocking slightly. "Can't."

"Amelia," Terrence said, still holding Jezebel close. "Why not take your father and . . . and clean him up?"

"Oh, yes." Amelia took Edgar by the arm. "Do come with me, Papa." She led him away. Edgar ran into bushes and plants and cursed continually as they went.

"Josh," Elizabeth pleaded, "please talk to me."

"Now you want to talk," Josh said, his face deathly pale.

"I believe we should go to another area," Terrence whispered to Jezebel, pressing her to move.

Jezebel shook her head. "I want to know why Josh is in his nightshirt."

Sighing, Terrence dropped his arms from her and picked up her hand. "And I want to know why you were throwing pots at Edgar." He tugged her along. "Now come."

"Very well," Jezebel said, flushing as he led her through the conservatory on a path away from Josh and Elizabeth.

"Josh, I am sorry," Elizabeth said, and could not help but put her arm around him. She felt complete mortification and guilt as she looked at his pained expression.

"So am I," Josh admitted in a tight, constricted voice. "You don't know how sorry." He blinked and suddenly grinned. " 'Course, now you can't be thinking I'm dallying with Betty, or any other for that matter. At least not for a while."

"What do you mean?" Elizabeth gasped.

He flushed. "Er, never mind."

"No, do tell me," Elizabeth cried. "You don't mean I've maimed you for life?"

"No, no," Josh said quickly. "But it was, ahem, a rather direct hit. Puts a fellow off for a while. But . . . but don't matter, wasn't planning to dally with anyone for a while, after all." His expression sobered. "That's what I was trying to tell you. Didn't do anything with Betty. All I know was I woke up and there she was. Said she wanted to help me dress. Had the devil's own time getting her out the door. Didn't think I did anything to make her come-hither that way, but there you have it."

Elizabeth looked at his earnest face, the golden face of an angel. She sighed. "You don't have to do anything. It's your looks. You're just too attractive."

He brightened. "You think I'm attractive?"

Elizabeth flushed. "Of course. That is why you are a rake, I suppose. Women can't help but throw themselves at you."

"Not you," he said. "You only throw flowerpots."

"Not always," Elizabeth said, looking down.

"Do you mean you forgive me?" Josh asked quickly.

"Yes." Elizabeth nodded.

"Are you still angry about the duel?" Josh persisted.

Elizabeth sighed. It still hurt to know how much he cared for Jezebel and that he would risk his life for the other woman, yet it was impossible not to forgive a man who sat bent over and maimed because of her. "No, I'm not."

"Good," Josh said, smiling. "Then you'll dance with me at the ball?"

Elizabeth looked at him and laughed. "You are unconscionable, but yes, I will dance with you at the ball." He looked so happy a warmth glowed through Elizabeth. To cover her feelings she asked, "Will you be able to rise?"

" 'Course," Josh said. "But only if you help me."

Elizabeth nodded. Sucking in his breath, Josh stood. He quickly put a strong arm around her and pulled her close. "Er, just need a little help."

"Oh, of course," Elizabeth said quickly and circled his waist with her arm. She flushed. Hugging a man with only a nightshirt between them felt scandalously delicious. Together, they walked through the conservatory. Both were silent, but it was a pleasant silence, almost as if they were a long time-married couple who did not need words. Elizabeth bit her lip at that thought. Only when they found the stairs did they encounter difficulties, for Letty was just descending them.

"Oh, my," Letty exclaimed as she saw them. Her faded blue eyes widened. But then she giggled and a hand quickly flew to her mouth. "Oh, my, Mr. Rakesham."

"Er, had a bit of a problem," Josh said. "Betty took my clothes."

"She did?" Letty's eyes sparkled, and her gaze was definitely glued to Josh's tall form. No maidenly blush painted her face. "How frightfully naughty of her."

"Yes," Elizabeth said, giggling herself, for it was Josh who was turning an embarrassed red. "Perhaps Her Grace should have a talk with Betty, don't you think, Miss Letty?"

"Oh, no," Letty said, a dazed smile upon her face.

"What?" Josh asked.

Letty blinked. "Oh, er, I mean we should try and be charitable. I'm sure she means to return them later."

"I don't think so," Elizabeth said. "I will see to that!"

Letty's gaze flew to Elizabeth's. "But Elizabeth, we certainly cannot have Mr. Rakesham remaining in his nightshirt, no matter what a pleasant sight it is." Then she gasped. "Oh, dear, I meant—"

Elizabeth giggled. "I fully understand."

Josh frowned. "I am pleased to amuse you ladies, but I believe I should proceed to my room."

"Yes." Letty nodded. "For you are dirty." Her gaze darted to the area where the most dirt was, and she giggled. "Oh, do forgive me." She moved forward, and Josh and Elizabeth shifted to permit her passage. Her laughter, however, floated back to them.

"Blast," Josh muttered. "Ain't that funny."

Elizabeth stifled her own giggles. "No, of course not."

Terrence drew Jezebel down to a bench amongst the conservatory foliage. He put a protective arm about her. "Now, tell me why you were throwing plants at Edgar. Did he make advances toward you?" His voice roughened and his grip became almost painful.

"No," Jezebel said quickly. "Not . . . not really. He did offer me carte blanche though."

"What! The cad!" Terrence said angrily. "I ought to—"

"No," Jezebel said quickly. "I already did."

Terrence's gray eyes flashed, and then he laughed. "Yes, I believe you did. Faith, was he a sight! But that he dared to even speak to you . . ."

Jezebel looked down. "He's under the impression that I will . . . will need new employment once you are married to Amelia."

"Forsooth," Terrence said. "The man is a bulldog."

Jezebel could not help herself. "Terrence, are you going to marry Amelia?"

His eyes widened. "No, never. Why do you ask?"

"I don't know," Jezebel said, shrugging. "I just wondered if you had changed your mind."

"Gad's no," Terrence said. "Just the thought! Amelia makes me all the more certain I will never marry."

"I see," Jezebel said in a small tone, surprised that his statement hurt. She turned and looked at him. "Terrence you . . . you do not wish to control me, do you?"

"What?" He quickly withdrew his arm from her.

"Edgar thinks you wish to control me," Jezebel said.

Terrence stared. Something passed through his eyes, but then he laughed. "That would be rather impossible, I would imagine. Edgar does not know you."

Jezebel's heart rose in her throat. "You are being honest with me? You don't . . . don't have other intentions than what we planned, do you?"

Terrence stood suddenly. He walked away from her, but then turned. "What intentions do you think I have, Jezebel? Since you are asking, since you clearly don't trust me, what intentions do you think I have?"

"I don't know," Jezebel shook her head. His eyes showed such anger Jezebel realized she must have been insane. Or perhaps, deep down, her intentions and desires for him had changed. Perhaps it was she who was not being honest. She forced a smile. "Forgive me. Edgar, I fear, has rattled me."

He seemed almost relieved. "Of course. I am sorry as well." He reached out a hand. "Let us forget it."

Jezebel nodded and rose. She walked over and put her hand in his. "I'd like that. I fear I was being silly."

Neither looked at the other as they dropped hands and walked quietly from the conservatory.

Thirteen

"They . . . they make such a lovely couple." Letty choked up and sniffed loudly, a tear rolling down her face.

"For goodness' sake," Dorethea said, shifting on her chair as they watched Jezebel and Terrence upon the dance floor. "What are you crying about now?"

"That dress Dorethea designed for Jezebel is fine as five pence," Theo put in. "Ain't a man here who can keep his eyes off of her."

"Especially Terrence." Dorethea chuckled.

"I know, and I wish it weren't so," Letty said, another tear trickling down her cheek. "You will say I am a widgeon and a noddy, but I cannot help it. I don't want Jezebel to be Terry's mistress. I want her to be his wife," she wailed.

The ladies fell silent a moment. Dorethea and Theo exchanged covert glances.

"You are a widgeon, Letty," Theo said gruffly.

Letty's face crumpled. "I'm sorry. But—but I've changed my mind. I . . . I do not think Amelia would be right for Terry. I don't. I don't."

"Do keep it down," Dorethea hissed. "And you are a ninnyhammer. I own it's a perfect coil, and I'm mostly at fault, but there is no sense of you blubbering about it. Oh, Lord," Dorethea groaned as Letty almost shrieked and then stared at her in surprise. "Do you want everyone gawking at us? Drat, Edgar is trying to cut in on Terrence."

The three sisters looked quickly toward the dance floor, all obviously tensing.

"He's in a bad skin tonight," Theo muttered.

"Swilling the champagne as if it was water," Dorethea observed. "Jezebel certainly put his nose out of joint. I wish the girl would behave herself, she makes everything more difficult."

"Now she's turned him away," Theo said, shaking her head. "Fueling the fire."

"Well, she certainly couldn't dance with him," Letty commented. "Not after yesterday."

"Letty," Dorethea said in exasperation, "Amelia is standing over there propping up a wall. Do go and find her a young man to dance with, please."

"Oh, yes, of course. Poor dear." Letty blinked and rose. She wafted away, swerving from one man to another in apparent indecision as to which might be a likely pigeon to pressure into dancing with Amelia, who indeed stood against a wall, resplendent in a green peacock-figured dress, looking like a brown wren borrowing far too brilliant plumage.

Dorethea and Theo sighed and then turned their gazes back to Jezebel, who at the moment laughed up at Terrence as he twirled her in a waltz.

"Red becomes the gel," Theo said.

"I knew it would." Dorethea narrowed her eyes. "If she doesn't have Terrence's heart at her feet tonight, I'll kill the boy."

"She is beautiful, isn't she?" Elizabeth asked softly, looking past Josh's shoulder as he spun her around in the waltz.

"Hmmm? Who?" Josh asked, his blue eyes trained upon her.

Elizabeth flushed. "Jezebel, of course." Josh turned his head to study his sister as she danced with Terrence. Elizabeth gazed at him while he looked at Jezebel, her heart twisting.

"Yes," Josh nodded. "Ain't used to seeing her in red, but since she's supposed to be . . . I mean, since she is . . . er, what she is, I guess it's all right." He turned his gaze back to her, and his blue eyes suddenly glowed. "But I say, it is you who are beautiful."

"Thank you," Elizabeth said, swallowing hard. The way Josh looked at her she could almost believe it. "But not as beautiful as Jezebel."

Josh frowned. "Yes, you are."

"No." Elizabeth laughed, shaking her head. "I am not."

"To me you are," Josh said, and his arms tightened about her.

"You are just saying that." Elizabeth flushed.

"I'm not." Josh's eyes sparked. "Why would I say it if I didn't mean it!"

"Because . . ." Elizabeth dropped her gaze from his. "Because as a . . . well, a rake, I am sure you must feel compelled to say it to all of us ladies, even those of us who are . . . are not beautiful."

"That's it," Josh exclaimed, halting abruptly.

"What is the matter?" Elizabeth asked.

"Tired of you not believing me," Josh said and grabbed up her hand. Elizabeth gasped, but he tugged her along. He dragged her out the doors and onto the balcony. Elizabeth's heart jumped when she noticed their solitude.

"Josh! I don't think—"

She never got out more words, for Josh jerked her into his arms and planted his lips firmly upon hers. She attempted a protest, but the strength of his kiss subdued it. Unable to withstand the swirling dizziness engulfing her, she succumbed happily.

Josh, of a sudden, pulled back. "Do you believe me now?"

"Believe what?" Elizabeth asked, passion dazed.

"That you are beautiful," Josh said, his voice rough. "Now say it!"

Elizabeth blinked. "I'm beautiful?"

"Damn right!" Josh exclaimed. He kissed her again, swiftly and thoroughly. Sensations tingled right down to Elizabeth's toes. He drew back, leaving Elizabeth clutching him for support. "And you're more beautiful than Jezebel. Say it!" Elizabeth shook her head. Josh growled and kissed her again, molding her body to his with a thrilling surety. He drew back again and panted. "Now do you believe me?"

Effervescent bubbles floated in Elizabeth where there once was blood. The sweet, confounding knowledge burst within her. She believed Josh, really believed him. Elizabeth smiled, but said, "I-I'm not sure."

"You will be," Josh threatened and smothered her with another fierce kiss. This time Elizabeth threw her arms around him and returned his kiss with all the fire and happiness she felt. Josh staggered back, groaning. He lifted his head, a strained expression upon his face. "You—you got to believe me soon, Elizabeth. I'm, er, I'm afraid I can't keep doing this without . . . well, just can't handle much more of this."

He was panting heavily. Pure female satisfaction purred through Elizabeth. Taking mercy on him, she said softly, "I believe you now, Josh."

"I ain't as good and proper as I should be." Josh gurgled to a halt, astonishment washing over his face. "What? You believe me?"

Elizabeth nodded. "I do."

Josh's eyes widened. "You mean . . ."

Elizabeth smiled mischievously. "I just liked being convinced."

A silly grin crossed Josh's face. "You did?" His smile widened. "You did!" Suddenly he picked her up off the ground and swung her wildly around. "You did! You liked it!"

"Josh." Elizabeth laughed. "Put me down!"

"You didn't slap me, by Jove," he cried. Suddenly his

face calmed and he set her down. The blue in his eyes turned to dark sapphire. "Elizabeth?"

She stilled. "Yes?"

"I love you," Josh said softly, his voice strained. "I love you."

"What?" Elizabeth asked, her heart racing.

He dropped his arms and stepped away from her. "I . . . I know I shouldn't have said that. You don't approve of me, and I can understand. Ain't as good as I should be for you. Haven't told you everything about me, b-but I can't."

"Josh!" Elizabeth exclaimed, swallowing hard.

"But, damn it, I love you," he said. Without another word, he turned on his heel and walked quickly from the balcony.

Elizabeth stood, gazing after him in shock and yearning. The words in her heart died upon her lips. He hadn't given her a chance to tell him. He had said he loved her and then had walked away before she could even answer!

"He'sh been dancing all the dances with her," Edgar slurred, sprawling in a chair. "He'sh only danced one with my Amelia. See, he's still dancing with that Jezebel! If she weren't hish mistress everyone would think they were engaged, when it'sh my Amelia he's going ta marry. Blast, look at that!"

"Yes, yes, Edgar, we know," Dorethea said, though she did not even glance in the direction in which he'd jabbed his finger, but rather craned her neck to view the balcony door better. "They haven't returned yet?"

"No," Theo said. "Bodes well. Bodes well."

"What the devil are you talking about?" Edgar asked. "It don't b-bode well. Terrence should be dancing with my Amelia."

"But, Sir Edgar," Letty said quickly, her own glance flickering repeatedly toward the balcony doors, "Amelia cannot be dancing with Terrence, she is dancing with that nice

Ellington boy who I . . . er, well, she's dancing with that nice Ellington boy."

"I don't care," Edgar bellowed. "It ain't Ellington she's going to marry. It's Terry, confound it. Something hash to be done."

"All in good time, Edgar, all in good time," Dorethea said. "But at the moment we are concerned about Josh and Elizabeth."

"Look at them," Edgar growled, pointing a finger at Terrence and Jezebel. "All lovey-dovey, billing and cooing. It'sh got to shtop."

"Lud," Dorethea exclaimed, "Josh is entering without Elizabeth."

"Bad sign," Theo said, shaking her head. "Bad sign."

"Do you hear me?" Edgar growled. "It's got to stop."

"Yes, Edgar, and so does everyone else," Dorethea said, without looking at him. "Why the devil did he leave Elizabeth out there?"

"Confound it," Edgar cried. "You ain't listening!"

"For heaven's sake, Edgar," Dorethea snapped, "do go have another drink and stop this."

"I will!" Edgar said, surging to his feet. "Shee if I don't!" He lurched toward the punch bowl.

"At last, here comes Elizabeth," Dorethea murmured.

"Looks like she's been hit over the head," Theo said.

"Oh, dear." Letty's eyes were tearing. "This is not turning out like we planned. Not at all."

"But wait!" Dorethea said. "Terrence is leading Jezebel from the dance floor!"

"Yes, yes." Theo nodded. "About time he did, about time."

"Oh," Letty said, her tears drying. "Perhaps that will be better. Oh, surely it must be!"

* * *

"Heavens, I love to dance," Jezebel sighed as Terrence led her onto the balcony.

" 'Tis clear." Terrence laughed. He gazed at her, his eyes softening. "You are the most beautiful woman here tonight."

"Thank you." Jezebel looked down at her ball dress, a figured red silk cut low upon the shoulders and with a skirt fanning out to whisper with her every movement. "I am still amazed the Duchess gave this to me."

"She is beginning to like you," Terrence said, stepping closer. "But then, who wouldn't grow to like you?"

Jezebel looked down, his closeness disturbing her. She had been in his arms for every waltz, touched hands with him in every country dance, and still it wasn't enough. She wanted to be in his arms once more. "I am certainly beholden to her," Jezebel said. "This is my very first ball, you know?"

"You have handled it with aplomb, my dear," Terrence murmured. "Evidently you were born for them."

"No," Jezebel said, shaking her head. "This is nothing like my life—my real life, that is."

Terrence's eyes darkened. He raised a hand and lightly brushed her cheek. "Perhaps this is your real life instead, perhaps this is what you were meant to be."

"What do you mean?" Jezebel asked softly, her heart skipping for no apparent reason.

Terrence shook his head. "I can't imagine you in that quiet life, in that dark house of your father's with Ruth your only companion, and your only objective to care for Josh." He slid his hand to the back of her neck. "You were meant to shine, Jezebel. To be the belle of the ball—to dance in my arms every night." His hand lightly commanded her to draw near, and he bent his head, his lips brushing hers.

"No," Jezebel said, pushing him back. He'd whispered the secret dream growing like a wildfire within her, and it flicked her on the raw. "This will all end, so do not speak that way."

Pain flashed in Terrence's eyes. "Does it have to end?"

"Of course it must!" Jezebel shoved Terrence away and turned from him, staring out into the dark night. "I-I cannot pretend to be your mistress for the rest of my life." Not when with every new day she grew to wish she really were, to imagine him where Mordrid, her guard dog, lay every night. God help her, she was growing to desire him past all reason or morality.

"No," Terrence said from behind. More pain thrummed within her as he placed his hands on her shoulders and she felt a whisper of a kiss in her hair. "I want it to be real, Jezebel." His voice was dark, tense. "I need it to be real."

Jezebel blinked back sudden tears. She needed it to be love. She needed it to be marriage. "Well," she said, a burning in her throat, "we don't always get what we need."

Terrence's hands gripped her shoulders and he spun her to him. "And what do you need, Jezebel? Can you honestly say you do not care for me, can you honestly say you do not need me as I do you?" He shook his head. "You lie, for you are trembling even now."

"I do not lie," Jezebel said in a ragged voice, "when I say I will not be your mistress. I will be no man's mistress. Someday I will be some man's wife, but I will not be his mistress."

Terrence's hands fell from her. "Some man's wife. Some man's. You talk of another when I talk of you and me!"

"No," Jezebel said, tears stinging her. "I talk of you and me, but when you talk of you and me, we cannot talk of marriage."

Terrence stiffened, his eyes turning dead. "Ah, yes, marriage! Amelia talks of it without even desiring me. You talk the same, without a word of need or want."

"Or love," Jezebel said, choking. " 'Tis another word not mentioned, isn't it, Terrence?"

He jerked as if she had slapped him. "Jezebel . . ." He reached out to her.

She stumbled back. "No, don't touch me. Don't touch me ever again."

Without waiting, she picked up her skirts and dashed past him.

"Lud," Dorethea cried. "Here comes Jezebel."

"Oh, dear," Letty said. "She doesn't look happy."

"And here comes Terrence," Theo observed, "looking like a blasted hang man."

"Drat it," Dorethea said, cracking her fan upon her lap. "What is wrong with these young people? Don't any of them know how to go about love?"

"Evidently not," Theo said as they observed Terrence overtake Jezebel and grab her hand. "He's acting like a coal heaver," she muttered as Jezebel apparently attempted to pull it from his grip and failed.

The music suddenly came to a whining and screeching halt. The dancers on the floor stumbled and faltered, as if caught off guard in a game of musical chairs.

"What now?" Dorethea exclaimed, casting an aggravated glance toward the musicians.

"Gad's hounds," Theo muttered, her gaze skewing over to them.

"Oh, dear," Letty said, jerking in her chair as if struck by lightning.

The hulking, disheveled figure of Edgar Arrowroot stood, or rather swayed, before the silent musicians. He waved a glass, which sloshed champagne in syncopated rhythm.

"Ladiesh and gentlemen," Edgar bellowed, his face red and his tone signaling drunken determination. "I have an announcement ta make. Indeed I do. Thish is a very important occasion."

"No," Dorethea said. "He wouldn't."

"He c-couldn't," Letty squeaked.

"I would like to announsh the engagement of Terrensh, the Marquis of Haversh-sham to my lov-ly daughter, Amelia."

"He did." Theo groaned.

The onlookers broke into an excited murmur. They turned and applauded Terrence, who stood frozen, a stunned expression on his face. Jezebel, whose hand he still held, blanched visibly. She swiftly jerked free of him and ran through the noisy crowd. Terrence didn't move, a frozen statue.

"Speech! Speech!" someone cried out, even as Amelia, beaming a wide smile, lifted her skirts and traipsed toward Terrence from across the ballroom. Edgar could be seen to stumble forward from the other side.

"Speech? Heaven forefend," Dorethea gasped, standing. "Ladies, hurry." Both Letty and Theo sprung out of their chairs, "Theo, you take Edgar. Letty, you take Amelia, and I'll take Terrence."

The crowd silenced slightly, and murmurs replaced the applause as Terrence stood, grim and silent.

Dorethea ungraciously swatted people aside as she marched to stand beside Terrence. " 'Tis surely to be a fine marriage, if it can finally make my grandson speechless."

The crowd laughed loudly, covering a bellow to the left. Dorethea glanced over. Theo had, in her own efficient manner, taken care of Edgar. He lay sprawled upon the floor. Theo was just then pulling back her foot.

Smiling, Dorethea looked to the right. Unfortunately, Letty did not show as much success in her errand. She was jumping up and down before Amelia, slowing, but not halting, the girl's fatuous progress.

"But let us permit the future bride a few words," Dorethea said, waving a hand toward them.

Amelia stopped in her tracks. Her smile fell. A light smattering of applause rose, and Amelia found her smile again. "I-I thank you," she said. "I am glad to share this night with you."

Dorethea did not wait one more moment. She grasped Terrence's sleeve. "I know you are bursting to dress me down. Let us go and do so in private."

"Grandmother," Terrence growled, glaring venom at her.

"In private," Dorethea said, lifting her head imperiously. "We shall not wash our dirty linen in public."

Terrence cursed, but permitted her to draw him along through the throng that listened to Amelia. Dorethea did not hear what Amelia said, but was grateful for whatever it was. She led Terrence into an antechamber and, turning, put her hands on her hips. "All right, fire away."

Terrence closed the door. "I cannot believe you did that."

Dorethea glanced down. "I suppose you wouldn't believe me if I said I didn't plan this."

"No, I wouldn't," Terrence snapped. "You told me from the start you wish me to marry Amelia. You've interfered in and manipulated my life since I was a child, but this time you have gone too far."

The hardness in Terrence's eyes frightened Dorethea. "Terry, I . . . I didn't do it. Edgar did this on his own."

"I don't believe you."

"He did!"

"Very well," Terrence said, his eyes narrowed upon her. "I shall talk to him, then."

"No!" The words were torn from Dorethea. In doing so, Terrence could only discover worse of her.

"Then you lie, Grandmother dearest," Terrence said. "But I already knew that. I could almost forgive you, but what you've done to Jezebel, I cannot."

Dorethea studied him carefully. "What have I done to Jezebel?"

"You gave her that dress tonight," he said softly. "She believed you were starting to like her. But it was only a parting gift, wasn't it? You made her the center of attention, and then embarrassed her by setting up this engagement announcement against my will."

"I embarrassed her?" Dorethea said. "Did I, Terrence? She is your mistress. A mistress should not be embarrassed by what is understood." She shrugged, even as a shiver went through her at Terrence's look. "Buy her a phaeton and pair and she will be appeased."

"Damn you, no!" Terrence roared. "Jezebel is not like that!"

"I know," Dorethea said, nodding her head. "And it confuses me."

Something hidden, agonized flashed through his eyes. "Yes, Jezebel is . . . confusing."

"What are you going to do, Terrence?" Dorethea asked softly. "You balk at marrying Amelia, yet 'tis patently obvious that if you marry her, you can still keep Jezebel as a mistress. And I fear Amelia is the only young lady I know who will accept the arrangement you have with Jezebel. You and Jezebel have made such a byword of yourselves there aren't too many fathers who will consider letting you near their daughters."

"Which is what I want," Terrence said. "I don't want to marry. I don't need to marry."

"Don't you, Terrence?" Dorethea asked angrily. "Has your devil-may-care life really pleased you? Do you truly not need a wife and companion? Or children? Legitimate ones, that is. Do you truly want to go on with Jezebel the way you are?"

Dorethea saw pain streak through Terrence's smoky eyes, but then a barrier dropped and he said with a coldness she had never heard from him before, "I intended to make you disown me, Grandmother, because I thought it was the only way. It never occurred to me it would be I who would disown you, but I will, Grandmother, I will."

"Terrence!" Dorethea cried, stretching out a suddenly trembling hand to him. "No!"

He turned and silently left her. Dorethea dropped her outstretched hand, in a daze. Age, cold and so frighteningly lonely, settled heavily upon her, and for the first time in her life, she slumped. She was nothing but a foolish old woman who could lose her most beloved grandson.

"I want to go home," Jezebel said softly, staring ahead as she sat on the bed in her room. "There isn't any reason to remain here."

"Now, now," Josh said, putting an arm about her and hugging her close. "Can't leave poor Terrence in the lurch."

"Is he in the lurch?" Jezebel asked tightly. "Or is everything happening just the way he wants?"

"What?" Josh exclaimed. "You can't think he really wants to marry that widgeon."

"I-I don't know anymore," Jezebel said, shaking her head as tears burned her eyes. "I just don't know."

Josh's eyes widened. "What are you saying? It was plain as a pikestaff he was bowled over tonight. He didn't expect that confounded announcement."

"No, I suppose not." Jezebel sighed.

"Then why do you want to go home?"

"Because . . ." Jezebel swallowed hard. She couldn't tell Josh that Terrence had asked her to become his mistress in truth, and not pretense. She couldn't bring herself to admit that he also did not love her. The tears finally escaped. "Oh, just because . . ." Jezebel sobbed, and laid her head upon Josh's shoulder.

"Here, here, nothing to cry about," Josh comforted. He patted her shoulder as Jezebel sobbed into his cravat and mangled his jacket with clenched fists. "Please, Jez, don't cry. You know I can't stand it."

There was the softest knock at the door, and it swung wide. Jezebel, shivering, quickly hid her face in Josh's neck. She didn't want anyone to see her crying.

"Elizabeth!" Josh exclaimed. "Thank God you're here. Make Jezebel stop crying."

Jezebel peeked to find Elizabeth gazing at them with the oddest expression. She sniffed and said, "I'm . . . I'm all right."

"No, she ain't," Josh said. "She's crying, and she says she wants me to take her home."

Elizabeth visibly paled, and she smoothed her skirts. "I see. Perhaps I should best leave you two to . . . to discuss it." Sudden tears glistened in her gray eyes and she added, "I-I can understand why . . . why Jezebel w-would wish you to take her home. Excuse me." Turning swiftly, Elizabeth ran from the room.

"What the devil?" Josh said, staring. "Why'd she do that?"

Jezebel pushed herself away from her brother's embrace, fully realizing what their position must have looked like to Elizabeth. "Go to her, Josh, she doesn't understand."

"But . . ." There was fright in Josh's blue eyes. "I-I think she's crying, and you know I ain't good with . . . with crying females." He tugged at his cravat, then quickly withdrew his hand and rubbed it on his satin britches. "Besides, I'm already wet."

"I'm sorry," Jezebel said, her lips twitching even as tears streamed down her face. "But you really should go to Elizabeth, she's mistaken your purpose in being here."

"No, I can't." Josh shook his head and flushed. " 'Fraid I said something to her I shouldn't have."

"Josh," Jezebel said. "What did you say?"

"Can't tell you." His voice was strained. "But now she's crying."

"May I enter?" Dorethea asked. Brother and sister glanced up. The Duchess stood in the door. Her face looked pinched, and her eyes shone suspiciously. "I would like to speak to Jezebel."

"Oh, no," Josh groaned. "You're crying too, ain't you?"

Dorethea sniffed, her chin lifting. "I never cry, young man. Never."

"Looks like you're going to cry to me," Josh said, his tone suspicious.

"Well, I'm not," snapped Dorethea, though her voice sounded perilously watery. "Now, I wish to talk to Jezebel."

"Yes." Josh sprang up, a harried expression on his face. "Will leave you to cry . . . er, mean talk." He shifted awkwardly from foot to foot. "Ain't no place for me when ladies . . ." He halted as Dorethea pinned him with a dark look. "Well, I'll be going." He bowed swiftly and darted from the room.

"Jezebel, I am sorry," Dorethea said and walked over to sit on the bed beside her.

Jezebel tried to hide both her tears and surprise. "Why? This is what you wanted, is it not?"

"Not like this," Dorethea said, shaking her head. "You must believe me, I would never have condoned an announcement in this irregular fashion. And not against Terrence's will. Edgar did it all by himself."

Jezebel studied Dorethea's tight, drawn face. "I believe you."

Dorethea reached out and clasped Jezebel's hand, causing her to start. "Terrence says he will . . . disown me."

Dorethea's grip tightened and Jezebel said, "I don't believe he will actually do that."

"No." Dorethea shook her head. "He will. I've done a terrible thing."

"I cannot say you haven't," Jezebel said softly, but in kinder tones than she ever imagined she would.

"No." Dorethea choked out the word. "You don't understand, I've done a truly terrible thing."

"Now, now," Jezebel soothed, for a tear slipped down Dorethea's face. "Trying to force Terrence into this marriage was unconscionable, but—"

"I forged Terrence's name to the marriage contract," Dorethea said, her voice low.

"I am sure you meant well— What?" Jezebel gasped. Then she gaped at Dorethea. "You . . . you . . . oh, my!"

Dorethea visibly shivered. "I was insane. I . . . I don't know what I was thinking, but it was before I had come to know you and I was truly frightened you were a Jezebel, and . . . and I forged Terrence's name to the contract. That is why Edgar arrived so quickly, and that is why this evening he thought he had the right to announce the engagement."

"Oh, my Lord," Jezebel breathed out.

Dorethea's face twisted. "Terry will never forgive me. I have ruined his life. Whatever shall I do?"

"Do? You must tell Terrence," Jezebel said. "He doesn't understand. I didn't understand. You must tell him."

"No," Dorethea said. She stood up swiftly, twisting her hands. "I can't. It is not just the scandal which would be created." She looked at Jezebel with hollow eyes. "Terrence, for all his easy ways, is a man of honor. I'm afraid he will marry Amelia to protect me. He . . . he will never let it be known to the world that I was a forger."

Jezebel paled. "You are right."

"I had counted upon it," Dorethea said. "And now I do not know how to change it. Terrence will marry Amelia to protect me, but he will never forgive me. I will lose him. And I-I cannot bear the thought." Tears slowly slipped down her face. "I cannot."

"Don't cry," Jezebel said, rising to go to Dorethea. "Somehow we will overcome this. I don't know how, but somehow we must."

Dorethea looked at her, stunned. "You will help me?"

Jezebel nodded. "I can understand how . . . how you do not wish to lose Terrence."

A small, wan smile crossed Dorethea's lips. "I believe you are very good for Terry." Then she frowned. "But I believe you should legitimize the relationship."

Jezebel stared. "What do you mean?"

"I mean, you should marry him," Dorethea said, sounding

more like herself. "You can't be his mistress all your life. Children need a name."

Jezebel flushed and looked down. "There will not be any children, and we will never marry." She looked up and caught a fleeting expression upon Dorethea's face. "Duchess, you must swear you will not do anything to contrive to get us married"

"I don't know what you mean," Dorethea said, lifting her chin.

"You know very well what I mean," Jezebel said. "You must swear it, or else I will not help you with Terry."

Dorethea's face paled. "I do not see—"

"Swear it!" Jezebel said curtly.

Dorethea's eyes narrowed. "And what would it matter if I swore it? You are talking to a woman who . . . who forged her grandson's name to a marriage contract. Would you honestly believe me if I swore it?"

Jezebel nodded grimly. "Yes, I would. So swear it."

Dorethea glared at her. "Very well, I swear I shall not contrive in your behalf."

Jezebel sighed in relief. "Thank you." She suddenly felt bone weary. "Now, I believe we should both retire. Do not worry, I will think of something."

"Yes," Dorethea said, looking far better. "You are right, perhaps there is a way out of this tangle after all."

Fourteen

"Terrence, may I come in?" Jezebel's voice came from the other side of his bedroom door.

Terrence stood silent, staring down into the weak, flickering flames in the fireplace. Unlike those mild flames, rage and caged fury blazed high within him.

"No, Jezebel." His fist clenched. "Not tonight."

"I must talk to you," Jezebel called.

He did not need to turn to know she had opened the door and entered. He could feel her presence in every fiber of his being. "Aren't you afraid I shall pounce on you and maul you?"

"No," Jezebel said softly.

"You shouldn't be here," Terrence said. "I am an engaged man, after all."

"What are we going to do?"

"Do?" Terrence spun about. Jezebel had moved to sit in the chair, her red skirts billowing about her. Her blond hair shimmered in the firelight, and its glow warmed her smooth skin. Her beauty wrenched at Terrence. It was a beauty he could not touch. "We shall leave tomorrow."

Jezebel shook her head slightly. Her calmness fueled Terrence's rage. "You cannot do that."

"Very well," Terrence growled. "I will kill Edgar Arrowroot first, and then we shall leave."

The slightest smile tipped her lips. "Leaving his corpse for the Duchess to dispose of, I presume?"

Terrence waved a hand even as a smile was drawn from him. "It would only be fitting. 'Tis her imbroglio, she should be forced to clean up after it."

Jezebel shook her head. "You know you cannot do that."

"Can't I?" Terrence asked, anger reclaiming him. "Just watch. Edgar and Dorethea think to force me to marry Amelia, but they'll have a difficult time of it when the groom has walked out on them."

He saw Jezebel's hands twist in her lap. She was not as calm as she pretended. "I do not think that is the best way to go about it. I think you should accept the marriage."

"What?"

"I mean, pretend to accept it," she said.

Terrence clenched his jaw. "I believe I've pretended enough. As I told you, I grow weary of it."

A flush rose to Jezebel's face. "Edgar has already announced your marriage. You cannot act as if it did not happen."

"Why not?" Terrence retorted. "He did so without permission or agreement, and I assure you, I do not care if I tell the world so."

"No!" Jezebel said quickly. "I mean, why not pretend to accept it for a while . . . and then make Amelia cry off."

"Amelia cry off?" Terrence asked. He snorted. "She'd not cry off if I were the Hunchback of Notre Dame."

"We can try," Jezebel said.

Terrence studied her. He could read tension in her every line. "Why do you want to do this?" He walked toward her, and she shifted back in her chair. "If we leave tomorrow you can be shed of me, isn't that what you want?" Jezebel remained silent. "Well, isn't that what you want?"

"Yes," she said, looking down. "I believe it would be the wisest."

"Then why do you—?"

"Because you cannot run away," Jezebel said, looking up, a desperation in her gaze. "We've come to this point, and no matter what, you should settle it now. We did not stop the Duchess, we did not stop Sir Edgar, but let us stop Amelia. If we make her realize she is engaged to a monster—"

"How kind," Terrence murmured.

"Yes, kind," Jezebel shot back. "Because if we make her finally cry off, you will be free. We need her on our side, rather than theirs. After all, it is only right, since she is the interested party."

"You mean the uninteresting party," Terrence said. "And don't you think I haven't tried that already? But ever since she saw that damn owl, she is certain we are destined to marry." He closed his eyes and said wearily, "Faith, to be shackled because some blind, idiot owl flew past me. She'll even suffer my kisses for that damn bird."

"Your kisses," Jezebel asked, her voice sharp. "You've kissed her?"

Terrence opened his eyes to see Jezebel sitting poker-straight in the chair. With an unworthy desire to hurt her as he hurt, he bent and placed his hands upon both sides of the chair. "Yes, I have. She said—"

"I don't need to hear what she said," Jezebel retorted, her eyes flashing.

"She said it was"—Terrence grinned cruelly and continued—"Was wonderful and earthshaking."

"Don't!" Jezebel paled.

Self-loathing filled Terrence and he jerked up, striding away from her. "She said it was not . . . unpleasant."

"Not unpleasant!" Jezebel gasped.

Terrence turned to see her gaping at him with astonished eyes. He smiled. "Which for Amelia is earthshaking no doubt. A lady does not need to feel passion, she need only marry."

Jezebel looked away. "I see."

"I had no doubt you would," Terrence said softly.

Jezebel's eyes flashed back to him in hurt and anger. She

stood abruptly. "We shall simply have to redouble our efforts and concentrate upon Amelia."

"We?" Terrence murmured. "You mean you and me?"

"Y-yes," Jezebel said, her voice but a whisper.

Terrence walked toward her, drawn like a magnet. "Why are you doing this?"

"What do you mean?"

He stood before her, aching to touch her. "Somehow I thought you would wish to leave."

"I'm not going to," Jezebel said. "Y-you will need me to help you w-with Amelia."

"Yes, I will need you. . . ." Terrence lifted a hand toward her face. Jezebel hastily stepped back. He dropped the hand quickly. ". . . To help me with Amelia."

Jezebel's smile was weak. "I think if we show her that her destiny is not as convenient as she thinks, she'll forget the owl. W-we simply must find her true desire and use it against her."

"She has no desire," Terrence said, and then laughed bitterly. "And if it requires any more kissing, you'll have to do it, because I'll not kiss Amelia again."

Jezebel stiffened. "Surely not." She seemed to shake herself, and then said, "I-I want you to understand that though I am willing to help, that is the only r-reason I am remaining. I do not wish you to think there is another reason."

"Of course not," Terrence said sharply. "You have stated the rules very clearly. I am not to touch you, I am not to kiss you."

"Yes," Jezebel said, looking away. "That is it. We will do what it is required t-to change Amelia's mind, but—"

"You will not change yours," Terrence said, anger tightening his voice. "No need to belabor the point, my dear. What we do will only be for the good of the cause, correct?"

Jezebel lifted dark eyes to him, an elusive emotion banked and hidden within their depths. "Correct. It will be for only one purpose and one purpose alone."

* * *

"When do you want the wedding to be, Terry-berry?" Jezebel asked in the broadest accent she could muster. She held a pen poised over a sheaf of paper as she sat at a round table, Amelia on her left and Terrence on her right.

Terrence shrugged, leaning back. "Whenever you two ladies decide to have it. It is of no moment to me."

"Ain't that just like a man," Jezebel said, winking at Amelia. "Always leaving the work to us women." She reached over and patted Amelia's hand. "Don't worry, ducky. I know all about weddings. Helped one of my, er, gentlemen with his. Everyone said it turned out right beautiful. 'Course the bride was busting the seams of her wedding dress. She was five months pregnant. I told him his bride should be wearing red, but he didn't see none of the humor in it." Jezebel brayed. "But you don't have to worry about that, do you, Amelia?"

Amelia gasped. "No, of course not."

"Best watch it after the wedding," Jezebel said. "My Terry, I mean our Terry, is a randy one. He'll have you big with child before you can blink."

Amelia did, indeed, blink. Then her eyes widened and she glanced at Terrence with a look akin to fright.

He grinned. "Now Jezebel, you two can have your girl talk when I'm not around."

"That's right," Jezebel said, and lowered her voice to conspiratorial tones. "Later I can tell you all his particulars . . . and peculiars."

"P-peculiars?" Amelia asked.

"Well, love"—Jezebel laughed—"You know the men. They all have their own little likes and dislikes. Now Terry, he don't have any nasty peculiarities—only naughty. So don't you worry none." She pretended to scratch on the paper. "Here, I'll write them down for you and you can study this."

"No!" Amelia said. "I . . . I don't think that will be necessary."

"We are straying from the subject at hand Jezebel," Terrence said. His mouth twitched slightly, but his expression remained solemn.

"Oh, yes," Jezebel said. Then she giggled. "But you know, love, I always stray to the subject I like the most." She turned a serious look upon Amelia. "I think we should have the wedding within the month. Mean, let's tie the knot fast and then we all can settle down cozylike."

"A-a month?" Amelia stammered. "Do you really think we . . . I mean, Terrence and I, should marry that fast?"

" 'Course, get done with all the pomp and ceremony, is what I say." She rapped Amelia's arm. "Besides, you won't be enjoying those connubial rights until you're leg-shackled. My Terry, I mean our Terry, is an honorable man, he is."

"Of course." Amelia nodded.

"Know you're impatient to get him under the covers," Jezebel said. "But there you have it. Have to wait a little longer."

Amelia blushed. "I . . . I believe I can wait that long."

"Oh, and the honeymoon!" Jezebel squealed. "Where should we go for the honeymoon?"

"I want to go to France," Amelia said, brightening. "There are birds that migrate there, and I've always wanted to study them."

Jezebel pulled a pout. "But I want to go to . . . to Greece. I've always wanted to go to Greece."

"Greece?" Amelia's face darkened. "I wish to go to France." Then her face lightened. "But there are some very learned scholars in Greece." She looked to Terrence. "Perhaps we could go to France and Greece both."

Terrence stiffened slightly. "I don't know."

"Please," Amelia said. " 'Twould be delightful." She turned imploring eyes to Jezebel. "Jezebel, do tell him that is what we want."

Jezebel gulped, feeling as if she had suddenly lost the advantage. Amelia's face, which had been dark and worried before, was now eager and bright. "Er, certainly. Terry, love, don't you think we could do both?"

Terrence's brows lifted, and it was clear he was nonplused. Then he grinned, a grin which Jezebel had come to know well. He intended some deviltry. A shiver ran through Jezebel, for that particular light in his eye had a tendency to make her knees weak. "I might be able to be persuaded."

Amelia, clearly oblivious to Terrence's mood said, "Oh, please, do say we shall."

"If Jezebel wants it," Terrence murmured and reached over to clasp her hand. Jezebel jerked it back, but he held on tightly. He picked it up and brushed it with his lips. "Anything for my sweets."

Jezebel, swallowing hard, glanced to Amelia. The girl only smiled. "Oh, I can hardly wait. Now where shall we stay? I know Papa spoke of a villa there. Perhaps we could rent it." She frowned, tapping the pencil. "Now what was the name of it?"

Terrence's lips hovered, grazing the back of Jezebel's hand. A curl of heat passed through Jezebel, and she bolted to a stand. "Amelia!"

Amelia looked up from her brown study. "What?"

Jezebel gaped at the girl as Terrence proceeded to nibble her thumb. "D-don't you . . . don't you n-notice anything w-wrong?"

"Wrong?" Amelia gazed at them. "What is wrong?"

"What Jezebel is asking," Terrence said, lifting his head and smiling, "is what will be the room arrangements?"

"Room arrangements?" Amelia frowned.

"Yes," Terrence said. "She wants to make certain there are plenty of rooms. She is partial to suites, in truth." He looked wickedly at her. "She says she does not trust herself to sleep safely without . . . knowing where I am."

"Oh, I see." Amelia nodded. "Well, I am certain there

are plenty of different rooms. But I will remember to ask Papa." She bent her head and scratched down a note.

"Her suite should be close to ours," Terrence said, and scooting back his chair, he tugged upon Jezebel's hand. She shook her head vehemently, but he relentlessly drew her to him. He swiftly toppled her onto his lap. "Very close."

"Terrence!" Jezebel hissed as he wrapped his arms about her.

"All for the cause, dear," Terrence whispered, nuzzling her neck.

"C-cause?" Jezebel stammered. She looked hastily over to "the cause" who still scribbled upon the paper with nary a glance to them, and groaned. "S—she can't be real."

" 'Fraid she is," Terrence murmured, his breath soft upon her ear.

"I have just bethought myself of all the different birds that inhabit the south of France," Amelia said. "I am writing them down, lest I forget them."

"Are there owls in France?" Terrence asked, his tone dry.

"Indeed, yes," Amelia said.

"Do not forget to write them down." Terrence's gaze deepened, and Jezebel's heart thundered an overture as it settled upon her lips. She licked them nervously. Terrence, smiling slightly, leaned over to kiss her.

Jezebel turned her head just in time. "Don't!"

"For the cause, Jezebel," Terrence murmured, brushing her cheek with his lips.

"For the cause, indeed," Jezebel said, shoving at him. Sudden anger mingled with her embarrassing desire. Terrence was toying with her, throwing her words back at her with a vengeance. She drew in a deep ragged breath and looked to Amelia, who still wrote upon the page. If this continued, Terrence could have her totally seduced before Amelia had scripted but a third of the birds in the south of France. "Amelia!"

"Yes?" Amelia asked, looking up without a mar to ruin

her brow. Jezebel's anger surged higher. It appeared she was the only one discomfited, and she'd not have it. "Here, ducky, you've got me feeling like a lazy one, sitting here while you do all the writing." She cast a challenging look at Terrence. "Why don't we trade places?"

"Jezebel," Terrence said, his arms tensing around her.

"Yes, Amelia"—Jezebel smiled, her eyes narrowed— "You come and have this comfy place on Terry's lap, and I'll do the writing."

"What?" Amelia asked. Her face was not so calm now.

" 'Course, dearie," Jezebel said, smiling with grim satisfaction. "Share the spoils, what? Or should I say the spoiled."

"Oh, ah," Amelia said, paling. "I-I don't think that . . . that would be proper."

"Terry don't need proper," Jezebel said, glaring at him. "So don't you fret yourself to flinders over that, love. Fact, he's got room for both of us, don't you, Terry-berry?"

"Do I?" Terrence gritted.

" 'Course you do," Jezebel purred. "Any girl sitting on your lap ought to know that. It ain't as if it can be a permanent position or anything." She skewered her head around and caught a stunned expression upon Amelia's face. "Come on board, Amelia."

Amelia rose to her feet with a twitch. "No, I do not think ladies do such."

"Sure they do," Jezebel cooed. "If they're around Terry, that is. And since you're getting leg-shackled to him you might as well get comfortable with it now."

"I-I cannot," Amelia stammered.

"You mean until after the wedding," Jezebel said.

"Y-yes," Amelia said. "I-I mean until after the wedding." She spun on her heel and scurried toward the door.

"Where you going?" Jezebel called.

"I'm going to see Papa about the villa," Amelia mumbled and disappeared.

"There," Jezebel said angrily, shoving at Terrence. "Now let me go!"

"With pleasure," Terrence said in a rough tone. He loosened his arms so fast that Jezebel lost her balance and toppled from his lap to the floor. He stood swiftly, glaring down. "In the future, please remember that it is my choice whom I invite upon my lap."

"It was all for the cause," Jezebel said nastily, scrabbling up and dusting herself off.

"No, it wasn't," Terrence bit out. "You were not doing that for Amelia's benefit."

"Neither was what you were doing!" Jezebel said angrily. "I told you before, I do not want you to touch me, and don't you think you can do it under any other guise."

"Indeed, madame," Terrence said, stiffening, "after this fine display, I assure you, I shall not be so unwise as to consider it again."

He turned on his heel and stalked from the room. Jezebel could almost feel the rage he left behind. It circled her heart like a dark, enveloping cloak.

Josh peeked into the parlor. Elizabeth sat quietly upon the settee, sewing on a sampler. He had finally run her to ground. He drew in a steadying breath. "Er, hello!"

Elizabeth looked up and then just as swiftly down. "Hello."

Josh halted, feeling at a loss. "Do you mind if I sit down?"

"You may do anything you wish," Elizabeth said in a cool tone.

What Josh wished to do was not something he thought Elizabeth would care to lend herself toward. "Er, thank you." He walked stiffly over to a chair and sat. Elizabeth did not look at him, her head bent over her stitching. Josh cleared his throat. "Ahem, about last night—"

"We need not discuss last night," Elizabeth said in clipped tones.

"W-we don't?" Josh asked, nonplused.

"No, we don't," Elizabeth said.

"B-but I said something"—Josh gulped—"Well, that w-we should talk about."

"No, Mr. Rakesham." Elizabeth finally looked at him, defiantly. "We do not need to talk. 'Tis clear what you said to me was . . . was of no importance."

"No importance!" Josh sat bolt upright in his chair. "But I said I loved you! That ain't important?"

"Not when I discover you holding another woman immediately afterward," Elizabeth said, and slammed her sewing down. She stood swiftly. "A woman who is your . . . ex-lover and whom you still love."

Josh sprung up. "You mean Jezebel?"

Elizabeth's hands curled into balled fists. "Of course I mean Jezebel, or were you also hugging another woman last night?"

"'Course not," Josh said, and then flushed. "Well, you of course."

"Yes, me of course," Elizabeth said, stepping angrily toward him. Josh pedaled back, his wary eyes upon her clenched fists "Well, do omit me from this charming threesome."

"I don't want to omit you," Josh cried.

Elizabeth's eyes shot fire. "You beast! Why don't you just leave? Take your beloved Jezebel home and get out of my life!"

"Jezebel isn't my beloved," Josh groaned. "She's my sister . . . I mean I think of her like a sister."

"Both of you hold to the same story very well," Elizabeth said. "But I am not fooled."

Anger rushed through Josh. "Yes, you are, blast it. That's what's the matter. You've got to believe me when I say I'm not in love with Jezebel, 'twould be ridiculous and—and damn impossible. I love you, confound it. Last night I was only consoling Jez, nothing more!"

Elizabeth lifted her head defiantly. "Then let her console you this morning, for I most certainly shall not."

"Fiend seize it," Josh exclaimed, shaking with impotent rage. "I said I loved you last night, that ought to mean something!"

"Yes, it does," Elizabeth said. "It means you are a womanizing, lying cad."

"No, I ain't!" Josh thundered. He stormed up to her and clasped her shoulders. "You don't believe that, you can't." He shook her slightly. "Now tell me the truth!"

Elizabeth looked up at him, her eyes widening. "Wh-what do you mean?"

Josh swallowed hard. "I want to know if you love me."

Elizabeth's eyes widened. "You dare to ask me that?"

"Yes," Josh said, flushing. "F-forgot to ask it last night."

Sudden tears welled in Elizabeth's eyes, and she said with a catch in her voice, "Y-you ask me that now?"

"Er, yes?" Josh said, but his hands fell from her shoulders. A glistening tear slid down Elizabeth's cheek, and he groaned. "But . . . but you don't have to cry about it. Please don't cry."

Elizabeth dashed the tear away and said with a sniff, "I can't believe you asked me that now, when . . . when . . ." She choked up and didn't speak.

"Don't cry," Josh stammered. Yet Elizabeth stood, shoulders shaking, head bowed. "Here now." He swiftly turned his cheek toward her. "Why don't you slap me?" He patted it. "It will make you feel better."

"No," Elizabeth sobbed. "No, it won't."

Josh straightened, anguish ripping through him. "But what do you want me to do?"

Elizabeth lifted her tearstained face. "I'll tell you. I want you to never, ever speak to me again and n-never a-ask me th-that q-question."

Josh blanched. "But—but I'd rather have you slap me!"

"No," Elizabeth wailed. Turning, she dashed from the room.

Jezebel sat on the bed in her room and stared into space. The scene between Terrence and her played round and round in her head. Mortification heated Jezebel. The simple truth was, she loved Terrence, and even when it was to be merely an act, she lost control.

A scratch at the door pulled her from her unpleasant reverie. She knew it well. Standing, she went and opened the door. "Well, what are you doing here?" she asked, gazing down at Mordrid. "You are usually with Theo at this time."

Mordrid cocked his head. Then he barked and barked again. He immediately turned his bushy tale and padded away. Surprised, Jezebel followed him.

"Where are we going?" she asked Mordrid as he doggedly led her through the different corridors of the left wing. He halted at a closed door and whined. Clearly he wished for her to open it for him. "What, you couldn't have found a footman for this?"

Shaking her head, Jezebel nevertheless opened the door. Glancing in, she froze. The room looked like a cyclone had whipped through it. Clothes were strewn about, the bedding tossed, and papers littered the Aubusson carpet.

In the middle of the unholy destruction Letty could be found with her head in an armoire, while Dorethea tossed letters from an escritoire, and Theo thwacked a cane with vengeful wallops upon the bed's mattress.

"What on earth are you doing?" Jezebel exclaimed.

"Eeks," squeaked Letty, and tumbled out of the armoire.

"Huh?" Theo said, her cane freezing in midair.

"Oh, Jezebel." Dorethea let a sheaf of papers slip from her fingers. "Thank heaven it is you. We'd be in a devil of a coil if it was Edgar."

"This is his room?" Jezebel exclaimed, stepping in and quickly moving to close the door. She almost caught poor Mordrid's tail as he scooted through the gap. "But what are you doing?"

"Dorethea told us about the marriage contract, and we are trying to find it," Letty said from her sprawled position on the floor.

"Get rid of the evidence." Theo nodded.

"And it's nowhere to be found." Dorethea's green eyes shone with indignation. "What kind of man doesn't leave a contract in his room where we can find it? I am growing to detest Edgar immensely. Why Theresa ever married him is beyond me. I told her not to marry the clod, but she would have him."

"Sweet Theresa." Letty sighed. "She was such a dear. But Edgar is another matter. And Amelia, I am sorry to say, is—"

"Is a bird of the same feather," Dorethea said. "Now, where haven't we looked?"

"Don't you think you should stop?" Jezebel looked about nervously. "Aren't you afraid Edgar will return before you can, er, tidy the room?"

"I sent him to the village for some thread," Dorethea explained. Then she snorted. "If I know Edgar, he'll stop by the tavern and won't be home for hours."

Suddenly Mordrid growled and paced to the door. The women were silenced. Voices sounded from the distance. Tiptoeing to the door, Jezebel cracked it open slightly. "Oh, Lord," she breathed out. Edgar and Betty, the maid, were strolling down the hall. Jezebel snapped the door shut. "Hide! Edgar is coming!"

With a muffled squeak, Letty scrabbled up and dove into the armoire. Cursing, Theo dropped to the floor and worked to squeeze herself underneath the bed. Dorethea sprang up and darted to the ruby red curtains, swishing behind them.

Jezebel stood there, amazed. For three old women they proved to be spectacularly spry.

"Oh, God," Theo suddenly grunted. "I'm stuck!"

"No," Jezebel breathed out. Theo was wedged halfway under the bed. Thinking quickly she said, "Mordrid, guard the door!" She pointed at it. "Guard!"

Then she bolted over and bent to tug at Theo. The older lady was as stuck as a spike driven into wood. "Oh, never mind," Jezebel gasped. She snatched up the tousled counterpane and flung it over Theo. "You'll just have to stay that way."

The door cracked open. Mordrid howled and flung his large body against it.

"What the devil!" Edgar bellowed from the other side.

"Jez, help!" Letty whispered. One hand flailed from the armoire whose door stood open. Jezebel darted across, almost skidding on the papers littering the floor, and slammed the armoire door shut.

The doorknob rattled, and Mordrid howled loudly again, having sat his big body down against the door. Edgar boomed, "Mordrid! Let me in you mangy cur!"

Jez looked swiftly around. Dorethea's wide skirts still showed from the curtains. "Hold him, Mordrid," she hissed. She dashed over and pulled the curtain well nigh from its valance as she covered the telltale skirt. "Next time wear the empire style, would you?" she muttered.

"Never," Dorethea's muffled voice shot back.

Jezebel sidled away from the drastically lumpy curtain and drew in a sharp breath. "All right, Mordrid. Come here!"

Mordrid yapped, bounded up, and trotted to her. The door, with its canine stop gone, burst open and Edgar tumbled into the room. He straightened. "Beda—" His eyes widened. "Bedamn!"

Betty peeked behind him. "Lord love a duck!"

"Hello," Jezebel said, striving for sangfroid.

"What happened here?" Edgar said.

"What are you doing here?" Betty asked.

"I'm . . . I'm . . ." Jezebel stammered. Mordrid growled, and she swiftly grabbed for his collar. "That's it! I mean . . . it was Mordrid. I-I came for Mordrid." It wasn't a complete lie. "I fear"—She flushed as she gazed around at the shambles—"I fear Mordrid was terribly naughty."

"The beast did all this?" Edgar asked. "I'll hide him to within an inch of his life."

The bedding stirred. "No!" Jezebel cried and swiftly jumped forward, attempting to block Edgar's view. "No! It wasn't just Mordrid!"

"Then who?" Edgar shouted, his face darkening to a plum hue.

"Ahem . . ." Jezebel thought furiously. "Geselda." A muffled thump came from the armoire. "Yes, yes. I will say it," Jezebel said, clapping loudly. Edgar and Betty looked at her as if she were cracked. "I must. Mordrid was chasing Geselda. He does on occasion, you know? I saw the two, but . . . but could not stop them when they ran in here."

"Those two animals did all this?" Edgar asked, his face astonished.

"They—they can be very, er . . . rambunctious," Jezebel said, rather weakly.

"Gor, they tore this place ta pieces," Betty said, stepping cautiously into the room. She reached down and picked up a jacket. "It will take all day to clean this up."

"No!" Jezebel cried as Betty walked toward the bed. "Leave it!"

"What?" Betty gasped, halting and gaping at her.

"I mean," Jezebel said, looking quickly to Edgar, "since I'm here, I would like to . . . to talk to Edgar." She narrowed her eyes and glared at Betty. She had a suspicion that the maid was the reason for Edgar's early, unwanted arrival. "Alone, if you please."

Betty flushed and turned to Edgar. "Sir Arrowroot, oughtn't

I to remain here?" She smiled broadly. "Help you make up the bed?"

"You can help him make up the bed later," Jezebel snapped. She turned and plastered just as fetching a smile on her lips as on Betty's. "That is, if Sir Arrowroot wishes it after I've finished 'talking' with him."

Edgar's anger disappeared in a flash. He puffed out his chest. "Yes, yes, Betty, we can talk later. I would like to hear what Jezebel has to say to me."

"Well!" Betty huffed. "I like that!"

"I'm sure you do," Jezebel cooed. Betty glared at her and stomped toward the door. "And do leave Sir Edgar's clothes. I know what a penchant you have for leaving the poor fellows without them." Betty glared and tossed the jacket at Edgar. She swished from the room.

"Hmmm," Edgar said, smiling. He swiftly dropped the jacket and stepped toward her. "Now what did you want to talk to me about, my beauty."

"I realized that I was terribly naughty to—to throw the flowerpots at you. And I . . . I apologize. I find I was much too hasty in—in refusing your offer," Jezebel said.

He grinned and took another step closer. "Told you Terrence was diddling you. I'd be a much better protector for you." Beside Jezebel, Mordrid growled, apparently taking this as an insult.

"But, I've been betrayed before," Jezebel said with a dramatic sigh. "If . . . I decide to become your mistress . . ." A muffled curse drifted from the curtains.

Edgar froze. "What was that?"

"Nothing!" Jezebel said. "The wind!"

"There ain't no wind!" Edgar declared, frowning.

"I must know," Jezebel cried loudly and threw herself at Edgar. "I must have proof that you can care for me."

"Proof!" Edgar grinned, wrapping his arms around her. "I'll give you proof." He lowered his lips to hers and Jezebel squinched her eyes shut, dreading his kiss.

It didn't happen. A growl and howl came instead. Jezebel snapped her eyes open, just as Mordrid sprang and sunk his canines into Edgar's calf.

"Owee!" Edgar howled. "Owee! Let go, you beast."

"Mordrid, no!" Jezebel gasped.

The dog's eyes rolled as he glanced at her, Edgar's calf sandwiched between his teeth.

"Let go, now!"

Mordrid growled, sounding terribly disgruntled, and unclamped his teeth.

"I'll kill him," Edgar raged, releasing Jezebel and bending to look at his ripped pantaloons.

"It's bleeding," she said. She realized she sounded rather too eager, and forced a sympathetic look. "We must go attend to it."

"I'll kill him," Edgar said, glaring toward the hound.

"Now, now," Jezebel soothed. "First we must attend the bite." She grabbed hold of Edgar and pulled him toward the door. "Come, Sir Edgar we must really look to it. Perhaps a brandy will help."

"Perhaps," Edgar said. He stopped fighting her and, with injured dignity, limped from the room. Jezebel was all too glad to shut the door upon the room, for the curtains were already puffing out and a lump was moving underneath the bedclothes.

Fifteen

"Now we men can talk, without the women's chatter," Edgar said, leaning back in his chair, a glass of brandy in hand, after the women had left the dining room.

Terrence glanced at Edgar, his brows raised. He should have said female, singular, chatter. The only one speaking during the long, drawn-out meal had been Amelia. The other ladies were noticeably silent. It amazed Terrence that Amelia had not noticed the below-freezing temperatures, but had prattled on and on about the wedding and honeymoon.

It was frighteningly obvious the scene he and Jezebel had performed in the morning hadn't phased her one whit. The only thing they had succeeded in doing was angering each other, not the silly Amelia. He stifled a pang of disgust. He had acted the cad. Yet the chance to hold Jezebel had been too tempting. Damn the woman. She had turned him into a desperate man.

He quaffed his brandy, cursing Jezebel and himself, and said, "Indeed, yes."

Edgar grinned. "My little puss is in high alt, 'tis clear."

"Don't think St. George's cathedral will allow all them doves she wants let loose during the w-wedding," Josh said, with a slightly slurred tone. He'd been hitting the bottle religiously during the meal. "Mean, they ain't housebroke or anything, you know."

"Humph," Edgar said, frowning. "We'll have to talk her out of that notion. Ain't fond of the thought myself."

"So, tell me, Edgar?" Terrence asked, wishing to talk of anything but Amelia. "What happened? I heard Mordrid took a bite out of you."

Edgar's face turned a mottled hue. "Er, nothing. Blasted beast should be shot."

"I like the cur," Josh said. "Temperamental fellow, but a fine guard dog."

"Yes, he is that," Terrence said, under his breath. He looked to Edgar. "Indeed, I have never known Mordrid to bite anyone unless he was guarding one of the ladies. So why did he bite you?"

"Well, he would have bitten that Frenchie chef," Josh said, grinning. "But can't fault the dog, the silly fool was chasing him with a hatchet. You weren't chasing old Mordrid with a hatchet, were you?"

"No, of course not," Edgar said, coloring. He wouldn't meet the men's gaze.

"Then what were you doing?" Terrence asked, frowning.

"Nothing, I tell you!" Edgar rose from his chair, then cursed. "This here bite is hurting like the devil. Think I'll . . . I'll turn in now."

Terrence and Josh sat, silent, as Edgar hobbled from the room.

"What was all that about?" Josh asked, blinking.

"I don't know," Terrence said, sighing. "But does it matter?"

"It's too smoky by half," Josh said, reaching for the brandy decanter. "He ain't acting natural." He poured himself another liberal dose. "But then, that chap, he don't ever act natural. And his daughter has a tile loose." He raised the decanter. "Want some more?"

Terrence sighed. "No, I've had enough tonight, I fear."

"Well, I haven't," Josh said, clanking the decanter onto the table and grabbing up his snifter. "Plan to get ape drunk. Only thing to do." He waved his snifter. "To the ladies."

Terrence frowned and then reached very deliberately for

the decanter. "If they're to whom we're toasting, I think I do need a drink."

Josh slumped back in his chair, shaking his head. "Don't understand them, don't understand them a'tall. Elizabeth don't even want to talk to me! I told her . . . Well, never mind what I told her. But blast it, laid my heart at her feet, and she don't even want to talk to me."

Terrence sighed, twirling his brandy glass and frowning into it. "Could be worse. Jezebel doesn't want me to even touch her."

Josh stiffened and glowered at Terrence. "Here now, you are talking about my sister, old man."

" 'Course," Terrence said, tossing his brandy back. "I wouldn't be talking about Amelia, would I?"

Josh considered a moment and then burped. "Right ho. But, you ain't supposed to be touching my sister anyhows."

"I know, damn it," Terrence said. "Don't you think I don't know that?"

Josh blinked. "Yes, yes, I guess so." He lifted his glass again. "As long as you know. Would have to call you out otherwise."

Terrence snorted. "Have no fear, it won't be necessary. Jezebel's seeing to that."

"Sorry. Shouldn't rip up at you," Josh said, looking downcast. "Know eg-zaclty how you feel. At least Jez will talk to you."

"I'd not claim that as a blessing," Terrence said.

"To blazes with them," Josh said. He lifted his glass. "Here's to man and bottle, 'tis far better than man and woman."

"Here, here!" Terrence said, grinning as he lifted his glass.

"Godmama, what are you doing?" Amelia gasped as Dorethea thunked a brandy decanter down upon the ornate table next to the tea service.

"We left the men to their drink," Dorethea said. "And it's time they left us to ours."

"Oh, Godmama, no!" Amelia exclaimed.

"You don't have to have any, child," Dorethea said. "Though if you are going to get married, you might like to learn to imbibe now. A good brandy always helps a woman, once she is married." She looked to the rest of the women. "Who wants brandy?"

"Oh, I'll take one," Letty said quickly, snatching up an empty teacup. "Just a nip."

"Me too," Theo grunted. "Could use a good spot."

"Elizabeth and Jezebel?" Dorethea asked.

Jezebel looked to Elizabeth, and Elizabeth looked to Jezebel. They both smiled.

"Perhaps a sip," Elizabeth said.

"Yes," Jezebel agreed and reached for a cup.

"I am still uncertain," Amelia said as the ladies all settled back with their brandies, "on where we should go upon our honeymoon, Jezebel. We shall go to Greece, since that is a place you wish to visit, but I have been thinking Italy is also a place I would like to see. There are even more scholars there I would like to study under. Do you think you would like Italy?"

"What? Jezebel is going on your honeymoon?" Theo asked, her heavy face working in astonishment.

"Yes!" Amelia nodded. "Terrence, Jezebel, and I have been planning it all day."

Theo stared. "Good God!" She quaffed her drink quickly.

"Yes," Jezebel said, taking a sip of her own brandy to quell her shiver. "I am sure it will be a delightful trip."

Elizabeth quickly swallowed from her glass as well. "Amelia, you do not mind that Jezebel . . . ? Well, you do not mind Jezebel?"

"No," Amelia said, frowning. "A lady should not consider such things. 'Tis the nature of men, and we ladies cannot understand it. Besides, I have discovered Terrence is not partial to the study of birds, and I intend to be spending much time with my research. Jezebel can keep him company at those times."

"Spoken like a true wife," Dorethea said. She shook her head, gazing with an almost morose look to Amelia. "My dear, I find you full of many surprises."

"Thank you, Godmama," Amelia said, evidently quite pleased.

Dorethea's eyes narrowed. "But I am not sure you understand the full nature of men . . . and women. Once you do, I do not believe you shall be as . . . as comfortable about the fact of Jezebel."

"Oh, yes," Letty chimed in. "You surely will not wish to share dear Terrence with Jez." She cast a harried glance to Jezebel. "I am sorry, my dear, but I am sure you understand what I mean. I-I have always been a maiden, but I am sure if I had a husband, I would not care to have you about. In fact I fear I would . . . would like to . . . to—"

"Scratch her eyes out?" Elizabeth asked dryly.

"Yes!" Letty nodded quickly. "Exactly that."

Jezebel glanced to Elizabeth, who flushed and looked down at her brandy-filled teacup. "You would?"

Elizabeth looked up. Her eyes were filled with a resigned pain as she gave a small nod. Instinctively Jezebel reached out to place her hand on Elizabeth's.

"There is no need, I promise you, not if you mean about Josh."

Elizabeth's chin lifted. "I was not talking about him."

"I see," Jezebel said softly, frowning. She had been so involved with her own problems she had not considered anyone else's. "Someday we must talk."

"No," Elizabeth said. "There is no reason to talk, I assure you."

"I see." Jezebel looked quickly around the room. The women were watching them, teacups raised. She smiled weakly. "Of course, not. Well, then what should we all talk about?"

"I think we should talk about whether we should go to Italy or not," Amelia said.

"I think we should talk about sex," Dorethea suddenly suggested.

Letty screeched, "Oh, my." But then she giggled. "Dorethea, you are naughty!"

"Yes, am I not?" Dorethea answered. "But since Amelia is motherless, I believe we should stand in her dear departed mother's stead. I would not have you going to your marriage bed with total ignorance, my dear child."

Amelia's brown eyes suddenly became those of the hunted. "Oh, oh, I am sure we need not . . . not discuss this now." She looked down. "Not with everyone in the room."

"But we are all your friends, dear," Dorethea said. "Certainly you know I am. Was it not I who helped arrange your marriage. And since I have, I believe it my duty to help you prepare for your wedding night."

"Need to know what you're getting into," Theo grunted. "Once you do, things are going to change. Will grow jealous of Jezebel, wish her in Hades. We women always get silly over men. They will drive you insane, so you'd best think long on it."

"I already offered to give her advice," Jezebel said.

"You did?" Letty asked. She smiled. "Dear, how sweet of you. You have such a good heart." She looked to Amelia. "You can take Jezebel's word." She leaned over and said, "She says our boy is quite excellent in bed. Isn't that reassuring to you?"

Amelia all but melded with the cushion behind her. She gazed at Letty as if she were an inquisitioner holding thumb screws. "Y-yes, I am sure, but . . . but I believe I am tired." She sprang up from the couch. "Yes—yes, I am tired. I must retire." She scuttled from the room.

"Well," Dorethea said with a grin, "I believe this calls for another round of drinks." She hefted up the brandy decanter, and the three older ladies' teacups shot out. Jezebel could only stare. She noted Elizabeth did the same.

"Fine job, Doro," Theo said. "Routed her quickly."

"Yes," Dorethea said. "The child does bolt from the subject. She truly has no notion what it is all about." She frowned. "Now if we could only route Edgar as easily."

"What are you talking about?" Elizabeth said, gazing at the women.

"Dear Elizabeth, you surely cannot believe Amelia is right for our dear boy?" Letty said. "Cannot you see that it will not work."

Elizabeth rightfully blinked. "But I thought—"

"We have had a change of plans," Dorethea said with a quelling look. "Now, Elizabeth, as you are my trusted companion I am sure I can have complete faith that you will not divulge anything we say."

"Of course," Elizabeth said. She settled back. "Do go on, do not let me stop you. I shall remain quiet, I assure you."

"What are we going to do with Edgar?" Letty moaned immediately.

Theo sat back with her second brandy, her gaze brooding. "Kill him is what I say."

"What?" Elizabeth gasped.

Dorethea quelled her with a frown. She then looked to Theo. "I believe we should try another course first."

"Then we kill him," Theo said.

"I think we should do what we were going to do with St. John," Letty said. "Let us kidnap him and hand him over to the press gang."

"Might have merit," Dorethea said. "Might have merit."

Elizabeth glanced to Jezebel with a worried look. Jezebel shook her head slightly and raised her finger. The ladies had suffered a rough day, and she felt it only right to permit them to air their disappointments. However, as the three elderly ladies continued to discuss their notions on how to rid the world of Edgar Arrowroot, she could not help but squirm.

Dorethea was holding to poison, listing a goodly number of which Jezebel had never heard. Theo, true to her character, recommended a good shooting to the gut. Letty, of course more kindhearted, still held with sending him to the press gang.

She had him first going to Australia, then America, then the West Indies. She finally settled on dropping him off in the middle of the jungles of Africa, where he could hunt to his heart's content. That was, if the animals there didn't eat him first, which she sincerely hoped they would do in order that Edgar could finally understand their displeasure at being shot and served up for dinner, their heads detached and hung upon walls. Letty thought it would be fitting if Edgar's head decorated some lion's den.

As Jezebel expected, the ladies' words became slower and more slurred as the decanter emptied. Gales of laughter riffled through their gruesome plans for Edgar Arrowroot's future. She finally cleared her throat loudly and said, "Well, it seems we have a multitude of plans for Edgar, but it is growing late. Perhaps we should wait until tomorrow to take a vote upon our final decision."

"Yes," Elizabeth said quickly, casting Jezebel a laughing glance. "Do let us sleep on this tonight."

"They are right," Dorethea nodded. She lifted the decanter. "No more brandy."

"Well, then," Theo said, "might as well go to bed."

The three elderly ladies stumbled to their feet. Jezebel and Elizabeth were quick to help them, kicking a footstool aside before Letty tumbled over it, opening the door after Theo ran smack into it, and freeing Dorethea's wide skirts when she snagged them upon the suit of armor in the hall.

"Thank you, my dear," Dorethea said as Elizabeth and Jezebel herded the stumbling ladies to the stairs. "You are s-so kind. Can't f-figure w-why I didn't l-like you at first."

"Perhaps my occupation." Jezebel laughed. "And my lack of discretion, of course."

"Discretion, meshun," Dorethea hiccuped. "You . . . you have s-spirit." She suddenly gripped Jezebel by the shoulders, gazing at her fiercely. "You ain't going to share our T-Terrence with th-that birdwit, are you? Amelia is my goddaughter, but I hate to say it, sh-she is cold." She all but rattled Jezebel. "You . . . you would scratch her eyes out for our T-Terry, wouldn't you?"

"Yes," Jezebel said, her heart tightening painfully. "Yes, I would."

"Promise?" Dorethea said.

Jezebel smiled. "I promise."

"Good," Dorethea said, nodding briskly. "Then w-we will t-take care of Edgar."

"No," Jezebel said quickly. "Let me do it, instead."

Elizabeth was holding up a sagging Letty. "I think you should let Jezebel do it instead," she said.

"It is my fight, after all," Jezebel insisted.

"But I want to shoot him." Theo was hugging the banister tightly.

"No, Africa," Letty said. "H-have his head upon a wall." She frowned. "Do caves have w-walls?"

"Poison," Dorethea persisted. "Nice, quiet poison."

"No, bed." Elizabeth chuckled. "All of you, do you hear?"

Letty hiccuped and looked around with a blurry gaze. "Wh-where are the men?" She straightened. "Must go back. Th-they'll be c-coming to s-see us after their . . . their drink. It wouldn't be polite to not b-be there."

"No," Jezebel said quickly. "Elizabeth and I will be there, but you should go to bed. Go to bed and . . . and—"

"Think things over," Elizabeth put in. "Now, let us help you to your rooms."

Dorethea rose to her full, short height. Her head lifted. "You overstep the b-bounds, Elizabeth. I h-have never n-needed help in g-getting to my bed."

"Me neither," Theo said, freeing herself from the banister and standing at a tilt. "N-never."

"We c-can do it," Letty said, waving off Elizabeth.

The three ladies, clutching each other, stumbled up the stairs. Elizabeth and Jezebel stood, silently watching. Even when the women disappeared at the landing, Elizabeth and Jezebel waited. After a few moments Elizabeth let out a breath.

"No thumps," she said. "Do you think they made it all right?"

"I hope so," Jezebel replied.

Both ladies looked at each other and then burst into laughter. Jezebel wiped a tear of mirth from her eye and said, "Elizabeth, I want you to know that . . . that I would be pleased to have you as a sister."

Elizabeth stopped laughing. She flushed. "I fear I cannot say the same. I like you very much, but . . ." She flushed. "Never mind."

Jezebel smiled. "Perhaps someday you will change your mind." Then she frowned. "What about the men? Letty is right, they haven't appeared."

Elizabeth raised a brow. "Perhaps we should see if they have retired. They must have forgotten about us."

"Perhaps," Jezebel said.

Both ladies, dubious expressions upon their faces, turned and walked toward the dining room.

Elizabeth raised her brows and looked quizzingly to Jezebel as they stood outside the dining-room door. Low rumbles and murmurs could be heard. Jezebel shrugged her shoulders and swung open the door. They stepped into the dining room.

"Oh, Lord," Elizabeth said, sighing. The sole occupants of the room were Josh and Terrence. Both men leaned over the table, their hands clutching brandy snifters.

"Didn't we just leave this scene?" Jezebel whispered.

Elizabeth nodded and straightened her shoulders. She strolled toward the men. "Hello, gentlemen."

Josh and Terrence swiveled their heads toward her, their eyes blurred and hazy.

"Hello," Terrence said. "What are you ladies doing here?"

"We grew tired of waiting for you," Jezebel said, walking over to stand by him.

He grinned up at her. "Did you now? Thought y-you wouldn't miss us."

"Thought you . . . you most likely w-wished for g-girl talk," Josh growled. "T-talking about clothes and wh-what-not."

"No," Elizabeth said, stifling a smile. She was tempted to tell the befuddled men just exactly what the ladies had been talking about, but deemed it too unkind. "That was not what we were talking about."

"We talked about . . . about sewing," Jezebel said. "Nothing else."

"F-figures," Josh mumbled.

"We were waiting for you," Elizabeth said, turning a dark eye to Josh.

"W-why?" Josh asked, sitting up. "Y-you don't want to talk to me. S-so what were you waiting f-for?"

"Josh," Jezebel said, her tone stern. "You are being rude. I believe you have had enough brandy."

"No," he said, shaking his head. "N-not enough."

"Yes, quite enough," Elizabeth said grimly, feeling as if she were dealing with a recalcitrant child. "It is time for you to retire. If you require assistance I will aid you, but retire you shall."

"Shh-shh," Josh said, lifting his finger and missing his lips. "You ain't talking to me."

"Then I will do so silently," Elizabeth said with narrowed eyes. "Now come."

"Very well." Josh lurched up from his chair. "B-but no t-talking."

"Come, Terrence, you should go too." Jezebel placed a hand on his shoulder.

"No, no," Terrence said, grinning drunkenly. "You ain't suppose to touch me, remember?"

"That's it!" Josh said, hooting with triumph. "You can't touch him, Jez." Suddenly he reached out and hauled Elizabeth to his side. He grinned down blearily at her and his breath well nigh sent her reeling. "At least y-you didn't say I c-couldn't touch you." Her blue eyes brightened. "M-means you like me a l–little, d-don't it?"

Elizabeth flushed, trying to keep him from swaying. "You said we weren't going to talk."

"Got the better part, old man," Terrence said.

"Indeed he does," Jezebel said, placing her hands on her hips. "For I am going to most definitely talk to you."

"Told you, Josh," Terrence said, pulling a face.

"Oh, oh," Josh slurred. "Am decamping, old man."

"Th-thought we were suppose to s-stick together," Terrence called as Josh lurched away, dragging Elizabeth with him.

"N-not now," Josh said. "Know Jezebel. Got a sh-sharp tongue." He grinned down at Elizabeth. "G-glad you ain't talking to me, after all."

Elizabeth glanced nervously back as Josh leaned heavily upon her and stumbled toward the door. Jezebel was glaring down at the drunken Terrence who was laughing. Elizabeth could tell she'd receive no help from that quarter, the pair clearly having difficulties. Josh pulled her closer to his side, and she realized she'd best look to her own problems.

"Don't hold me so close," she said, shoving at him.

"Shh-shh!" Josh almost capsized. Gasping, Elizabeth grabbed him quickly. He grinned down at her, his drunken eyes smug. "Ain't talking, you know."

"You are as drunk as a wheelbarrow," Elizabeth muttered

as the two progressed erratically through the hall and to the stairs. Josh merely grinned and wagged his head. She glared. "Your behavior is reprehensible." Josh patted her shoulder and chuckled, but speak he did not. Nettled, Elizabeth said, "It is not bad enough that you tell women you love them— all women." She gritted as they stopped at the first step. "But you must drink excessively." Josh did not speak, but slipped his hand to her waist and tickled her. Elizabeth slapped his hand away. "Stop that! This is not humorous!" She helped the mum Josh up the stairs. When they stopped at the top landing, Elizabeth caught her breath and then said, "You are a cad and a bounder! Now what do you have to say about that, sirrah!"

Josh but smiled a foolish smile and hugged her close.

"Let me go," Elizabeth cried, frustrated to her very core. "I call you a bounder, and all you can do is try to make up to me." She thought she heard Josh chuckle, but she ignored it, striving for as much dignity as she could gather as they thumped and bumped their way down the hall to his bedroom door.

"I have never known a man with such low character as yours," she bit out as she propped him against the wall and opened the door. "Rake does not even describe you. You are below reproach." Fuming, she once again took his arm and dragged him into his room. "And as for this childish game in which you will not speak to me, I have had enough!" She released him and put her hands to her hips. "I want you to talk to me, do you hear? I want you to tell me what you have to say for yourself!"

A darkness filled Josh's blue eyes. Swiftly, before Elizabeth could move, his arms snaked out and hauled her to him. He lowered his head and kissed her, kissed her so wildly that all words disappeared from Elizabeth's head. So did all thoughts.

Josh suddenly released her. "There," was all he said. He

turned and walked over to the bed. Elizabeth's eyes widened as he fell down upon it face first.

"Josh?" she said. Swallowing hard, she walked over to him. "Josh?" A snore arose from him.

Elizabeth sighed. He had not spoken, but what his kiss had said was enough for her. Crossing her arms about her, Elizabeth tried to chase the chill from her heart. She could do all the talking she wanted, but his kiss always changed it all. She was helplessly in love with the snoring rake upon the bed.

"I cannot believe your behavior," Jezebel said angrily. "Sitting here with Josh and getting as drunk as a lord."

"I am sure you'll make me as sober as a judge," Terrence sighed, slowly rising from the chair.

"Here, let me help you," Jezebel said, despite herself. She reached out.

"No!" Terrence waved her away. "Do not touch me, or I will not be responsible for the consequences."

An anger blazed through the haze in his eyes, and Jezebel stepped back instinctively. "Very well."

He studied her a moment, and Jezebel shifted nervously. Then he barked a laugh. "That's right. Y-you would avoid the consequences at all cost, w-would you not?"

Jezebel bit her lip. "You are drunk."

"Yes, we have divined this already," Terrence said. The rage disappeared from his eyes, and a weariness replaced it. "But not drunk enough, for I still have this damn problem of wanting you." He stumbled past her. "But th-that's my problem, isn't it?"

"Terrence," Jezebel said, "wait!"

"Wait for what?" he called, lurching toward the door. "Wait for me to f-find myself tied to Amelia? Wait for you to go back to y-your cold little life?" Jezebel, fighting off the shiver his words had caused, hurried after him. She was puffing when she finally caught up with him at the foot of the stairs. He spun about and raked her with a scathing glance. "Is that what I'm waiting for, Jezebel?"

She skidded to a halt. "I . . . I . . ." She bit her lip.

"That's what I thought," Terrence murmured. He turned away and started climbing the stairs, holding heavily to the banister. "And you rail at me for d-drinking. Ha!"

Jezebel followed behind, not wanting to hear his words, but unwilling to leave him, lest he fall and hurt himself.

"I have such a fine life!" Terrence said. "S-surely I should wish to f-face it sober, dutifully. As my dear grandmother has told me, I sh-should marry Amelia. She will make a fine wife. Bring lands with her, b-bond our beknighted families together." Jezebel saw his body cringe. "God, what a thought." He reached the landing. "And Amelia and I should have ch-children." His chuckle was low, rasping. "Le-git-i-mate ones, of course. C-can you imagine m-more little Amelias?"

"Terrence, it won't happen!" Jezebel said, pain lancing through her.

"No?" Terrence demanded. "Won't it?" He shook his head. "I'm caught, Jezebel. I might as well quit kicking and f-face it."

"Don't do that!" Jezebel said, anger rising in her.

Terrence's face twisted. "Just leave me, Jezebel. Leave me."

Jezebel stiffened, and she choked out, "I am not going to leave you."

"Oh, but you will," Terrence said softly. "But you will."

Jezebel looked down, knowing full well what he was saying. "I will see you safely to your room."

"Yes," Terrence said. "You will see me safely to my room, but not safely to my bed." He turned and ambled down the hall. "And will you see me safely wed?" he asked. Reaching his door, he shoved it open and disappeared.

"No," Jezebel protested, chasing in after him. "No, Terrence, I will not see you safely wed."

He turned, standing at the foot of his bed. "But you've always been a pr-proponent of marriage."

"Yes," Jezebel said. "But love and marriage."

"Ah, love," Terrence sighed, walking over to sit on his bed. "Let us not discuss that!"

"No," Jezebel said, feeling terribly hurt. "No, of course not. But you will not marry Amelia." She gripped the bed's post. "You hired me so you would not have to marry, and I will see to that."

"H-hired you," Terrence said. He shook his head. "I went to f-find an actress and a hussy, and I got you instead. God, what did I do?"

Jezebel swallowed hard. "I know I am not what you wanted—"

"I did not say that," Terrence said, glaring at her. Their gazes met and held, and Jezebel felt an ache rising in her. "You know that." He sighed and looked away. "But it would have been better had we never met."

"Perhaps," Jezebel said in a small voice. "But since we did, I promise you, you will not be forced to marry Amelia. You . . . you mustn't give up. I-I think we made her nervous this morning."

"Who are you lying to, Jezebel? We did not." His laugh was hollow. "You heard her tonight, p-prattling on about the wedding and wanting damn doves set free in the cathedral!" He sighed. "No, my dear. Amelia could find us in bed together and she'd not b-be stopped from traipsing down the aisle with me." He groaned. "I am trapped and there is nothing you can do. I could run like I had first thought—but why run? What is there to run to?"

"Your freedom," Jezebel said softly.

"Freedom?" Terrence looked at her. "Do you think I'll ever have that again, Jezebel?"

She could not speak, dared not speak. His eyes deadened and he sighed.

"As I said, we should never have met. Leave me, Jezebel, I believe I need to sleep this off." He lay down then.

Jezebel stood a silent moment and then walked from his room. She stumbled down the hall, almost feeling if she were drunk. She knew she wasn't, but the emotions warring within her made her dizzy.

She silently let herself into her room. She heard a soft woof and turned. "Hello, Mordrid." As she crossed to the bed the large hound, already well ensconced on the counterpane, sat up. She reached over and hugged him, closing her eyes. "I love him, Mordrid," Jezebel whispered softly. "I love him. What am I going to do?"

Sixteen

Jezebel awoke with a start. Perspiration heated her skin. Her dreams had been frightful. Dorethea, Theo, and Letty had killed Edgar. Unfortunately they had employed Theo's method of shooting him. They had been carted off to Newgate. She had seen them in a dank cell. Oddly enough, Mordrid, Sir Drake, and Geselda were there as well. Mordrid was a rack of bones and had not even possessed the energy to growl at Geselda.

The dream had changed then, to an even stranger one. Terrence, dressed in groomsman's attire, was confined in a huge golden cage, while Amelia, in her wedding gown, sat staring at him from the midst of a group of scholars, all pointing and speaking in foreign languages. Amelia was saying, "Yes, yes, he is my husband; is he not an unusual specimen?"

Terrence then rattled the cage and shouted, "I should never have met you, Jezebel, I should never have met you!"

Jezebel tried to go to him and free him, but the scene turned into a mist with only his words ringing out. Then the oddest vision appeared. Her head was mounted on a cave wall, and African lions prowled underneath. One licked his paw and said, "He should never have met her."

Jezebel shook her head wildly and sat up quickly. Yet, still the grotesque visions swirled within her mind. "No!" she said fiercely. Mordrid, beside her, jerked and then sat up with a growl.

"I'm sorry, Mordrid," Jezebel said, "but something must be done." She looked around and noticed the room was growing light. It would soon be morning. Picking up her pillow, she hugged it close. It was clear. Edgar had to be gotten rid of, not literally but must definitely figuratively, and Amelia must be finally forced to jilt Terrence.

Jezebel stared into space, deep in contemplation. It was simple really, she only had two objectives to accomplish. The exact hows were the difficult part, yet slowly a plan formed in her mind. It would take great initiative, but having been tutored, so to speak, by the ladies of the house, Jezebel decided her plan was not so strange, certainly not as strange as her nightmares.

Jezebel tossed her pillow aside and sprang out of bed. She had much to accomplish this day, for she couldn't afford to wait, not with the ladies plotting murder and the men drinking themselves into oblivion.

"My dear, I am so glad you wished to see me!" Edgar said, rushing into the parlor. He had the look of an eager schoolboy, unfortunately a lustful, eager schoolboy.

"Yes," Jezebel said, fanning out her bright fuchsia skirts as she sat on the settee. "It was a shame that our discussion yesterday was, er, cut short."

"Damn dog," Edgar growled.

"Do let us forget him." Jezebel forced a smile. She patted the cushion next to her. "Come and sit down."

Edgar beamed and limped over to sit beside her. He grinned at her. "I . . . I have something for you."

"You do?" Jezebel asked, rather stunned.

"Yes." Edgar nodded. "You wanted proof that I can care for you." He reached into his pocket and withdrew a slim case. With elaborate display he cracked it open.

"Oh, my!" Jezebel exclaimed. A diamond necklace sparkled from its satin bed. "Heavens!"

"Diamonds for my diamond," Edgar proclaimed. His thick hands jerked the necklace out of its satin nest. "Here, put it on, put it on!"

"No," Jezebel said. "Really—"

"Here, here," Edgar said, leaning over. "Don't have to thank me. Told you I could take care of you." He wrapped Jezebel's neck with the diamond strand and clasped it shut.

It felt like a noose to Jezebel. "Er, yes."

When Edgar's hands slid to her shoulders, Jezebel truly felt strangled. "Now, doesn't that show you proof of my ability to care for you?" His heavy face moved closer. Jezebel could feel his breath.

"P-perhaps," Jezebel said, slipping swiftly from his grasp and springing up. She darted across the room. Drawing in deep breaths, she forced a calm and turned, dragging up what she hoped was a winsome smile. "But this is only one diamond necklace."

"One!" Edgar asked, his jaw dropping. "What do you mean only one? Haven't noticed Terry giving you any diamonds."

"Er, no," Jezebel said. She lifted her chin. "But that is my point. If I change my protector, how do I know you won't be a nipfarthing once I've, er, thrown my bonnet over the windmill." She sashayed over to him. "I mean, Terry is a Marquis. He ain't got the lettuce now, but he is the Duchess's grandson."

Edgar puffed out his chest. "Never you mind, I'll have plenty of money. Even more once Terrence marries Amelia."

Jezebel flicked her head, making her curls bounce. "If he marries Amelia."

"He will," Edgar said with a growl.

"You know," Jezebel said, narrowing her eyes. "Terrence still says you announced the engagement without his permission, that he never signed the marriage contract with you."

"What!" Edgar sprang up. "The boy lies. He's duping you, I tell you!"

"Maybe so," Jezebel said, looking coyly down. "But if you would show me the contract, so's I can make certain it ain't you who's lying, then see for myself that you ain't puffing off the sum you're claiming you'll get and I'll believe you. Which, considering the shabby way Terry has treated me, I want to do. I'm thinking . . . thinking that you—"

"I'm what?" Edgar asked quickly.

"That you're just the fellow for me," Jezebel said. Then she sighed heavily. "But I-I don't want to leave Terrence if he isn't really going to marry Amelia. He has such prospects you know."

"I'll show you," Edgar said, rubbing his hands together. "I'll show you. But if I do, will you promise to be mine?"

"Yes," Jezebel said. She batted her lashes. "So why don't we go and get the contract now?"

Edgar flushed. "Well, I don't have it with me at this moment. It's at my solicitor's."

"Ah," Jezebel said, nodding. Edgar wasn't as stupid as one could wish. She thought swiftly. "Then let us meet tonight."

"Yes, yes," Edgar nodded.

"But only if you have the proof," Jezebel said as he charged toward her. "I want to see it with my own eyes."

"I can get it!" Edgar said, stretching out his arms for her.

Jezebel smacked a hand to his chest, holding him at bay. "Then do. I will . . . will meet you at . . . eleven o'clock . . . in—in your room."

Edgar grinned. "Done!" He clenched her wrist and jerked it up to slather a wet kiss on her palm. "Only wait until tonight."

"Yes, tonight," Jezebel said, controlling a shiver. "But we must keep it secret. We . . . we are under the Duchess's roof and I am still under Terrence's patronage until you prove to me otherwise."

"Of course," Edgar said, chuckling. He balled her hand in a tight grip. "That's what I like about you. You appear almost the lady."

"Yes," Jezebel gritted out. "Don't I?"

"What is going on in here?" Terrence's voice rapped out from behind them. Edgar jumped, swiftly dropping Jezebel's hand.

Jezebel swung around, her heart pounding. "Nothing, nothing at all."

"Er, ahem," Edgar said. "Only talking to Jezebel a moment. That's all."

Terrence stood tall and still, his eyes shooting sparks.

"Well, now. I'll leave you to have a chat with Jezebel." Edgar swiftly darted past Terrence and out the door.

What a fine protector Edgar would make, Jezebel thought inconsequentially. She clasped her hands together and tried not to look at Terrence. "Were you looking for me?" He did not answer. Jezebel peeked up. His gaze was trained upon her neck.

"Where did you get that necklace?" he asked softly.

"This?" Jezebel laughed. It came out nervous and hollow. "Oh, it is mine. Paste, of course."

Terrence stalked up to her and placed a hand on the diamonds. Jezebel had shivered at Edgar's touch, and she did so at Terrence's, but in a totally different manner. "They are not paste," Terrence said softly. "And I know you did not have this before. Where did you get it?"

"Very well," Jezebel said, stepping back. "If you must know, Edgar gave it to me."

"He what!" Terrence shouted.

Jezebel walked stiffly to the fireplace. "He—he was asking to be forgiven for his behavior toward me."

"I don't believe you," Terrence's voice cracked.

Jezebel spun about. "You don't believe me?"

"No," Terrence said. "I don't. A man doesn't give a woman a diamond necklace to apologize." He stalked closer. "Not unless he intends to receive something more than forgiveness for it. What are you doing, Jezebel?"

She stared at him. His face was dark, suspicious. He was giving her a look no lady should receive, not when she had done nothing to warrant it. Her chin jutted out. "What I am doing is none of your business."

Terrence's eyes narrowed. "Yes, it is."

"No, it's not," Jezebel shouted, shaking. "You do not own me. And you . . ." She choked up, then went on. "And you wish you had never met me, so what does it matter what I do? If I choose to accept a necklace from Edgar Arrowroot, I will!"

"Oh, you will?" Terrence closed the gap between them. "If you accept that necklace from him he will expect you to be his mistress."

"And what if he does?" Jezebel asked, angered.

Terrence appeared stunned. Then his eyes narrowed. "So, the truth comes out. All this time you deny me your bed, talking of love and marriage, but what you are really doing is holding out. What was the matter, Jezebel, did I not give you diamonds? You must forgive me, for at the time, I was under the impression you were a true lady."

Jezebel gasped. Without thought, she swung out and slapped Terrence. His head snapped back.

"Oh!" she quickly darted past him and put the settee between them. Terrence turned, rage in his eyes, even as a red mark stained his cheek. Jezebel drew in a ragged breath and said, "I am leaving."

"So I gather," Terrence said, his eyes turning cold.

Jezebel stifled the shooting pain ripping through her. "But before I go, we are going to do one last thing."

"We are?" Terrence asked.

"Yes," Jezebel said "We are going to have Amelia find us in bed together."

"What!" Terrence exclaimed.

Jezebel's nails dug into the satin of the settee back. "I have thought about it. You said last night you thought she'd marry you even if she found us in bed together, but I don't think so. The only thing which seems to unsettle Amelia is . . . well, that kind of thing. And if we really force her to confront it, she . . . she might cry off."

"No!" Terrence said, his voice curt.

Jezebel stiffened. "You said you want your freedom, and this is the one thing we haven't tried."

"I said no," Terrence snapped.

"Why?" Jezebel asked. "You said you won't kiss Amelia again, but it is either that or . . . or go to bed with me."

"What charming choices," Terrence said.

Jezebel stiffened. "It is not appealing to me either, but that is what you paid me for and I am going to see it through."

Terrence's lip curled. "You can give me that necklace there. I am sure it is worth what I paid Molly."

"No," Jezebel said, gritting her teeth. "I will not!"

"And I will not go to bed with you!" Terrence roared.

Jezebel started back. "We wouldn't really. It would be . . . be an act of course."

"Of course," Terrence said curtly. "You are such a fine actress, after all."

"I will be able to act it," Jezebel said lowly. "Are you saying you cannot?"

"No, damn it!" Terrence said. "If you can act it, so can I!"

"Fine!" Jezebel said tightly. "Come to my room at twelve. I will make certain Amelia will discover us there. She will jilt you, and it will be over. You can have your freedom and I will . . ." She halted. She couldn't say she would return home and die slowly without him. "I will do whatever I wish."

"Fine!" Terrence said. He bowed. "Madame, until to-night."

He stalked from the room. Sudden tears stung Jezebel's eyes.

"Drat it," she exclaimed, and her hand rose to grip the necklace around her throat. Furious, she ripped it from her and flung it across the room. "Damn him!" she said, tears streaming down her face. "Damn him!"

"Duchess?" Jezebel's voice called softly through the darkened bedroom.

Dorethea cracked open her eyes and closed them immediately as nausea overtook her. "Yes, dear?"

She heard and felt Jezebel come to her and sit down upon the bed. "I-I was wondering . . ."

Jezebel didn't finish. Sighing, Dorethea opened her eyes. She focused them upon Jezebel. "My dear," she said, striving to sit up in the bed. Her world spun, but the look on Jezebel's face forced her to persevere. "You look frightful."

"I-I do not feel well," Jezebel said.

Jezebel's eyes looked red and puffy. "I know," Dorethea said. "We should not have drunk so much last night."

"Yes," Jezebel nodded. "Do you think you could give me some . . . some laudanum. I . . . I know you said you had some."

"Of course, dear," Dorethea said in concern. The girl really did look pale and drawn. "It is over in that drawer." Dorethea pointed to the dressing table. "Do you mind if I do not get it?"

"No," Jezebel said quickly. "You just lie back down."

Dorethea sighed in gratitude and sagged back against the pillows. "Thank you, my dear."

She watched as Jezebel rose and walked over to the table. Jezebel found the bottle and turned. "Thank you."

"It is all right, my dear," Dorethea said. "Take a little of that and then get some rest."

"Yes." Jezebel nodded. She walked toward the door and then turned. "I-I do not want you to worry about Edgar or Amelia. Everything will work out, I promise you."

"Of course, dear," Dorethea said and closed her eyes. In truth, the only thing she worried about at the moment was whether she was going to be sick or not.

"Goodbye," Jezebel said, closing the door.

"Goodbye," Dorethea murmured, thinking Jezebel had the right of it. Laudanum might very well be beneficial.

"I do not understand," Amelia said, blinking at Jezebel. "Why are you leaving?"

"I have found another protector so I am leaving, but I will need your help."

Amelia shook her head, still confused. "But we had the honeymoon all planned. Do you not want to go?"

"No," Jezebel said. "You'll want Terry all to yourself, won't you?"

Amelia flushed. "I do not mind if you travel with us. I am sure I will be very busy with my . . . my studies and with the scholars."

"I meant at night," Jezebel said, her eyes narrowing.

Amelia stiffened. "I do not see that we need to discuss the matter."

Jezebel's eyes were implacable. "But I am sure you don't wish to be unprepared for what will happen on your wedding night."

"Papa says I need not worry my head over such," Amelia said, lifting her chin. "Once I am married, it will be time enough to deal with that."

"I see," Jezebel said. "Tie the knot, and then, when it is too late, discover the truth."

Amelia shook her head. "Papa says all I need to do is think about God and country, and I'll do fine."

"And birds," Jezebel said, her tone crisp. Amelia flushed, for Jezebel studied her with a deep, frowning concentration. "You know, Amelia, there is another reason I shouldn't travel with you and Terrence. You must realize you are going to become a married woman. As a matron rather than a girl, you will command far more consequence. All those professors and learned men you wish to meet and study with on the trip will certainly respect you. But they are foreign, and I fear they will take it amiss if your husband's mistress travels with you."

Amelia frowned. "But Papa said—"

"Yes, I know, however, they are foreign. They will lose respect for you."

"I see." Amelia certainly didn't want her future professors to think badly of her. "Very well." She nodded. "If you need me to help you, I shall."

"Thank you," Jezebel said, rising. "Now remember, you must come to my room at fifteen after twelve. You promise me?"

"Of course," Amelia said.

"Very well." Jezebel walked to the door. Then she turned. "Remember, what your father accepts and what the rest of the world accepts are different. Many people frown at the thought of a man having a mistress openly. They will also say it is because you are not wife enough to keep him from straying."

"Straying?" Amelia asked.

"Yes, from your bed," Jezebel said.

Amelia flushed. She wished everyone would stop talking about bed and such. It made her terribly uncomfortable. She knew very well she must face the frightful prospect, as all ladies who wished to become wed did, but she didn't see why she should also have to talk about it, or think about it, until it happened. Perhaps it was a good thing Jezebel was leaving, since the actress had taken to bringing up the dreadful subject so often.

"I will help you leave tonight," Amelia said quickly. "I promise to be there fifteen minutes after midnight."

"You wish for what, Miss Jezebel?" Stilton asked, knowing his look of composure was slipping.

"I would like you to take a chilled bottle of champagne to Sir Arrowroot's room before ten o'clock," Jezebel said. "And also have another bottle in my room before twelve o'clock."

"Yes, miss," Stilton said, stiffening.

Jezebel smiled at him, her blue eyes almost sad. "I would have you know you are an excellent butler. You take care of the Duchess very well."

Stilton colored. "Thank you, miss."

Suddenly she reached out and touched his sleeve. "Do not worry, Stilton. If all goes well, I will be helping your mistress and Terrence, not harming them."

"I am glad to hear it, Miss Jezebel," he said, frowning. "But, if you will permit me to ask, you are not doing anything which might harm you, are you?"

A flush rose to her cheeks. "No, no of course not." She ducked her head and left. Stilton stared after her, wondering just what Jezebel was about and why she needed so much champagne, in different rooms at that.

Jezebel glanced nervously to the gilt clock on the mantel. She had only ten more minutes before she must be in Edgar's room. She paced around the bedroom, her negligee rustling, her hand reflexively clenching the vial of laudanum. She had not allowed herself enough time. She had only one hour to steal the marriage contract from Edgar and be back here in the room for Terrence.

She prayed everything would go right. This simply must go more smoothly than the dinner had. A more tense meal had never been eaten, and Jezebel thought she had survived some very tense ones under the Duchess's roof. Everyone had watched each other and had attempted to appear nonchalant at the same time. It did not help matters when Stilton had dropped his tray the moment she had risen and announced she did not feel well and would retire early. Terrence had glowered at her, Amelia had given a small gurgle, and that blasted Edgar had winked. Only Josh had shown sincere concern and had followed her into the hall. Soothing his cares, while not raising suspicion, had taken a monumental effort. Yet she knew Josh would not be amenable to her plans. Indeed, if he had divined her intentions, she had no doubt he would have objected strenuously, very strenuously.

Jezebel halted her pacing and drew in a deep breath. There wasn't time to worry over it anymore. She must go to Edgar's room. She went and picked up a cloak, already prepared for the evening, and put it on hastily. The last thing she wished was for someone to catch her in her negligee. She slipped the vial of laudanum into the cloak's pocket, since she hadn't found a decent place to hide it in her negligee.

She then sneaked out the door and came to a standstill. Stilton stood in the hall, a bottle of champagne and a bucket in hand. She flushed. "Oh, hello, Stilton."

"Miss Jezebel," Stilton said, bowing.

Jezebel flushed. "I see you are quite on time. Did you . . . did you . . . ?"

"The bottle of champagne is already in Sir Arrowroot's room," Stilton said. "So is Sir Arrowroot, I might add."

"Already?" Jezebel gasped "Drat, I am late." She hustled past Stilton and dashed down the hall. She was out of breath by the time she reached Sir Arrowroot's room. She rapped quickly upon the door.

"Come in!" Sir Arrowroot called.

Jezebel pushed open the door and entered, quickly closing it. She turned and then all but peddled back into the closed door. Sir Arrowroot stood beside a table laden with the champagne. He held a filled glass in his hand and was dressed in a silk smoking jacket.

"Oh, my," Jezebel said. "How . . . how were you able to change so fast?"

He smiled broadly and winked. "I slipped out early myself. Thought I'd change into something more comfortable."

Jezebel pushed herself away from the safety of the door with great effort. "You seem very certain of yourself."

"I am," Sir Arrowroot said. "I am." He waggled his brows. "And what do you have under that cloak, my dear?"

"You will see," Jezebel said, dragging her feet as she walked over. "But I must see the contract first."

"Of course, of course." Sir Arrowroot nodded. He then set his glass down and walked over to the bureau to open a drawer.

Jezebel could not believe her good fortune. She dashed over to his abandoned champagne glass. Delving into her pocket she pulled out the vial.

She had snapped open the lid and was just beginning to pour the laudanum when Sir Arrowroot said, "Here it is, my dear!" Jezebel jumped and vial and all splashed into the glass.

"Oh," she said, turning swiftly and blocking table and glass.

Edgar stood not two feet from her, waving a paper. " 'Tis not I who lie."

Jezebel stilled. "May I see it?" Grinning, Edgar handed it to her. Jezebel snatched the paper up and scanned it rapidly. Her eyes widened at the terms. 'Twas no mistake why Edgar wished Amelia to wed Terrence. She glanced at the signature. The Duchess was an excellent forger. "Yes." Jezebel sighed. "He signed it."

Edgar pulled the contract from Jezebel's fingers before she could object. "As you can see, I will be well able to provide for you, my beautiful ladybird." Jezebel watched with sinking heart as he pocketed the contract in his smoking jacket.

"Let us have a toast," she said, smiling weakly. She turned her back to him quickly. Without conscience, she plucked the vial from the champagne and tossed it under the table. Most of the contents floated in the glass, turning the golden liquid murky. "A toast to us," she said breathlessly and picking up the glass swung around. "Here!" She shoved the glass into Edgar's hand. "Drink up."

He, however, stood with the glass held out. "But where is yours?"

"Yes, mine," Jezebel muttered. She turned back to the table and the bottle, splashed champagne into the empty glass remaining, and picking it up, turned once more. "Toast!" She lifted her glass and then quickly drank from it, watching closely as Edgar swallowed the contents of his.

His face twisted. "This tastes bitter."

"It must be a poor year," Jezebel said. Edgar lifted the glass to peer at it. Cursing to herself, Jezebel said loudly, "Well, I suppose I should make myself comfortable as well." Edgar's gaze immediately deviated from the champagne to her. Forcing herself not to cringe, Jezebel lifted a hand to the cloak and undid its clasp. She let the material fall to her feet.

"Gads, you're beautiful," Edgar whispered, almost awed as he stepped toward her.

"No," Jezebel said swiftly. "Finish your drink first!"

"What?" Edgar said. "Oh, yes." He promptly quaffed the glass, never tearing his hot gaze from her. Suddenly he sputtered and coughed.

"Here, have another," Jezebel exchanged her glass with his as Edgar wheezed and blinked away tears.

"Gad's hounds," Edgar said. "Something was in the champagne."

"No," Jezebel said. "I am sure you are wrong. I thought it tasted divine. Try it again."

Since Edgar was still making choking sounds and had very little choice if he wished to clear his throat, he drank. His face cleared and he sighed as he withdrew the glass from his lips. "Ah, that is much better."

Jezebel feigned a frown. "This glass does look dirty. We must speak to Stilton about it." She sashayed over to the fireplace and tossed the glass into the flames. "To us!" she cried and then turned to smile as seductively as she could.

"Oho, you're a spirited filly," Edgar breathed. "Come to me, sweetings." He reached out his arms and charged toward her. Jezebel squeaked and dashed away. She found herself cornered at the bed as he panted, "Take me to heaven!"

"With pleasure," Jezebel said, vaulting onto the bed, and thinking she'd like a pistol at the moment in order to dispense him there. She bounced across the mattress and landed upon the other side. "But let's not rush it!"

"Ah, the chase," Edgar breathed, his brown eyes flaring. "Here I come, my little vixen." He threw himself across the bed. His reach barely tagged Jezebel, and she skittered over to a chair. Edgar rolled over and looked at her. Miraculously his gaze appeared slightly blurred.

"Come here, my fine fellow," Jezebel said, her courage returning. She crooked a finger at him. Edgar was indeed slower as he rolled from the bed. "Make my dreams come true," Jezebel cooed, envisioning him lying out cold.

"W-will do, my darling," Edgar said, and stumbled from the bed.

If Jezebel had harbored any liking for Edgar her conscience would have stung her mightily, but it didn't. She called encouraging endearments, and flitted away before Edgar's slowing hands could reach her. She had to give

Edgar credit, however, for he was game. He repeatedly stifled his yawns while he stumbled and bumbled after her.

"Come to me, my little dove," he breathed out, halting in the middle of the room. His arms wavered, in more of a flap than anything else, and then he toppled forward, face first.

"You mean pigeon," Jezebel murmured, and tiptoed to him. A snore greeted her. "Finally!" She bent down and rolled him over. Without compunction, she reached into his pocket and withdrew the contract. She sprung up and rushed to bury it in her cloak's pocket. Then she put the cloak on, her fingers fumbling with the clasp in nervous relief.

Collecting her thoughts, she bent and looked under the table until she discovered the vial she had tossed beneath it. She exclaimed in delight, and it joined the contract in her pocket. Then she turned to study the sprawled figure of Edgar.

She had learned far more from the actresses than acting. Delia was a very lazy actress, and from her Jezebel had learned how to make a man think he had experienced a wondrous night, without a girl ever having to tax herself. Smiling grimly, she trod over to Edgar. Bending, she struggled to divest Edgar of his smoking jacket. Gratefully he wore a nightshirt underneath. According to Delia, she was supposed to take that off as well, but that was where Jezebel drew the line.

She stood, holding the smoking jacket. Grinning, she walked over to the window, opened it, and tossed it out. If Edgar wondered where his jacket and contract were in the morning, he'd have to go hunting for them.

Then she went to the bed, ripped the pillow and sheets from it, and strewed them about Edgar. Remembering Delia's last tip, she grabbed up the champagne bottle and spilt the wine liberally over the snoring Edgar. She set the empty bottle close to his head, then pulled from her cloak pocket the necklace he had given her that morning. She garnished the bottle with it and rose, nodding at her handiwork.

"Good night, Edgar," Jezebel said and tiptoed from the room.

Jezebel's father would be rolling in his grave at her scandalous actions, but she was feeling rather proud of herself as the contract crackled in her pocket. She flitted down the hall, deciding she was surely ahead of schedule. She should have remembered to look at the clock. "You can't think of everything," she murmured to herself and let herself into the room.

"Where have you been?" Terrence's voice cracked.

Jezebel gasped and turned. He lounged in a chair, a glass of champagne in hand. He, too, wore a silk smoking jacket. It made Jezebel's mouth go dry, for he looked dangerously handsome in it. She shook her head. She hadn't cared to see Edgar in bedroom attire, yet she feared she enjoyed seeing Terrence in it far, far too much.

"You . . . you are early," Jezebel said. Then she muttered, "Can no one stay on schedule?"

"Well?" Terrence glowered at her. "Where have you been all this time?"

"Ahem . . ." Jezebel drew a blank. Hoping to distract Terrence, she quickly took the cloak from her shoulders. Unfortunately the gesture did not have the desired effect. He was not distracted as Edgar had been. His eyes did not light, and he did not call her beautiful. Rather, his face darkened even more, if that were possible. "My God, you had nothing under your cloak and you were outside?"

"I am so glad you like my negligee," Jezebel said, anger rising in her. "And yes, I was out in this attire. I . . ." Jezebel halted; then inspiration hit. "I'd forgotten Mordrid, you see. I had to go and tie him up." She walked over to the champagne and poured a glass as calmly as she could. "He is out in the barn with Sir Drake." Which was the truth, but

Mordrid had been secured out in the barn with Sir Drake for the better half of the day, for she had not forgotten him.

Terrence laughed, not pleasantly. "Gads, I'm finally in your bedroom without that hound."

Jezebel looked worriedly at him. "You are not drunk, are you?"

Terrence stiffened. "No, madame, I am not drunk. I believe being forced to enact this scene is sobering enough."

"I assure you," Jezebel said, stung, "I do not look forward to it any more than you do!"

"You need not remind me," Terrence growled. He cast a withering glance over her. "Where is the necklace from Sir Edgar?"

"That's none of your affair," Jezebel snapped.

"No, it is your affair, isn't it?" Terrence said. "I keep forgetting."

"Well, try to remember," Jezebel shot back. "Now, let's get this business over with."

"We still have time."

"Not the way things have been going tonight," Jezebel said in bitterness. "Amelia will most likely be early." She glared. "Like some other people I know."

"Very well." Terrence slapped his champagne glass onto the side table. He sprang up. "No sense prolonging it."

"Of course not!" Jezebel said.

"Indeed!" Terrence said. They glared at each other.

"Well?" Jezebel said, a breathlessness rising within her.

"Ladies first." Terrence waved a hand toward the bed.

Jezebel looked that way and swallowed hard. "Very well!" She quickly lifted her glass and drank a deep gulp, then stalked to the bed and slammed her glass down upon the bedside table. Muttering under her breath, she crawled under the covers, scooting all the way to the other side. She lay stiff, gripping the sheet. "Well?" she asked, when she sensed no movement from Terrence. "It's your turn!"

"Of course, it's my turn," Terrence said, striding to the

bed. "You don't have to tell me." He ripped off his smoking jacket. "I know how it's done, I assure you. And plenty of women can attest to that," he said, crawling into the bed upon his side. "Plenty!"

"I have no doubt." Jezebel looked straight ahead, all but shredding the sheets with her fingernails. "Most likely scores."

"Scores and scores," Terrence growled. "And scores!"

"I get the point!" Jezebel snapped.

Silence fell. Then Terrence said, "I was under the impression 'twas you didn't know how. But since you are planning this scene so well—"

"Be quiet!" Jezebel gritted out. "Just be quiet!"

"Of course," Terrence said. "Anything to please a lady!"

"Stop calling me that in that nasty tone," Jezebel said.

"Certainly," Terrence said. Once again silence fell. "Well, madame, when do we start?"

"W-we can wait until . . . until we hear Amelia c-coming," Jezebel said with a stammer.

"Fine," Terrence said.

"Fine," Jezebel said.

Both lay there, staring straight ahead.

Seventeen

Amelia opened the window and looked out into the night sky. She was exhilarated. Visions of her future as a learned and respected matron swirled within her head. It had taken Jezebel to show her how it would be for her. She would gladly help the woman pack so that she might leave and Amelia could go forth into her grand future.

Smiling, Amelia turned from the window. *Coo-coo-chw* sounded. Amelia halted. She had never heard such a bird call before. She dashed back to the window and peered out. *Coo-coo-chw* trilled again. She peered into the darkness and waited. *Coo-coo-chw* arose to her from somewhere below.

She turned from the window in eagerness. She simply must discover what kind of bird it was. Then she remembered she had to go see Jezebel. She had promised, and Jezebel had seemed desperate for her to do so.

Coo-coo-chw drifted through the window again.

"She's got to be coming soon," Jezebel said.

"Yes," Terrence replied. "Now is about the time."

"All right." Jezebel stiffened. "I suppose w-we should start."

"On command," Terrence said. It sounded as if he were gritting his teeth. "Very well."

He rolled toward her, and Jezebel gripped the sheet, closing her eyes. Already, she was strung and tense, lying beside

Terrence having proven a wicked torture. Every salacious and seductive thought of what it would be for him to kiss her again had cavorted through her mind, mocking her into anger and self-disgust. This was going to be nothing but an act, not the real thing.

Terrence shifted on top of her and Jezebel wheezed. It was amazing how different it was when both bodies were stiff and tense. His elbow dug into her rib.

"Ouch," Jezebel cried at the very moment Terrence kissed her. Their teeth clicked painfully together.

"Damn," Terrence cried. He rolled swiftly away, sitting up.

Jezebel snapped her eyes open, swiveling her head to glare at him. "You hurt me!"

"I hurt you?" Terrence said, his hand nursing his mouth. "You hurt me! There was no reason to bite me."

"I did not bite you!" Jezebel gasped. "You dug your elbow into me!"

"Well, it would help," Terrence said, "if you wouldn't clutch the damn sheets so much." He reached over and tugged at her hands. They were locked, of their own accord, to the material. He shook them. "Let go, Jezebel."

"I will," Jezebel promised, but her hands refused to budge.

"Let go!" Terrence commanded, and ripped her hands from the sheets. He almost fell back with the effort.

Jezebel swiftly scrabbled up. "This is not going to work!"

"Yes, it is," Terrence said, his face stiff and determined. "I have done this before. I know I can do this."

Jezebel swallowed hard. "And if you can do it, I can do it."

Terrence's brow lifted. "Really?"

"Yes!" Jezebel almost shouted.

He looked at her warily. "You won't bite me?"

"I did not . . ." Jezebel stopped. "All right, I won't bite you. But don't jab your elbow into me."

"Agreed," Terrence said. "Now let me direct this scene, we'll fare better, I hope."

Jezebel made to object, but he shot her a warning look. She bit her lip. "All right."

"Now come here and put your arms around me," Terrence ordered. Jezebel, nodding, scooted close. Shutting her eyes, she clamped her arms about him.

"Jezebel," Terrence gurgled, "I can't breathe."

Since she lacked that particular ability herself, she felt no sympathy for his complaint. She did, however, release him and retreat.

Terrence shook his head, running a hand through his hair. "Let's try this a different way. You"—He cast her a stern look—"Don't do anything."

"Nothing?" Jezebel asked.

"Nothing," Terrence said. "I might come through this alive that way." He shifted on the bed so that he sat extremely close to her. Lifting a hand to her chin, he cupped it. Then he leaned over and lightly kissed her. It was a feather touch, and a tingle flowed down Jezebel's spine. She drew in a gasp, her eyes fluttering shut.

"Don't move," Terrence murmured softly, and just as softly kissed her cheek, her temple, and her closed lids. One of his hands slid to the back of her neck, gently kneading it. The other found the curve of her waist, sending heat through the sheer silk. Jezebel sighed, as her tension drained away, replaced by a glowing warmth.

Terrence's mouth claimed hers then, with a taste of need, the very need building in Jezebel. She moaned slightly and pressed into that kiss, opening to it. Reaching out, she wrapped her arms about him, bringing her body close to his. Terrence groaned, his kiss deepening with a fierceness. Jezebel ignited, and she met his searching lips with an equal passion. Needing more, she pulled at him, dragging him to her.

"Jez, you are moving," Terrence rasped, as they toppled

back. No sharp elbows interfered as their bodies entwined in far more difficult moves until they lay supine. It was soft flesh and hard melding in an orchestration of passion.

Jezebel welcomed Terrence's weight on top of her, stretching her body to feel the new and wondrous length of his.

"Jez," Terrence panted, his lips close to her ear. "For God's sake, don't move."

"Hmmm, yes," Jezebel said, splaying her hands and running them along the strong cording of his shoulders.

"That's right," Terrence said. "Don't move."

Groaning, Terrence grazed her neck with kisses, his hands learning her curves, leaving a brand of heat and sensation. "Jez, Jez," he whispered as his lips trailed to the curve of her breast.

"Yes? Yes?" she murmured, afloat on a sea of sensation. Her name rang in her ears, as if called from every direction. Yet in her mind she only heard Terrence's name, feeling and needing only him.

"Jez!" Suddenly it was a roar. Confusion shot through Jezebel. It wasn't Terrence's voice this time. It was Josh's. "What the devil is going on in here!"

"Josh!" Cold water doused every heated nerve in Jezebel. She screeched and pushed at Terrence as reality crashed in upon her. Terrence groaned, but rolled from her. She sat up quickly. "J-Josh," Jezebel said stupidly as she discovered her brother staring at her from the open door. "W-what are you doing here?"

His face was white, his eyes a startling blue. "I called. You said yes. I came in."

"Oh," Jezebel said, gulping. She didn't remember it, but was not about to confess that.

"Hello, Josh," Terrence said, his voice roughened.

"Don't hello me," Josh said, his fists clenching. "You bounder. You loose screw. Had me gulled, didn't you? I thought you were a gentleman, when you've been doing—doing that all along."

"Not long enough, I assure you," Terrence said, his teeth clearly clenched.

"No, Josh," Jezebel cried. "We haven't been doing . . . well, doing that. I-I mean this. We—we were only . . . only acting."

"Acting!" Josh cried. "That ain't acting! It's . . . well, it's—"

"Doing that." Terrence sighed.

"Damn you," Josh yelled. He paced across the room to Terrence. "How dare you seduce Jezebel! How dare you defame her! You are going to marry her and make an honest woman of her."

"M-marry?" Jezebel blinked.

"Honest?" Terrence asked. His face settled into cold lines. "Since it is you two who set me up, I don't see where honesty is necessary."

"What?" Jezebel asked, stunned.

"Set you up?" Josh cried.

"Yes." Terrence glared at Jezebel. "He doesn't look much like Amelia. You had this planned all the time, didn't you?"

Jezebel's mouth fell open and she gaped. His meaning finally snaked into her numb, passion dazed mind. "Why you . . . you . . ." She reached out and slapped him soundly. "Beast!" She scrambled away, stumbling from the bed.

"Dog!" Josh cried. Even before Terrence could recover from Jezebel's stinging slap, Josh grabbed him by his nightshirt. "How dare you suggest a thing like that. Jezebel ain't like that!" He shook Terrence. "She ain't, and you'll marry her else I'll call you out and put a bullet through your dark heart."

"No!" Jezebel cried, aghast. "No, Josh!"

"I accept," Terrence said, and gripping Josh's arms tossed him onto the bed. The two men rolled upon it, the pillows flying.

"No, no," Jezebel cried, hopping up and down with rage. "I'll not go through it again." The men continued to punch and roll. "I don't know how I'll stop another duel, so don't do it!"

Suddenly both men froze.

"What did you say?" Josh asked, letting loose of Terrence's shirt and sitting up.

"Yes, Jezebel," Terrence said, following suit, his eyes narrowed, "what did you say?"

Jezebel blinked. "Er, nothing. I only meant—"

"You did it, didn't you?" Terrence said. "You made St. John draw off."

"No," Jezebel said, biting her lip. "Of course not."

"You're lying," Josh exclaimed. "I can tell."

As both men looked at her in accusation, sudden rage shot through Jezebel. Glaring at them in defiance, she said, "Very well, I did it. And why in heaven I did, I don't know. I wish I hadn't. I wish St. John had put a ball through both of your thick male hides." She spun about, sheer frustration driving her. "Telling us when to behave, telling us when not to behave." She cast a look of loathing toward Terrence. "Telling us not to interfere with men's honor, and all the while trying to take ours." She halted abruptly, her pain and rage exploding. "I hate you! Do you hear me? I hate you!"

"Don't matter," Josh said, his face reddening. "You are going to marry Terry, and that's that."

"No," Terrence said. "I won't marry a conniving, scheming hussy."

"Oh, yes, you will," Josh said. "And don't call her a hussy."

"He can call me anything he likes, because I won't marry him," Jezebel said, drawing herself up, in fury. "I wouldn't marry him if he were the last man on earth. I'll become . . . I'll become any man's mistress before I become his wife."

"No, you won't," Terrence roared, springing from the bed. "You won't become Edgar's mistress."

Jezebel started, but then said, "I didn't mean him, but he'll do. Thank you for the suggestion."

"Damn it," Terrence said. "I won't allow it. You'll marry me first."

"Right," Josh nodded vigorously. "It's only proper!"

"Proper?" Jezebel rolled her eyes. Shaking with anger, she sashayed up to Terrence. "You mean you'll marry me to save my honor and keep me from becoming Edgar's mistress?"

A muscle jumped along Terrence's cheek, but he said, "Yes."

"Right," Josh said. "Only thing to do."

"Wrong!" Jezebel roared. She glared at Terrence, determined to hide the pain ripping through her. "I'm that conniving, scheming hussy, remember? The one who just entrapped you. I don't have any honor to save. Besides, a man of your 'character' does not marry his mistress."

"You aren't my mistress," Terrence said.

"And I never shall be," Jezebel said, the burn of tears stinging her eyes. "Nor shall I be your wife."

"Here now," Josh exclaimed, scrabbling from the bed. "Stop saying that. Terry said he'll marry you and you've got to marry him."

"I won't," Jezebel said, a catch in her voice. "I won't."

"Be sensible, Jez," Josh said. "You've got to marry him, he and you were . . . well, you've been compromised."

"I'll be more compromised if I marry him," Jezebel protested.

Terrence stiffened, a dull flush staining his cheeks. "She's right, Josh. We would never be able to marry."

"Yes, you would," Josh yelped. "You'd be perfect together."

"We'd make each other miserable." Jezebel's heart tightened.

"Yes," Terrence said. "She'd be always managing and manipulating."

"And he would always be longing for his freedom."

"She'd rather have Mordrid in bed than me," Terrence complained.

"And he'd have actresses on the side," Jezebel said.

"Stop it!" Josh roared. Terrence and Jezebel turned, stunned. His blue eyes flashed anger. "You both talk rot. You love each other, and that's what counts!"

"No!" Terrence and Jezebel said in unison.

"No?" Josh said. He jabbed a finger to the bed. "I know what I saw, and it was a damn sight more than—"

"Be quiet!" Jezebel cried.

"Shut up," Terrence said. He refused to look at Jezebel. "She says she won't marry me, and I said I won't marry her. You can call me out, you can call her out, but we will not marry." He spun on his heel and stalked from the room.

"Jezebel," Josh said, his voice pleading.

"No, Josh," she said. "N-now please leave."

"Very well," Josh muttered. He walked stiffly from the room.

Finally the tears fell. Jezebel, choked up, threw herself upon the bed. As her wracking sobs subsided, the thought of her and Terrence and what they had been doing upon this very bed swamped her. Crying out, she scrambled from it.

Dashing away her tears, she walked to the armoire. She opened the door and began pulling out a few dresses of the cheaper and less virulent variety. She would take only those, only enough for the travel home.

Jezebel slipped out of the Duchess's room. She had found she could not bring herself to write her goodbye. She had merely left the contract upon the bedside table with a sheaf of paper saying "With love, Jezebel." In truth, that line said it all.

She went to Josh's room and rapped on the door, cringing inside. Talking with him would be the hardest. She rapped again. "Josh, wake up."

Suddenly the door opened. Josh stood before her, still dressed, still apparently awake. "Oh, good," she said, looking down and brushing past him. "I was afraid you were . . ." She halted. His bags were set upon his bed. She spun about. "Josh . . ."

He grinned sheepishly. "Since you won't marry Terrence, thought you might wish to leave tonight."

Those disgusting tears welled in Jezebel's eyes. "Oh, Josh!" She rushed toward him, and he enveloped her in his arms. "Oh, Josh. I'm s-sorry."

"I'm sorry too," he said, his voice hoarse. "I acted like an idiot back there."

"No." Jezebel sniffed into his jacket. "Y-you didn't. But . . . I want to go home."

"We will," Josh soothed. "We will."

Jezebel suddenly withdrew to look at him. "But are you sure you wish to come with me? Don't you want to stay?"

Josh's expression stiffened and his eyes grew dark. "No reason for me to stay if you don't."

"What about Elizabeth?" Jezebel asked softly.

He shook his head. "There ain't no reason to stay."

"But, Josh, you love her."

Anguish flickered in his blue eyes. "You should know th-that just because you love someone doesn't mean you two will marry."

Jezebel looked down, her heart wrenching. "No, no it doesn't."

"Elizabeth don't love me," Josh said, sighing.

Jezebel shook her head. "I think she does. But you need to tell her I am only your sister."

He hugged her tight. "You ain't 'only' anything. So don't you say that."

Jezebel chuckled through her tears, "I am so glad you are my brother."

"Are you?" Josh asked. "Even after I've muffed it like I have?"

"I am," Jezebel said, nodding and smiling. She frowned. "But if you would only tell Elizabeth the truth . . ."

He grimaced. "I'll promise not to call Terrence out, or ask you to marry him, if you don't ask me to tell Elizabeth the truth. She hates me enough as it is, and for her to find out that I lied . . . well, don't think I could bear it."

Josh's face showed such hurt, Jezebel swallowed. "All right."

He straightened, and suddenly there was an air, a strength, to him she had never seen before. "Best be going. Ain't no use in thinking what might have been. We got to do what's best for . . . for them."

"Yes," Jezebel said, her voice sad. "Yes, we do."

Terrence set his teacup down with a rattle. He was seated at the breakfast table, and conversation flowed around him, forks scraped on plates, racks of toast were passed. Everything seemed somewhat normal. Dorethea appeared in fine fettle, a smug look upon her face. Every time she looked at Edgar she would break out into a feline grin. Terrence could not smile when he looked at Edgar, for a strangling jealousy would swell within him. Gratefully Edgar appeared silent and sullen that morning, else Terrence feared he would have ripped the man's head off.

As Terrence's gaze roved to two empty chairs, tension built in him. When would he have to face sister and brother? When would he be forced to face the woman who had declared she'd never marry him? The woman who had set his blood on fire and set him up, only to turn him down. Damn you, Jezebel, he thought, even as he picked up his fork, damn you.

"Don't know what's the matter with Mordrid," Theo was saying. "In an odd mood. Came to me this morning, dragging a man's smoking jacket in his teeth and whining."

"Blast it, he didn't!" Edgar yelped. Everyone looked to

him at this outburst. He flushed. "Well, the infernal beast gets into everything. Damn him."

"Do you think it was your jacket?" Dorethea asked, setting her cup down.

"Wouldn't know," Edgar said quickly. "Didn't look . . . er, wouldn't know."

Everyone stopped of a sudden, watching Edgar. He stared down at his plate, shoving his food around.

Into the silence came Stilton. He walked to Dorethea, a surprising alarm upon his face.

"Yes?" Dorethea said, her gaze still upon Edgar. "What is it, Stilton?"

"Your Grace," the butler said. "I do not wish to overstep my bounds. However, even though the stable boy informs me it was with your full knowledge, I wish to ensure that you knew Miss Jezebel and Mr. Rakesham departed in a carriage early this morning."

Dorethea's head snapped to her butler, her green eyes shocked. "What?"

"Yes, Your Grace," Stilton said. "They told him that you had approved it, and that he could expect the carriage back in three days."

"Good God!" Dorethea said.

"Jezebel left?" Letty exclaimed. "But . . . but I do not understand."

"Stole the carriage as well," Theo said. "Learns fast, that girl."

"She left?" roared Edgar. "With that damn Mr. Rakesham?" His face reddened, and he appeared about to suffer an apoplexy. "She chose to run off with that Rakesham fellow instead of me?"

"And why shouldn't she?" Elizabeth asked, her face whiter than a sheet. "I-I would have."

"The Jezebel," Edgar cried, slamming his fist upon the table. "I give her a necklace and she tosses it back in my face."

"She didn't?" Letty asked, amazed. " 'Twas rude, and I've never known Jezebel to be so. Well, upon occasion, but only with unsavory characters who deserve it." Her eyes widened as she looked at Edgar. "Oh, dear . . . well."

"Cheer up, Edgar," Theo said. "Should be pleased. At least it wasn't a flowerpot this time."

"Harrumph!" Edgar looked down. "She didn't exactly toss it back in my face. She left it . . . er, in my room last night."

"She left it?" Terrence said, a sudden joy bounding within him. "She returned it to you?"

"Yes, blast it," Edgar growled. Terrence couldn't help it. He started to laugh, uproariously. Edgar's face darkened, and he said, "Don't you laugh, young man, 'cause it was only after we spent a wonderful night together."

Terrence stiffened, and stood slowly. "You lie!"

"No, I don't!" Edgar bounded up. "The little vixen wore me out."

"That is why," Amelia gasped, "she was not in her room when I went to see her."

Terrence, stunned, looked at her. "When did you go to see her, and why?"

Amelia flushed. "She . . . she said she was leaving you and that . . . that I should come to her room and help her pack. I-I had no notion she was leaving you for . . . for Papa."

"She didn't," Elizabeth said in a dead tone. "She left him for Josh."

Terrence glared at Amelia. "Did she tell you when you were supposed to come to her room?"

"Yes," Amelia said, flushing. "I-I was supposed to help her at fifteen after twelve, but . . . but I was late. There was a bird, you see. I heard him call, and I fear I went to find him."

A cruel reality gripped Terrence. Jezebel had not lied. She had planned for Amelia to be there. He raked Amelia with a scathing eye. "You let a damn bird stop you from coming to Jezebel's room?"

"It had the most un-unusual call," Amelia said, cowering.

"I can't believe it, because of you I accused Jezebel of . . ." Terrence stopped and shook his head, remembering the terrible things he had said. "All because you took it into your little brain to chase after a bird." He laughed bitterly. "Well, I'll take it as a sign."

Amelia frowned. "What do you mean?"

Terrence grinned evilly. "I hope to blazes you found your bird, because this particular one is flying the coop. You took the owl as a sign we were supposed to marry. I take that bird last night as a sign we are not going to marry."

"What?" Amelia was stunned. "But . . . but—"

"Divine intervention," Terrence said, laughing. He felt a weight rolling off him, a light as bright as the sun bursting through him. "I'm not going to marry you, Amelia. You can take your damn birds and . . . and travel to the south of France, or even to a much warmer climate than that, and I won't give a rap. You can meet all those other scholars too, but beware. They'll find you more of a birdwit than the creatures they study. But once again, I don't care, better they suffer your inanity and frigidness than I. I'm going to marry Jezebel!"

"Huzzah!" Theo exclaimed, while Letty clapped her hands and Dorethea chuckled.

"What?" Edgar shouted. "You can't toss my little girl over for the likes of that strumpet. Why, Jezebel spent the night with me, a night like you wouldn't believe!"

"No, I wouldn't," Terrence said with a grin, his heart suddenly opening up and knowing it would trust Jezebel no matter what. "Whatever you say, I wouldn't believe you. I know Jezebel."

"Excuse me," Stilton said. "If I may be permitted to speak . . ."

"No, you can't," Edgar said, glaring. "You're just a damn butler."

"Do speak, Stilton," Dorethea invited. "I am enthralled."

Stilton bowed. "Miss Jezebel could not have spent the entire night with Sir Edgar, not unless you, Master Terrence, did not meet her at twelve o'clock." He turned a raised brow to Terrence. "And I do hope you were not so ungentlemanly as not to do that?"

Terrence laughed. "No, I wasn't." He turned an accusing eye upon Amelia. "Unlike some people I know, I arrived when I promised I would. I was even early."

Stilton bowed. "As was Sir Arrowroot. Miss Jezebel was quite in a turmoil over that."

"What?" Edgar exclaimed. "How—how did you know that?"

"A butler should know everything," Dorethea said. "That is why I employ Stilton."

Stilton nodded. "I was the one who delivered the bottles of champagne upon Miss Jezebel's request." He looked apologetically to Dorethea. "She assured me she would do nothing to harm you or Master Terrence, but, rather, would help you."

"So she did," Dorethea said. "So she did."

The butler turned back to Edgar. "Her request was for me to deliver a bottle of champagne to your room before ten-thirty, and one to her room before twelve o'clock. She left her room for your room at twenty-five after ten, and if she met Master Terrence—"

"And I was early," Terrence said. "So she couldn't have spent more than an hour with you." He laughed. "She said she went to take care of Mordrid, but I now see she went to take care of a different dog."

"Impossible!" Edgar blustered. "I know better. When I woke up this morning . . ." He flushed. "Impossible."

"Impossible or not," Terrence said. "I trust Jezebel."

"But we . . . she . . ." Edgar said.

"Even if you did"—Terrence's jaw clenched—"I do not care. I will not marry Amelia. I am going to marry Jezebel."

"You are not!" Edgar roared. "I will sue you for breach of promise! I will—"

"You shall not, Edgar," Dorethea said, rather calmly from the end of the table.

"What?" he exclaimed. "I most certainly shall."

"No." Dorethea smiled smugly. "I fear you did not only lose your smoking jacket—and Jezebel—last night but something else."

Edgar stared at her, frowning. Then his eyes widened and he almost choked. "You mean . . . ?"

Dorethea nodded. "My grandson and I will both deny that there was an agreement for a marriage. And since you announced it without his consent, without even notice to the papers, I do not believe you will have much to stand upon."

Edgar blanched. "You mean . . . she . . . you—"

"I had a very pleasant fire this morning." Dorethea smiled.

Edgar fell back into his chair, stunned. "The Jezebel."

Terrence lifted a brow and looked to Dorethea. "Are you going to tell me what this is all about?"

"Upon my deathbed," Dorethea said. "Or upon your wedding day."

Terrence grinned widely. "Then I'd best hurry if I want my answer, for I find I don't wish to wait until your death, which I hope will be many years from now."

"Yes." Dorethea nodded. "After the grandchildren. But you must do it on your own. Jezebel made me promise not to do anything in that respect."

Terrence grinned. "Outgunned you, did she, Grandmother?"

"She is a Jezebel," Dorethea said, cracking another smile.

"I can't believe it," Edgar said, sitting hunched. "I can't believe it."

"Believe it," Terrence said. He laughed. "Believe anything about Jezebel you wish, because she is a surprising woman. And she is going to be my wife." He glanced at Amelia. "I should say I am sorry, but—"

"Sorry!" Amelia's face was as flushed as her father's. "You . . . you insulted me. You insulted my birds. You've insulted the fine scholars with whom . . . I will study. Jezebel was right, I would never gain their respect with y-you as my husband. I won't marry you!" she cried out, shaking her head. "I refuse! I won't think of God and country. I won't!"

Terrence sighed, but his lips twitched. "I wish you hadn't said that. Now I will have to find another ploy to entrap Jezebel." He grinned. "Well, I must leave you."

"I wish to go with you," Elizabeth said, standing. Her face was pale, but her gray eyes flashed fire. "I hope you succeed with Jezebel, because I-I refuse to let her have Josh."

Terrence studied her, and then smiled. "There are things about him you do not know."

"I do not care," Elizabeth protested. "No matter what he's done, I do not care."

"Do you trust him?" Terrence asked softly.

"Yes," Elizabeth replied. "I do."

He nodded. "As I do Jezebel." He laughed. "They are two of a kind, I assure you. In fact, they could be of the same family."

"Good God!" Dorethea exclaimed. Her eyes widened. "That is why . . . My Lord!"

Terrence looked at the thunderstruck Duchess and chuckled. "Outgunned again, Grandmother darling?"

Dorethea stiffened. "But . . . but if they are—"

"Come, Elizabeth," Terrence said, chuckling. "You must steal Josh from Jezebel, and I must steal Jezebel."

Elizabeth's eyes shone, and she nodded. "Fair enough."

"Terrence," Dorethea roared, standing. "I demand to know—"

"Goodbye one and all," Terrence said, and strode from the table. Elizabeth was right behind him.

"Terrence, I demand an answer!" Dorethea bellowed. "I demand one now!"

Eighteen

Josh stared down at his tankard of ale, not really seeing it or hearing the men about him in the taproom as they laughed and swapped tales. He and Jezebel had stopped at an inn she knew about, and the innkeeper, who had given them two rooms, had been surprisingly gracious to Jezebel. She still lay asleep upstairs, exhausted, no doubt. She had asked him to wake her, for she had wanted only a few hours sleep before they continued to London.

Josh lifted his tankard and sipped from it. He'd let her sleep, for he saw no reason to hurry. It wasn't as if they were escaping. He swallowed hard. It wasn't as if they were going anywhere either. A bleakness enveloped him at the thought of returning to his life in London, never to see Elizabeth again.

"Hello, Josh." It was Elizabeth's voice.

Josh closed his eyes with a sigh. Faith, he even heard her voice as if she were there with him.

"I believe when a lady addresses you, you should give her an answer." Elizabeth spoke again, "I refuse to be ignored."

There was a definite edge to that voice, not at all like one in a dream. Josh popped his eyes open, stunned. Elizabeth, partnered by Terrence, stood before his table.

"Elizabeth!" Josh exclaimed, stumbling up. "What . . . what are you doing here?"

"She came with me," Terrence said, grinning.

"Yes. I figured if you could run away with Jezebel, I could run away with Terrence," Elizabeth explained.

"Run away with . . . ?" Josh gurgled, and his eyes slid to Terrence, jealousy striking him. "Why, you cad—"

"No, don't call me out," Terrence said, raising his hands. "In truth, we are here to stop you two lovers from fleeing. It is *you* who are the cad. For shame, to steal Jezebel right from under my nose, you villain."

Josh began to protest, but Terrence asked, "Where is Jezebel by the way?"

"Sh-she's sleeping," Josh stammered, his eyes still wide and fixed upon Elizabeth. On her face was a mixture of anger and anguish.

"Is she?" Terrence said. "Good! I always fare better when she is unconscious. Well, I'll leave you two. I need to go and find Bentwood, for the key."

"What?" Josh asked, tearing his gaze away from Elizabeth. Terrence was already strolling away. He looked back to Elizabeth, and his mouth turned dry. "Er, it isn't what you think, Elizabeth."

"No." Elizabeth's voice was strained. "Please, before you speak, I-I wish to say something."

Josh tensed, ready for her angry words. He glanced hastily around, realizing the men in the room were watching them. He did not relish an audience when Elizabeth raked him down. "It . . . it ain't proper for you to be here in the taproom. Y-you're a lady."

"I'm not," Elizabeth said. One of the men laughed, and she flushed. "What I mean to say is, I need to speak now or . . . or else I'll lose my courage."

"Elizabeth," Josh said. "Let us go to someplace more private."

"This isn't easy for me," Elizabeth said, twisting her hands and appearing as if she had not heard him. "I-I know you are running off with Jezebel, even though you said you loved me."

A mumbling rustled through the taproom. "And . . . and I can understand. She is very beautiful, far more beautiful than me."

"I think you're just fine, lass," a burly man from the corner table called out. "Likes your looks, I do!"

"Here now," Josh said, glaring at the man. "Don't be saying that to her! You're a stranger."

"I've got eyes in my head." The man grinned. "If'n you don't!"

"And . . . and she . . . she is very charming," Elizabeth said, obviously set and determined. "I mean, if I didn't wish to scratch her eyes out, I w-would love her too."

Josh looked back to her in shock. "Scratch her eyes out? Why'd you want to do that?"

"Because . . ." Elizabeth looked down. "B-because—"

"You ought to scratch his eyes out, lass," the man called out once again. "It's him that's done you wrong."

"I told you not to talk to her," Josh cried, spinning toward the man. "Damn you, don't talk to her!"

"Why?" the man shot back, heaving up from his chair. "If you're tossing her over, she's fair game."

"She ain't," Josh roared and charged toward the table.

"No!" Elizabeth cried. "Josh, you've got to listen to me. I'm trying to tell you something!"

"I'll tear your tongue out!" Josh growled, as he met up with the man. He clamped his hands on the man's neck.

"Right, bucko," the man said, wrapping iron arms around him.

"Josh, you're not listening to me," Elizabeth cried. "I'm trying to tell you I love you!"

"What?" Josh exclaimed. With Josh's attention diverted, the burly man moved swiftly, shifting him into a full head-lock. "What! Wh-what's that you say?"

"I want to marry you!" Elizabeth said.

"You . . . you want to marry me?" Josh wheezed. He slapped at the man, attempting to break free. "Damn it, let me loose! She wants to marry me!"

"You saying yes to the lass?" the man grunted, holding firm.

"Yes," Josh cried. "Yes!"

"The devil." The man sighed and released him. "There go my chances."

Josh didn't take notice, for he finally could see Elizabeth, who stood there, beautiful and with an amazingly hesitant look in her eyes. He shook his head. "You want to marry me?"

"Yes," she nodded. "I do."

"You do!" Josh hooted and bounded across the taproom, snatching up Elizabeth and swinging her around. Finally he let her feet touch the ground, only so he could kiss her wildly. And she kissed him back with a fervor which awed him to his very heart. Only the laughter and the applause of the men around them caused him to draw back. Flushing, he said, "I love you."

"And I love you too, Mr. Rakesham." Elizabeth's smile was tremulous.

Josh's face suddenly fell. "Oh, Lord."

"What is it?" Elizabeth asked.

Josh glanced about. The men still watched with smirking faces. He grabbed hold of Elizabeth's hand. "Let's talk elsewhere," he said nervously, and then dragged her with him.

"Josh, what is it?" she gasped.

He tugged her along the bar and into the small room behind it. Bottles and mops and towels littered the small space, but it was empty of human kind. Gripping Elizabeth's hand he turned to look down at her, mustering his courage. "I-I've got to tell you something."

He could feel her stiffen. "What?"

"Well, m-my name ain't Rakesham," Josh confessed.

Elizabeth shook her head. "It isn't?"

"No," Josh said. "It's Clinton. Jezebel is my . . . my sister."

Elizabeth's eyes widened. "Sh-she's your sister?"

"Yes," Josh said, as Elizabeth's face paled. "She ain't really an actress either, or . . . or Terry's mistress. They . . . they were just pretending. And when I came, well, things got in a tangle." He flushed. "Y-you was telling everyone such stories about me, and . . . and it was easier t-to go along with those in-instead of the real one."

Elizabeth stared, mute, as if she were turned to stone.

"I wanted to tell you," Josh said, anguished. "But I'd promised Jezebel I-I wouldn't. And the Duchess seemed like she would let me stay when she thought I was a rake, but I didn't think she would if she knew who I truly was."

Elizabeth slowly came to life. The color swept back into her face, and her gray eyes flashed. "Then who was that Molly you talked about th-the first night?"

Josh groaned. Of all the questions she could ask, she had chosen that one. "Ahem, she . . . she was my mistress and is an . . . an actress. That's how it all started. She—"

"I don't want to hear it." Elizabeth stepped back quickly from him. "I don't!"

"But she was the only one, Elizabeth!" Josh cried. "I swear. And I didn't love her. I-I know that now."

"The only one?" Elizabeth asked, her tone darkly suspicious.

"Y-yes, the only one." Josh flushed to an even fierier degree, shifting upon his feet. "I'm sorry. Lied about that, too. I-I ain't a rake. In fact, ain't much with the ladies."

"You aren't?" Elizabeth said. "You could have fooled me. In fact, you did fool me."

"Well, when I'm with you, I can't . . ." Josh stopped. "I-I can't seem to behave proper. You—you make me feel l-like a rake."

"I see," Elizabeth said, looking down.

"Pl-please Elizabeth," Josh said. "W-will you forgive me?"

Her gaze rose to his, and her chin lifted. "I most certainly shall not. Because of you, I proposed to a Mr. Rakesham, and . . . and in front of all those men in the taproom."

"I know," Josh nodded, his heart sinking.

Elizabeth looked at him sternly. "So what are you going to do about it, Mr. Clinton? At this moment I am engaged to a rake and a bounder."

Then Josh saw it. A glimmer of a twinkle in her eyes. It brought a bit of hope to him. Heart thudding, Josh fell to one knee. "Please Elizabeth, do not m-marry Mr. Rakesham, r-run away with me instead. I promise I'll be faithful and love you forever. I'll be as proper as you want."

"Or don't want?" Elizabeth asked softly.

Josh's eyes widened. "Or . . . or don't want."

"Good." She sighed. "Because you see, I've known this one rake, and I've . . . I've grown fond of him."

Josh sprang up and with a fierce joy pulled Elizabeth to him. "I promise, I can do better than that f-fellow. Much better!"

Josh Clinton lowered his lips and kissed Elizabeth ruthlessly, far more ruthlessly than Mr. Rakesham ever had.

Jezebel sat at the piano in her father's study, hitting the keys one by one. Why there was a piano in the study she could not fathom, but one was there. She was trying to find the notes to the song she and Terrence had sung that night upon the stage; "My True Love." The words and tune escaped her, and she desperately wanted to remember them, needed to remember them.

"What are you dreaming, sweetings?" Terrence asked.

Jezebel looked up, stunned. Suddenly he stood beside the piano, looking handsome and devilish. He was there, just when she knew she was never going to see him again. "Terrence?"

"Yes," he said, walking over to sit down upon the bench

beside her. He reached up and smoothed her hair. "What are you dreaming about?"

She frowned and her heart sank. "I'm dreaming?"

Still he smoothed her hair. "Yes, you are. Are you dreaming about me?"

Jezebel looked at him. It was a rather foolish question since he was sitting right next to her. "Of course."

"Do you dream about me often?" he asked.

She looked down. "I don't want to, but I do."

"Do you love me, Jezebel?" Terrence asked.

She looked up at him, shook her head. "I-I can't tell you that."

Terrence smiled. "It's only a dream, dear, you can tell me."

He was right, it was only a dream. "Yes, I love you."

He brushed her cheek. "Will you marry me?"

It was a wonderful dream! "Yes, yes, I will!"

Terrence smiled and leaned over and kissed her. Jezebel wrapped her arms about him, feeling exhilarated. She kissed him desperately.

"Jezebel, we've got to stop," he said, unaccountably drawing away.

"It's only a dream." Jezebel sighed happily. She hugged him close, but he pulled her arms from around his neck.

"Wake up, Jezebel!" Terrence said. Suddenly Terrence's form shimmered, turning hazy. "Wake up!"

He vaporized.

Crying out, Jezebel snapped open her eyes. Her world careened and then everything came into focus. Terrence leaned over her, her arms folded around his neck "Wh-what?"

He freed himself quickly and bounded from the bed. Shaking her head in confusion, Jezebel sat up. Terrence now stood across the room, a devilish look upon his face, the same one he'd had in the dream. Only this was reality. "Terrence, what are you doing?"

"Making sure you won't kick me out of bed again." He laughed, though his eyes were dark, passion filled. "But I am glad to know you will marry me. I wouldn't want you to take advantage of me again unless your intentions are honorable."

"Take advantage of you? I never did." Jezebel gasped as the gist of his words sunk into her befuddled mind. "Marry you! I didn't say I would marry you!"

"Yes, you did," Terrence said, smiling. "Just a moment ago." He shook his head. "Your memory is slipping, sweetheart."

"A moment ago?" Jezebel thought a second, and then understanding flushed through her. She glared at him. "But that was in my dream."

"And I'll take that dream," Terrence said, softly. "With all my heart."

Jezebel's throat constricted. "But—but I was unconscious."

"I find you adorable when you are unconscious," Terrence declared. "But since we both know your dangerous tendency when you are asleep, I really think we should wed soon, so that I can protect you, as it were."

"Protect me!" Jezebel said. She was coming fully awake, and mortification engulfed her. "The only one I need protection from is you!"

"And I am offering it to you," Terrence said.

"You took advantage of me!" Jezebel protested, finding safety in anger. "I was sleeping, and I was—"

"I know." Terrence nodded. "You were unconscious." His eyes darkened. "So now I am asking you, awake and conscious, will you marry me?"

Jezebel gaped at him. "I-I don't understand. Why are you asking me? You . . . you didn't want to marry me last night."

"Last night I was unconscious," Terrence said softly. "But I've wakened from my nightmare. I just didn't realize that was what it was."

"B-but what about Amelia?" Jezebel asked.

He grinned. "She's cried off. I insulted one too many of her feathered friends for her liking. And Edgar . . . well, I don't know what you did to him last night, but he's rolled up. I know Grandmother and you were both involved, but she says she'll not tell me until her deathbed—or until our wedding day."

Jezebel flushed. "Indeed."

"Though I'd like to know what trick you used." Terrence smiled. "Edgar claims you and he spent a wondrous night together."

"He did?" Jezebel asked. "Then it did work. Delia was right!"

"Delia?"

"Delia. You know, the one who played the maid instead of me?" Jezebel said "She's the one who told me how to do it. I put laudanum in Edgar's champagne, and when he passed out, I arranged the room so that when he woke up he'd think he'd . . . ahem, had a wonderful night."

Terrence cracked a laugh. "I hope you don't intend to do that on our honeymoon."

She looked down, unable to speak.

Terrence walked toward her, but halted at the foot of the bed. "Jezebel, you know I want you, and need you. But it is because I love you."

She looked up, her heart pounding. "You do?"

"Yes," he said softly. "And I'm afraid it's a love that's going to last a lifetime. You gave me my freedom from Amelia, but now I don't want it. I want us instead."

Tears stung Jezebel's eyes. "And I want us. I love you!" She crawled across the bed and, standing, threw her arms about him.

Terrence kissed her and they toppled back. As their kisses deepened, Jezebel groaned, her hands roving over Terrence's strong back out of sheer pleasure. This time he wasn't a dream, he wouldn't vaporize. They would be together, always.

Then Terrence stiffened. Groaning, he rolled away and sprang from the bed. Not until he stood at the door, as if prepared to make an escape, did he halt.

"What are you doing?" Jezebel asked, blinking.

His smile was loving, his eyes warmly laughing. "I'm not going to let you tempt me, you Jezebel."

"Me, tempt you?"

He chuckled. "This time I'm going to make certain I have the exclusive! Now do get dressed. I left Josh and Elizabeth down in the taproom. Either she's killed him or they are discussing the very notion we are." His eyes turned serious. "She's stealing him from you, Jezebel. Will it upset you?"

"No," Jezebel said, smiling. "It won't, as long as she doesn't steal you from me."

"Not a chance," Terrence said, his eyes turning wicked with promise. Blowing her a soft kiss, he slipped out of the room.

Jezebel and Terrence, Josh and Elizabeth, all sat about a table in the taproom. It was a rather unusual setting for them, but amongst them, none were well funded. Indeed, Josh had the most money, but having paid for the shot, he had enough only for their drinks. The men nursed tankards of ale and the two women wine. Luckily, the taproom was all but deserted, except for two men in the corner engaged in a game of cards.

"Well?" Josh said. "What is our plan? Are we returning to the Duchess's or not?"

Elizabeth smiled. "I certainly must. I need to tell her of . . . my change of plans."

"And Jezebel and I better if we care for our lives." Terrence laughed. "I have no doubt the ladies are wondering what happened this very minute."

"The only thing I'm wondering," a stern voice said from the entrance, "is what you are doing in the taproom?"

They looked up to discover Lady Dorethea, hands to her hips and foot tapping. Theo and Letty stood behind her. Bentwood, Stilton, and a strange little man could be seen flanking them.

"Grandmother," Terrence said, rising. He bowed. "Do forgive us, but I fear we've found ourselves at point nonplus. None of us have the ready for a private parlor."

"Damn common," Theo grunted.

"Perhaps," Letty said. "But it will be a treat. I have never been in a taproom before." Her eyes brightened, and she looked to Jezebel. "Do you think you could sing for us like you did at the tavern, the one where you caused poor Lord St. John to kiss you? Oh, and dance on the bar as well?"

"For goodness' sake, Letty," Dorethea said, sailing into the taproom. "Do not encourage Jezebel. She will never learn discretion if you continue in such a manner." She noted the two men in the corner and lifted an imperious brow. "Sirs, if you could kindly remove yourself from the premises, we are preparing for a wedding."

"Grandmother," Terrence said stiffly as the two men threw down their cards, snatched up their tankards, and left the room.

Dorethea turned to look at him. "Are you telling me you have not asked Jezebel yet? I told you, you would have to do it yourself."

"Yes, I have asked her."

Dorethea's brows snapped down and she frowned at Jezebel. "And did you not say yes?"

"Oh, please do," Letty said. "I would far rather have you as Terrence's wife than mistress. He is quite unattached now. Amelia threw him over this morning, and I was never so grateful. Besides, if you do not marry him, Dorethea will feel pushed to find him a wife, and I do not think my nerves could survive the stress."

"Letty, you are dithering," Theo barked. She looked at Jezebel. "But she's right. I ain't generally one to shove another female into the line of matrimony, might as well shove her off a cliff is what I say, but I can't help it. If ever two should run in tandem it's you and our Terry."

"Now who is dithering?" Dorethea exclaimed. She narrowed a demanding gaze upon Jezebel. "Did you accept Terrence or not?"

Jezebel laughed. "Yes, Duchess, I did."

"Very well," Dorethea said more calmly. "I knew you would not fail me." She then turned her gaze to Josh and Elizabeth. "Have you two decided to marry? And please speak quickly before Letty and Theo interrupt."

"Yes, we have," Elizabeth said, laughing.

"Excellent," Dorethea said. Turning, she waved to Stilton. "Do proceed, Stilton. No, one moment." She walked over and perused the drinks upon the table. "Ale and wine? For a wedding celebration?"

"Terrence is waiting for his next quarter's allowance." Jezebel giggled.

"And I'm saving to go up to Eton," Josh said, flushing.

"Stilton, be sure to bring the champagne first," Dorethea instructed.

"Yes, Your Grace," Stilton said, cracking a smile and turning.

"And, Bentwood," Dorethea went on, "since it seems our gentlemen have not thought ahead, please prepare rooms for us all, and two suites for our engaged couples."

"Two suites . . . ?" Bentwood flushed. "But, madame, both are occupied."

Dorethea flicked a dismissing hand. "Then find them other rooms or send them on their way."

"Y-yes, Your Grace," Bentwood stammered, and, bowing, departed swiftly.

"Tsk, Grandmother," Terrence said, his eyes twinkling.

"Airing our sleeping arrangements in public, and even arranging them. 'Tis quite improper."

"It won't be," Dorethea said, drawing up a chair and sitting. "Not since you will be married within the next two hours."

"Indeed," Letty said, coming to sit. "No one can find fault with that. It is quite respectable to share a suite upon your honeymoon. Now when you and Jezebel shared a room before, it was not the thing; indeed—"

"Letty," Theo said, coming to sit down as well. "Do stop it."

"Oh, yes," Letty said, and smiled. "Sorry."

Terrence raised a brow. "We are going to be married so soon?"

"Yes," Dorethea replied, even as Stilton appeared with a basket and Dorethea's other footmen entered, carrying some white linens, flowers, and dishes. "After we have a toast and dinner, that is." She suddenly peered to the little man who still hovered at the door. "I am sorry, Reverend, would you care to join us?"

"No," the man said quickly, coloring. "This is highly irregular, but I will wait until you are ready for the ceremony." He peeked at Jezebel, turning a brilliant red.

"Very well, tell Bentwood to find you a private room," Dorethea ordered as Stilton withdrew a bottle of champagne. The reverend muttered something unintelligible and scuttled away.

"How did you command him so fast?" Terrence asked.

Dorethea shrugged. "It was simple. I told him Jezebel was enceinte and that you were desperate to marry her."

"What!" Terrence roared.

"I did not lie completely, did I?" Dorethea said. "You are desperate to marry her, are you not?"

Terrence eased back, laughing. "That I am, Grandmother."

"See," Dorethea said. "I would not lie to a man of the

cloth. Though I own, 'tis a shame Jezebel is so knowledge-able in the ways of the world, for I wouldn't mind if she were in the family way. I'd have my grandchild quicker, but"—She picked up her glass of champagne—"I can wait."

"How kind of you," Terrence said dryly.

Dorethea looked to Josh. "And you, Mr. Rakesham, do you have any objections to marrying this afternoon?"

"Er, no," Josh said, flushing. He looked at Elizabeth. "Not if Elizabeth don't."

"I hope not," Dorethea said. "You are a charming rascal, but you have been drinking far too much. Elizabeth needs to start reforming you as swiftly as possible."

"Oh, I am already doing so." Elizabeth laughed. "He's now a different man, in fact."

Dorethea's eyes narrowed. "Hmmm, yes. Unfortunately I only tumbled to it this morning." She looked at Josh. "Just who are you, and what is your true name?"

Josh flushed. "Er, actually I'm Josh Clinton."

"You are Jezebel's brother?" Letty asked. Then she sighed. "Thank heaven. I cannot explain it, but every time I thought of you two as lovers—or ex-lovers—it always seemed—"

"Incestuous," Theo said baldy. "Too beautiful and blond not to be related."

Terrence laughed. "And you, Grandmother?"

"I am quite satisfied," Dorethea said, not batting an eye-lash. "For a moment I was worried Jezebel was a Rake-sham."

Terrence cracked a laugh. "Was that all that concerned you?"

"No," Dorethea said, with a withering look. "I do not condone deception, but since I had already acquired the spe-cial licenses a few days ago, it was of moment."

"You did?" Terrence asked, his eyes narrowing.

Jezebel looked stern. "You promised you would not do anything in that regard."

"I didn't," Dorethea said. "I only wished to be prepared if Terrence and you came to your senses." She smiled a small smile. "At least this time, I can say I finally signed the right names to the right contracts."

Jezebel laughed. "But for Rakesham."

Dorethea waved a hand negligently. "That is not difficult to alter."

Jezebel giggled. "No, I have no doubt."

Dorethea lifted a brow. "But is your name actually Jezebel?"

"Yes it is," Jezebel answered, looking down. "We . . . we did not lie about that."

"Do you mind telling me, since you are now going to be part of the family," Dorethea said, "what you did lie about?"

"Dorethea," Letty exclaimed. "How very rude. Jezebel has already told us she does not care to talk about her unfortunate past. To press her on the matter is quite unkind. And on her wedding day at that!"

"Letty," Jezebel said, flushing, "I am afraid I have no unfortunate past. I am not an actress, you see."

"Oh, don't say that dear," Letty protested. "You mustn't give up on your art no matter how much of a failure you seem. All artists have their trying setbacks, and merely because you haven't learned the knack of acting yet—"

"Oh, she has," Terrence said, laughing. "What Jezebel is trying to say is she never was an actress until I met her and . . . commissioned her."

Dorethea's brow winged up. "Commissioned her?"

"Yes," Terrence said, casting Jezebel a warm, teasing glance. "There was a slight confusion. . . ." He halted as Josh broke into a fit of coughing. "But when I heard her name was Jezebel, I just knew I needed to bring her home to you, Grandmother."

"Repulsive boy," Dorethea said, without heat.

"Tsk, for shame," Terrence teased. "I went through a great deal of trouble on your behalf, Grandmother. You have no notion how steep the price is for a professor's daughter."

"What!" all the ladies, except Jezebel, exclaimed.

Jezebel flushed. "I'm sorry, but that is what I am. I—I have no colorful past to speak of."

"Gads," Theo said.

"The poetry book," Dorethea said, snapping her fingers.

"You're not an actress?" Letty asked. Her face fell. "Oh, dear. And here I thought when your speech had improved it was due to our company."

Dorethea laughed of a sudden. "Faith, a professor's daughter. I'd entertained all different notions, but I had never thought of a professor's daughter." She raised her glass. "I applaud you, my dear." Then she leveled a stern gaze upon Terrence. "But you, my boy, what a lot of trouble you have caused. You have taken a perfectly respectable professor's daughter and turned her into an actress of notorious repute. Now we will have our work cut out to turn her back into Jezebel, the professor's daughter, and not Jezebel, the actress."

"But if I hadn't needed an actress," Terrence said, "I wouldn't ever have met Jezebel."

"Gadzooks," Theo said, "he might have brought home a real actress."

"Yes," nodded Letty, her eyes wide. "She no doubt would have accepted our five thousand pounds in a winking. And she wouldn't have saved Geselda or Sir Drake."

"And she wouldn't have saved Mordrid," Theo said.

"Or me," Terrence said softly, clasping Jezebel's hand.

Suddenly, there was a great commotion at the entrance of the taproom. The party looked up to discover Lady Kellair charging in, her thin face twitching, her eyes snapping. Lord Kellair and Bentwood dragged along behind, both with that particular look of alarm men display when women seem beyond their control.

"I refuse," Lady Kellair said. "I refuse to be thrown from my room, tossed out for the likes of—of that hussy!" She jabbed the air with a shaking finger. "That Jezebel!"

Dorethea did not even deign to rise, but narrowed her eyes and lifted her head. "If you are referring to my future granddaughter-in-law, Lady Kellair, I suggest you keep a silent tongue in your head. She will be the future Lady Haversham, so do not dare to show her disrespect."

"She . . . is going to be . . . ?" Lady Kellair's eyes widened as her face purpled. "Impossible!"

"Not at all," Dorethea said. "And since I have taken great pains to ensure that very fact, you may rest assured that I stand behind Jezebel completely."

Lady Kellair almost swayed. "Well . . . well, I never!"

"We's all knows that, ducky," Jezebel suddenly said, her accent broad, as she stood. "But you ought to at least once, yer know, it'd be good for your heart and soul. Not to mention the old indergestion. And Lord Kellair 'twould like it too. I'd bet me red and gold corset on it, I would." She sashayed over to Lady Kellair, grabbed up her hand and pumped it. "Congratulates me, love, I'm going ter be a proper lady, I am." She leaned over and whispered. "Going ter have me own suite as well. And since Granny ordered it, we'd ought to let her have her way." She waved toward Dorethea, whose face was a picture of imposing dignity. "She's kinder high-in-the-instep, yer know. Likes ter get what she wants. Fact, can turn mighty fractious if she don't, like a cat with its tail in a knot." Lady Kellair reared back, but Jezebel merely patted her arm kindly. "Now now, I'd let yer have that there suite, 'cause truth is, me and Haversham don't need but one bed, 'cause I have a sleeping disorder that he's powerful conscious about taking care of, but it's me wedding night, and if I'm going ter be a proper lady, I've got ter do it all right and tight."

Dorethea sighed and shook her head. "I told you we'd have trouble getting rid of the actress Jezebel."

Terrence laughed in delight and, as Jezebel patted Lady Kellair once more, winked slowly at Lord Kellair, he said, "Of which I am forever grateful."

He grinned even more broadly as Jezebel swayed and rustled back to him. He didn't need direction, but scooted his chair back and she plopped down on his lap. He wrapped his arms around her tightly, and they looked at each other in shared amusement. Jezebel pursed her lips and blew him a silent kiss. "Forever grateful!"